the

magic

strings

of

Frankie

Presto

the
magic
strings
of
Frankie
Presto

Mitch
Albom

HARPER

An Imprint of HarperCollins*Publishers*

THE MAGIC STRINGS OF FRANKIE PRESTO. Copyright © 2015 by ASOP, Inc. All rights reserved. Printed in the United States of America. No part of this book may be used or reproduced in any manner whatsoever without written permission except in the case of brief quotations embodied in critical articles and reviews. For information, address HarperCollins Publishers, 195 Broadway, New York, NY 10007.

HarperCollins books may be purchased for educational, business, or sales promotional use. For information, please e-mail the Special Markets Department at SPsales@harpercollins.com.

FIRST EDITION

Grateful acknowledgment is made for permission to quote from the following:

"A House Is Not a Home" (from the film *A House Is Not a Home*), written by Burt Bacharach and Hal David. © 1964 Sony/ATV Music Publishing LLC. All rights administered by Sony/ATV Music Publishing LLC, 424 Church Street, Nashville, TN 37219. All rights reserved. Used by permission.

"Jonah," words and music by Paul Simon. Copyright © 1978, 1980 Paul Simon (BMI). All rights reserved. Used by permission.

"Just Waitin'," written by Hank Williams Sr. and Bob Gazzaway. © 1951 Sony/ATV Music Publishing LLC. All rights administered by Sony/ATV Music Publishing LLC. 424 Church Street, Suite 1200, Nashville, TN 37219. All rights reserved. Used by permission.

"Lost in the Stars," words by Maxwell Anderson; music by Kurt Weill. © 1946 (Renewed) Chappell & Co., Inc., and Tro–Hampshire House Publishing Corp. All rights reserved. Used by permission of Alfred Music.

"Lost in the Stars," from the musical production *Lost in the Stars*, words by Maxwell Anderson; music by Kurt Weill. TRO-© Copyright 1944 (Renewed) 1946 (Renewed) Hampshire House Publishing Corp., New York, NY, and Warner/Chappell Music, Inc., Los Angeles, California. International copyright secured. Made in the USA. All rights reserved, including public performance for profit. Used by permission.

"Nature Boy," by Eden Ahbez. © 1948, 1976, 1995 by David J. Janowiak DBA Golden World Music. Used by permission.

"Parlez-Moi d'Amour," by Jean Lenoir. Copyright © 1930 by Societe d'Editions Music Internationales, copyright renewed. All rights reserved. Used by permission.

Library of Congress Cataloging-in-Publication Data

Albom, Mitch.

The magic strings of Frankie Presto / Mitch Albom. — First edition.

pages ; cm

ISBN: 978-0-06-229441-8

ISBN: 978-0-06-243324-4 (BAM Signed Edition)

ISBN: 978-0-06-243323-7 (B&N Signed Edition)

I. Title.

PS3601.L335M34 2015

813'.6—dc23

2015016184

15 16 17 18 19 OV/RRD 10 9 8 7 6 5 4 3 2 1

To my uncle Mike, the first of many
musicians in my life who made me say,
"I want to play like *that*."

Here's to all the boys who came along

Carrying soft guitars in cardboard cases

All night long

And do you wonder where those boys have gone?

—PAUL SIMON

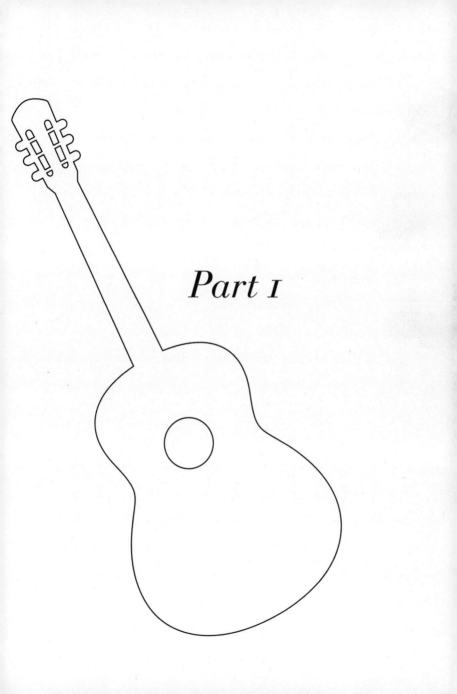

Part I

1

I HAVE COME TO CLAIM MY PRIZE.

He is there, inside the coffin. In truth, he is mine already. But a good musician holds respectfully until the final notes are played. This man's melody is finished, but his mourners have come a great distance to add a few stanzas. A coda, of sorts.

Let us listen.

Heaven can wait.

Do I frighten you? I shouldn't. I am not death. A grim reaper in a hood, reeking of decay? As your young people say—*please.*

Nor am I the Great Judge whom you all fear at the end. Who am I to judge a life? I have been with the bad and the good. I hold no verdict on the wrongs this man committed. Nor do I measure his virtues.

I do know a great deal about him: the spells he wove with his guitar, the crowds he enthralled with that deep, breathy voice.

The lives he changed with his six blue strings.

I could share all this.

Or I could rest.

I always make time to rest.

Do you think me coy? I am at times. I am also sweet and calming and dissonant and angry and difficult and simple, as soothing as poured sand, as piercing as a pinprick.

I am Music. And I am here for the soul of Frankie Presto. Not all of it. Just the rather large part he took from me when he came into this world. However well used, I am a loan, not a possession. You give me back upon departure.

I will gather up Frankie's talent to spread on newborn souls. And I will do the same with yours one day. There is a reason you glance up when you first hear a melody, or tap your foot to the sound of a drum.

All humans are musical.

Why else would the Lord give you a beating heart?

☙

Of course, some of you get more of me than others. Bach, Mozart, Jobim, Louis Armstrong, Eric Clapton, Philip Glass, Prince—to name but a few of your time. In each of their cases, I felt their tiny hands at birth, reaching out, grabbing me. I will share a secret: this is how talents are bestowed. Before newborns open their eyes, we circle them, appearing as brilliant colors, and when they clench their tiny hands for the first time, they are actually grabbing the colors they find most appealing. Those talents are with them for life. The lucky ones (well, in my opinion, the lucky ones) choose me. Music. From that point on, I live inside your every hum and whistle, every pluck of a string or plink of a piano key.

I cannot keep you alive. I lack such power.

But I *infuse* you.

And yes, I infused the man in the coffin, my mysterious and misunderstood Frankie Presto, whose recent death during a festival concert was witnessed by a sold-out crowd, his body lifting to the rafters before dropping to the stage, a lifeless shell.

It caused quite a stir. Even today, as they gather in this centuries-old basilica for his funeral, people are asking, "Who killed Frankie Presto?" because no one, they say, dies that way on his own.

That is true.

 ᶜ⌒

Did you know his first name was actually Francisco? His managers tried to hide that. "Frankie," they believed, was more palatable to American fans. The way young girls would scream it at his concerts—*"Frankie! I love you, Frankie!"*—I suppose they were right. Shorter names are more suited to hysteria. But you cannot change your past, no matter how you craft your future.

Francisco was his real name.

Francisco de Asís Pascual Presto.

I rather like it.

I was there the night it was bestowed.

℮

That's right. I know the unknown details of Frankie Presto's birth, the ones historians and music critics—even Frankie himself—always labeled a mystery.

I can share them if you like.

Does that surprise you? My willingness to begin with such a coveted story? Well. Why delay? I am not one of the "slower" talents, like Reason or Mathematics. I am Music. If I bless you singing, you can do so from your first attempt. Composing? My best phrases often lie in the opening notes. Mozart's *Eine kleine Nachtmusik? Dum, da-dum, da-dum da-dum da-dum?* He burst out laughing when he played that on his fortepiano. It took less than a minute.

You want to know how Frankie Presto came into this world?

I will tell you.

Simple as that.

℮

It happened here, in Villareal, Spain, a city near the sea that was founded by a king more than seven centuries ago. I prefer to begin everything with a time signature, so let us set this as August 1936, in an erratic 6/5 tempo, for it was a bloody period in the country's history. A civil war. Something whispered as El Terror Rojo—the Red Terror—was coming to these streets and, more specifically, to this church. Most of the priests and nuns had already fled to the countryside.

I recall that evening well. (Yes, I have memory. No limbs, but endless memory.) There was thunder in the skies and rain pounding on the pavement. A young expectant mother hurried in to pray for the child she carried. Her name was Carmencita. She was thinly framed with high cheekbones and thick, wavy hair the color of dark grapes. She lit two candles, made the sign of the cross, put her hands on her swollen belly, then doubled over in pain. Her labor had begun.

She cried out. A young nun, with hazel eyes and a small gap between her teeth, rushed to lift her up. "*Tranquila*," she said, cupping Carmencita's face. But before the women could make for the hospital, the front doors were smashed in.

The raiders had arrived.

They were revolutionaries and militiamen, angry at the new government. They had come to destroy the church, as they had been doing all over Spain. Statues and altars were desecrated, sanctuaries burned to a char, priests and nuns murdered in their own sacred spaces.

You would think when such horror occurs, new life would hold in frozen shock. It does not. Neither joy nor terror will delay a birth. The future Frankie Presto had no knowledge of the war outside his mother's womb. He was ready for his entrance.

And so was I.

The young nun hurried Carmencita to a hidden chamber, up secret steps built centuries earlier. As the raiders destroyed the church below, she laid Frankie's mother on a gray blanket in a corner lit by candles. Both women were breathing quickly, creating a rhythm, in and out.

"*Tranquila, tranquila*," the nun kept whispering.

The rain rapped the roof like mallets. The thunder was a tympani drum. Downstairs the raiders set fire to the refectory and the flames crackled like a hundred castanets. Those few who had not fled the church were screaming, high, pleading shrieks, met by lower barking orders of those committing the atrocities. The low and high voices, the crackling fire, whipping wind, drumming rain and crashing thunder created an angry symphony, swirling to a crescendo, and just as the invaders threw open the tomb of Saint Pascual, ready to desecrate his bones, the bells above the basilica began to chime, causing all to look up.

At that precise moment, Frankie Presto was born.

His tiny hands clenched.

And he took his piece of me.

Ah-ah-ah. Am I committing to this tale? I must consider the composition. It is one thing to tell the story of a birth, quite another to tell the whole life.

Let us leave the coffin and go outside for a moment, where the morning sun is causing people to squint as they emerge from their cars, parked along the narrow streets. Only a few have arrived so far. There should be many more. By my measure (which is always accurate) Frankie Presto, during his time on earth, played with three hundred and seventy-four bands.

You would think that means a large funeral.

But everyone joins a band in this life. Only some of them play music. Frankie, my precious disciple, was more than a guitarist, more than a singer, more than a famous artist who disappeared for a good chunk of his life. As a child, he suffered greatly, and for his suffering, he was granted a gift. A set of strings that empowered him to change lives.

Six strings.

Six lives.

It is why, I suspect, this farewell could prove interesting. And why I will stay to hear the mourners speak—Frankie's remarkable symphony, as played by those who knew him. There is also the matter of his strange death, and the shadowy figure who was following him just before it.

I want to see this resolved.

Music craves resolution.

But for the moment, I should rest. So many notes already shared. Do you see those men on the church steps, smoking cigarettes? The one in the tweed bowler cap? He is also a musician. A trumpeter. He had nimble fingers once, but he is old now and battles illness.

Listen to him for a moment.

Everyone joins a band in this life.

Frankie was once in his.

Marcus Belgrave

Jazz trumpeter, Marcus Belgrave and His Quintet; the Ray Charles band; sideman with McCoy Tyner, Dizzy Gillespie, Ella Fitzgerald, and others

LEMME HAVE A LIGHT. . . . MMM . . . MMM . . . THANKS. . . .

No, uh-uh, I can't believe it neither. Nobody dies like that. But I'm telling you, Frankie had some strange stuff going on, magic, voodoo, something . . . I never told no one this story, but I swear it's true.

We were playing a club up in Detroit, maybe 1951 or '52, in the part they called Black Bottom. Used to be a nice buncha clubs there, but after the war, it got pretty dicey.

Anyhow, we're playing a Friday night, four sets—eight, ten, midnight, and two a.m.—and Frankie's with us, just this skinny teenager playing the guitar. This was way before he made them hit records or even started singing. Shoot, I didn't even know his last name. Just "Frankie." He wasn't supposed to be there on account of how young he was, but he never asked for no money, and to the guy who owned the club, that made him twenty-one, know what I mean? We let him sit in the back, out of the spotlight, his big mop of black hair bouncing in the shadows. At the end of the night, he got a free plate of chicken, and we got us a free guitar player.

I know, I know, I'm getting to it. Like I said, the place was low-end now, some bad elements, and at one point we were playing "Smokehouse Blues," and a big bearded fella is sitting in the corner with this pretty young blond thing who's wearing too much lipstick, maybe trying to look older.

Well, something musta happened, because the Beard jumps up and pushes the girl against the wall, his chair goes flying backward, and he's got a knife to her throat. He's choking her, screaming, calling her every kind of name. Tilly, our piano player, walks straight out the door, because that was how he was—"Don't-Want-No-Trouble Tilly," we used to call him—but the rest of us were riffing on the chords with that frozen kind of look when you don't wanna watch, but you can't turn away? It was almost like if we stopped playing, the Beard was gonna kill this girl. He's screaming, waving that knife, she's choking, and nobody was doing nothing, because this guy was *big*.

Well, next thing I know, Frankie jumps up front and starts playing real loud, and fast. He's playing so good, people kinda don't know where to look. And Frankie yells,

"Hey!" and the Beard looks over and hollers something drunk. But Frankie just plays faster. Me, Tony, and Elroy, we're trying to keep up but he's off into something, fingers moving like they're possessed.

"Hey!" Frankie yells again, and he's playing like lightning, still getting every note clear and true. And damn if the guy doesn't turn and point the knife at him now like he's taking the challenge.

"Faster," the Beard grumbles.

So Frankie goes faster. Some people start whooping, like it's a game. And now Frankie's off "Smokehouse" and he's on to "Flight of the Bumblebee," you know, from that Russian opera? I'm trying to find the notes on my horn, and Elroy is banging the pedal so hard his damn foot is gonna snap off.

And again, the guy yells, "Faster!"

And we're thinking there's no way on the Lord's earth anyone can play faster than—but before we even finish that thought, Frankie's upped it again, his fingers running from the bottom strings to the top strings so fast I swear a buncha bumblebees is gonna come flying out of that guitar. He's not even looking at his hands. He's just staring at the guy, with his lips kinda open, hair falling onto his forehead, and everyone is clapping now, trying to keep pace with Elroy's beat, and Frankie starts this run from the far end of the neck up to the highest frets and the Beard is damn near hypnotized and he comes closer for a better look. Frankie's staring at the lipstick girl and she's staring at him, and then he jerks his head and she's outta there, quick as a bullet.

And now the whole place is whooping in that way crowds do—you know, "Whoo! Whoo! Whoo! Whoo!"—and the kid squeezes his lips and he's up in the highest notes, sounds like he's pinching baby birds it's so damn high, and the Beard is by the edge of the stage and Frankie points the neck right at him like some kinda machine gun— *bangadedybangedybang*—and then he's done. Finished. And he whips the guitar over his head and the whole place is going crazy, just breathing hard, like, man, that boy can play and we're glad nobody's dead.

And then Frankie races out the door, chasing that girl.

But here's the thing.

I look at his guitar, and one of the strings has turned blue. I swear. Blue as the middle of a flame.

I thought to myself, I don't know where this kid come from. Maybe I don't want to know.

2

WELL.

There's a hint.

The young blond girl with too much lipstick would have died had Frankie not done what he did. But he was too young to understand such things, or to even know he possessed such power. . . .

My apologies.

Up here.

On the windowsill.

I have been listening to a kitchen radio playing Blondie's "Heart of Glass" into the alley behind the church. Did you ever notice how music sounds different played outdoors? A cello in a garden wedding? A calliope in a seaside amusement park?

That's because I was born in the open air, in the breaks of ocean waves and the whistling of sandstorms, the hoots of owls and the cackles of tui birds. I travel in echoes. I ride the breeze. I was forged in nature, rugged and raw. Only man shapes my edges to make me beautiful.

Which you have done. Granted. But along the way, you have made assumptions, like the more silent the environment, the purer I am. Nonsense. One of my disciples, a lanky saxophonist named Sonny Rollins, played his horn for three years on a bridge in New York City, his tender jazz melodies wafting between the traffic noises. I would pause there often, on the girders, just to listen.

Or my beloved Frankie, born amid the cacophony of ringing bells and clamorous destruction. Remember that night, inside the burning church? Carmencita, Frankie's mother, had to keep her newborn child from crying, lest they be discovered by a murderous militia. So, lying together on the gray blanket, she hummed a song in his ear. It was a melody from the past, well known in the town of Villareal, written by one of its native sons, my brilliant guitarist Francisco Tárrega. Carmencita hummed it as purely as any song has ever been hummed, tears falling from her cheeks to the newborn's skin.

He did not cry.

A good thing, since, within minutes, the raiders had reached the main altar and could be heard destroying everything below. They were drawing closer and would soon ascend the steps. The nun with the hazel eyes and the gap between her teeth was trembling. She knew the new mother could not be moved; she was too weak, there was blood everywhere.

She also knew the raiders would kill any nun they discovered.

She mouthed a prayer, pulled her tunic off over her head, and pressed her fingers against the flames of the candles, extinguishing the light.

"*Silencio*," she whispered.

Carmencita halted the only melody she would ever sing to her son.

The song was called "Lágrima."

It means "teardrop."

~

Of course, all this seems incongruous if you only knew Frankie Presto from his most popular years, the late 1950s and early 1960s, when they called him "the next Elvis Presley" and he made records that led to television appearances and raucous concerts and an iconic photo of him smiling in a tan sports coat and a pink-collared shirt, leaning out a car window to sign the hand of a pretty brunette.

That photo, used by *LIFE* magazine, became the cover of his most commercial album, *Frankie Presto Wants To Love You*. It sold millions of copies and earned him more money than he ever imagined during his childhood days on the poor streets of Villareal, where men transported oranges in horse-drawn carts.

But by that stage of his life, Frankie was an American artist with an American manager and there was no trace of a Spanish accent in his singing. Even his guitar playing had been pushed to the background. The songs they made him play, quite frankly, were beneath his talent.

But I haven't even told you of his first instrument, or the hairless dog, or the girl in the tree, or El Maestro, or the war, or Django or Elvis or Hank Williams, or why Frankie disappeared at the height of his popularity.

Or how he died, rising over a stunned audience.

Frankie's journey. Such a rich tale to share. You show interest. That is tempting. I am always tempted by an audience.

The cars arrive. The sun climbs above the city. The priest is still dressing in his chambers.

There is time, I suppose.

Let us jump right in then, as befits a man named Presto. Today it may be a word you exclaim after a magic trick. But it was once used by composers to signal my quickest tempos, bright, jumpy, and energized. *Presto.*

It also means "ready."

Are you ready?

Here is the rest of my child's story.

3

EVERYONE JOINS A BAND IN THIS LIFE.

You are born into your first one. Your mother plays the lead. She shares the stage with your father and siblings. Or perhaps your father is absent, an empty stool under a spotlight. But he is still a founding member, and if he surfaces one day, you will have to make room for him.

As life goes on, you will join other bands, some through friendship, some through romance, some through neighborhoods, school, an army. Maybe you will all dress the same, or laugh at your own private vocabulary. Maybe you will flop on couches backstage, or share a boardroom table, or crowd around a galley inside a ship. But in each band you join, you will play a distinct part, and it will affect you as much as you affect it.

And, as is usually the fate with bands, most of them will break up—through distance, differences, divorce, or death.

Frankie's first band was a duo—mother and child. By the Lord's good grace, they had not been discovered by the raiders that night, and had managed to escape the burning church. But traumatized by the horrific events, the woman moved to the farthest end of town and never spoke of what she endured. There was great distrust in Spain during those years; you kept your secrets to yourself. When townspeople walked past, the mother lowered her head, avoiding eye contact.

"*Qué niño más guapo!*" they would exclaim. *Such a beautiful boy!*

"*Gracias*," she would mumble, quickly moving on.

The child developed a full head of dark hair. As the months went by, the woman noticed he would turn whenever church bells chimed. Once they passed a street musician playing the flute, and young Francisco held his hands out as if to grab more of me (although he had quite enough already, thank you).

He was a normal infant in most ways, except that, for the longest time, he did not cry. He barely made any sound at all. They lived in a one-room flat above a *panadería*, and when they went hungry, which was often, the mother would go downstairs and wait for the elderly baker to ask about her quiet baby. She would lower her eyes, and he would sigh sympathetically. "Don't worry, señora, I am sure he will speak one day," he'd say, and he would give her a plate of rolls soaked in olive oil. Occasionally she earned money from sewing or washing clothes. But the country was struggling with its crippling war, money was scarce, and alone with a baby, she could hardly work. Month after month, she barely kept them going.

"Go to the church, let them help you," the neighbors said. But she never did. She wanted no part of a church anymore.

When Frankie's first birthday arrived, to break the monotony, she carried him to the one paved street in town, Calle Mayor, and into Casa Medina, its largest store, to look at things they would never own. She lingered by the new strollers, wishing she could afford one. The store also featured a wind-up gramophone, and on her way out, she stopped to admire it. The owner, a well-tailored man with a thin mustache, stepped forward, noticing perhaps that she did not wear a wedding ring. He smiled as he put on a new shellac disc.

"Listen please, señora," he said proudly. The artist on that disc was a Spanish guitar player named Andrés Segovia. What he played that morning held the baby Frankie mesmerized. His head tilted. His little hands clenched.

And when the song finished, he finally cried.

Loudly.

The baby's voice was as powerful as a grown man's. The owner grimaced. Customers made faces. The embarrassed mother shook him harshly, hissing "*Silencio!*" But his piercing noise continued, so loud it could be heard from one end of the store to the other. Another salesman grabbed a piece of candy from a counter dish and pushed it at Frankie's lips to make him stop, but the child waved his hands wildly and cried even louder.

Finally, the flustered owner put the gramophone's arm back on the disc.

Segovia played again.

And Frankie fell silent.

You don't need me to tell you the song.

"Lágrima."

◦

From that day forward, the child was never content. He would cry all the time. No hour was immune. No bed or blanket soothed him. He wailed louder than the roosters or the alley dogs. It seemed he was screaming for something he could never have.

"Enough!" the neighbors would yell out the windows. "Give him milk! Make him stop!"

But nothing seemed to work. Night after night he howled, even as fists banged on the walls and broomsticks pounded on the ceiling. "Do something!" "We need to sleep!" No one could recall a baby that loud. Even the baker downstairs ceased giving the mother bread, in hopes that they would find someplace else to live.

Without aid, and with food so scarce, the poor woman was at her wit's end. She didn't sleep. She grew depressed.

She ached from hunger and her health deteriorated. As winter approached, she caught a fever and suffered fits of delirium. She would walk the streets with a red towel around her neck, leaving Francisco to cry alone in the flat. Sometimes she mumbled words she thought were being spoken to her.

One cold morning, with nothing to feed the child and no way to stop his shrieking, she carried him to the outskirts of the town, where the Mijares River runs to the sea. She descended a hill to the riverbank. A strong wind blew, swirling leaves from the muddy ground. She looked at the child, wrapped in a gray blanket. For a moment he fell silent, and her face softened. But then the distant church bells rang and his howling resumed. She threw her head back and exhaled a shriek of her own.

She flung the baby into the water.

And she ran.

A mother should never do such a thing. But this woman did, tears falling from her hazel eyes and past her gap-toothed mouth. She ran until her lungs nearly burst, and she did not look back, not on the child, not on the river.

A mother should never do such a thing. But this woman was not Frankie's mother. That woman died in the chamber of the church, draped in the tunic of a nun.

Clem Dundridge

Backup singer, the King-Tones, the Jordanaires, the Frankie Presto Band

HOW YA DOIN'? . . . YOU WITH A TV STATION OR SOMETHING? . . . What time they gonna start this here funeral, any idea?

Me? Nah . . . I never been to Spain—but I kinda like the music. Ha! You know that song? . . . Who was that? Dang . . . Three somethin' . . . Three Dog Night! That's it . . . What kinda stupid name is that?

Shoot, I know. Where I live, funerals never start on time, neither . . . Greenville, now. South Carolina. America . . .

Naw, I hadn't seen Frankie in about twenty years. Just lost touch, you know? Most people lost touch with him, right? That's how he was. I didn't even know he was still playin' until I heard how he died. . . .

Met him? Ha! You ready for this? I met him with Elvis Presley on the *Louisiana Hayride* circuit, 1957. . . . Yes, ma'am. . . . Yes, ma'am. . . . Well, hell yeah, it's a true story. I don't mind sayin' it now. I was supposed to keep quiet till the day Elvis died and the day Frankie died. But they're both gone now, and I'm eighty-two years old. What am I waiting for? I'm figuring to maybe tell it in the church. Are we allowed to speak during the service? It's Catholic, isn't it? Maybe they don't let you . . .

Right now? . . . Tell you what. You lemme have some of that coffee you're sippin', I will . . . Thank you . . . much obliged. . . . Mmmph . . .

Okay. So this is what happened. I was singin' those days with the Jordanaires, which was Elvis's backup group. Lot of guys came in and out of the Jordanaires over the years, mostly gospel singers, some of them was ministers who eventually went back to the church. I was with them just a brief stretch, but during that time, Elvis was catchin' fire. Every show was bigger than the last.

Now Frankie looked a lot like Elvis, there's no denying that. They both had them toothy smiles and all that hair, real dark, although Elvis was dyeing his, its natural color was more like reddish-brown, and Frankie was a little taller and a little skinnier. But in those days, nobody knew Frankie could do anything besides play guitar. I'm not even sure how he got to Louisiana. Someone said he came from Detroit in the trunk of a car. Seriously. But he kept to himself and didn't smoke or carouse, and if you don't do that in a band, there ain't hardly time to get to know you. . . .

So anyhow, this one afternoon, we're at the Shreveport Municipal Auditorium—that's where they taped the *Louisiana*

Hayride, a real big radio program down there—and we're doing our sound check for that night's show, and Elvis was out with a girl somewhere doing who knows what. Colonel Parker, Elvis's manager, was so angry he was ready to jerk a knot in someone's tail. The Colonel ran a tight ship, and he hated anyone being late—even Elvis. We waited five or ten minutes, he kept looking at his watch, and finally he screamed, "Play somethin'! Let's get going!" Well, you didn't cross the Colonel, no, sir, so the band just started into the show's first number, "I Want You, I Need You, I Love You," and the Jordanaires did our background parts. But of course without Elvis it sounds kinda stupid, just a lot of "Whooooo, whoooo," and you can feel the Colonel's anger from a hundred feet away, his face is getting all red, he keeps looking at the doors, pacing back and forth. And suddenly we hear a voice singing the words, you know? And it sounds like Elvis, except it's Frankie, up on the mike. He's singing it perfectly. And I look at the other guys, thinking, the Colonel is gonna string this kid up! Imitating Elvis in front of the boss? I mean, you just don't do something like that. The Colonel stares real hard, pushes his jaw out and bites on that cigar he always had in his mouth, and I'm thinking, Nice working with you, Frankie. But the Colonel doesn't stop him. We finish the song, and all he says to the sound guy is, "Are we done here?"

So we walk off, kinda shaking our heads, and I remember Hoot, the piano player, he handed Frankie a beer right after that, and when Frankie asked him what for, Hoot said, "Because you're still in one piece."

So, okay, flash ahead now, about a month later, we're on a tour of the Pacific Northwest with Elvis and we're booked to play in Vancouver, Canada, in a football stadium. Well, we come to find out Colonel Parker is talking to the army about Elvis getting drafted. The army wanted Elvis to start his service, and the Colonel is desperate to get them to delay until he can get more recordings in the can. He's got a million-dollar tiger by the tale, and he'll be doggone if anybody, even the United States government, is gonna take it away.

So the army agrees to meet with Elvis and the Colonel, but it's a secret meeting and it's in Virginia, on the day we're supposed to play in Vancouver. They're not budging, because some big-shot general is gonna be at that meeting, he wants to meet Elvis, and it's either meet that day or get a draft notice, I reckon.

Now, most people woulda just canceled the show, but most people ain't Colonel Parker. He didn't want to give up the gate from a football stadium, not for nobody. There was supposed to be like twenty thousand people there. That was big money.

So the night before, up there in Vancouver, me and the fellas get called by the Colonel to come down to a little theater at midnight. It's empty, no sign of Elvis, just a stage with all our equipment, and the Colonel is already there with—guess who?—Frankie. And he's whispering, and Frankie's nodding his head. We don't know what's going on. Finally the Colonel turns to us and says, "I want y'all to run through the show with the boy singing." And we look at each other like, *What?* But we don't say nothing. We do as we're told. We play. Frankie sings. And sure as I'm standing here, by the end of that rehearsal, if I shut my eyes, I couldn't tell if I was listening to Frankie or Elvis. That boy was so musical, he coulda made a kick drum sound like a nightingale, you know what I mean?

Still, we're wondering, how is this gonna work? He *looks* like Elvis, but he *ain't* Elvis, you know? But when we're finished, Colonel Parker says, "Now, listen here. The boy is gonna stand way back by you. He's not to come to the front of the stage, ya hear me? And no talking in between the numbers. Y'all just go from one song into the other. Fast."

Then of course he added his warning. "Any of you pickers tell one soul 'bout this, I'll sue you so fast your head'll spin off your neck." He needn't have said that. None of us was giving up the Elvis gig. We had a tiger by the tail as well.

So the next night comes. The real Elvis is somewhere in Virginia, with the government, and we're out in Vancouver, Canada, in a black sedan pulling up to the stadium. Frankie's in the back, sitting between us, dressed in that gold satin jacket, wearing sunglasses, being real still. I couldn't tell if he's super relaxed or scared to death. *I* was scared to death, I can tell you that. We were told to surround him when we walked to the backstage area, and not to let anyone, not even the police, get too close to him. We hustled Frankie to the edge of the curtain, and I can hear the rumblin' of the crowd out there. And I'm thinkin', There ain't no way on God's green earth we are gettin' away with this.

But when we take the stage, we look at the fans, and they're so far away, up in the stands, and there are these sawhorses on the field the Colonel set up, telling everyone they were for Elvis's safety. We got a good forty-yard cushion, nobody is gettin' close, which is just how the Colonel wanted it. And it's still kinda light out, because this is late summer, so the spotlights aren't on, which makes it harder to see details from far away. And I whisper to Bill, one of the other singers, "What do you reckon?" and he said, "Clem, if it goes bad, run to the right, that's where the cars are."

And then the announcer yells, "Ladies and gentlemen, Elvis Presley!" and the place becomes one big scream. And out steps Frankie, wearing that gold jacket and a black shirt, a guitar around his neck, high on the straps, the way Elvis wore it. I braced myself for something, people booing or throwing stuff. But it never happened. They believed it one hundred percent! And Frankie stayed back with us like the Colonel told him, didn't go out front where the cameras could catch him alone, and he didn't do no talking, neither, just started right in with *"Well, since my baby left me"*—you know, from "Heartbreak Hotel"—and from that point, it might not have mattered if Frankie, me, or Pearl Bailey was singin', it got so crazy you could barely hear. And suddenly all them kids come running out of the stands and out onto the field. And Frankie tears into "I Got a Woman" and "Rip It Up" and "Ready Teddy." We're looking at each other, smiling like bandits, because he's good and we're getting away with it. And the police are chasing the kids back up into the stands, but then they come running back onto the field again. With each song, Frankie is getting more and more into it, doing some of Elvis's leg shakes and the way he'd thrust his hips. A couple times I shook my head at Frankie, like, Don't do it, man, just lay back. Let's get out of here safe. But then comes "Hound Dog," and I guess he couldn't help it, he just cuts loose. He pops out front and he's shakin' and windmillin' his arms and he's got that sneer on his lips just like Elvis—and that did it. The crowd mobbed the field, all of them—the police were trying to hold them back, whistles were shriekin' and people were gettin' knocked over. And as soon as "Hound Dog" was done, security hustled us off the stage, Frankie grinnin' and wavin' at the crowd like, good-bye, see ya!

Twenty-two minutes. That was the whole show. Twenty-two minutes. We pulled it off. To this day, people talk about that concert as one of the wildest and craziest of Elvis's career—and his last one ever in Canada. And only the band, the Jordanaires, the Colonel, and Elvis his own self, God rest his soul, knew what went on.

And Frankie, of course.

He left the band the next day. I don't think he wanted to face Elvis. Maybe Elvis didn't want to face him. Either way, he was gone, and I didn't see him again until he asked me to come on tour with him a couple years later. He was different by then. More confident. More like a star, you know? I think that concert changed him. He had a taste of it, and he wanted it for himself.

Nobody said nothing about that night for damn near sixty years. But I'm eighty-two now, and Frankie's dead, so the hell with it, he deserves the credit. You think about all them people who became Elvis impersonators, made whole careers out of it. But Frankie was the first—and you gotta say the best.

I mean, if the point is to make people feel like they're seeing the King, he's the only one who ever really pulled it off.

4

THERE WILL BE MORE STORIES LIKE MR. DUNDRIDGE'S. IT
is why that Spanish news crew is camped on the church
steps, the large bearded man with a television camera, the
well-coiffed young woman standing next to him with a
microphone. A death as spectacular as Frankie's will draw
interest. But whatever tales are shared, none will tell the
whole truth. Because no one knows the whole truth but
me. Well. There is one other person. But that person, I can
assure you, will not be here.

Where were we? Ah. Yes. The Mijares River. A winter
morning. A fleeing woman. And a child tossed aside with
no protection in this world beyond a gray blanket and the
sound of his own misery.

None of this, mind you, would the boy remember. For
Frankie Presto, memory would only crystallize in the next
phase of his life, the part he would call his "beginning."

But even beginnings have beginnings. Take the prelude,
an established form of musical composition. Today, it can
be beautiful and elaborate, a song unto itself, yet originally

—in *its* beginning—a prelude was something an Italian lute player in the sixteenth century called *tastar de corde*, "testing the strings." Not very poetic, but accurate. One must indeed test the strings in this life, bounce the bow, wet the mouthpiece, prepare for the deeper music that follows.

The prelude for Frankie Presto began with his calamitous birth and ended with a splash in the Mijares. In one year's time, he had witnessed death, siege, hunger, and abandonment, and now the cold river water dripped into his eyes and made him blink repeatedly as the current began to carry him downstream. He should have quickly sunk and drowned, and I was present to collect his unfulfilled talent should that have happened. But there are moments inexplicable in your world, and all I can relay is what I witnessed: that the gray blanket—the same blanket that once lay beneath Frankie's true mother, Carmencita—did not submerge. It acted as a vessel for at least three minutes, carrying the child back toward the city, while Frankie rubbed his eyes and cried at an incredible volume—crying until even the Lord above could not ignore the sound.

e~

At this point, I will share something you are yet to fully discover. It is not just humans who are musical. Animals, too. This should be obvious in the thousands of birdsongs I have spawned, or the clicking of dolphins, or the moaning of humpback whales. Animals not only make music, they hear it in unique fashion.

On the river that day, Frankie's crying rose to a sound beyond the human ear. Suddenly, a hairless dog, with thin, sinewy legs and black skin that seemed to be painted on, came charging down the riverbank. A leash, hooked to its collar, was flopping wildly. As Frankie's squeals grew higher and more intense, the dog ran and yelped, and at a bend in the river, splashed in. The infant grabbed for the barking sound, his fingers ensnaring the leash. The dog bit down on the blanket and scrambled backward, until both of them were safe on the bank.

The child rolled over. The blanket slipped into the water, disappearing downstream. The dog put one wet paw on each side of Frankie's head and lay its own head down, panting heavily.

Prelude complete.

No talent to collect.

5

LET US NOW, IN THE INTEREST OF SPEED (BECAUSE A PRIEST can take only so long to dress and cars are filling the narrow streets), jump ahead and place Frankie in his next home, a residence on Calvario Street with a tile roof and a horseshoe arch and two slots in the doorway through which a cart's wheels could roll. It was the house of a Mr. Baffa Rubio, the owner of a small sardine factory, an Italian automobile, and that hairless dog.

The man who found Frankie on the riverbank.

Baffa, unmarried and in his forties, went to church regularly and kept a cross on the wall of his bedroom, so the discovery of an abandoned child was, for him, a divine act, like finding Moses in the reeds. He took the boy in. He bathed him. Fed him. Rocked him to sleep at night. Not many men would do this. But I pay great attention to labels (*allegro* means you play me fast, *adagio* means you play me slow, and so on), and while Baffa's last name, Rubio, means "blond" or "fair-haired," his scalp was covered with thinning black bristle. This confirmed a man who could alter his destiny.

He named the child Francisco Rubio.

The child called him Papa.

Baffa was potbellied, with a sagging chest, thick jowls, a drooping forehead, and a downward-bending mustache, so that when he sat, he seemed like a layer of frowns stacked in a chair. But the boy made him happy. Having inherited his family's sardine factory, Baffa was an oddity in Villareal, a town full of orange growers, orange pickers, orange packers, and orange shippers. He'd grown used to being alone, a fat man with a fishy smell, yet suddenly there was a small human to share in his daily routine, which during the week meant riding to work in his Italian automobile, and on the weekends meant sitting in his small garden listening to the radio, with the hairless dog sleeping near a bed of pomegranate flowers. The radio was constantly on, morning to evening, and young Frankie was content as long as music emerged. He would squat near the speaker and sing along with any melody, in a high, pleasing voice. When Baffa turned the dial to hear the news (there was a terrible war brewing in Europe), Frankie cried until the man gave up and returned to whatever music he could find, a concert by an orchestra, an opera, or a Spanish *jota*, with its 6/8 tempo and endless energy. Frankie seemed to like that most of all.

One day, just shy of the child's fifth birthday (not his real birthday, but the sardine maker had made a guess), Baffa saw him standing at the edge of a table, his fingers drumming to the sound of a complex flamenco guitar piece. He was keeping perfect rhythm, even though finding the beat in 6/8 time can be like cooking an egg under a blanket.

"Come here, little one," Baffa said proudly. The boy, with a full head of black hair, turned, smiled, and walked smack into the leg of a chair, tripping and landing badly. He cried and Baffa lifted him and soothed him against his chest. "It doesn't hurt, it doesn't hurt," Baffa whispered, but he realized the boy's vision was still not right. The water from the river trauma had infected his blue eyes, and the slightest sun would make him squint, his corneas would redden, sometimes he couldn't see anything to his sides. Doctors had warned that his sight might one day go altogether. The irritation left him constantly rubbing, and the neighborhood children would mock him: "Are you crying *again*, Francisco?" As time passed, they called him Llorica—"crybaby." While they played a ball game called *trinquete* in the street, Francisco sat alone, humming to himself.

Baffa, a practical man, worried for his boy's future. What if he grew up without any friends? And if his vision was bad, what kind of work would he find? How would he support himself? That day in the garden, as the *jota* music played, Baffa had an idea. Musicians, trained properly, could always work, even blind, right? He recalled a *taberna* several years ago where a guitar player with dark glasses performed to great applause, and afterward a beautiful young woman took him by the hands and led him off the stage, planting a small kiss on his lips. Only then had Baffa realized the man could not see.

This, Baffa decided, could be a future for his divinely sent child. Through music, he could work. He might even find love. Never one to waste time (efficiency had always attracted Baffa, even in sardines), he took the boy to a small music school on Calle Mayor, the paved street in the center of town. The owner had a long chin and round glasses.

"Can I help you, señor?"

"I want my son to play guitar."

The man looked down. Frankie rubbed his eyes.

"He is too young, señor."

"He sings all day."

"He is too young."

"He keeps a beat on a table."

The man lowered his glasses.

"How old is he?"

"Almost five."

"Too young."

Frankie rubbed his eyes again.

"Why does he keep doing that?"

"What?"

"He rubs his eyes."

"He is a child."

"Is he crying?"

"An infection."

"He cannot play if he always rubs his eyes."

"But he sings all day."

The man shook his head.

"Too young."

This, by the way, is hardly the first time one of yours has discouraged one of mine. If I possessed a metal link for every tongue-clucking human who said a child was too young, the instrument too large, or the very idea of pursuing music was "a waste of time," I could wrap your world in chains. Disapproving parents, dismissive record executives, vindictive critics.

Sometimes I think the greatest talent of all is perseverance.

But only sometimes.

For while Baffa argued with the music school owner, young Frankie gave me a special moment. He wandered into the back room, where the instruments were stored. There his eyes widened at a treasure trove heretofore unseen in his young life: a spinet piano, an old viola, a tuba, a clarinet, a snare drum—and a guitar. The guitar was lying on the floor. He walked over and sat down next to it. It had a simple wooden body with a red and blue rosette around the sound hole. Most children would have grabbed its neck, plunked its strings, twisted its tuning pegs as if they were toys. But Frankie just stared at it. He studied its shape. He cocked his head as if waiting for it to talk. I found the respect he showed most satisfying. And, given what he had just endured with that long-chinned naysayer, I felt the moment was right for a little magic. Now and then, we talents can surge inside you to create the inexplicable (well, inexplicable to you). You call these "flashes of genius." We call it stretching.

Frankie reached out and pressed a finger on the third string, just behind a fret. He quickly released it. A soft note rang out. He smiled and did it again, the next fret up, using what guitar players call the "hammer-on" technique—a hard and quick push and release. Another note. Then another. He quickly figured out the relative sounds made by pushing behind each fret. Simply put, he was teaching himself a scale.

So I gave him another nudge.

Soon he was sounding out a melody. His eyes widened with each new note, because playing a song for the very first time is my greatest revelation, like discovering you can walk on a rainbow. He began to hum along. Had the two grown men in the front room stopped their arguing, even for a moment, they might have heard the little miracle of Francisco de Asís Pascual Presto, not yet five years old, fingertipping his way through a tune he'd heard many times on a Saturday-morning radio program, a nursery rhyme turned jazz standard:

A-tisket, a-tasket
A green and yellow basket

I wrote a letter to my love
And on the way, I dropped it

It was Frankie's first guitar performance.

And no one heard it but me.

Down the hall, Baffa lost his patience with the owner. He yelled, "Francisco! We are leaving!" The child stood up and gave a farewell pat to the guitar, realizing he had found what he was looking for, and he was no longer rubbing his eyes.

℮

This still left him shy of a teacher. Clearly the music school was out, and it was the only one in Villareal. Baffa felt defeated. On the way home, he stopped and bought a bag of oranges. He peeled one for the child and gave a piece to the hairless dog, who chomped it loudly. They walked together, Frankie's second band, a trio with eight legs.

"That man was an idiot," Baffa mumbled.

The hairless dog barked in agreement.

"Idiot," Frankie repeated.

Baffa laughed and rubbed Frankie's hair. That made Frankie happy, even if he didn't know what "idiot" meant. They walked home with Frankie humming "A-Tisket A-Tasket" and the hairless dog singing silently along with him.

℮

That night, Baffa returned to the *taberna* where he had once seen the blind guitarist play. The bartender remembered him as well, but said the man had been fired several years ago. Too much drinking. Too many late arrivals. He believed he was staying in a flat above a laundry on Crista Senegal Street—if he wasn't already dead.

"Dead?" Baffa said.

The bartender shrugged. "He drank like a man who wanted to get this life over with."

The next day was Sunday. After attending morning mass, Baffa took the boy and the hairless dog to Crista Senegal Street, hoping to catch the guitar player in a good mood. Even a drunk, Baffa reasoned, might give Sunday to God.

He found the laundry. Above it, he saw faded blue shutters, latched shut. The bell button was covered with a long piece of masking tape, so the three of them had no choice but to walk up the steps. It was a hot day, and Baffa, still in his church suit, was dripping sweat when they reached the landing. He wiped his face with a handkerchief, then knocked. Nothing. He knocked again. Nothing.

Baffa shrugged at Frankie, who stepped up and banged with his small fists, two at a time, as if playing a conga drum.

"*Sí? . . . Qué pasa?* . . . What is it?" came a voice. It was gravelly and loose, as if still waking up.

"Señor, I would like to speak to you about teaching."

"Teaching what?"

"Guitar?"

"Go away."

"It is important."

"Go away."

"I will pay you."

"Teaching who?"

"My child."

"Girl or boy?"

"Boy."

"Girls are better students."

"He is a boy."

"How old?"

Baffa paused, remembering the music school.

"Seven."

Frankie looked up.

"Small for his age."

"No boys."

"He is very talented."

"No boys."

"He is very talented."

"So am I."

"I would pay you."

"Of course you would pay me."

"So you'll teach him?"

"No."

"Señor—"

"Go away."

Baffa turned to Frankie. "Sing something," he whispered.

Frankie shook his head.

"*Sing* something," Baffa repeated.

Now, most children will not sing when asked. At the early ages, talents yield to fear. (Sometimes at the later ages, too.) But this moment, I knew, was too important in the overall map of Frankie's life. So I gave the child another nudge.

"*Da-da-dah, duh* . . . ," he began, slowly.

Baffa raised his eyes. He had never heard this tune.

"*Da-da-dah, duhh* . . . ," the boy continued.

It was a simple melody, childish but haunting. It went high and came down on the major notes, like something you might hear played on a xylophone. "*Duh, duh, duh, da-da-da, deh duh, dah, dahhhh* . . ."

Frankie stopped.

"*Qué canción es esa?*" Baffa asked.

Suddenly the door opened. A tall man with dark sunglasses, thick stubble, unkempt dark hair, and a sleeveless undershirt with a large coffee stain over the belly was gripping the doorframe like a guard.

"It is called 'Lágrima,'" he said. "By Francisco Tárrega."

He lowered his chin in the direction of the boy.

"He does not sound seven."

Darlene Love

Singer, solo artist, member of the Blossoms, the Crystals;
inductee, Rock and Roll Hall of Fame

YOU SEE THIS PICTURE? THAT'S ME AND FRANKIE AT THE
Hollywood Bowl. I kept it all these years. Silly, isn't it?
But when you're that age and love hits you, you want to
keep every little thing, every ticket stub, every flower
petal, every kewpie doll you win at the arcade, whatever
makes you think of it, you know?

I was just eighteen, still in high school, and completely
new to the music business. I was singing with some girls
from my church choir and we'd won a contest to back up
Nat King Cole during his Hollywood Bowl performance.
It was our first time singing in a place like that, and even
the drive up through those fine neighborhoods was an eye-
opener. We didn't know people could live in houses that
big!

Backstage, while we were waiting, that's where I met
Frankie. The girls and I were laughing, we were so nervous,

we'd shush each other and then we'd laugh and shush again. And suddenly, from the next dressing room over, I heard a man laughing and shushing, too—imitating us, you know? And that made us laugh harder. His voice sounded young but deep, and even laughing, it was sexy. I yelled, "Who's there?" And he yelled, "Frankie," and we giggled and my girlfriend said, "Frankie who?" And the door opened, right on cue, and he stepped in and said, "Presto."

And I lost my breath.

I had never seen a boy like that. None of us had. Not in our neighborhood. Those dark eyebrows, those baby blues, that sweep of hair that was as close to black as I've ever seen.

"Presto?" My girlfriend laughed. "Like the magic?"

"Presto, like the magic," he said, and she stopped laughing. I mean, that boy froze you in your tracks. He was wearing this bright yellow sports coat and a black shirt and pants and he said he was one of the opening acts, he was supposed to sing one song, because the record company had put him on at the last minute—I think it was Capitol, the same label Nat King Cole worked for. I said he looked a lot like Elvis, and he looked down and said, "There is only one Elvis," and someone said it was too bad Elvis had to go in the army.

Then a photographer came by to take our picture and Frankie went to leave but all of us girls said, no, don't go, take a picture with us, and I got one by myself and here it is. I still have it, all these years later. I didn't know he would become a star, but I had a sense he was going to be special. Sometimes you can just tell.

After the show was over, we were driving back along Hollywood Boulevard, and my girlfriend pointed out the window and said, "That's him! That dreamy singer!" And sure enough, Frankie was walking all by himself, holding a guitar case in one hand and his yellow sports coat in the other. We rolled down the window and yelled, "Where are you going?"

"To the ocean," he said.

"You're walking?"

"Yes."

And we laughed again because he was a long way from the ocean. I said to our chaperone, "Can we drive him? We know him." And the chaperone said all right, and Frankie got in.

It was Saturday night and the weather was good and we drove to the Santa Monica Pier and promised the chaperone we'd be back in half an hour. Of course we weren't. There were parties on the beach, small bonfires and teens playing radios and dancing and making out. We ran into some kids we knew and the other girls went to sit with them and Frankie and I wound up alone, walking on the sand. I couldn't take my eyes off him. We were both barefoot and he had his pants rolled up and every time the waves reached our feet I jumped back, but he stood dead still.

"The ocean's so big," I said, something silly like that. And he said, "I sailed across it once." And I said, "This ocean?" And he said, "Another one." I asked where he came from and he said, "A lot of places." I asked where his parents lived and he said, "They're gone."

All this time, by the way, he was carrying his guitar case. He wouldn't let it go. He hadn't played it at the Hollywood Bowl, he'd just sung with a band, so I teased him and said, "Do you only carry a guitar to impress girls?" And he smiled (Lord, those teeth!) and said, "No."

And that's how I got my own private Frankie Presto concert, in the sand by the Santa Monica Pier.

To this day, I will never forget it. He put the guitar over his knee, and he turned his ear to the ocean. "Listen," he said. I could see lights from a faraway ship, way out there, but Frankie had his eyes closed. And he began to tap, real softly, once, then twice, and I realized he was finding the beat of the waves.

And then he played a song. I thought he'd play some rock and roll—everyone who had a guitar played rock and roll back then—but it was a classical piece. Slow, delicate, played up high on the strings. And when he finished, I was crying. I'd never heard anything that beautiful. I asked what the song was called and he said, " 'Träumerei,' " and I asked who wrote it and he said, "Schumann," and he saw my tears and—I know this sounds strange—he said, "Don't cry, you're a great singer." And I kind of burst out laughing.

"How would you know that?" I said.

"I heard you."

"We were singing in a choir."

But he said he could hear a voice within voices, and mine was beautiful, and I could be a famous singer one day.

Well. I was wondering what to do with my life at that point, should I pursue music, should I just finish high school and find a job? And what he said was exactly what I needed to hear. It gave me the confidence to keep singing.

We looked at each other, all goofy. And I bet you think we kissed, because that's how these little moments go. But I never kissed Frankie. I thought about it. I wanted to. But he hooked his arm around my arm and I leaned my head against his shoulder and we sat like that, kind of intertwined, with the waves crashing, and honestly, for that night, it was perfect. I felt so relaxed and so safe, like I'd known him all my life. I was totally, head over heels in love with him.

And with music.

We promised to stay in touch and I gave him my phone number and when I got home—after my mom and dad let me have it—I shut the door to my room and I wrote in my diary, "Today I met the boy I'm going to marry," which, a few years later, was actually the name of one of my biggest hits. When the songwriters first showed the lyrics to me, I smiled inside because I knew I was meant to sing it.

Of course I didn't marry Frankie. I didn't see him again for forty years. But when I heard he died, everything came rushing back. That's why I'm here, I suppose. You're never in love with anyone the way you are when you're eighteen, on a beach, at night, with your shoes off.

I still can't believe he's gone.

6

AH, LOVE AND FRANKIE PRESTO. PERHAPS LATER I WILL explain why women always fell for him. (Or were they falling for me?) But right now our story has reached a critical moment.

In every artist's life, there comes a person who lifts the curtain on creativity. It is the closest you come to seeing me again.

The first time, when you emerge from the womb, I am a brilliant color in the rainbow of human talents from which you choose. Later, when a special someone lifts the curtain, you feel that chosen talent stirring inside you, a bursting passion to sing, paint, dance, bang on drums.

And you are never the same.

It was a blind guitar player who did this for Frankie on a Sunday afternoon in the kitchen of the small flat on Crista Senegal Street, while Baffa and the hairless dog waited in the laundry downstairs.

"Set two chairs across from each other," the blind man

said that day. His sleeveless undershirt hung loose over his dirty tan trousers, and he did not wear shoes.

"Now what, teacher?" Frankie asked.

"Are you ready for your first lesson?"

"Yes, teacher."

"Good. Learn how to light a cigarette."

The man pulled a crumpled pack from his pocket. His fingers found a single cigarette and he put it in his mouth. Then he took out a silver lighter and flicked it open. A flame appeared.

"You see what I did, boy?"

"Yes, teacher."

"You do it."

Frankie took the lighter nervously. Baffa had told him to never go near fire. But he'd also said to do whatever this man told him to do.

"Go ahead, boy."

Frankie snapped the lighter open.

"Is there fire?"

"Yes."

"Now take the cigarette and light this end for two seconds. . . . One, two . . . then shut it."

Frankie did as told, then snapped the lighter shut. It fell to the floor.

"Give me the cigarette," the man said.

Frankie gave him the cigarette.

"Pick up the lighter."

Frankie picked up the lighter.

"Congratulations. You have passed your first lesson."

"Thank you, teacher."

"Now what do I call you?"

"Francisco."

"Francisco." He grasped for the chair, steadying himself as he sat down. "Like our great Francisco Tárrega, whose music you were singing."

"I don't know him."

"What? Stupid child!"

He rapped his hand along the kitchen table until he found an open bottle. He gulped a mouthful, and slammed it down.

"Why are you singing his music if you can't say his name?"

"I don't know—"

"Again, stupid boy! Did the song write itself?"

"No—"

"Did it fall from the sky?"

"No—"

"No. That is right. It did not fall from the sky."

He snuffed out his cigarette on the kitchen table (which was full of burn marks from previous cigarettes) then reached to find his guitar in its stand, nearly knocking it over. Frankie felt badly for this man, flailing around for everything. He wondered why he wore dark glasses if he could not see.

"Listen, now, very carefully," the man insisted, hunching

over the instrument, lifting its neck, placing his fingers by
the frets. "Listen to the great Francisco Tárrega."

He took a deep breath.

And began to play.

The song, of course, was "Lágrima," the same one
Frankie had sung by the door. The blind man played it
passionately, with great care, pausing for emphasis, shaking his head at certain notes as if absorbing their smell.
Frankie stared at the fingers moving deftly up and down
the neck of the guitar. He heard the sweet, warm tones of
the strings, the way the high notes seemed to blow gently
across the lower ones, the way it sometimes sounded as
if two people were playing at once. His mouth fell open
slightly.

The blind man finished.

"Now, tell me, boy. Does that composer deserve to have
his name remembered?"

Suddenly, he felt two small arms hugging his neck.
Frankie was resting his head on the man's shoulder, the way
he once rested against his mother. Hearing "Lágrima" had
lifted a curtain not only on Frankie's future, but on his past.

"Get off me," the blind man grumbled. Frankie hugged
tighter. The teacher could smell the scent of soap in his hair.

"Look, boy, I am sorry I yelled. But you cannot go forward without knowing your history. Do you understand?"

"*Sí*," Frankie whispered.

"Learn the names of musicians you would study."

"*Sí.*"

"Say 'Tárrega.'"

"Tár-re-ga."

"He was a Francisco, like you."

"Francisco."

"How do you know that song, 'Lágrima'?"

"I just know it."

"Did your papa teach you?"

"No."

"Your mama?"

"I don't have a mama."

The blind man swallowed. His own story was rising in his throat.

"I am sorry to hear that."

"Can you see anything?" Frankie asked.

"No," the man replied.

"How come?"

"I just can't."

"Sometimes my eyes hurt."

"My eyes do not hurt."

"I rub them a lot."

"My eyes do not hurt. I am blind. That is all."

"Are you Francisco, too?"

"No."

"What is your name?"

"Get off me now."

The child pushed back and touched the man's face below his dark glasses. It was wet with tears. He returned to his chair as the man wiped his cheek with his palm, then fumbled again for the bottle.

"You will call me El Maestro," he said.

7

TALENT IS A PIECE OF GOD'S SHADOW. AND UNDER THAT shadow, human stories intersect.

Young Francisco Presto shared a story with another Francisco—Tárrega, the great Spanish guitarist born in this very town back in 1852. There is a street named for him just behind this church, and two statues honoring him, one depicting him sitting in a chair, guitar on his knee, fingers ready to play. Children in Villareal run around that statue and grab at Tárrega's bronze feet.

Like Frankie, Tárrega took a fat handful of me upon entering your world. Like Frankie, he was mistreated by a caretaker early in his life—a nanny, from whom he ran away, landing in a drainage ditch and injuring his eyes. And like Frankie, he came to the guitar because his father thought he could earn a living should blindness overtake him.

As a child, Tárrega lived in a convent adjacent to the church, where his parents served the nuns. Perhaps they envisioned a similar life for their son. But once the boy became infatuated with me, he (naturally) thought of nothing else. He ran away to Barcelona, where he attempted to play in taverns until someone returned him to his father. He was only ten years old.

He ran away again, a few years later, to Valencia, where he made music in the street with gypsies. Again, someone returned him to Villareal.

A few years later, he ran away once more.

His wandering would affect his music. Tárrega—who eventually became famous and in demand all over Europe—found himself in London once, alone and depressed. He missed the sunshine of his country. Someone encouraged him to capture his sadness in music, so he wrote a composition that embodied his yearning.

That composition was "Lágrima"—"Teardrop"—the beautiful melody hummed in Frankie's ear in the church chamber, the one that kept him from crying, the one that, in truth, saved his life. It was a favorite of Frankie's real mother, Carmencita, because, like others raised in Villareal, she knew the music of her city's most famous son.

So did El Maestro, the blind teacher in the sleeveless undershirt, who played Frankie many Tárrega compositions. This is how talents weave from generation to generation, how the shadow stretches, and how an artist born nearly a hundred years earlier begins to fill the soul of a child who shares his name.

For the longest time, by the way, that was all El Maestro did during their lessons. Play. Frankie sat in a kitchen chair, mesmerized, absorbing every note, watching the man's fingers and wondering if his eyes were open or closed behind those dark glasses. After every song the man would smoke or drink from a bottle of red wine or the cheap but higher-alcohol *aguardiente* ("burning water"). When at last he'd drop his head back and lower his arms, Frankie would rise from the chair.

"Good-bye, Maestro."

"Yes, yes, good-bye."

Frankie would walk downstairs to find Baffa and the hairless dog and they would go home together, no sheet music, no assignments.

No guitar.

"Señor," Baffa asked El Maestro one day, "why is the boy not playing the instrument?"

"Go sit in the laundry," El Maestro growled.

Two weeks later, Baffa asked again.

"Señor, shouldn't the child be playing by now?"

"Go away. Your dog smells."

Baffa dared not get angry, for he had great respect for an artist's talent, something that always endeared the fat sardine maker to me. But he was persistent. Two weeks later, he brought Frankie to the door and raised the issue again.

"Señor, I must insist—"

"No, you mustn't."

"But I am paying for lessons."

"Do you want an artist or a monkey?"

Frankie felt himself smiling. *A monkey.*

"Of course, señor, I want an artist, but—"

"Then stop talking. I am getting a headache." He scratched under his armpit. "Do you have my money?"

Baffa sighed. "Yes."

Frankie watched Baffa hand him some bills, which El Maestro stuffed into his pants pocket with his cigarettes.

"You cannot write if you do not read," the blind man said. "You cannot eat if you do not chew. And you cannot play if you do not"—he grabbed for the boy's hand—"listen."

He yanked Frankie inside and slammed the door.

8

ALL TOLD, IT TOOK ONE FULL YEAR BEFORE EL MAESTRO LET
the boy touch a string. "First your ears, then your hands,"
he insisted. Meanwhile, he *explained* music. He explained it
in Spanish—and in English, which, having learned himself
when he was younger, he deemed vital for Frankie's progression, believing the rhythm, syntax, and pitch of languages helped the understanding of such things in music.
Week after week, jumping between tongues, he demon-
strated my chords, my scales, my voicings, laying them out
like fine silverware until Frankie could identify them by
sound. He made Frankie memorize the names of each composer and composition. Sometimes they listened to music
on the small kitchen radio, and El Maestro squeezed Frankie's hands at certain parts. "Do you hear? Right there! That
is a minor key . . . that is a triplet . . ."

As far as Frankie could tell, El Maestro had no other students. He was often sleeping on the couch when Frankie
arrived, the door unlocked, and Frankie would push him

on the shoulder until the man growled and rolled over and Frankie knew he was awake.

Still, as the months passed, the blind man seemed to grow less angry with his young student and stopped calling him "stupid boy," which made Frankie happy. Baffa, meanwhile, gave up arguing over the guitar. Instead, he took his laundry with him to Crista Senegal Street and made use of the time, coming home each week with clean socks and underwear, wrapped in string.

℮

When the big moment came, Frankie was so excited he could barely hold still. El Maestro had him sit in the chair, so he could position the instrument correctly, but the guitar he had chosen was too large. It came up to Frankie's chin.

"You are very small for eight," El Maestro said, reaching around the boy's frame. "Does your father not feed you?"

"Yes, Maestro, he feeds me."

"Give me your left hand."

Frankie did.

"Your nails are too long. You must cut them."

"Cut them?"

"The left hand. Every day."

"Yes, Maestro."

"You cannot play the guitar if your nails are not cut."

"All right, Maestro."

"Do you know why this is?"

"No, Maestro."

"No, you do not. Most people think it is because the nails get in the way of pressing on the strings. But I say it is something more."

"What is it, Maestro?"

"The nails protect the fingertips. The fingertips are sensitive. Only by cutting the nails back can you truly be in touch with the music."

"Yes, Maestro."

"Only then can you feel the pain of every note."

"Yes, Maestro."

"There is no protection."

"Yes, Maestro."

"Music hurts. Do you understand me, boy?"

"Yes, Maestro."

"Now show me to the closet."

Frankie stood and led his teacher across the flat, taking tiny steps.

"Walk faster, boy. I am not a cripple."

Frankie walked faster.

"We are at the closet, Maestro."

"Open the door."

Frankie pulled on the knob, revealing stacks of shoe boxes, some clothes hanging from a bar, and four guitars, each one smaller than the next.

"Give me the smallest one," El Maestro said.

Frankie took the instrument with both hands and lifted it toward his teacher. He looked down and noticed a pair of shoes, but they were for a woman, and on the hangers were several dresses and a handbag.

"Do you have a wife, Maestro?"

"Back to the chair," the teacher said.

Frankie closed the closet door.

⌒

That guitar, the one that would introduce Frankie Presto to his destiny, was, in fact, not a guitar at all, but a *braguinha*, an instrument similar to a ukulele. It had just four strings. The neck fit in the cup of Frankie's small left hand, and the curve of the body fit on his bony left knee, which protruded from the short pants he wore in the hot weather. It was a perfect size, as if molded to his body.

He would take it everywhere.

"Bend your right arm and relax your right hand," El Maestro instructed. "Do not squeeze it in; you are not choking something. And do not push down; you are not drowning something. Your right fingers are talking to the strings. Would you talk to someone by choking or drowning them?"

"No, Maestro."

"No, you would not."

"What do I do with my left hand?"

"The left hand finds the beauty. She makes the notes and chords. You can show off all you want with your right hand, boy, but you are nothing without the left, understand?"

"Yes, Maestro."

"Show your left hand respect. Each time you play, begin by holding it out like this." He straightened Frankie's palm. "Like you are asking for something."

Frankie thought of people in church, on their knees at the pews, hands out before them.

"Like I am asking God?"

El Maestro smacked Frankie's hand.

"Stupid boy. God gives you nothing. God only takes."

❧

At that stage, all Frankie knew about God was that He had a big house and He slept a lot. The big house part he assumed after Baffa told him his mother lived with God—and all the other good people who died—so it had to be a big place, right?

The sleeping part Frankie deduced after Baffa showed him the basilica in Villareal, which had been burned and destroyed by bad men. God would never allow such a thing to happen unless He slept through it, Frankie figured, just as Frankie sometimes slept through the hairless dog whining at the door and woke up to see a puddle on the floor.

Bad things can happen when you sleep, Frankie reasoned, and bad people could get away with evil if they knew when God closed his eyes.

Or maybe God was sometimes like his guitar teacher, wearing the dark glasses.

"Did you ever see anything?" Frankie asked El Maestro one day.

"Will my answer make you a better guitarist?"

"No, Maestro."

"Then why ask the question?"

"I am sorry, Maestro."

"What would I see if I saw you?"

Frankie smiled at the idea.

"A boy."

"A boy who is not playing his lessons."

Frankie's smile went away. He had been practicing for months now, every day in the garden, with the hairless dog at his feet. He wanted to play songs like the ones El Maestro played. But for now, all he got to play was exercises.

"My fingers hurt, Maestro."

"Music is pain."

"But they look funny."

"Those are calluses."

"What are calluses?"

"When you start playing, your fingers are not used to pressing strings. You get lines in them, yes?"

"Yes, Maestro."

"And they feel puffy?"

"Yes, Maestro."

"Maybe they bleed?"

Frankie swallowed. He had not wanted to tell his teacher that. But in the beginning, he played so much, he had to sometimes wipe the blood from his left hand with his shirt.

"Sometimes they bleed, yes, Maestro."

His voice quivered.

"Are you crying, Francisco?"

"No, Maestro."

"Do not cry over losing blood. Not for something you love."

He fumbled with a cabinet by the sink and reached inside to find a small bottle and a bowl.

"Soak your fingers in that," he said.

"What is it?"

"Why do you care, boy? If I tell you something will help you, do you need to ask questions?"

"*Lo siento*, Maestro."

"Say it in English. 'I'm sorry.'"

"I'm sor-ry."

El Maestro tapped on the table until he found his bottle of *aguardiente*. "There is a big war going on, boy. We are all going to be speaking English or German soon. Personally, I prefer English. German sounds like someone is scolding you."

He took a swallow and grimaced. "Also, they are murderous criminals. And our country won't do a thing to stop them."

Frankie had heard the word *war* before. Baffa spoke about it with the men at the factory. It didn't sound good. And Frankie didn't want to learn a language that sounded like scolding. The calluses were hard enough. He decided to do as his teacher said, just think about music. He wondered if he should tell El Maestro that he was only six years old.

Leonard "Tappy" Fishman

Music agent, record executive

WHERE? INTO THE CAMERA OR AT YOU? . . . OKAY . . . YES . . . Sure. My name is Leonard Fishman, originally from Brooklyn, New York. My age is eighty-six. This was a helluva trip for me. Overseas. In coach, no less. But I wanted to be here. Broke my heart when I heard the news. Honest to God. Poor Frankie. I was his first agent, during the fifties and sixties. We didn't have such a good end, it's true. He went a little nuts. Who knows why? I don't believe half the crap they wrote about him. You shouldn't either. Especially the stuff about me. His marriage? The movie fiasco? They want to say it was my fault. What do they know?

You want to hear the truth? I discovered him. Someone else might tell you different, but I found him when he was just a *pisher*. You know what that means? A *pisher*? It's Yiddish. It means a kid, young and innocent.

Innocent. Ha! I laugh, because Frankie Presto was never *that* innocent.

Huh? . . . Sure. Here's an example. I love this story. We were in California. This was in February of 1959. I'll tell you why I remember in a second. I had signed Frankie the year before, when he came to my office and said he'd been in Elvis Presley's band. I was representing a lot of acts, but you mentioned Elvis, you got in the door.

Frankie could really sing—he stood by my desk and did "You Are My Special Angel," his hands crossed in front of him, and it knocked me out—and obviously he was a good-looking kid. I knew I could make money with that face. I had a secretary, and every time Frankie dropped by, I thought she was gonna faint. He later got involved with her and broke her heart, like he usually did.

Over the years, I saw him with a lot of women like that, secretaries, waitresses, hotel receptionists. He was like a machine, honest to God, I wish I had that energy. His long-time girl left him just before his career took off, and I used to say, "Kid, if you're trying to get back at her, I think you won."

And he'd say, "Oh, Leonard, come on."

That was Frankie. He called me Leonard. Everyone else called me Tappy, 'cause I was always tapping my foot or my fingers, a nervous habit, look, even now, I'm doing it, see? But Frankie was different. Crazy. *Mashuga*. But I loved him. He had heart. The world forgot about him, and that's a shame. Him dying like this? It's tragic. . . .

What's that, now? . . . Oh, yeah. So in California in those days there was this circuit of county fairs, where they had amusement rides and zoo animals—goats, horses, all that crap—but at night, to keep the teenagers interested, they had rock and roll shows. And I booked Frankie on one with, lemme see, the Drifters maybe, the Everly Brothers, Eddie Cochran, Buddy Knox, Fats Domino, a few others. They'd each do two songs. A real assembly line.

Anyhow, the promoter for this circuit was a Romanian— big, hairy guy with a mustache. He ran the whole thing. The animals, the rides—*and* the music. All the money went to him. Every night the workers had to line up to get paid, waiting in his tent until all the receipts were counted. He kept the money in this one gray cash box, and with this big cigar in his mouth, he'd count out every dollar. Meanwhile he kept the tent boiling hot—he even had heat blowers going—so that the workers would get so hot and fed up, they'd leave. But Frankie stayed. Him and the Everly Brothers, Phil and Donald—Don, they called him. They stood there on the first night, sweating until they were soaked. But when they finally reached the front, the Romanian had given out all the money from the cash box.

"I'll pay you tomorrow," he said.

Well, they put up with this for four straight days. Same routine. "I'll pay you tomorrow." Finally, it's the last show on that circuit. Frankie and the Everly boys were beside themselves now. Frankie loved the Everlys. He said they were better musicians than they let on, which was the case with him, too, you know. I heard Frankie sing their song once, "All I Have to Do Is Dream"—honest to God, it made you weep. His voice? That song? I told him, "Frankie, lemme record that with you," but he refused because—get this—he met the couple who wrote it, a husband-and-wife team, and he said the woman told him she'd dreamed of her husband's face when she was eight years old, and when she was nineteen, she saw it across a room, and they'd been together ever since. True story. That's where the "all I have to do is dream" part comes from.

Anyhow, Frankie said a song like that should only have one home, just like the couple only had each other. So he wouldn't record it because the Everly Brothers already had. Of course about a thousand other people have recorded it since. He had more heart than brains, Frankie, but what are you gonna do?

Huh? . . . Oh, yeah. The Romanian and the money. So the last night they do their show—Frankie kills 'em, by the way. I was there. He was doing "I Want To Love You"—he hadn't even recorded it yet, but you could see it was gonna be huge by the way the girls were jumping up and down. So when the show finished, again the musicians line up at the tent, and I went down, too, because it was the last chance to get the money, see? It's hot as hell. Frankie's nowhere to be found. We're all waiting for the big Romanian. Suddenly there's this screaming and yelling and everyone scatters because—you ready for this?—the *elephants are loose!*

You ever hear such *mishugas*? The elephants are loose? So everyone runs. You don't want to get crushed by an elephant, right? The police cars arrive, the sirens, it's crazy, and suddenly a car pulls up and Frankie is driving with a girl next to him, and he yells to me and the Everly boys, "Get in!" And we take off. And everyone is a little shaken up—except Frankie, who seems perfectly calm. He drives us to the hotel.

"Where did you get this car?" I ask him. And he just smiles. You know that Frankie smile? Those God-blessed white teeth? Ach, I wish I had his chompers. Mine are mostly gone now, all bridgework . . .

Anyhow, I know not to ask again, and the Everly boys get out at the hotel, and Frankie runs after them and he says, "Hey, hold up." And he gives them this envelope, and I see it's money. And he whispers something and they pull him around by the neck, give him a hug, and when they leave, I say to him, "Just tell me you got paid, too," and he smiles and says, "Leonard, come on." And then he remembers the girl, and that was the last I saw of him that night.

But here's what I was telling you about the date, February 1959. The next morning, I'm in my office and the phone rings. It's Frankie. And he says, "Where is Pacoima?"

Well, Pacoima is this little town in the San Fernando Valley. He says he wants to go there. Right away. I say okay, what, you want me to drive with you? And he says he doesn't have a car. I say, what about the car from last night? He says he doesn't have that car anymore. Don't ask.

So a few hours later I drive out to pick him up, and I turn on the radio. That's when I hear the news. Buddy Holly, Ritchie Valens, and the Big Bopper were killed in a plane crash. You know that story? In Iowa, that's right. A snow-storm.

Well, Frankie makes me drive to Pacoima, because that's where Ritchie Valens was from. Valens was just a kid when he died, maybe seventeen, but he met Frankie once, on a road show, and since he was Mexican and Frankie was from Spain, they took to each other. Frankie loved that Ritchie actually had a hit song in Spanish, "La Bamba." He thought that was the greatest thing.

So we drive to Pacoima, and we stop at a gas station and Frankie goes in and he comes out with an address. It's Ritchie Valens's mother's house. We drive over and there's a bunch of cars and some reporters outside. So Frankie makes me wait. We wait maybe four hours, sitting in that car parked on the street, until all the people are gone. It's dark out now, and he says, "Okay, I'll just be a minute," and he gets his suitcase from the back. And he opens it. And what do you think he takes out?

A gray cash box.

Yep. The Romanian's cash box. He's got it. My right hand to God.

And he walks up to the porch and he leaves the cash box there, just inside the door. Doesn't even knock. Then he gets back in and says, "We can go."

I said to him, "Frankie, what did you do?" But he never really answered me. He just said losing a kid had to be hard, and Ritchie's mother would need some help now. Can you believe that? He'd orchestrated the entire fiasco—the elephants, everything—just so we'd get paid. Then he gave it all away. The whole ride back, I'm looking in the rearview window, hoping that crazy Romanian isn't coming after us.

9

MONEY. A MYSTERY, I MUST ADMIT. WHILE IT CLEARLY MEANS a great deal to humans, it seems, to me, an enormous burden. I have never held it. Never experienced its benefits. All I know is that while some of my disciples have grown quite rich, many more, in need of money, have chosen to abandon me. Why? Wealth has never defined music. What is played from the heart can be played anywhere.

On anything.

Frankie made his first music on his cheap *braguinha*. He graduated to a six-string when El Maestro approved, directing him to take one from the closet, a caramel body with a mahogany neck. Because Frankie was now going for lessons several times a week, often while Baffa was at work, Baffa purchased him a wagon the color of a pale green apple, which Frankie used to pull his new guitar through the streets.

A boy with his guitar in a wagon stood in marked contrast to the war that was overtaking the country—and the world. I was quite busy during those years collecting talent that was snuffed out before its time, left on battle-fields, drowned in sunken ships, shot out of the sky. Such a waste. Why humans kill each other is beyond my compre-hension, but I can testify that you have been doing it since your inception. Only the weapons change.

The war affected everyone. Baffa began to have trouble at the sardine factory, because some of his workers were given blue uniforms and taken away to fight. Others argued over party allegiances. The government ordered Baffa to pro-duce a certain amount of sardines to help the war efforts—something, I gather, he did not wish to do. Baffa came home at night, dropped in his chair, and placed a wet towel across his forehead. The hairless dog crouched at his feet.

"Go outside to practice," Baffa would tell Frankie. The boy was sad to see his papa this way, and he made him cheese and mustard sandwiches before going to the garden with his gui-tar. He cut the nails on his left hand each day before playing, then practiced the arpeggios that El Maestro had taught him, breaking down each chord by notes and playing them in a dif-ferent order. He practiced all his scales. He walked his fingers along the frets like a spider's legs, fast and faster, but never crossing.

"Have you ever seen a spider trip?" El Maestro had asked.

"No, Maestro."

"No, you have not. And your fingers must not trip, ei-ther."

"*Sí*, Maestro."

"Say 'Yes,' boy."

"Yes."

"Speak English."

"The teachers say we must speak only Spanish."

"With them, you speak Spanish. With me, English. You don't tell them about me or our lessons. You understand?"

"*Sí.*"

"Our secret."

"*Sí.*"

"Say 'Yes.'"

"Yes."

"Keep practicing."

"Yes."

El Maestro had good reason to be secretive. Politics is not my concern, but the repression in Spain was widespread, and as the months passed, more and more people were arrested in Villareal for being antigovernment. Many of them were artists. A piano player I had gifted was pulled from his home in the middle of the day and thrown into a prison cell. So were two cellists, a flutist, and several singers. As I understood it, the reigning Spanish leader—a balding man named Franco—had created a tyrannical society in which any deviation was viewed as criminally disloyal. I have witnessed such governments before. Their citizens always look the same. Tired. Glancing back and forth. And battling a constant, choking fear.

Art suffers under such conditions, and it suffered in Spain. People were afraid to express themselves. Afraid to write or to dance a certain way. Poets were jailed. Regional music was banned. The varied radio music programs were replaced with traditional Spanish fare.

"This Franco," El Maestro grumbled. "If he had his way, we would play only flamenco."

Still, sometimes good is found amid bad, just as major-key notes can be played over minor chords. One day, as Frankie was pulling his wagon toward Crista Senegal Street, past a new sign that warned IF YOU ARE SPANISH, SPEAK SPANISH!, he saw a commotion in front of the city's biggest store. Policemen in gray uniforms were pulling people out, and merchandise was being stacked in the street. Frankie moved through the crowd and heard whispered words he did not understand. He heard others cheering, "Franco! Franco! Franco!" As people began to push one another and the yelling increased, Frankie's eyes fell on something amid the stacks of goods. A phonograph machine. He had seen one in the store window once, and Baffa explained that it played music on round discs. When Frankie asked if they could get one, Baffa said, "They are too expensive."

But now here was a phonograph just sitting on the curb, atop a stack of recordings—music from America, England, France, and the outer regions of Spain. Frankie was too young to understand that under this government, such recordings were considered subversive. He figured if they were in the street, someone didn't want them.

So as gray-clad police began clubbing people into submission, Frankie quickly loaded the phonograph and the records into his pale green wagon, covered them with a blanket, and pulled a big chunk of me away from the fighting.

He had no idea he was being watched.

10

e~

I SHOULD SPEAK FOR A MOMENT ABOUT FRANKIE'S ABSENT
mother, and the shadow she cast on his young life.

Frankie, of course, remembered nothing of Carmencita,
the prayerful woman with hair the color of dark grapes.
And Baffa, who never knew her, could not tell Frankie the
truth—that he had been found in a river by a hairless dog—
because what child wants to think he was once thrown
away?

So a legend was constructed. It is how you humans re-
mold your history. Baffa told Frankie that his mother was
a saintly woman, Baffa's one and only love, who died trag-
ically on a trip they took shortly after Frankie was born.
This, Baffa figured, would explain why they never visited
her grave at the cemetery in Villareal.

It was not a good lie. And unfortunately for Baffa, Frankie
was nearly as curious as he was musical.

"Where was the trip, Papa?"

"America."

"Where is that?"

"Far away."

"How did Mama die?"

"A car crash."

"Was she driving?"

"Of course not."

"You were driving?"

"Yes."

"Were you hurt, Papa?"

"No. Well. I was hurt, but not badly."

"Did you try to save Mama?"

"Of course."

"Did you try really hard?"

Baffa sighed. You should never construct a lie based on a child's questions. It is like writing music based on cymbal crashes.

"Yes. I tried everything."

"Where was I?"

"You were here."

"By myself?"

"With a friend."

"Which friend?"

"You don't know him."

"How come?"

"He died."

"How?"

"A car crash."

"Was he driving?"

Baffa rubbed his head. He was a practical man, with a good heart. But I am rather certain when he came into this world, his little fists did not grab the talent for storytelling.

"I don't remember, Francisco. It was a long time ago."

"What happened to Mama?"

"When?"

"After she died?"

"She was buried."

"What does that mean?"

"When you die, you are put in the ground."

"Then how can she live with God?"

"After you are buried, *then* you live with God."

"Where is Mama buried?"

"In a cemetery."

"Where?"

"In America."

"Where?"

Baffa barely knew America. His sister, Danza, had moved to Mexico years ago, and had married an American man from Detroit.

"Detroit."

"What is that?"

"A city."

"Where?"

"In America."

"And you went there?"

"Yes."

"Why did you go there?"

"To get a car."

"Our car?"

"A different car."

"The one that crashed?"

"That is the one."

"Was Mama pretty?"

"Very pretty."

"Did she love me?"

"Very much."

On this, Baffa told the truth, even if he didn't realize it. And then, with his head pounding, he shut down the tale.

"No more questions, Francisco."

"What did she look like?"

"Please."

"Is this her?"

Frankie held out a photograph. In it, a younger Baffa had his arm around Danza, his sister, a plump woman with light hair and dark lipstick. The picture was from years ago, the last time he had seen her, before she left for Mexico.

"Where did you find that?"

"In the closet."

"Why were you in the closet?"

"Is this Mama?"

Baffa sighed. "Yes. That is her. No more questions, all right?"

Frankie gazed at the photo. So the plump woman hugging his father was his mother, the saint, who had died in a car crash in a faraway country and was buried in the ground so she could live with God.

He had his story. Years later, inspired by this tale, he would write his first guitar composition, which he called "Lágrimas por Mi Madre."

"Tears for My Mother."

Truth is light. Lies are shadows. Music is both.

11

SPEAKING OF ME, YOU HAVE MANY WORDS FOR HOW I SHOULD be played. In classical music, most of them are in Italian. *Adagio. Moderato.* This goes back to what you called the Renaissance, when Italy was at the center of creativity and musicians who went there invented hundreds of phrases for my tempos. *Vivace. Andantino. Prestissimo.* So far in Frankie's story, we have been going *largo*, slowly, or at least *larghissimo*, as slow as it makes sense. But with the looming funeral service, we must employ *accelerando*, going faster, perhaps reach *adagietto* or *allegro*.

The next three years of Frankie's life—from the day he stole the phonograph to the day he left Spain in the bottom of a ship—contained the following developments: he grew nine inches, lost six baby teeth, got in four fights at school, took his first Holy Communion, mastered a soccer kick, put pomade in his hair, had a girl plant a kiss on his ear (and run away laughing), learned to ride a bicycle, pray in Latin, and make *bocadillos* with sausage and olive oil. He wore his first bathing suit, saw his first tank, asked Baffa, constantly, to point out America on a globe, and slept with that photograph of the light-haired woman under his pillow every night, the one he believed to be his mother.

He also practiced his guitar at least three hours a day in the garden, learning more than a hundred songs and serenading the hairless dog with arpeggios and finger drills.

Of his lessons with El Maestro, I can attest that he made extraordinary progress, measured by the fact that his blind teacher actually smiled sometimes when Frankie played. El Maestro even gave up smoking cigarettes, although this may have been due to the time when Frankie, using the lighter, accidentally set fire to a tablecloth, then doused it with wine before his teacher could warn him that alcohol might set the whole place ablaze. (It did not. But such a scare can break a habit.)

Frankie spent more and more time in that flat above the laundry on Crista Senegal Street, learning the proper classical techniques, turning the guitar neck away from his left shoulder, tilting it upward, putting his foot on a stool. El Maestro made him hold an orange in his right hand for hours to simulate the proper setup position for plucking the strings, and he constantly grabbed the boy's fingers to show him the fleshy part of the thumb and the angle of the nails that would bring out the purest sound. He taught him every inch of the guitar, the piercing high sounds of playing up on the neck, the volume and tone relative to the sound hole, how each string vibrated and could be picked, tapped, plucked, fingered, or strummed.

Frankie also learned to work the phonograph he had stolen from the curb. El Maestro, at first, was furious. He insisted they throw the machine away. ("If the *policía* shut down the store, what do you think they would do to me, stupid boy?") But when Frankie put the needle on a recording of Duke Ellington's orchestra doing "Don't Get Around Much Anymore," El Maestro slumped in his chair with his mouth open and made the boy put the needle back thirteen straight times.

Eventually, he and Frankie listened to every disc that was in that pile, many times over. El Maestro's favorite was a shellac recording of a gypsy guitar player named Django Reinhardt, whom the teacher labeled "not of this earth." Frankie was partial to Louis Armstrong and the song "Bill Bailey, Won't You Please Come Home?" the lyrics of which he memorized. One day, as El Maestro ate one of Frankie's sausage *bocadillos*, the boy sang it for his teacher in perfect imitation.

"Won't you come home, Bill Bailey?
Won't you come home?"
She moans the whole day long.
"I'll do the cookin' honey; I'll pay the rent.
I know I've done you wrong . . ."

When Frankie stopped, the blind man finished chewing, then rubbed his chin with two fingers.

"Francisco, you are going to have a problem."

"What problem?"

"You sing well."

"Thank you, Maestro."

"Too well. You must decide what you are going to be—a great singer or a great guitar player."

"Can I be both?"

El Maestro sighed. "Being both means being neither."

Frankie looked at his teacher, the dark glasses, the unshaven whiskers. He didn't mean to let him down by singing.

"I am sorry, Maestro."

The blind man smacked his teeth.

"And stop trying to sound like Louis Armstrong. You are going to hurt your throat."

12

I HAVE PROMISED SPEEDY MOVEMENT THROUGH THESE remaining Spanish years. So let me focus on two days only: the day Frankie fell in love, and the day he left.

The first took place in the early autumn of 1944, on a cloudless afternoon when Baffa drove Frankie to the sardine factory near La Vilavella. Not long after arriving, Baffa was drawn into another argument between laborers, and he told Frankie to take the hairless dog for a walk. Frankie understood this to mean his papa did not want him hearing what was being said, and that was fine, since he wanted to finish learning the latest song El Maestro had taught him.

With the guitar slung over his back, he led the hairless dog down the long path out of town. He whistled as he walked, and he sang a tune to himself and threw a stick, which the hairless dog retrieved.

Before long he had wandered far from any houses and deep into a thicket of woods. Figuring he could lean against a tree stump to practice, he meandered until he found a good spot. He sat down, adjusted his guitar, held his left hand out (as El Maestro had taught), and began to play his scales.

"Shhhhh!"

He looked up.

"Shhhhh!"

Frankie could not see who was shushing him. His eyes worked their way through the woods until he spotted a figure in a tree, straddling a huge branch. It was a boy, about his size, in brown pants, a yellow shirt, and a cap pulled down tightly over his forehead.

"*Quién anda ahí?*" Frankie said.

"I don't speak Spanish. Be quiet!"

"I can speak English," Frankie said.

The child squinted.

"Do you want to see dead bodies?"

Frankie gripped his guitar neck.

"I have to practice."

"Are you scared?"

"No."

"It's all right. Most people aren't as brave as me."

The boy's English sounded strange. (It was Frankie's first British accent.)

"I'm not afraid."

"Prove it."

"How do I prove it?"

"Climb up."

Part of Frankie wanted to run. He had no desire to see

dead bodies. But he had never encountered an English-speaking child before. And he didn't have many friends, since most of the schoolkids still teased him for rubbing his eyes. He wondered if this boy knew any songs.

"All right," Frankie said. "I'll come up."

He wrapped his arms around the trunk and tried to climb. He got a few feet before falling awkwardly.

"That was stupid," the boy said, laughing.

Frankie wiped the dirt off his shorts. The hairless dog licked his bare legs.

"Here. Catch."

The boy dropped a rope that was tied around the branch. Gripping it and jumping, Frankie pushed his feet against the tree and began walking up the trunk. When he reached the branch, he collapsed.

"Hmmph," the boy said.

Only then, breathing hard, did Frankie realize that this was not a boy at all, but a girl with blond hair tucked under a cap. Her teeth formed a perfect little curve beneath her lips, and her skin was whiter and her cheeks pinker than any Frankie had ever seen. Her eyes were the shade of pool water, which made her seem a bit dreamy, even when she was looking straight at him.

"You have proven you are brave," she said matter-of-factly. "So you can be my friend."

Something warm spread inside Frankie. He felt as brave as she suggested.

"Help me pull the rope up," she said.

"Why are you in this tree?"

"I'm spying."

"What does that mean?"

"You don't know what spying means?"

Frankie shrugged.

"I'm seeing secret things that no one is supposed to see."

"Why?"

"So I can tell my daddy. He is very important, you know."

Frankie shrugged again.

"Only brave people can be spies. Like my daddy."

"Where is he?"

"I don't know. He's on a secret mission. But when he comes back, I shall tell him what I saw."

"What did you see?"

"The dead bodies. Look."

⁓

Frankie had almost forgotten about this part. He looked to where she was pointing and saw a large clearing in the woods, where the dirt appeared different from the dirt surrounding it. It had been dug up, churned, and replaced, as if covering something. Nearby was a deep, empty hole beside another mound of dirt.

"They dug it this morning," the girl whispered. "That's where they'll put them."

"Put what?"

"The new ones."

Before she could elaborate, a military truck came rumbling into the woods, crushing weeds and twigs in its path. The girl stiffened and grabbed Frankie's forearm. He stared at her small white hand, her fingers thin and delicate in their grip. Frankie spent a great deal of time looking at fingers—guitarists often do—and he would never forget his first look at hers.

"Don't talk," she whispered.

The military truck came to a halt. With the engine still running, a band of men jumped out. They wore scarves over their mouths and noses. There was fast movement, something was unlatched, and then the men were pulling bodies from the back—six bodies, barefoot, still wearing clothes, which were darkly stained and wet. They seemed, to Frankie, to be deeply asleep, so asleep that they bent when carried, like long sacks of rice. He wanted them to stir, to say, "Hey, put me down. I'm awake now." But they never even flinched.

With the rumbling engine drowning out any sound, the soldiers silently threw the bodies in the hole, one atop the other, with no more emotion than dockworkers unloading crates. They returned to the truck and brought out long metal shovels.

Minutes later, enough dirt had been thrown on the

corpses that Frankie and the girl could no longer see them. The soldiers didn't speak. They just packed the dirt with the back of their shovels and stomped on it with their feet. Once finished, they hurried back into the truck, pulling the doors shut as it rumbled away.

Suddenly it was terribly quiet, as if the earth itself were too stunned to breathe. I know this sound; silence is part of music. But just because something is silent doesn't mean you aren't hearing it.

Frankie looked at the girl. A single tear fell down her cheek. As she stared at the freshly covered graves, she put her hands together in front of her and spoke in a soft, deliberate voice. Her words were from the Catholic ritual of *Sancta Missa*:

" 'Come in haste to assist them, you saints of God. Come in haste to meet them, you angels of the Lord. Enfold in your arms these souls, and take your burden heavenward to the most high.' "

She turned to Frankie.

"Somebody has to say that for them, or else they won't get to heaven."

She wiped the tear away with a knuckle.

"We can climb down now. And you can play me your guitar."

Here is what I know of love. It changes the way you treat me. I feel it in your hands. Your fingers. Your compositions. The sudden rush of peppy phrases, major sevenths, melody lines that resolve neatly and sweetly, like a valentine tucked in an envelope. Humans grow dizzy from new affection, and young Frankie was already dizzy when he and the mysterious girl descended from that tree.

They walked together without talking. She led him to the lip of the burial field.

"Not so close," she said, when he edged up on her heels.

"Sorry."

She smiled.

"You're still afraid."

"No, I'm not."

"The soldiers won't come back."

"How do you know?"

"They never do."

"Were all those people dead?"

"Yes."

"How did they die?"

"They probably got shot."

"Why?"

"Because there's a war. My daddy says the Generalísimo kills whoever he wants."

Frankie had heard this name before. Generalísimo. It made him shiver.

"I don't like war," he said.

"I hate war."

"Me, too."

"You talk funny."

"No, I don't."

"Where did you learn English?"

"From my teacher."

"Your schoolteacher?"

"My guitar teacher."

Frankie swallowed, realizing he had just violated El Maestro's trust.

"You can't tell anyone."

"I won't."

"It's a secret."

"I can keep a secret."

She looked at his guitar. The hairless dog looked at her looking at it.

"Can you really play?"

"Yes."

"Play something."

"For you?"

She turned to the freshly dug field.

"For them."

"What should I play?"

"I don't know. Something that says we won't forget them."

Frankie wanted very much to please her. He thought about all the music he'd learned. He recalled one of the stolen discs, a song from the Philippines that his teacher said was "sad enough to melt the phonograph needle." El Maestro had taught it to Frankie. Its title was "Maalaala Mo Kaya," written by a Filipino composer named Constancio de Guzman. ("An elegant name," El Maestro had mused.) It depicted two people from different social classes promising not to forget their love. On the record label, the translated title was "Will You Remember?"

Frankie sat on a rock and put the guitar on his knee. He was keenly aware of his new friend watching him, and he tried to play perfectly. I felt it in the touch he applied to the strings, in the tenderness he draped over each and every note.

Had you watched the scene from a distance, it might have seemed odd, two children near a mass grave, one playing the guitar, one listening, the sun hot in the sky, the tracks of a Spanish army truck still fresh in the dirt.

But I saw something else. I saw a boy all but bending the strings in a girl's direction. It was the first time Frankie Presto attempted to give his music to someone else.

Which is how I knew he was in love.

"How do you play like that?" she said when he finished.

"I don't know."

"It's quite good."

"Really?"

"Yes."

"Do you think they heard it?"

She looked at the dirt field. "I don't know. It's not a proper grave."

"What does *proper* mean?"

"It's when you do something the right way."

"What is the right way?"

"For a grave? You make it very nice. You put the body in a box. The family comes to say good-bye. And they put flowers on top."

"Why flowers?"

"So the dead people have something pretty to look at as they go up to heaven."

"Oh."

"Have you never seen a grave?"

"My mother has one."

"Your mother died?"

"Yes."

"Was she nice?"

"I never met her."

"Where's her grave?"

"America."

"So you never saw it?"

"No."

Frankie wondered what that grave looked like, and if anyone had put flowers there. He wished he could ask Baffa. He suddenly missed his father very much.

"We should put flowers on *this* grave," the girl said.

"All right."

"Do you see any?"

"What about those?"

"Those are weeds."

"You can't use weeds?"

"No. They're ugly."

They stood in silence. Frankie looked at his guitar.

"There were six people, right?"

"Yes."

"I know what we can do."

He lowered his guitar and began twisting a tuning peg backward. He untied the string from its peg and its bridge. With the loose string in his hand, he squatted down and the girl squatted with him. He looped the string several times, then bent it at a ninety-degree angle and tied it all in place, creating a stem that stuck down from the circles. He had done this before with El Maestro's old strings, making toy shapes while his teacher slept on the couch. But he had never removed a string from his guitar before.

He pushed the end into the ground and pressed it with two small stones so it stood upright.

"A flower," the girl marveled.

"So they can go to heaven," Frankie said.

"But now you can't play."

Frankie knew she was right. Still, he loosened another string, then another and another.

"Can I try?" the girl asked.

They squatted together. This time she didn't tell him, "Not so close." They made five more string flowers and spread them around the dirt that covered the bodies. Then they stood and rubbed the dirt away. The sun lowered in the sky. The girl mumbled a small prayer and Frankie repeated her words, even though he didn't comprehend them.

As they gazed at the grave, she hooked her fingers in Frankie's. He squeezed hers in return. There are moments on earth when the Lord smiles at the unexpected sweetness of His creation. This was one of those moments.

"What's your name?"

"Francisco."

"What's your last name?"

"Rubio."

"Does it mean something? Francisco?"

"It is the name of a famous guitarist."

"Oh."

"What's your name?"

"Aurora."

"What's your last name?"

"York."

"Does it mean something? Aurora?"

"It means 'dawn.' "

"What's dawn?"

"When the sun comes up. Everybody knows that."

Frankie looked away. He would have to ask El Maestro to teach him more English.

"You play very well, Francisco."

Frankie blushed.

"I think you are the best guitar player in the world."

"Really?"

"I wouldn't lie to you."

The hairless dog whimpered.

"Have you ever been kissed by a girl?"

"Once."

"Where?"

"In school."

She laughed. "No. *Where?* On your cheek?"

"On my ear."

"Which ear?"

He pointed.

"I'll kiss the other one," she said.

And she did. Softly. Quickly. And then, as if quite happy with herself, she leaned over and patted the hairless dog's head.

Frankie blinked.

"Aurora," he said, as if practicing. "Au-ro-ra."

She smiled as he said her name, and he smiled back, and without even knowing it, he had joined another band. From that moment on, Aurora York was in Frankie's music. That day. That night. And forever.

13

NOW, UNDERSTAND, IN MY WORLD, THINGS SHIFT QUICKLY from major to minor. It's a simple chord change, a flatting of the third; you move one finger, and it's done. Frankie left the woods that day in a dreamy state, the hairless dog walking beside him. But when he returned to the factory, he knew something was wrong. There were police trucks outside. Men in gray uniforms were leaning against the front wall. The hairless dog growled.

"What do you want, boy?" a policeman asked.

Frankie swallowed.

"My papa."

"Where is your papa?"

"Inside there."

"Yes? Inside here? Really?" The policeman stood up straight. Another truck pulled up. Frankie recognized it as the one he had seen in the woods. The soldiers who had earlier been burying bodies stepped out and lit cigarettes. Frankie's heart was racing.

"Who is your papa?" the officer asked.

The hairless dog began to bark.

"Shut up, beast!"

The man pulled his gun.

"No!" Frankie screamed.

The man fired and missed, the bullet raising smoke from the dirt. The dog raced away.

"Now," the policeman continued, "who is your papa?"

Just then the front door of the factory swung open, and one of Baffa's workers came stumbling out with his arms tied at the wrists. Two policemen stepped out behind him.

"Luis!" Frankie yelled. "Luis! Where is—"

Luis glared hard and shook his head. Frankie went silent.

"Is this man your father?" the policeman said.

"His father isn't here!" Luis yelled. "He's out sick."

"Quiet!" shouted the officer holding him. He jammed a stick into his ribs, then pulled Luis toward the truck and shoved him inside. Frankie saw two other workers already in the backseat. They looked terrified.

"Is that true, music boy?"

Frankie felt tears running down his face.

"Speak, boy! Is that true? Is your father sick at home?"

"*Sí*," Frankie finally whispered.

"Then why did you say he was inside?"

Frankie stared straight ahead. "I wanted . . . water."

"Get water somewhere else. And give me that guitar. I'll show you how a Spaniard plays."

Without waiting, the officer yanked the instrument from Frankie's back. He flipped it over.

"What is this? There are no strings."

He spat.

"You need strings to play a guitar, boy. Has your papa not taught you that?"

He flung the guitar, and it landed in the dirt. The others laughed.

"Francisco, go home!" Luis yelled from the truck.

The officers laughed again.

"Yes, Francisco, go home. Tell your father there won't be any work tomorrow. Or the next day."

Frankie turned and ran, his feet making a crunching sound on the gravel as he broke away. He ran nine or ten paces, then stopped, ran back, and scooped up his guitar. The policemen laughed again.

"Better find some strings!" one of them yelled, but Frankie was already disappearing, his breath filling his chest so deeply he felt as if he'd swallowed all the air in his country.

He ran a long way. When his legs gave out, he walked. Then he ran again. A truck of gypsies pulled alongside him. They offered to take Frankie to Villareal for all the coins in his pocket—and his guitar. He reluctantly handed it over. He crawled in the back, the gypsies' eyes upon him, and wedged between a sack of potatoes and a snoring woman in a black shawl.

As the truck headed west, it was passed by a military vehicle that would stop at the sardine factory and unload an officer who, upon hearing that a boy had been there and had run away, slapped the face of a soldier and yelled, "That was the bastard! The Rubio boy!"

But by that point Frankie was bouncing in the back of a flatbed, trying not to cry. It seems cruel to say that he never saw Baffa again. But it is true. On the same day Frankie Presto found love, he lost his home.

Major to minor.

Abby Cruz

Songwriter, producer

I MET FRANKIE PRESTO IN A CUBICLE.

It's true. I was twenty years old, and had just started working for Aldon Music in New York City, in an office building on Broadway. They put songwriters like me in cubicles, one next to the other. Neil Sedaka was there. Carole King. Gerry Goffin. Cynthia Weill. Barry Mann. Our job was to write hits. You had your piano and your little table and your ashtray—everyone smoked back then—and you pounded away. It sounds strange now, because we could hear each other working through the walls. But that actually inspired us. It was a competition. An awful lot of famous music came out of those cubicles. "On Broadway," "Breaking Up Is Hard to Do," "Will You Still Love Me Tomorrow."

I never had any hits that big. I was struggling, hoping they wouldn't fire me. They paid fifty dollars a week, and they expected you to make them money in return.

I was the only Latino writer working there, so there was never any call for speaking Spanish. But one day, in 1961, I was pregnant with my first child—so I was really hoping they wouldn't fire me—and everyone was out to lunch except me. I was desperate to write something big. I was playing the piano, this one hook that I thought was good, and all of a sudden I hear a guitar. It caught my ear because, for one thing, there weren't a lot of guitars around—and this one was playing a solo *over my piano chords.*

I stopped. And it stopped.

So I started again. And sure enough, the guitar starts playing again, a fast little solo. So I tried something tricky. I played a song my Colombian grandmother had taught me. "La Malagueña." And I heard that guitar take off on it, playing like crazy.

So I stopped and said in Spanish, "Okay, who's doing that?" And from the next cubicle out pops the most handsome man I've ever seen—black hair, blue eyes, wearing a pink shirt and black slacks. And he says, *"Hola, me llamo Frankie."* I knew him right away. He'd been on *The Ed Sullivan Show*—twice—and *American Bandstand.* "I Want To Love You" had been the number one record in the country. I mean, everyone in the business knew Frankie Presto. But I had no idea he spoke Spanish. We all thought he was from California.

Anyhow, there I am, pregnant out to here, and I say, "Hi, I'm Abby." And he says, "How do you know 'La

Malagueña'?" And I say, "What are you doing here?" And he says, "Hiding." He points to the window, and I walk across and look down and there's a mob of young girls holding his records, crowding around the front entrance.

It turns out he was there with his manager, Tappy Fishman, who was meeting with our company about songs for Frankie's next album. I got excited because I thought maybe I could write for him, but he told me he didn't really want to record other people's material. He was just going along to be polite.

"I think an artist should sing his own songs," he said.

"You wrote 'I Want To Love You,' right?"

"Yeah."

"For a girl?"

"Uh-huh."

"Did she like it?"

"I don't know," he said. "She disappeared."

I couldn't believe I was alone with him. I asked what it was like to be that famous—he was in *LIFE* magazine, was friends with Sinatra and Bobby Darin, all that kind of stuff—and he laughed and said it was usually fun, except when he had to run from screaming women. He'd actually hurt his ankle once jumping from a fire escape.

Only when he was leaving did he ask, "When's your baby coming?" I appreciated that, since with most men, it was the first thing they mentioned. I told him six weeks, and I was just hoping they wouldn't fire me before then. He said, "They won't fire you. You write good hooks." And then he said, "One day, I want to teach my kids music."

So my daughter was born, and I took a few months off. When I returned to work I discovered, in my cubicle, a basket of toys and a note that read, "Congratulations!" signed "The Guitar Player Next Door." Inside the basket was a piece of sheet music for a song called "No, No, Honey." Under the title it said, "Written by Frankie Presto and Abby Cruz."

Well, I must've stared at it forever. Then I slapped it on the piano and played it. The hook was the chorus I'd been playing the day he came in. I don't know how he remembered it! But he gave me cowriting credit for the whole piece. And as you probably know, "No, No, Honey" became a top-ten song. My first gold record. And I promise you, it kept me from being fired. Carole and Gerry had written major hits for the Shirelles and the Drifters, Neil Sedaka had done it for Connie Francis, Barry and Cynthia had done it for the Crystals. But I had a hit with Frankie Presto. That was huge!

Over the next few years he'd send me little notes at the office, congratulating me on writing this or that. He always added, "Sing your own songs!" and he always signed it, "The Guitar Player Next Door." And then the notes stopped. I didn't hear from him for years. I know he went through a lot, and he stopped making music for a long time.

Still, when I heard how he died, I was shocked. I wanted to come. Pay my respects. He was so kind to me early on. Without him, I might have been out of the music business altogether. "No, No, Honey" put my daughter through college. I do find it strange, him being buried in Spain, because I remember him saying something very harsh about this country once.

It was the last time I saw him, in New York, 1964, an industry thing at a big hotel. By that point, he'd had all those other hits, like "Shake, Shake" and "Our Secret," but he seemed a little less happy-go-lucky. He was wearing a yellow suit and sunglasses, and was standing with his manager and his fiancée, the actress, I forget her name. I had my little girl, so I didn't want to bother him. But as soon as he saw us, he raced over.

"This is the baby?" he asked.

"This is her," I said.

"How old?"

"Three."

"Wow."

"Your fiancée is beautiful, by the way."

"Thanks."

"Is she the one you wrote 'I Want To Love You' for?"

"Nah."

He bent down to talk to my daughter and sang her "Do Re Mi." When he finished, she hugged him.

"Where are you getting married?" I asked.

"Hawaii."

"Really?"

"Tappy is taking care of everything."

"Do you have family in Hawaii?"

"I'm from Spain, remember?"

"Then why not get married in Spain?"

His face tightened up.

"I'm never going back there again," he said.

14

THE SECOND DAY I PROMISED TO SHARE WAS THE DAY YOUNG
Frankie left his homeland for good. This occurred eleven
months and nine days after Baffa was imprisoned for something made up by disgruntled workers that was, frankly,
beyond my comprehension. You humans are always locking
each other away. Cells. Dungeons. Some of your earliest
jails were sewers, where men sloshed in their own waste.
No other creature has this arrogance—to confine its own.
Could you imagine a bird imprisoning another bird? A
horse jailing a horse? As a free form of expression, I will
never understand it. I can only say that some of my saddest
sounds have been heard in such places. A song inside a cage
is never a song. It is a plea.

Frankie had come home the night of the factory raid hoping to find Baffa in the house on Calvario Street, but it was
empty when he entered and still empty when he woke up.
He noticed the front-door lock had been broken and furniture had been pushed out of place. His stomach growled.
He wished Baffa could make him his breakfast. He peeked

out the windows and saw people going by, but after Luis had deliberately lied to protect him, Frankie understood not to trust anyone. He stayed in the dark, praying for his papa. He washed his face and behind his ears, in case good behavior might hasten Baffa's return. Without a guitar, he could play no music, and he was too afraid to turn on the radio for fear someone might hear him. Soon the silence grew so loud, Frankie put his hands over his ears.

I wanted to comfort him. To drape him with a soothing melody. But I knew at that moment he was once again being watched, and I dared not interfere with such fates.

Instead, Frankie hid inside for two days, eating from jars and drinking water from the sink. He saw Baffa's face with every blink of his eyes, saw him humming behind the wheel of the Italian automobile, tapping his foot as Frankie practiced, leaning over to kiss the boy good night.

On the third morning, Frankie heard a scratching at the door. He feared it was the soldiers and ran out back to the garden, hiding behind the table where he once drummed a *jota* beat. He waited, expecting someone to kick the door open. Instead he heard a whimpering sound, and he slid out to see the hairless dog slinking toward him, his breath labored and his pink tongue drooping and wet.

I cannot tell you how that creature made the journey, but Frankie had never been so happy to see anything in his life. He grabbed the dog by the neck and hugged it, burying his face in the animal's coat and crying for a long time. They lay there together in the garden, two members of the trio, missing their third.

Everyone joins a band in this life.

One way or another, the band breaks up.

e⌒

That afternoon Frankie changed his shirt, tied his shoes, pulled on a tweed cap, and took the hairless dog with him out the back gate of the garden. An hour later a police car would arrive, and two officers would again search the house. This may seem highly fortuitous, but when a higher power has plans for you, life can be full of near misses.

Frankie walked with his head lowered and the cap pulled down until he reached the laundry on Crista Senegal Street. He climbed the steps. He banged on El Maestro's door. No answer. He banged again.

"*Quién es?*" came the raspy voice.

"It is me, Maestro."

"Your lesson was yesterday."

"Yes, Maestro."

"Is today yesterday?"

"I am sorry, Maestro."

"Go away."

"Please, Maestro."

"Today is not your day."

"May I come in, Maestro?"

"Go back to your papa."

"I can't, Maestro."

"Why not?"

Frankie didn't answer.

"Why *not*, boy?"

Frankie couldn't breathe.

"I am going back to sleep now—"

"My papa is gone!"

Frankie began crying the moment he said "gone." Everything he'd held inside came gushing out. His knees buckled. He dropped to the floor. His sobs were more inhale than exhale, and the hairless dog nudged his face with his nose, whimpering with him, harmonizing his misery.

Finally the door swung open. Frankie grabbed the bottom of his teacher's legs and squeezed them tightly. The blind man stood with the dark glasses on his nose, tilting his chin upward.

"You will come inside and eat," he said softly. "Then you will tell me what happened." He shook his head. "This country has gone to hell."

ᕫ

Suffice it to say that Frankie and the hairless dog lived with El Maestro from that day until the night Frankie boarded a ship. I will skip over most of the details for now (we do have a funeral service to get to), but I will tell you that student and teacher had a profound effect on each other, as humans thrown together by trauma often do. Frankie slept on a sheet beneath the kitchen table, and in the morning he swept the flat and wiped dust from the guitars. He bought food from the markets until the money in El Maestro's drawer was gone, then he stole from bakeries and fruit stands. He backed up to their edges and slipped the goods into his jacket pocket. When El Maestro discovered what Frankie had been doing, he scolded him harshly.

"You have lost enough, boy. Don't lose your soul as well."

"How will we eat?"

"Are you hungry again?"

"Yes, Maestro."

The blind man fumbled for his wine. Having never had children, he'd been unaware of how much you had to feed them. He heard Frankie take his place under the table and mumble, "Good night, Maestro." He heard the hairless dog whimper, as if echoing him. He stayed in his chair until the last of the wine was gone. Then he rose and went to bed.

The next day he woke up early, bathed, shaved his face, put on a pair of leather shoes, and tucked in a clean white shirt. He asked Frankie how he looked, and when the boy said, "Like you are going to work," he informed Frankie they were heading out.

"Where are we going, Maestro?"

"Just take me where I tell you." He paused. "Bring the dog."

Minutes later, Frankie was leading them through the streets of Villareal, along the Calle Mayor and down a side street of shops and awnings. They were going back to the old *taberna*—the place where Baffa first saw the blind man perform. When they entered, El Maestro lifted his nose and turned his face both ways, as if recalling the room by scent. He then announced, loudly, "I wish to see the owner!" When the man approached, El Maestro sensed him before he spoke and immediately held out his hand.

"We meet again," El Maestro said.

"So we do," the owner said, cautiously.

"I come today with a proposition. I am offering to allow you to host my playing again."

"Why would I do that?"

"Because I am good."

"Not when you are drunk."

"No longer a concern."

"So you say."

"So I do."

"What are you proposing?"

"Two shows each night. In exchange for a fair wage, of course."

"We do not play the same music as before."

"This I know."

"Only what the Generalísimo approves."

"This I know as well."

"You still want to work?"

"Am I not here in front of you?"

"What about the drinking?"

"I do not drink anymore. The child makes sure of it. Right, boy?"

He tapped Frankie's shoulder, and Frankie forced a smile.

"My nephew," El Maestro said. "And our lovely dog."

The dog whimpered.

The owner pursed his lips.

"You have changed your life quite a bit."

"As you can see."

"You've even shaved."

"Indeed."

"Well . . . You *are* the best who ever played here."

"I agree."

"But I cannot have the customers upset."

"Of course."

"You must arrive on time."

"Early, even."

"If you drink, you are out, understood?"

"Understood."

He looked at the new trio, man, boy, dog.

"You start tomorrow."

"As you wish," El Maestro said.

℃

When they got home, Frankie gathered the bottles of wine and *aguardiente* and put them in a garbage pail.

"What are you doing?" El Maestro asked.

"It's not right to lie," Frankie answered. "You told him no more drinking."

El Maestro groaned, but he didn't stop the boy. Instead, he slumped into the couch, as if resigned to a new fate. He held his face in his hands, then lurched forward until he found his guitar. Frankie was privately happy to get rid of the alcohol. He liked El Maestro better without it. As his teacher began playing a Segovia composition, Frankie carried the bottles downstairs and gave them to the woman who did the laundry, in exchange for several months of free washes and a promise she would make them dinner that night.

And thus did Frankie Presto, in his newest band, influence its blind leader, who, despite swearing he would never do it again, returned to a stage to play his beautiful music.

15

PERHAPS YOU ARE WONDERING ABOUT BAFFA, THAT POOR, simple soul. Frankie wondered, too. In the beginning, he asked El Maestro about his papa every morning, but there was no word. I have mentioned how the fear of tyrants chokes humans; to even inquire about a "disappeared person" in those years meant you might be next. The world was at war, Spain was under martial law, and anything that offended the Generalísimo's political or religious beliefs was punished by prison, even death. El Maestro told the boy it was too dangerous to speak about Baffa outside the house. In time, Frankie stopped asking altogether.

But being silent is not forgetting. And the child never forgot his papa. Each night, before crawling under the kitchen table, he would turn on the stolen phonograph and listen softly to an Ella Fitzgerald recording of "A-Tisket A-Tasket," the song about losing a brown and yellow basket.

In the song, Ella pined for her basket and wondered where it could be, and the men in her band responded, "*So do we! So do we!*" Frankie felt the same way about Baffa. *So do I! So do I! Where could he be?* The song gave him comfort. That is often why you come to music, isn't it? To feel that you are not alone?

Meanwhile, during the daylight hours, Frankie studied intensely with his newly sober teacher. It would be the boy's most fertile musical growth period. As he no longer went to school (an arrangement that did not bother Frankie at all), the two of them worked hours at a time on the guitar. Before he turned nine years old, Frankie could already play multiple styles, from jazz to flamenco, turning his fingernails inward to strum in the *rasgueo* technique. Going classical, he could finger-pick with great speed through difficult arpeggios that made it sound as if one hand were playing a bass line while the other hand played a cascade of notes. El Maestro, despite his blindness, painstakingly taught Frankie to read music, through description, listening, more description, more listening. The teacher could hear even a single note out of place, and insisted Frankie check the sheet music and read him where every dot, line, sharp and flat occurred.

Although his cheeks were still soft and his thick hair carried the sheen of youth, the boy's music displayed a sensitivity beyond his years. "An old soul" is how you sometimes describe it. But talents like me have been inside you since creation. Every artist is old in that way.

Frankie even mastered the much-revered twelve études of Heitor Villa-Lobos, which were extremely demanding in how they stretched his left fingers. If he complained about

how hard they were, El Maestro would tell him, "Mr. Lo-
bos lived with cannibals in the Brazilian jungle to learn his
music. *That* was hard. What you are doing is not."

"Is that really true, Maestro?"

"What?"

"That story?"

"Of course."

"Cannibals?"

Maestro sighed.

"Man suffers for his art, Francisco. That is what you
must remember. Sometimes it is cannibals. Sometimes it
is worse."

❧

Although Frankie asked many times, he was forbidden to
accompany El Maestro to the *taberna*. "You must have your
sleep," El Maestro said. Instead, a mustached conga player
named Alberto came by each night to take the blind man
to work.

"*Tu tío es un gran artista*," Alberto often said. *Your uncle is
a great artist.*

"*Yo sé*," Frankie replied. *I know.*

Sometimes the boy would wake up in the morning and
smell a faint trace of perfume. He thought about the dresses
in the closet and he wondered if a lady had been there while

he was sleeping. It made him think about the pink cheeks and the thin white fingers of Aurora York, and the afternoon they had together before everything changed.

"Maestro?" he asked one day as they ate breakfast, "When is the right age to get married?"

"Are you not telling me something, Francisco?"

"No."

"Have you met a girl?"

"Once."

"And you want to marry her?"

"Maybe."

"Where did you meet her?"

"In the woods."

"Was she a fairy?"

"I don't think so."

"Did she have strange eyes?"

"Yes."

"Was she kind and helpful?"

"Yes."

"Have you seen her again?"

"No."

"She was a fairy. An *anjana*. Don't fall in love with fairies, Francisco. They are not real."

"She was real."

"She sounds like a fairy."

"She was not a fairy!"

"All right. She was not a fairy." He chewed and swallowed, and then tapped the table until he found his coffee cup. "If she was real, you will see her again."

"When?"

"When it is time."

He sipped his coffee. Frankie scowled.

"Whose dresses are in the closet?"

He didn't mean to ask that. He was angry, and it just slipped out. The blind man put down his cup.

"Finish eating, Francisco."

$$e\sim$$

Every loss leaves a hole in your heart. El Maestro, as you may have surmised, suffered a great loss earlier in his life, one that led him to a drunkard's despair. His wife died. The beautiful woman who would lead him from the stage and plant a kiss on his lips. Once she was gone, he wanted nothing from this earth. He let himself sink—into melancholy, into drinking, into a haunted, restless sleep. If he could have unplugged his heart and shut the lights on his memory, he would have.

But over the months with his new protégé, the teacher healed considerably. He walked better. His belly shrank. His head hurt less. His skin had more color. Without the constant cloud of alcohol, he gradually returned to a sense of purpose. He found himself almost glad to be waking up, smelling the toast that Francisco was making. He enjoyed the respect that the child showed him, pulling out his chair, handing him his guitar. He liked hearing Frankie sing around the flat, songs the two of them shared in their secret library of shellac recordings. He even, begrudgingly, accepted the dog. Sometimes, the creature would lay its head in El Maestro's lap and he would scratch its ears.

"He likes you," Frankie said.

"He smells like gutter water," El Maestro said.

Deep down, the blind man knew that Frankie remained heartbroken over his father. And having come to care about the boy himself, he could only imagine what pain Baffa was going through. So one night, at the *taberna*, El Maestro took a chance. He asked the owner if there were any soldiers in the audience.

Yes, he was told, a group of them sitting near the front.

"Introduce me," El Maestro said.

Throughout the evening, he played many flamenco favorites—the kind of music the Generalísimo approved of—and he dedicated them all to the "brave men serving our leader." People clapped and the owner smiled and the soldiers were appreciative. Later they invited the guitar player to sit with them. He bought them drinks and told them stories and bought more drinks and laughed in a way that he never usually laughed. It was, deep down, agonizing for El Maestro. He had an ugly history with war, and had no use for soldiers or generals. But, like practicing scales, some things you endure for a reason. As the soldiers drank more and more, he braved a few questions.

By the end of the night, he had learned the fate of a sardine maker named Baffa Rubio.

℮

On August 3, 1945, two days before Frankie left the country for good, El Maestro paid a visit to a prison many miles outside Villareal. It took lies and bribes and a gypsy on a motorcycle to accomplish. More details are unimportant to this story. What is important is, that afternoon, in an empty yard behind a redbrick jail, a final conversation took place between the unmarried man who found a baby in a river and the blind guitarist who taught him his destiny.

They spoke for twenty-four minutes, in a whispered, *mosso* pace, 7/4 time—a jerky, interrupting rhythm. Baffa Rubio, who was pale and bruised and much thinner than he had ever been, saw the man with the dark glasses and began to tremble. He waited for the guards to move away. His first two whispered words were: "My son?"

"I have him—"

"Thank God."

Tears. Breathing. Silence.

"He is all right?"

"He is all right."

"Does he ask for me?"

"Of course."

Tears. Breathing. Silence.

"I am a poor father. I never planned if something happened to me."

"I am watching him, Señor Rubio."

"You must not tell anyone he is mine."

"Why not?"

"The factory. Three workers—they hated me—they told the police I was Socialista, that the others were from trade unions. When I denied this, they said I lied. They said the boy was proof. That a good Catholic would never take in a bastard. That his mother was a leftist—"

"Wait. He is not your child?"

Tears. Breathing. Silence.

"I have done nothing wrong."

"Of course not."

"I saved a life."

"Of course."

"These pigs—"

"Softly, Señor Rubio."

"This Franco—"

"Do not speak of him, Señor Rubio."

"I have done nothing wrong."

"I understand."

Tears. Breathing. Silence.

"Are you teaching him guitar?"

"Every day."

"And his playing?"

"It is exceptional."

"I wish I could hear him."

"How long will they keep you?"

"Twelve years and a day."

"Twelve years?"

"That is my sentence. How can this be? When I get out, Francisco will be a man."

"I am very sorry."

"I must ask you a favor. Will you do it?"

"I will do it."

"Send the boy away."

El Maestro felt his stomach tighten.

"Away?"

"Yes."

"Where?"

"America. I have a sister."

"America?"

"He will be safe there."

"Such a journey."

"There is no future here."

"But I can watch him—"

"It is too risky"

"He can stay with—"

"Please, Maestro. Someone will talk. I have heard what they do to children of traitors. They are beaten and starved."

"But you are not a traitor."

"Yet I am still here."

El Maestro rubbed his face. He was sweating now.

"How would I do this?"

"I have money. Hidden. You will get it. Pay the men at the docks."

"Which men? Which docks?"

"Enough money will get you any man at any dock."

"But how—"

"Listen. We have little time. Take this."

He grabbed the blind man's hand and slipped him a piece of fabric ripped from a shirt. On it was some writing.

"There is an address in America. It is where he must go."

"All right."

"Give the boy a new name. Mine is poison."

"All right."

"Tell him one day I will find him."

"Yes."

"Not to forget me."

"Yes."

"That I love him."

"I will tell him, Señor Rubio."

Tears. Choking.

"I've done nothing wrong, Maestro. You must believe me."

"I do."

"He is all I had."

"I'm sorry."

"Do what I ask."

"I will."

"Keep what money is left."

"I do not want your money, Señor Rubio."

"I meant no offense. You cannot know what it is to give up a child."

Beneath the dark glasses, tears began to well.

"No," the blind man said. "Of course not."

16

THAT NIGHT, AFTER FINISHING AT THE *TABERNA*, EL MAESTRO and Alberto the conga player slipped into the house on Calvario Street (which had been looted and emptied of its possessions) and found a tin box hidden beneath a floorboard, just as Baffa Rubio had detailed. In the box was a velvet sack containing 600,000 pesetas—profits from the sardine factory—enough money to bribe a small army. The two men left quickly through the back garden and went to the laundry on Crista Senegal Street where they sat, by candlelight, as Alberto separated the money into rolls of 10,000 pesetas, each one wrapped in a rubber band so El Maestro would know how much he was handing out.

"Take three for yourself," he told Alberto.

"Maestro, I cannot—

"Yes, you can. Please. Then find some paper. You must write down what I tell you."

He gave instructions for eight minutes. When he finished, Alberto exhaled, looked at his list, then gripped the guitar player's arm.

"This is a great deal in a short time, Maestro."

"The boy is in danger."

"I will do as you ask."

"Thank you, Alberto."

Alberto stared at the velvet sack of money. El Maestro, of course, could not see his face. But I could. I saw a look that I have seen many times when new riches are within reach. The eyes get smaller. The lips tighten.

"Do not worry, Maestro," Alberto said. "God is on our side."

El Maestro did not sleep well that night. In the morning, with Frankie still dozing, he got dressed in the clothes stacked on the bathroom counter (the boy did this for him every evening) and made his way to the closet. He fumbled until he found a purse draped on a hanger. He undid the clasp and reached for something inside: a set of new strings, coiled together in a circle. He remained in the closet for several minutes, as still as a statue. Then he stepped out, shut the door, and moved to the kitchen.

"Get up, Francisco," he said.

The boy opened his eyes. The hairless dog lifted its head.

"Did I sleep too long, Maestro?"

"No," the blind man said, gripping the strings. "But we have much to do today."

The remaining hours of August 5, 1945, were ripe with activity, as if a trumpet player were blowing eighth-note triplets to fill each measure. El Maestro told Frankie to pack a bag with a toothbrush, comb, soap, and all the clothes he could fit in, especially underwear.

"Where are we going?"

"An adventure."

"Where is *your* bag, Maestro?"

"I will get it later. Now hurry."

They left the flat and, holding the boy's hand, the blind man had Frankie lead him first to a shop on San Miguel Street, where guitars and violins hung on the walls. Frankie had never seen such a place. It smelled of wood and oil. When a bearded man came out from the back, he approached El Maestro and hugged him. They spoke in quiet voices, a conversation Frankie could not hear.

"Maestro, is it you?"

"It has been a while, old friend."

"How may I help?"

"Today I must leave with your finest guitar. Make sure it is strong enough to travel."

"I have an Estruch. Spruce, rosewood, an ebony neck."

"Excellent."

"But this would be expensive."

"Get it for me now. And your most solid case."

"You are playing again, Maestro?"

"It is for the boy."

"That boy?"

"Yes. And one more request. Cover the maker's seal."

"But that will devalue the instrument."

"He does not need to know its value."

"Nor do those he might encounter?"

"Precisely."

"And the strings?"

"No strings."

"As you wish, old friend. But may I ask one thing?"

"Certainly."

"Is this too fine a guitar for a boy so young?"

"No. It must be with him the rest of his life."

"Why?"

"Because I cannot be."

El Maestro handed him a roll of bills from a sack in his jacket pocket, and the man disappeared for a few minutes. Frankie approached and touched his teacher's elbow.

"What are the black boxes, Maestro?" he asked, studying a row of small amplifiers.

"Do they have knobs?"

"Yes."

"And a cord?"

"Yes."

"A waste of time."

"What do they do?"

"They make your guitar very loud, so people can hear you from far away."

"Is that bad, Maestro?"

The blind man found Frankie's shoulder.

"Remember this, Francisco," he said. "The secret is not to make your music louder, but to make the world quieter."

The shop owner emerged with a guitar case. He called El Maestro over. They whispered and hugged once more, and El Maestro turned, carrying the new purchase. He held out his left hand. Frankie led him out the door.

"Did you buy a new guitar, Maestro?"

"Yes."

"When will you play it?"

"Walk to the right."

e‿

They made three more stops. At each place, Frankie was surprised to see El Maestro greeted by people who seemed to know him. The boy had hardly heard his teacher speak to anyone. In fact, the only person the blind man ever addressed by name was Isabel, the woman who owned the laundry downstairs and who now and then cooked them *peladillas*, almonds wrapped in a candy shell.

But on this day, people were embracing the blind man as if welcoming him home. Frankie could not know that years earlier, before the war, El Maestro had been a well-known guitarist and a popular nightclub performer, acquainted with certain men who liked to stay out late listening to music, drinking, and courting women. Musicians often grow friendly with those who stay to the end. They bond in an hour when all the world seems asleep but them. Some of these men scared Frankie, with their craggy faces and large bellies. But they reacted quickly when El Maestro gave them a roll from his pocket. Each conversation ended with a whisper and a handshake. Then El Maestro turned, reaching out for Frankie, and on they went.

In between stops, he bought the boy food, and at the bakery he told Frankie to get extra bread and small jars of honey to put in his bag. Overall, it was an exciting day for the boy. But he kept waiting for El Maestro to pack his own suitcase, and he noticed the hairless dog sticking close to him, sometimes bumping against his leg.

Late in the afternoon, El Maestro asked, "Where is the sun?"

"Almost gone," Frankie answered.

The blind man told the boy to take him to a nearby restaurant. Frankie and the dog waited outside. Frankie ran his hand gently over the new guitar case. He hoped El Maestro would bring out some food. He was hungry again.

An hour passed. It was nearly dark. When the teacher finally emerged, he had nothing with him. His voice was deep and slow.

"Let's go, Francisco."

"Where, Maestro?"

"To the *taberna*."

"I can see you play?"

"This one time. Yes."

Frankie, at first, was so excited he forgot about his hunger. But El Maestro did not share the enthusiasm. His breathing was labored. He made groaning noises. As he walked, holding the new guitar, he wobbled a bit. Frankie realized that his teacher had not been eating in that restaurant. He had been drinking.

"What color are your pants today, boy?"

Frankie frowned.

"I asked you a question."

"Brown, Maestro."

"And your shoes?"

"Also brown."

"And your hair?"

Frankie didn't want to answer. He felt sad that his teacher had broken his promise, as if bad things were going to start happening again.

"Your hair, boy?"

"It looks black."

"And your eyes? I don't even know."

"My eyes are blue, Maestro."

"Ah. Blue."

He inhaled deeply through his nose. He dropped his chin into his chest. He sang something in a half mumble.

"Am I blue? . . . Am I blue? . . ."

He coughed.

"It's a song, boy. You will learn it one day."

❧

Man searches for courage in drink, but it is not courage that he finds, it is fear that he loses. A drunken man may step off a cliff. That does not make him brave, just forgetful.

That night, on the *taberna* stage, the drink helped El Maestro forget about restrictions imposed on artists in his country. The result was the most fearless performance of his career. Barely pausing between songs, he played American compositions like "St. Louis Blues" and "Tiger Rag." He played "Parfum" from the gypsy legend Django Reinhardt. He did a haunting rendition of the French classic "Parlez-Moi d'Amour" ("Speak to Me of Love"), as well as works by Schumann and Vivaldi and Ferdinando Carulli. His guitar sounded powerful and passionate, and I must confess, I surged through him that night like a shooting fountain. He rocked back and forth, feeling the vibration of every note. People in the crowd were so silent, at times it seemed as if the room was empty. Such music was forbidden by the government. But when performed that beautifully, I can mesmerize a crowd. For the next two hours, no one raised a protest. Not even a heavily clothed figure who was watching from the back.

Toward the end, El Maestro reached up under his dark glasses to rub his eyes. Then, for the first time all night, he spoke.

"This last song, my fellow countrymen, is for the finest student I have ever had."

He turned his head toward where he had put Frankie in a chair, near the kitchen.

"Come, boy. Let's play together."

He began to strum the chords of "Avalon," a song by Al Jolson that Frankie loved to listen to on the stolen phonograph. Customers looked back and forth. Some pointed at the child in the corner.

Frankie felt his whole body shiver. He slid off the chair and nervously approached, touching his teacher's shoulder to let him know he was there.

"Come now," El Maestro whispered over the chords. "Take the other guitar and sing the song."

"But I don't want to."

"Why not?"

"I'm scared."

"Yes. And you will be scared again. All your life. You must conquer this. Face them and pretend they aren't there."

"Maestro—"

"You can do it. Always remember I said you can do it."

Frankie was petrified, but his trust in his teacher was complete. He picked up the guitar, put the strap over his shoulder, and began strumming the chords that he and El Maestro had practiced. Finally, after waiting through the intro, he sang his first song for an audience.

I found my love in Avalon
Beside the bay . . .

The people glanced back and forth. He was singing in English!

I left my love in Avalon
And I sailed away . . .

I will admit, I enjoyed watching their reactions. Frankie's voice was so rich and true, they could not help but admire it (meaning, of course, they were admiring me). And he and El Maestro played their guitars in perfect balance, Frankie driving the rhythm, his teacher lacing solo notes, like sprinkling sugar atop a cookie. For one entire verse, the crowd marveled. For one entire verse, art overtook politics, and beauty overtook fright.

I dream of her in Avalon
From dusk till dawn
So I think I'll travel on
To Avalon.

Frankie's voice, like a strong drink, had made the patrons momentarily forget their fear. But like a drink, it did
not last. A man in a beige suit was the first. He banged his
glass in protest. Once. Then again. Others followed. Soon
the whole *taberna* was slamming its glasses or silverware.
Fear pulled down the curtain. Frankie stopped singing.
Tears formed in his eyes. He spun to his teacher, who, as if
expecting this, stopped playing.

"Help me up," El Maestro said.

He rose, holding Frankie's hand. As the customers
booed, El Maestro leaned toward Frankie and said, "Now
we take a bow, like this."

He bent at the waist. Frankie did the same. The jeers
grew louder. Someone yelled, "*Traidor!*"

"Always thank your audience," El Maestro whispered.
He squeezed Frankie's hand.

"Now lead us out the back."

℮

The rest, for Frankie, was a blur. He would remember Alberto, the conga player, waiting behind the wheel of a car
in the alley. He would remember a long ride in the dark.
He would remember crying much of the trip, thinking of
how he made those people angry. He would remember El
Maestro, the new guitar case between his knees, saying

very little, until he felt the car bump and he asked Alberto, "How much longer?" and Alberto said, "Twenty minutes, my friend."

He would remember his teacher handing him a silver flask and telling him to drink, that they had a long journey ahead and Frankie needed to sleep. He would remember a sweet but stinging taste to the liquid. He would remember El Maestro handing him the guitar case.

"This will be yours now, boy. It is a fine instrument, made of rosewood and spruce, with an ebony neck. The builder is from an old family of guitar makers. This is important. There should be history in whatever you play."

Frankie wanted to be happy. A new guitar. But too many emotions were swirling inside him.

"Why did I have to sing, Maestro?"

"One day, you will understand."

"But they banged their cups."

"And you showed courage. You will need that in life."

"Where are we going?"

The blind man turned away.

"Do you remember your first lesson?"

"Yes, Maestro."

"What did you do?"

"I listened."

"That is right. And where you are going, you will also

have to listen. When you listen, you learn. Remember that. In music and in life."

"But, Maestro—"

"When you started to play, the first time, what do you remember?"

"It hurt."

"Yes," the blind man said. His voice choked. "And this will hurt as well." He cleared his throat. "But you will form your calluses. And it will get easier."

The car bumped. The blind man rubbed his face.

"Francisco."

"Yes, Maestro?"

"There are strings inside this guitar case. You will put them on this guitar."

"All right, Maestro."

"They were very special to me."

"Why, Maestro?"

"They were from my wife."

"You have a wife, Maestro?"

"No longer."

"Where did she go?"

"She went to heaven. The strings were a present. I never used them."

"Because she died?"

"Yes, before she could give them to me. I found them in her purse."

Frankie tried to imagine what the woman looked like.

"Were those her dresses in the closet?"

"Her dresses. Her shoes. A bottle of her perfume. You don't need much to remember someone, Francisco. Even one thing will do."

He reached over and patted the boy's knee.

"You have those strings from me. That is enough."

Frankie felt even more scared now.

"Are we leaving our home, Maestro?"

"It is just a flat."

"Are you coming with me?"

"Above a laundry."

"Are you coming with me?"

No answer.

"Where are we *going*?"

The blind man leaned over. "What do you see outside?"

Frankie squinted against the windowpane. It was very dark. But as they came over a rise, Alberto slowed the car, and in the distance, small diamonds of moonlight glimmered to the horizon.

"The sea," Frankie whispered.

❧

Dizzy Gillespie, the jazz trumpet player, once said, "It's taken me all my life to learn what *not* to play." He was one of my special ones. And he was quite correct. Silence enhances music. What you do not play can sweeten what you do.

But it is not the same with words. What you do not say can haunt you. El Maestro was an artist (his soul was surely mine), but his instincts were too musical for this life. He left out words as he left out notes.

And so that night, as they sat at the Valencia harbor, he let Frankie fall asleep without telling him everything. And an hour later, when they got the signal, he carried the boy in his arms, walking up a long ramp to a ship, following behind Alberto, who held the bag and the guitar and whispered, "Straight ahead, Maestro . . . watch this plank, Maestro . . ." Many times the blind man lifted the child's head to his face, rubbing his cheeks against Frankie's nose and chin, as if memorizing its shape.

He hadn't told him so many things. That they were not making this journey together. That the boy would awaken, somewhere in the belly of this ship, in the company of men who had been bribed to ensure his passage. That he would find, in his guitar case, a roll of money, traveling documents, a piece of fabric with an American address, and a note that read, in the wiggly letters of a blind man's penmanship:

Francisco—
It is time for you to leave. It is too dangerous here.

This is your papa's wish. He loves you and will find you one day. I am sorry that I cannot continue to teach you. But you can teach yourself now. Find your aunt in America. When you need money, play your guitar. If you miss me, as I will miss you, close your eyes and play the strings that I gave you. I will be in your music always.

—*Maestro*

He did not tell him anything else—not the details of the prison visit, not the length of Baffa's sentence, not the answers to any of Frankie's many questions, including the one about El Maestro ever being able to see. The truth was, yes, his teacher once had sight. He lost it fighting early in his country's civil war, protecting his wife's younger brother, who had raced off to fight with the Republic. He followed the brother into battle. During a violent attack, he saved the young man from a grenade, which exploded, instead, near El Maestro, containing a poison gas that smelled like mustard. In the days that followed, his skin grew blotchy and his eyesight slowly disappeared, like a curtain lowering on his life.

The brother, ashamed, fled the country. El Maestro returned home a blind man.

"We have arrived, my friend," Alberto said.

"Where are our contacts?"

"Right in front of us," he answered, nodding at two unshaven sailors from the engine room.

"Is he blind?" one sailor asked.

"He is a great artist," Alberto said.

"You know what to do with this boy?" El Maestro said.

"Yes, yes. England, then America. Hurry up."

"Alberto? Can they be trusted?"

"They can be trusted, Maestro."

"We've done this many times," the sailor said. "Where is the money?"

"In my pocket. Take the child. Careful."

El Maestro held out the sleeping Frankie, and felt his arms being relieved of their burden. Suddenly, he gasped. He was not prepared for the emptiness that overwhelmed him.

"Wait. Where is he? *Where is he?*"

"Right here, for God's sake."

"Francisco!"

"Calm down! We have him. See?" The sailor took El Maestro's hand and tapped it against Frankie's face. "All right? Keep your voice low."

"Yes. Forgive me."

"He'll be safe."

"Good."

"This is hard for him," Alberto interjected.

"The money. Now." The sailor spat. "It's not my fault the man can't see."

Of course, had El Maestro been able to see, our story would be different, for long before handing over the boy in the moonlight, he would have recognized something in Frankie's dark grape hair and deep blue eyes and the curl of his lips. He would have seen in the boy's face the unmistakable reflection of his wife, Carmencita. He would have somehow realized she was Frankie's mother, and the burned corpse left behind in the church was only half the murder he had thought.

He would have realized, when Baffa confessed to not being the child's father, that he, El Maestro, was. That for years he had been teaching the very child he had been mourning.

But this is the note that fate chose to leave out, shading the melody by making it heartbreaking. Instead, the blind man unknowingly handed his only son to two sailors from the engine room. He gave them ten rolls of pesetas from the velvet sack in his jacket pocket. They took the boy, his bag, and the guitar, which contained the gifted strings and the traveling papers signed by a Carlos Andrés Presto, listing the boy not as a Rubio but as Francisco Presto.

In losing his father, Frankie regained his name.

❧

Minutes later, the boat pulled away from the harbor. El Maestro heard the croaking engine, the splash of waves against the hull, all the sounds of disengagement. He remained there on the ramp, high above the water, until the sounds were gone and the ship was far away. He took off his dark glasses and rubbed his eyes with the back of his hands. Suddenly, he could not stop his tears.

"Why do you cry, Maestro?" Alberto asked.

He had no words to answer. Only that he felt as hollow as the inside of his guitar. He held out his arm until he found the conga player's shoulder.

"My friend . . . Thank you for helping me."

He could not see the blank expression on Alberto's face. He could not see his eyes get smaller or his jaw set. He only felt the man's hand slip quickly inside his pocket and steal the velvet sack of money.

"You're welcome," Alberto said. "Good-bye."

He pushed the blind man over the ledge, dropping him twenty feet into the water, where his tears and the sea became one.

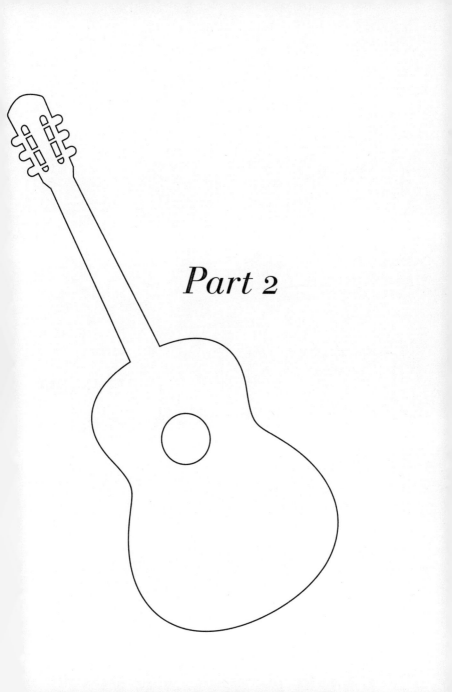

Part 2

Niles Stango

Music historian, author

FRANKIE PRESTO HAD STAGE FRIGHT.

Did you know that? It's true. He said it stemmed from his childhood, some performance he did here in Spain where the audience booed him. He never got over it. He had to kneel down and take deep breaths before every show. A lot of great ones suffer that way. Streisand. Adele. David Bowie. Carly Simon. They sweat. They vomit.

But as soon as Frankie Presto got onstage, you never saw nerves. He could sing and play—and he could dance. Really dance. I would rate him in my top-five performers of early rock and roll. Want to know the five? James Brown. Elvis. Chuck Berry. Frankie Presto. Little Richard. That's my list. I keep a lot of lists.

The first time I saw him? The Buffalo Municipal Auditorium. I had just started writing for *LIFE* magazine, fresh out of college, and they assigned me to do a story about "The Twist"—the Chubby Checker dance, that's right—so

I went to Buffalo to interview Chubby, who was on the bill with a bunch of other acts, including Frankie Presto. And let me tell you, Presto stole the show. He did four songs—only played guitar on one of them—yet he was clearly the best musician on the stage. He took a solo on a fast version of "My Girl Josephine" that was stunning. He was bending the strings and accenting the upbeat—I think he threw a few jazz licks in there—and he did it all while he was *dancing*, sliding to the left and right, dipping and swinging the guitar like a sword. I saw the band look at each other and shake their heads. That's how you know someone's good, when even the *band* can't believe it.

I asked him about it backstage that night. "How come you don't play guitar all the time? You're great." He just laughed and said, "Oh, I have to be careful with that guitar. It's mighty powerful."

Now I remember those words, "mighty powerful," because that's something you'd say if you grew up in Mississippi, not Spain, right? But as we later found out—I wrote about this in my second book, *Profiles of Rock*—Frankie Presto grew up all over the place: England, Detroit, Nashville, Louisiana, California. I could never get the real story about his time in this country. He'd say, "I don't remember much about Spain." I always thought he was lying. Who doesn't remember *something*?

But you wanted to know about his greatest hits? I have a list for that, too. Here's my top three:

Number one, of course, is "I Want To Love You." It sold two million copies—which in those days was just an unbelievable number. Nobody started records with a naked drumbeat back then. But Presto did. The pounding rhythm. *Ba-bump-bump.* Then that screaming guitar lick. Then he sings, *"Ah-ahhhh want to love you . . ."* Crowd goes wild. Oh, yeah. I'd put it as my top rock and roll song of 1960.

Number two, for me, would be "No, No, Honey," which he wrote with Abby Cruz. That was a coy little song about a man begging a woman not to leave, despite his behavior. And of course it has that brief female vocal at the end, which is uncredited, where the woman sings, "Yes, yes, honey," and takes him back. To this day, people are still guessing who that was. I thought Darlene Love, it sounded like her, but she denied it. Anyhow, "No, No, Honey" is my clear number two. And it sold a ton of copies.

And last—number three—I go with "Our Secret." It's sparse. It's haunting. Burt Bacharach produced it, of all people. He put that reverb on Presto's voice and it really sounds ghostly. That one didn't sell as well as the other two, but it's still his best ballad. I asked him once about the inspiration for "Our Secret" and he said, "You wouldn't know her.''

Friends? I can't say we were friends. He was nice enough to me over the years, but let's be honest; a reporter's job is to pry into things. And Frankie Presto had a lot of secrets, so he wasn't crazy to see me coming around, especially when I started working for *Rolling Stone*. He once said, "Niles, what I play, you can't write, and what you write, I can't play."

I could never find any information about his parents, how he got to America, even what school he went to—if he went to school at all. He was like a ghost that suddenly materialized into a rock and roll star. The last time I interviewed him was maybe forty years ago, the late 1960s, before his long disappearance. He was into the drug thing, like all of us back then, and we were at some club in New York and he said something strange. He said, "Niles, I've got three strings left." I assume he was referring to his age. . . .

Me? Seventy-two. Retired, for the most part. I live in Paris now and I'm working on a new book. When I heard that Presto had died—and how he died, lifting above the crowd like he was flying, then falling like some circus act— well, I jumped on a plane to Barcelona and drove down. I guess my old reporter's instincts were kicking in. I thought I'd do a piece for somebody, *Newsweek* or *Time*—you know, "the life and death of a mysterious pop star"—but most places I've talked to just want to know if Presto was murdered, not about his career. That's why your crew came, isn't it? Death sells. Music, not so much.

I'll tell you what, though. There's a story here. Something weird. I've been asking around and a couple of people told me they saw Presto the morning of the day he died, near the statue of Francisco Tárrega, and he had his guitar and someone was with him.

I wish I could have heard him play again. He hadn't made a record in decades—unless you believe in the legendary "unreleased" album, the one they call *The Magic Strings of Frankie Presto*. Who knows if it's him? There're so many rumors. A writer once asked Frankie what his bravest performance was—ever—and he said the time he played alone in the bottom of a boat. I'm thinking, "Yeah, right." Bottom of a boat? What is he, a pirate? It's like that song from *The Sound of Music*. How do you solve a problem like Maria? How do you tell a story like Frankie Presto? Who knows what to believe?

17

1969

"CAN I HELP YOU?" THE MAN BEHIND THE COUNTER ASKED.

"Eggs," Frankie whispered.

The man put a finger to his ear. "Can't hear you, fella."

Frankie was unshaven, his eyes glassy behind aviator sunglasses. As he leaned in, his long black hair fell over his angular cheekbones and you could barely see his face at all.

"I need to buy . . . some eggs."

A grinning teenager suddenly pushed up to the counter, jostling Frankie's shoulder. He wore a floppy green hat.

"Hey, man, you sell beer?"

"The eggs are over there," the man said, ignoring the teen, pointing at a refrigerated shelf behind a crowd of young people, men with scruffy beards and headbands, alongside women in print dresses or blue denim shorts, many of them shoeless. The store's floor was covered in muddy footprints.

"Sixty cents for the eggs." The man pushed up his glasses. "Do you have sixty cents, fella?"

Someone screamed, "I'm so high!" and others roared in approval. A ceiling fan spun overhead. Frankie reached into his pocket and went wobbly on his heels. He could feel his guitar in its soft case on his back, but he couldn't see the man in front of him anymore. He felt as if he were in the middle of a balloon being squeezed from the outside.

"Here," Frankie mumbled, fingering a twenty-dollar bill off a wad in his hands.

"Can I have one?" the teen asked.

Frankie let another bill drop.

"I'll take twenty beers!" the teen announced.

Frankie found a carton of eggs and stumbled away. The man yelled after him, "You want your change?" but Frankie was pushing out the screen door into the sticky summer air.

This was America, the calendar year 1969, the month of August, the state of New York, during the three-day music festival known as Woodstock, where half a million people gathered on a six-hundred-acre dairy farm. Frankie, now thirty-three years old, was tall and lanky, with deep blue eyes, high shoulders, large hands, and dark stubble on his chin and cheeks. His life at this precise moment was, in musical terms, *lontano*—distant, or from a distance—and in such erratic time signatures it is impossible for me to notate. This was due to something he drank or swallowed behind the festival stage. I cannot tell you what it was. I doubt Frankie knew himself.

In a moment, I will explain why we have advanced our story so far, and why Frankie's journey at Woodstock would mark a major turning point in his life, his music, and his love affair with Aurora York, the little girl in the tree whom he would spend much of his youth pursuing.

But first, I wish to say something about being in an altered state, like the one Frankie was in now. It does not bring you closer to me.

It just makes me dizzy.

For centuries, musicians have sought to find me at the end of a needle or the bottom of a drink. It is an illusion. And it often ends badly.

Take my cherished Russian disciple, Modest Mussorgsky. In 1881, he lay facedown in a St. Petersburg tavern. This man once composed marvelous works, *Pictures at an Exhibition* and *Night on Bald Mountain* (later made famous through an animated film called *Fantasia*). He composed nothing on that barroom floor, believing alcohol made him an artist. He died at forty-two.

I was there to collect his talent.

I was there at the hospital deathbed of my beloved Billie Holiday, just forty-four, her liver destroyed by drinking; I was there inside the hotel room of Charlie Parker, my singular jazz saxophonist, who died in his midthirties, but whose body was so ravaged by drugs the coroners thought he was sixty.

Tommy Dorsey, the bandleader, choked in his sleep when he was fifty-one, too deep in pills to awaken. Johnny Allen Hendrix (you called him Jimi) swallowed a handful of barbiturates and expired. He was twenty-seven.

It is not new, this idea that a purer art awaits you in a substance. But it is naive. I existed before the first grapes were fermented. Before the first whiskey was distilled. Be it opium or absinthe, marijuana or heroin, cocaine or ecstasy or whatever will follow, you may alter your state, but you will not alter this truth: I am Music. I am here inside you. Why would I hide behind a powder or a vapor?

Do you think me so petty?

❧

But let us return to Frankie's dazed journey through a muddy dairy farm, carrying a guitar and a dozen eggs. A band named Santana was on a stage far from view, and the lead singer's voice seemed to come out of the sky:

You've got to change your evil ways . . . baby

Frankie was lost. The chemicals in his system, which he'd ingested just before sunrise, had led him to wander far from the musicians' area. This is all he remembered:

He had been with Aurora York, who was now his wife, and she was sleeping on a cotton blanket, pregnant with their first child. He did not want to wake her, but he did.

"Francisco?"

"Aurora," he whispered.

"It means dawn."

"I know."

"I'm hungry, Francisco. If you love me, you'll get me breakfast."

She crinkled her eyes and smiled. Frankie told her to wait there, he would get some eggs and cook them for her. But after that, things got foggy. And now, outside the grocery store, he was not sure how long ago that was.

"Was she a fairy?"

"I don't think so, Maestro."

"Did she have strange eyes?"

"Yes."

"Was she kind and helpful?"

"Yes."

"She was a fairy."

He shook his head to clear El Maestro's voice, which often popped into his brain. He tried to locate the stage area where he'd left Aurora, but could see only an ocean of spectators, some of whom appeared to have comet tails as they moved. He stepped awkwardly over sleeping bags and blankets.

A man's voice blasted over the loudspeakers.

"WE GOT A FEW ANNOUNCEMENTS TO MAKE, PEOPLE . . . ALL RIGHT, THIS IS COOL . . . THE NEW. YORK STATE THRUWAY IS CLOSED! WE CLOSED THE THRUWAY, MAN!"

There was a sweeping roar of applause and Frankie rolled his head. Everything was too loud. In the midst of the people slapping hands in celebration, he stared at the egg carton until his ears detected the music.

Lord knows you got to change . . .

He stumbled toward the sound, trying to use me as a compass, and to remember when—and with which band—he was supposed to play.

18

1946

"PLAY SOMETHING. *JOUE.*"

Frankie looked up. He was ten years old, wearing tattered clothes, sitting by his open guitar case on the docks of Southampton, a port on the South coast of England, two hours south of London. A French-speaking man with a thin mustache had wandered over.

"*Joue*," the man said again, shaking his wrist. "*Pompe.*"

"Beg your pardon, sir?"

"*Pompe.* Your geetar. Like dees."

The man made a pumping movement, as if scratching his chest. It was already dark, and Frankie glanced at the two coins in his case. It was not enough to buy a single potato, which was all he had eaten since morning. The ships were in for the night. This foreigner was his last hope.

"Please, sir. I'm hungry. I can play a song for a shilling."

The man bit on his cigarette and pulled a coin from his pocket.

"*Joue*," he said, dropping it. "Something happy, *oui*?"

Something happy. Even the idea seemed foreign to Frankie. It had been more than a year since he'd left Spain on that ship. After three days below deck, he'd been awakened at night and told to crawl beneath a dirty red blanket.

"For your protection," one of the sailors said.

"Where is my teacher?"

"He is coming."

"My guitar——"

"We are bringing your things. It's a fun game, yes?"

"I want El Maestro!"

"Lower your voice! This is how you play. You hide and then he finds you."

"But——"

"Quiet! If you speak, he will not come!"

Frankie inhaled as the world went dark. Enveloped in that blanket, he was carried off the boat by two of the men. He heard splashing water, the creaking of wood, flapping sails, his own accelerated breathing. He was laid upon a hard surface, and the guitar case was slid under the blanket. He grabbed it with one arm, holding on as if it might keep him safe.

"Your teacher comes soon," a sailor whispered. "Stay in the blanket until you hear him."

ᥱ

Of course, his teacher never came. Nor did anyone else. The sailors abandoned him on this British port, and in the months that passed, young Francisco Presto joined a long line of talented predecessors, begging, through his music, to keep himself fed. How far back does this go? Francesco Corbetta, my Italian virtuoso of the baroque guitar, had to play in the streets of Florence in the seventeenth century; three hundred years later, Irving Berlin was singing for pennies on the Lower East Side of Manhattan. You should be ashamed to treat my children this way, no better than dogs pleading for scraps.

Frankie, with his omnipresent guitar, rarely wandered beyond these docks. He knew from the note that he was supposed to find his aunt in America. But the smugglers had taken his money, so that was imposssible now. Each night he dreamed of seeing El Maestro stepping off a ship, led by Alberto the conga player; Frankie would run to his teacher and take his hand and the blind man would ask, "Have you been practicing, Francisco?" and things would be good again. So the boy remained, waiting in this smelly harbor, playing for travelers, dancing if they wanted him to. He went from musician to performer, and some days he ate and some days he did not.

Now he adjusted the guitar on his knee, which was bone thin. His fingernails were uneven from biting to keep them short. *Something happy.* He chose an upbeat song called

"Billets Doux," by the Belgian-born Django Reinhardt, the famous gypsy who was widely considered the greatest jazz guitarist in Europe. (El Maestro had once said of him, "*He is not of this earth.*")

The song was quick and lively, like a child skipping, and it demanded Frankie's full attention—so as he played, he didn't notice the Frenchman's stunned expression, or see the cigarette fall from his lips.

"What is name, this song?" he asked.

" 'Billets Doux.' "

"Who write it?"

"Django Reinhardt."

"Who he?"

"A great guitar player."

"What mean? 'Billets Doux'?"

"I don't know. I just know the names."

"You play nice."

"Thank you, sir."

"Where you mama?"

"Dead, sir."

"Where you papa?"

"I don't know, sir."

The man lit another cigarette and looked at the water.

"I go on trip. Far away."

"You're lucky, sir."

"No want go."

"Why not, sir?"

"Have baby. Boy like you."

"That's good, sir."

"Baby die. Two month ago. No want to go on trip." He tapped his hand on the rail. "No want to do anything."

Frankie didn't know what to say. The water lapped against the wooden pylons.

"*Parles-tu français?*" the man asked suddenly.

"No, sir. Just English."

"You are no English."

"Yes, sir, I am."

"*Hablas Español?*"

Frankie didn't respond.

"*Bueno,*" the man said anyhow, and from that point on, he spoke in broken Spanish. "Now where are you really from?"

Frankie shrugged.

"Spain, yes? What part?"

"I'm not from there anymore."

The man tapped his foot against Frankie's guitar case.

"Listen to me. Where I am supposed to go, I need someone to speak English. My English is bad."

"So?"

"Your English is good. You come? Translate my words? Then maybe I go."

"No, thank you."

"I pay you."

"No, thank you."

"Give you bed."

"No, thank you."

"Give you food."

"Why are you going?"

"To make music."

"You're a musician?"

"*Oui*. Not as good as you, perhaps."

The man held out his right hand, motioning at Frankie's guitar.

"Let me try."

"Don't break it."

The man adjusted the strap around his shoulder. He placed his left hand on the neck. Only then did Frankie notice the man's fingers were badly damaged; two of them were mutilated, and only his first and second digits lined up by the frets.

"Is good guitar."

"I know."

"Where you get such strings?"

"My teacher."

"Of what they are made?"

"I don't know."

He purred as if stroking velvet. "*Magnifique*."

"Do you really play?" Seeing the two fingers, Frankie had his doubts.

"I try 'Billets Doux,'" the man said.

He rolled his chin, exhaled deeply, then played the same song—but so fast that Frankie stopped breathing. The man's two fingers shot across the frets, holding a note then springing to many others, spilling octave runs as smoothly as oil poured down a funnel. Those two fingers produced more music than any five fingers could, and he finished with a sweeping of chords, using the "pump" technique he'd been trying to explain, a syncopated strum that made the guitar sound like a train engine.

"'Billets Doux,' no?" the Frenchman said, handing back the guitar. "It means 'love letters.'"

"How do you know that?"

"I write it."

The man smiled for the first time, his mustache lifting.

"I am Django."

"You?"

"*Oui*. I just said so."

Frankie took the guitar. He felt goose bumps.

"What happened to your hands?"

"A fire."

"You got burned?"

"When I was young."

"You play with two fingers?"

"I play with this."

He touched his chest near his heart.

Frankie couldn't believe it. He had listened to this man's recording so many times, sitting beside El Maestro in the flat above the laundry, both of them imagining a guitarist with large, powerful hands and incredible reach. It was the first time my child realized the utter disconnect between a man's body and the music he can make.

"You are gypsy?" Django asked Frankie.

"No."

"I am gypsy. Come with me, I show you how to play like gypsy."

Frankie bit his lower lip. He was so hungry. And this was Django Reinhardt!

"When?"

"We leave in morning."

"*Tomorrow* morning?"

"Yes."

"Why so fast?"

"I play with band. They are waiting."

"What band?"

"Duke Ellington."

"*The* Duke Ellington?"

"*Oui.*"

"Where?"

"America."

Frankie shivered. America? Where his aunt was?

Django held out his palm.

"You go, I go?"

"Okay," Frankie said.

They shook hands. Frankie looked at his guitar.

The bottom string had turned blue.

19

1969

"WHIP, WHOP! WHIP, WHOP! WHOOO!"

As the sun set over Woodstock, Frankie passed a large group of spectators screaming, dancing, and banging on drums.

"Whip, whop! Whip, whop! WHOOO!"

Some wore ponchos and some were shirtless and two blond men who might have been brothers had wrapped green towels around their necks like capes. They were passing a bottle as they chanted. One brother handed it to Frankie and motioned for him to drink.

"Whip, whop, man!"

Frankie took a swig.

"Whip, whop," he said.

"Join in! Play!"

The man pointed to Frankie's guitar.

"C'mon, man. Rock us!"

"Rock us! Rock us!" the crowd started chanting. The drumming continued.

"Hey, I know you! You're Frankie Presto!"

"Whoa!"

"Really?"

"Who?"

"Frankie Presto, man! Shake, shake! Remember?"

Frankie, even in his cloudy haze of consciousness, felt a flight reflex kick in. *You're Frankie Presto!* He was supposed to move away when someone said this.

"Shake, shake, Frankie! Shake, shake, Frankie!" They passed the bottle and banged the drums and now all of them were chanting, calling him in. "Shake, shake, Frankie!" He turned and staggered off, hearing "Booo!" and "No!" and "Awww!' and "He's freaking out." He felt his heart racing and once he was safely away, he fell to the muddy ground in an area of yellow buses, each of them spray painted with colorful messages. He breathed heavily, in and out, letting his ears find the music in the sky, another band that he could hear but not see, Canned Heat, singing something called "Going Up the Country." Was that a flute? Frankie thought. Yes. A flute.

"Hey, man," a female voice said, "take it easy."

He turned to see an attractive, dark-haired woman sitting inside a purple van. She wore a sleeveless orange top and denim shorts and her skin was tan and her toenails were painted different colors. She made him think about Aurora. Where had he last seen Aurora? The eggs. He had to take her the eggs. *If you love me, you'll get me breakfast.*

"What's your name?" the woman asked.

"Frankie."

"Come here, Frankie . . ." she said.

20

e

1946

"COME HERE, FRANCISCO," DJANGO YELLED. "THEY ARRIVE!"

Frankie ran back toward the Frenchman, who was wearing a red ascot and a blue sports coat as he stood by a gate at the railway station called Grand Central in New York City. Frankie had been jumping between the streams of sunlight cascading through the upper windows of the terminal. He had never seen walls so high. Frankie's world, until he was nine, began and ended in the streets of Villareal. It expanded on the docks of Southampton. But it exploded upon landing in America. Everything he saw was bigger and grander than what he'd seen before. The cars. The buildings. The bags people carried. The hats they wore.

"Look, Francisco. Is him, no?"

From the waves of commuters, Frankie saw two strangers approaching, one a tall, striking man with a thin mustache, his hair slicked back. Frankie had seen his face on a record album. It was like seeing paper come to life.

"Monsieur Django, I presume?" Duke Ellington said, offering his hand.

"Monsieur Duke, pleasure great is."

Frankie was dumbstruck. He remembered the night El Maestro made him play Duke Ellington's record over and over until he said they could keep the phonograph.

Django touched Frankie's shoulder and mumbled "*chavo*" (the gypsy word for "boy"), then rambled in his Spanish-French mix. Frankie spat back the words in English.

"Mr. Django says he is very excited and honored to meet you and to perform with your orchestra," Frankie said. "Also, he would like to hear Dizzy Gillespie play somewhere."

"And you, young squire?" Duke Ellington asked, smiling.

"Huh?"

"Are you his son?'

"No. I am . . ." Frankie didn't know what he was. "I am his talker."

"Very well, talker. Tell him we leave for Cleveland in an hour."

Frankie did as asked, although he didn't know the word for Cleveland so he just said "Cleveland." The man with Duke Ellington said, "I can carry Mr. Reinhardt's guitar."

"That's mine," Frankie said.

"Where is Mr. Reinhardt's?"

"He didn't bring one."

"He didn't bring a guitar?"

Frankie translated. Django looked embarrassed, almost angry. He rattled off a stream of words.

"He says he thought someone here would give him one."

℮

On the train to Cleveland, Frankie was too excited to sit still. He now wore a new coat that Django had purchased at a store in the train station. And he was traveling with musicians! He marveled at their luggage on the platform—trumpets, drums, an upright bass. Some opened their cases and tooted a few notes for him.

"What do *you* play?" Frankie asked a group of men.

"Saxophone," they answered.

"You all play the same instrument?"

"Tenor."

"Alto."

"Baritone."

Frankie was awestruck. The musicians even let Frankie hold different horns, gold-colored, silver-colored, a long trombone with a valve that slid back and forth. He felt as if someone had opened a treasure chest. Best of all, he'd been given the tour schedule, and on it Frankie read the word *Detroit*. That was the city! The one on the piece of cloth that he kept in his guitar case! He would find his aunt and she would help him return to Spain and Papa and El Maestro.

He was back on his path.

Frankie allowed himself a giddy feeling that he had not experienced since Villareal, a tickle in his stomach that made him anxious for the next day. He was given a lower berth in the sleeping car but as he stood beside a heavyset trumpeter, Frankie blurted out, "Can I have the top one?"

"Hell, yeah," the man said. "I don't need to do no climbing."

Frankie scrambled up and bounced on the mattress. He put his hands behind his head. The train jerked forward and began to rumble, and he heard the scattered laughter of the musicians and someone humming a song. He liked the camaraderie of these men, who were more like boys than the men in Spain. They even had childish names, like "Cat" and "Taft" and "Shorty." Lying in his bunk, Frankie smiled.

He had joined another band, this one without even playing.

That night, Django came back to see Frankie's accommodations. The musicians were dressing for bed, and Django noticed they all wore boxy underpants with colorful floral patterns.

"*Que están usando?*" he said, laughing.

"He wants to know what you are wearing," Frankie said.

The men seemed surprised.

"Ain't he ever seen nice skivvies before?"

"You are crazy," Django blurted out.

"He says you are crazy."

"We heard."

"We ain't the ones with a pint-size translator."

"Go tell it to Duke."

Frankie followed Django to the compartment he shared with Mr. Ellington. When they entered, the bandleader was also undressing. Django was shocked to see his undergarments were even gaudier, with hearts and flowers in a colorful pattern.

"Is something wrong?" Duke asked.

"*Non, non*," Django said.

He leaned over to Frankie and said in whispered Spanish, "*Chavo*, this is a strange country."

21

1969

"YOU GONNA COOK THOSE EGGS?" SAID THE WOMAN IN THE van. She wore blue eyeshadow, her lips were glossed and three necklaces draped around her neck.

"Cook them?" Frankie looked at the carton. "Yes."

"Where?"

He pointed in the direction of the music—or what he thought was the direction of the music.

"Back there."

"Where are you from?"

"Me?"

"Yeah, handsome." She smiled. "You."

Normally when someone asked this, Frankie said California. This time he said, "Spain."

"Far out," the woman cooed. "You came to hear music?"

"To play it."

"Onstage?"

"Yes."

"You're a long way from the stage."

"I have these eggs."

"You said that——"

"For breakfast."

"Are you really from Spain?"

"*Sí.*"

"You're funny."

He felt his knees wobble. He steadied himself against the van door.

"Why don't you come in?"

"Where?"

"Next to me."

Frankie stepped inside. He would only stay a minute, he told himself.

"How did you get here?" she asked.

"I walked from the store."

"No," she laughed. "You said you're from Spain. How'd you get *here*?" She spread her arms. "America."

Frankie dropped his head against a large embroidered pillow. He watched her roll a cigarette.

"With a band," he said.

22

1946

THE ELLINGTON BAND TOURED FOR THREE MONTHS. DURING that time, Frankie saw his first cow (out the train window), his first hand-dipped ice-cream cone, and his first American movie theater. He continued to learn the gypsy guitar techniques from Django—and perfect the Spanish-French language they forged together. He also learned that Django's baby was named Jimmy and that he died after living only a few weeks and that Django chose Bach and Handel and Mozart to be played at the funeral mass, and that the little boy was buried in a French cemetery. It was the second time he had heard about a proper burial (Aurora York had told him of the first), and he thought about seeing where his mama was buried when they got to Detroit.

He also learned that Django was ready to cancel what would prove to be his only trip to America—until Frankie had agreed to go. The idea of traveling with a boy made the journey after his son's death more bearable. I can see all futures, the ones my talents will make and the ones they will turn away from (just as I can hear all melodies on a keyboard, those played and those yet unplayed) and I can tell you had Frankie not been there, Django would never have experienced America, or the way it influenced his life and art.

This is why Frankie's bottom string turned blue when they met.

But we will return to that. First, the opening night. When they reached Cleveland, Django was forced to buy a new guitar for the concert, which made him furious. "This is travesty," he told Frankie as he tuned the new instrument. "Why they not have a guitar for me? A Selmer, as I love? I am Django. They should give me a guitar of gold."

"You can play mine," Frankie said.

"Yes?"

He put down the new one and took the instrument from Frankie. After plucking a few notes, he stopped.

"Is perfect. Did you tune already?"

"Yes, sir."

Django studied Frankie. "I will play your guitar tonight and show them who I am. But I will give it back and you must never let it go. Never sell it. Never lose it. Never give it to someone and hope it returns. Don't let go of your music, *chavo*. Or you will let go of yourself."

"Yes, Mr. Django."

That night, from the wings of the stage at the Cleveland Music Hall, Frankie experienced something that would stay with him forever. The first blasts from an orchestra. The syncopated punches of a horn section. The elegant twirling of clarinets and saxophones. The dragging power of trombones and basses. Even the look of the band—the uniformity of them all, handsomely dressed in dark tuxedos—made an impression. And the crowd! Nearly two thousand people! Their roaring ovation was a response Frankie never imagined. It jolted into him, spreading through his bloodstream. He did not understand the physics of applause, but he knew, from that moment, that he wanted to hear it for himself one day.

Django did not come out until the end, and was accompanied only by Duke Ellington on the piano and a bass player who tried to follow. There had been almost no rehearsal. But someone once said of Reinhardt, "He is music made man," and I accept the compliment. He was one of my prizes. His playing that night, on Frankie's well-traveled guitar, was so remarkably original, even the band members were yelling, "Go to it, Master! Go to it!" He did four songs, each one making a bigger impression than the one before.

The next morning, in the hotel, Django asked Frankie to find a newspaper and read him anything that was written about him. Frankie turned the pages until he saw a headline: FRENCH GUITAR ARTIST STEALS DUKE'S CONCERT.

"Hmph," Django said, sipping his coffee. "As it should be."

Their time together was so eventful and so fast, that years later, it would feel to Frankie more like a dream than a memory. But one night in the city of Chicago, Frankie watched the band setting up, and noticed the bass drum featured a drawing from the RCA Victor record label—a dog staring into a gramophone.

Frankie's stomach went weak. He thought of the hairless dog and the phonograph in El Maestro's flat. He thought of all the parts of his life he had left behind. He was suddenly and profoundly sad. This trip was exciting, but he was still a child, and all children eventually want to go home.

When the tour reached Detroit, he set out to do it.

23

1969
―――

THE WOMAN IN THE VAN RAN HER TONGUE OVER HER TEETH.

"That is such a mind-blowing story," she said. "You just traveled all over when you were a kid? With Duke Ellington?"

"Yeah."

"So cool." She dragged on her rolled cigarette then handed it to him. She leaned over his legs.

"I want to see this guitar."

She undid the clasps and opened the case.

"Careful," Frankie mumbled.

"Why careful?"

"It does strange things."

"Like what?"

"Magic. Stuff like that."

She grinned.

"You're funny."

"I'm not."

"I think you are."

Frankie looked at his hand. It seemed huge. The smoke left him blinking. The woman slid closer.

"Take one of these."

"What is it?"

"A Lemmon. Don't you like Lemmons?"

She put a small green pill in his mouth, then swallowed one herself. She curled up against him.

"What's with the eggs?"

"My wife. They're for my wife. I have a wife. We're having a baby."

"Where is she?"

"I don't know . . ."

"You don't know?"

"At the stage."

She smiled.

"Then she's not here, is she?"

She put her face close to his.

"What happened next?"

"Next?"

"The story. After you left the band?"

"I don't remember."

"Try."

Frankie closed his eyes.

"It was cold."

24

1946

IT WAS COLD. SNOW WAS FALLING. FRANKIE TUGGED ON THE wool jacket Django had bought him and adjusted his thighs on the concrete stoop. At this point, he had been in America for October, November, and part of December. He didn't know how people lived in such weather. Once again, for the thousandth time, he opened his guitar case and took out the piece of cloth with an address written in Baffa's handwriting, the address of his sister: 467 Claret Street, Detroit, Michigan.

Frankie had already knocked, many times. No one had answered. He'd been waiting on the steps most of the afternoon. Django had offered to come with him, but Frankie, quite bold in his independence by this point, told the guitarist his aunt would likely want to hear all about Baffa, so he would be there for a while. And she would probably want him to live with her until she could get him back to Spain.

"If this is so, you must come to say good-bye, *chavo*," Django said. "We leave tomorrow, yes?"

"Okay," Frankie said.

He tugged on his coat. The small brick house resembled others on the block; each had a short, straight driveway, like frets lining a guitar neck, with parked cars collecting snow. Big cars. Long cars. It seemed to Frankie that everyone in America had a vehicle, unlike Villareal, where people still used carts and horses.

Frankie closed his eyes and pictured Baffa's house on Calvario Street, sitting in the garden, listening to the radio, the hairless dog by his side. He remembered those days as warm and sweet.

"Are you lost, son?"

Frankie opened his eyes. A mailman with a blue uniform and a large leather bag was in front of him. Snowflakes dotted the brim of his cap.

"No, sir."

"What are you doing?"

"I'm waiting."

"In the snow?"

"Yes."

"Who for?"

"My aunt."

Frankie held out the piece of cloth.

"Well, you got the right house. She's your aunt, huh?"

"Yes, sir."

"How'd you get here?"

"Mr. Django paid a car."

"You mean a taxi?"

"I think so."

"Does she know you're coming?"

"I'm late."

"Were you supposed to be here this morning?"

Frankie shifted on the concrete. "Later than that."

The man pressed his lips together, considering the boy in front of him. He handed over several envelopes.

"Want to give them their mail?"

Frankie took the letters.

"Stay warm," the man said. "They should be home from work any minute."

Who was "they"? Frankie thought. He watched the man finish his route, stopping at every house, until he couldn't see him anymore. It grew dark. Frankie wondered if he'd have to sleep here.

Just then, a pale green Chevrolet turned down the street with its headlights on. As it slowed, Frankie's heart sped up.

Stop here, he willed it silently. *Stop here. Stop here.*

It stopped. Frankie rose. He did not truly understand the purpose of an "aunt," having never had one before. But since the moment he'd read El Maestro's note in the hull of that ship, he had been waiting to meet her, hoping she

would fix things, get him back home, reunite him with his
original band.

What he saw changed all that.

What he saw was the car doors open and a man step out
of one side and a plump woman with light hair step out of
the other. Frankie had seen her face before, countless times,
in a photograph with her arm around Baffa—a photograph
he'd kept under his pillow. A chill ran through his young
body and a cymbal crashed inside his head. He dropped the
letters, leaped from the stoop, and as the woman's mouth
fell open in confusion, he ran across the snow-dusted grass
with his arms held high, screaming, "Mama!"

℘

In Western music, things resolve. A suspended fourth
moves back to the third. A diminished chord slides to its
tonic. Dissonance to consonance. I make peace that way.

Humans follow no such rules. So that night on Claret
Street, Danza Rubio, the woman who'd stepped out of the
pale green Chevrolet, was startled by the boy running toward her. And, having had no contact with her brother,
Baffa, for many years, she was suspicious at the sudden
appearance of a child. She stood motionless when Frankie
tried to hug her. And when he exclaimed, "I am your son!"
and told her the story Baffa had told him (about his wife,

the car, the accident in America) she grew angry and broke the truth to Frankie right there in the street, like a series of hard rim shots on a snare drum.

Thwack!

She was not his mother.

Thwack!

She was not Baffa's wife.

Thwack!

Baffa never had a wife.

Thwack!

He could never get a wife.

Thwack!

He had never been to America.

Thwack!

There was no accident.

Thwack!

There was no grave site.

Thwack!

Baffa was a liar.

Thwack!

He hadn't spoken to her in years.

Thwack!

She assumed he was dead.

All of this took less than three minutes. Each blow stunned Frankie into a deeper silence. By the end, when Danza's husband gruffly interjected, "Look, boy, we're not giving you any money, if that's what you expect," the dazed child felt his jaw trembling. It took all he had to grab his guitar case and run. Danza yelled after him, but he did not turn back. He disappeared into falling snowflakes under pools of lamplight, tears rolling down his cheeks.

I have said that music allows for quick creation. But it is nothing compared with what you humans can destroy in a single conversation.

Burt Bacharach

Songwriter, performer, composer, producer

FRANKIE PRESTO LOVED THE STUDIO. HE WOULD HAVE LIVED in there if they'd had a bed.

Oh . . . sure . . . my name is Burt Bacharach . . . America . . . Los Angeles. But I met Frankie in New York. I produced his song "Our Secret" back in 1964. Great ballad. Did a reverb thing on his voice that made it eerie. And the string part we came up with around midnight. I started making calls and found a couple of violinists to come in at three or four in the morning. Frankie and I were from different parts of the world, but we had one thing in common: we didn't leave a studio until it was perfect. Some musicians don't like that. I keep them there for twenty takes, thirty takes. But what's the point in making art if it isn't right?

Frankie got that, you know? He was a beautiful soul— and if I had known he was still playing guitar I would have flown around the world to hear it. I really had no idea where he'd gone—or if he was still alive—until I heard about him dying a few days ago. Was it really on the stage? . . . My God . . . that's awful. . . .

The first time I heard him play? . . . Yes, I do. That's really how we met. I was at Bell Sound Studios in New York, before a recording session with Dionne Warwick. I got there early and the big room was empty except for this one guy who had his back to us. He wore headphones and was leaning over an electric guitar. I asked the engineer to bring up the sound, but before I could tell the guy to get out, I was frozen. His playing was incredible. He was switching between classical riffs and the jazz tune, "Body and Soul." I said, "Who the hell is this?" And the engineer said, "You won't believe it. That's Frankie Presto." And I said, "The singer?" and he said, "The singer plays a mean guitar."

I guess he had been cutting a record just before us, and everyone had left but he'd stayed in there another two hours, messing around on all the instruments, moving from the drums to the piano to the guitars. My guys were coming in now, so I clicked on the room microphone and said, "Hey, sorry to interrupt genius, but we're on the clock."

He pulled off the headphones and waved like he was apologizing. I said over the speaker, "That was fantastic, you should have blasted it all over the building," and he leaned into the mike and said, "I was just messing around."

He came out and I introduced myself and he knew who I was right away, which surprised me, because I wasn't recording back then, just writing, but he said he'd really liked some things I'd done, "Baby, It's You" by the Shirelles and "Only Love Can Break a Heart," the Gene Pitney song. He said something about trumpets and flugelhorns—which was unusual for a rock and roll guy—so I said, "Where did you learn about horn sections?" and he said, "Traveling with Duke Ellington," and I laughed and said, "What were you, his water boy?" I mean, he was way too young for Duke.

He was taller than I thought, and very striking. When the band guys came in, even they were staring at him. He had a presence, you know? And he was wearing a bright red sports coat, which didn't hurt. When I told him we were recording Dionne Warwick, he said he loved her voice and asked if he could stay. Normally, I don't like outside distractions when I work, but Frankie had a good vibe, you know? He was musical, you could feel it. So I said, "You can hang out here in the booth if you want." And he said okay.

The song we were doing was for a movie called *A House Is Not a Home*. Hal David wrote the lyrics. I wrote the music. To be honest, we were rerecording it because Brook Benton had done the original but I wanted Dionne to take a shot at it. We did a lot of takes with a full orchestra, string section, background singers—like I said, that's how I worked—and I sort of forgot about Frankie sitting back there. Then, during a playback, I happened to turn around as Dionne was singing the part:

But a room is not a house,
And a house is not a home
When the two of us are far apart
And one of us has a broken heart.

I saw Frankie crying.

"You all right?" I said.

"Yeah," he said.

But you could see it got to him. He didn't even wipe away the tears. I didn't learn until much later that he was an orphan. No mother. No father. "A House Is Not a Home." No wonder, right? Could there be a tougher thing to hear?

25

1950

"DID YOU HEAR ME?" THE NUN YELLED. "I SAID LINE UP!"

The children lined up.

"Now move!"

They marched to the cafeteria. A tall boy shoved Frankie in his back.

"Knock it off," Frankie whispered.

"Make me," the taller kid said.

At this point in our story, Frankie was either thirteen or fourteen. He hadn't decided. Once he'd discovered that Baffa was not his real papa, Frankie ignored the birth date he'd been told, figuring that was a lie as well.

"Begin!" the nun barked.

The children, standing by cafeteria tables, recited their prayers out loud. Then they sat down, and the nuns poured orange juice into their glasses, followed by spoonfuls of cod liver oil.

"It tastes horrible," one boy complained.

"Be grateful you have it. Drink!"

Frankie lifted the juice to his lips, and the sweet smell brought back memories of Villareal, the orange carts rolling down the streets. But such memories only made Frankie angry now. Baffa was never his father. The woman in the photo was never his mother. His only identification papers listed him as "Presto"—a name he didn't even know. It was all a lie. There was nothing sweet about oranges anymore.

At this point, Frankie's life was in rigid formation, a 4/4 cadence, with a tempo best described as *mosso*—or agitated. He'd been living for three years in the Greater Detroit Catholic Home for Orphans, sharing a bedroom with nine other boys. He had been taken there when the police discovered him sleeping in an alley behind a restaurant, after he'd missed the train that took Django and the Ellington band to their next stop. (By the time Frankie found a way to the station, they were gone. He sat and cried, his elbows on his guitar case, until a man in a uniform told him he couldn't sit there anymore and should "go home to your mother.")

He returned to begging and eating from trash cans. The ones behind the restaurant offered the best scraps. He was actually surprised when the police found him (he'd become quite skilled at hiding from authorities) but was happy when the nuns said he'd get his own bed. He accepted their blue pants and white shirt and black leather shoes and he didn't even mind when they threw away his old clothes saying that, unlike his soul, they were beyond salvation.

Frankie had been scrawny when he'd arrived, but in three years he'd sprouted into a lanky teenager, with prominent white teeth, large hands (a great boost to his guitar playing) and a deep set to his blue eyes that drew nervous smiles from the girls in his class.

The boys were another matter. Children in orphanages take note of the slightest preference, and the other boys hated that Frankie played the guitar so well that the nuns let him accompany them in Christmas and Easter ceremonies. Or that he got private time in the library each night to work on his music. He was different, so they looked for ways to mock him, like the slight accent that still tinged his English.

"Hey, Spic," they would tease. "No spic-a-the-language?"

"Hey, Coconut. Are you brown or white?"

"Hey, Gyppo, tell us about your gypsy friend again."

One night the tall boy, named Rafael, handed out cupcakes after his birthday celebration. He deliberately skipped over Frankie.

"They don't eat in the alley where you came from," he whispered.

"I don't want your cupcake," Frankie said, "if it makes me as dumb as you."

Instantly, they were scuffling on the floor. The other boys cheered and whooped. Frankie socked Rafael in the eye, and Rafael howled. He pushed Frankie down, ran to Frankie's bed, reached beneath it, and pulled out Frankie's guitar. Frankie jumped on him and they wrestled, the guitar slamming around between them. By the time they were separated, Frankie saw the bottom string had snapped— the same string that had once turned blue on the British docks.

Frankie burst into tears, screaming, "I'll kill you! I'll kill you!" He tackled Rafael again and had to be restrained by the woman from the cafeteria. As punishment, both boys were forced to sleep on the floor that night, Rafael in the rectory, Frankie in the kitchen. Frankie stared at the ceiling and felt an emptiness that he'd never felt before—but not because of the fight.

Until that moment, his strings had never broken.

This was quite unusual, seeing that guitar strings often break after a few months of use. Frankie figured it was because he had played carefully, even gently, as his teacher had taught him.

"Do not attack the strings, Francisco."

"No, Maestro."

"Coax them."

"Yes, Maestro."

"Make them hunger for your next note. Same as in life."

"In life, Maestro?"

"When you want someone to listen to you, will you attack
    them?"

"No, Maestro."

"No, you will not. You will make them hear the beauty of
    what you are offering, and they will want it for themselves."

Frankie missed those lessons. He even missed lighting El
Maestro's cigarettes and cleaning up his wine spills. He
cherished the guitar; it was, as Django had suggested, his
most precious possession. The strings were all he had left
from his teacher. And now someone had broken one.

That night, Frankie could not sleep. He thought about
El Maestro. He thought about Aurora York, the girl in the
tree, and he wondered if his teacher was right, had she been
a fairy? It seemed so long ago. He did not often pray by
himself (since the nuns were always leading them in prayer
someplace) but he closed his eyes and asked God if he could
please go home to Spain. He was tired of America. He
crawled under a long table and lay on his side, humming
"How Great Thou Art."

Minutes later, his eyes opened. He heard a scratching
noise from outside the building. He pulled a chair to the
wall and climbed to the window above the sink. At the
sight of something out in the alley, his face changed, and
he quickly pushed the window open and wedged himself
through, falling to the ground.

What happened next may seem incredible. I can only tell you it is true.

Frankie opened his eyes to feel the wet tongue of the hairless dog, licking his cheeks.

26

WE SHOULD SPEAK ABOUT THOSE STRINGS.

You know that they came from Carmencita, Frankie's beautiful, dark-haired mother.

You know that she intended them for her husband, El Maestro, who was really Frankie's father.

You know that they sat unused for nine years—inside a purse in El Maestro's closet—until he gave them to Frankie the day the boy left Spain.

What you do not know is where Carmencita acquired them.

Or from whom.

It happened on the last morning of her life. Sleep had been restless, the unborn child stirring inside her. Carmencita rose with the dawn, dressing quietly so as not to wake her husband. She pulled on a shawl and walked toward the Mijares River. A mist hung over the earth, washing all colors in a filmy white. It was so thick she almost didn't see a gypsy family sitting on the riverbank. The man had large ears and thinning hair. The woman next to him seemed older. Behind them was a little girl with long auburn braids. She was brushing a horse.

"God be with you, señora," the man said.

These were dangerous words during the war. But Carmencita replied, "God be with you as well."

"Your baby comes soon," the woman said.

Carmencita put her hand on her belly.

"May I offer you a scarf?" The woman reached into a wooden box of possessions.

"I brought no money," Carmencita said.

"We are not selling these things," the man replied. "We are giving them away."

"My husband thinks of others—"

"We have no need for them—"

"He is a man of God—"

"I am but a horse trader—"

"They want to kill him, señora!"

The woman began to cry. Carmencita lowered her hand from her belly. So many in her country were like this, fleeing from one side or the other. The war was ruining lives. Her husband had lost his eyes. Her brother had disappeared. Priests were being hunted, and families like this one were on the run. She wondered about the world her baby was about to enter.

"You can stay with us if you wish," Carmencita said.

The gypsies looked at each other.

"Where?"

"In our home. We do not have much room, but you are welcome."

"But we are strangers to you."

"Tell me your names and you will not be strangers."

The man smiled. "Does a name make such a difference?"

"Of course not," Carmencita replied. She knew, in war, it was sometimes better not to know a name.

"Thank you, kind woman," the man said. "But we could not endanger you that way."

He held his wife's hand and summoned their daughter, who put down the horse brush.

"We have little to offer in return for your generosity. But perhaps a song?"

The child began to sing, a soft gypsy melody.

"Such a pretty voice," Carmencita said.

"You enjoy music?" the man asked.

"My husband is a guitarist."

"As am I. Or was. I would play songs to the Lord. Sadly, my guitar is gone."

"Taken," his wife said.

"I am sorry," Carmencita said.

"Your husband, will he teach your child to play?"

"It is all he speaks about."

"Then you must have these."

He reached into the box and removed a set of strings, coiled together by a yellow band. They seemed brand new, almost shiny.

"I could not," she protested.

"For your kindness."

"It is not nec—"

"Please. To connect the child and the father. They are special strings." He lowered his voice. "They have lives inside them."

His wife slapped his arm. "He means they were made from silk, and the silk came from worms, and the worms were once alive."

She gave him a harsh look. "Do not speak in riddles."

He smiled and rocked back and forth. When his wife turned to tend to the horse, he leaned in toward Carmencita.

"I don't mean worms," he whispered.

He removed from his pocket a rosary, with simple black beads and a small black cross. Carmencita realized the rosary was held together by a guitar string like the ones he'd just handed her. As he pulled on both ends, the string began to glow blue, like the inside of a flame.

"*Le duy vas xalaven pe,*" he said, a gypsy expression that translates to "the hands wash each other"—meaning we are all connected.

When his wife approached, the man stuffed the rosary back in his pocket. He gazed at the white sky.

"Best to be on your way, señora."

"Are you certain you won't come?"

"God will protect us. As I pray He protects you."

"I will light a candle for your family at the basilica."

"San Pascual?"

"Do you know it?"

The man's eyes grew far away.

"We were there once. With our other daughter. Be mindful. These are dangerous times for prayer."

Carmencita looked at the strings.

"May I ask your name?" she said. "Even if it does not matter?"

"He is known as El Pelé," the wife said.

Carmencita walked into the mist. A minute later, she turned, but they were gone.

ᥱᐤ

On her way home, Carmencita put the strings inside a small purse, planning to give them to El Maestro upon the birth of their child. That night, during the storm, she had the purse with her in the cathedral where she went to light a candle not only for the baby, but for the gypsy family she had met that morning. She said her prayers, fell over in pain, dropped the purse, and never saw it again. Never saw the rack of candles overturned by the raiders. Never saw the fire from her lighted prayer candles join the larger fire, consuming everything in its path.

The next day, when police in Villareal searched through

the ruins, they found the charred remains of Carmencita's badly burned corpse. The raiders, having assumed she was a nun—due to the tunic that draped her—had desecrated her body. It was too gruesome to identify, and her bones were quickly buried in an unmarked grave.

Two days later, a teenage boy was scavenging through the wreckage; he found a small purse, which had inexplicably survived the flames. Inside was an identification card. The boy returned the purse to the listed address, handing it to the person who answered the door.

A tall, blind man named Carlos Andres Presto.

Better known as El Maestro.

He grabbed the purse and stumbled to a chair. He realized what this meant—why his wife had not returned in three days. He spilled the contents on the wooden table. He felt a coiled object.

"What is this?" he asked the boy.

"It looks like strings."

"For the guitar?"

"Yes."

El Maestro bit his lip.

"Leave me alone. Now!"

The boy left quickly.

Holding the undelivered gift, his wife's final kindness, El Maestro broke down. He wept until nightfall, never leaving the chair. Then he put everything back inside the purse and hid it in a closet. Those strings, with the "lives" inside them, remained unused for years, just as the story of a stranger's kindness remained untold.

Weeks later, the man known as "El Pelé" rushed to help a priest who was being beaten by Republic soldiers. He was arrested and ordered to surrender his rosary. When he refused, a firing squad shot him. The killers saw his body crumple, but they did not see something else: the rosary, at the moment of his death, turning a burning shade of blue.

Decades later, El Pelé would be canonized by the Catholic Church as its first gypsy saint. People still speak about his courage, his humility, and, of course, that rosary.

No one mentions the strings he gave away.

They would tell a story of their own.

27

1969

THE WOMAN IN THE VAN WAS KISSING HER WAY UP FRANKIE'S neck. He felt so heavy, he couldn't move. He gazed down the side of her body, the orange cotton top; the denim shorts; the tan legs; and the painted toenails, red, black, purple.

"No blue," he mumbled.

"Hmm?"

"You don't have blue."

"Blue toenails? You're funny."

"Am I blue . . . ," Frankie half-sang.

"I know who you are."

"Hmm?"

She kissed him some more.

"You're the singer—"

"My wife is waiting—"

"Frankie Presto."

"Breakfast—"

"Are you really gonna play onstage?"

"I have to cook these eggs."

"You didn't finish the story. After you ran away."

"I played my guitar."

"You were just a kid."

"I was good."

"How good?"

"I saved her life."

"Who?"

"Aurora."

"Who's Aurora?"

Frankie's eyes went glassy.

"Keep singing to me . . ." the woman said.

But Frankie's jumbled thoughts were on the blue strings and Aurora York and where he left her, pregnant, sleeping on a blanket. He knew he had to get back, he didn't want to disappoint her, to be irresponsible, as he'd been so many nights before.

"I have to go—" he suddenly said.

He pushed up so quickly that the woman slid off him, thudding to the floor. He grabbed his things and stumbled out the sliding doors, which growled like lions as he pulled them apart.

"Hey, what the hell?" she yelled after him.

28

1951

"*WHAT THE HELL?*" A MAN SCREAMED, OPENING HIS CAR TRUNK. His name was Hampton Belgrave, and he was staring at a teenaged Frankie curled around his dog.

"I can explain," Frankie said, blinking.

"You 'bout give me a heart attack!"

"Is this Tennessee?"

"Is this my car?"

"Yes, sir."

"Then I ask the questions!"

"Yes, sir."

"Who the hell are you?"

"Frankie, sir."

"Frankie who?"

"Presto, sir."

"Whose dog is that?"

"Mine, sir."

"Why you in my trunk?"

"Marcus Belgrave, sir."

"My cousin Marcus?"

"Yes, sir."

"The musician Marcus?"

"Yes, sir."

"He put you in this trunk?"

"No, sir."

"Then why you in it?"

"To get to Tennessee, sir."

"Whynchu take a train?"

"Can't afford it."

"Take a bus, then."

"Can't afford that, either."

"So you hide in my trunk?"

"Yes, sir."

"With a damn dog?"

"Sorry, sir."

"How long you been in there?"

"Since Detroit, sir."

"I left Detroit yesterday!"

"Yes, sir."

"You ain't eat since then?"

"No, sir."

"Ain't drink since then?"

"No, sir."

"Ain't pee since then?"

"No, sir."

"You think I give a damn?"

"No, sir?"

"Damn right, I don't! You a stowaway—"

"No, sir—"

"—want to go to Tennessee."

"Yes, sir—"

"You best not peed in my trunk, boy."

"No, sir."

"That dog best not peed, neither!"

"No, sir—"

"How you know where I'm going?"

"Are we there, sir?"

"I ain't said where we are. But I got me a gun in my glove compartment—"

"Marcus told me, sir!"

"How did Marcus know?"

"You're his cousin! Your name is Hampton! You told him you were driving back to Tennessee!"

"Why would Marcus tell you that?"

"I work for him."

"White boy work for Marcus? Come on now. What you do?"

"I play music."

"Tell the truth."

"In his band."

"You play with Marcus?"

"Yes, sir."

"You just a kid!"

"I'm about fifteen, sir."

"About?"

"Don't know for sure, sir."

"What you play?"

"Guitar. It's right here, sir."

"Wait a minute . . ."

"You see?"

"Take that hat off!"

"Why—"

"You that boy! The one who play so fast!"

"Yes, sir."

"I was there! I saw that! You done hypnotized the man with the knife!"

"Yes, sir—"

"You the devil!"

"No, sir!"

"In my trunk!"

"Please—"

"The devil in my trunk!"

"No—"

"With his devil dog!"

"I just play—"

"No earthly man play like that—"

"She was in trouble, sir—"

"What you want with me, devil?"

"I'm not the devil!"

"Swear it!"

"I swear it!"

"Swear to Jesus!"

"I swear to Jesus!"

"Why you here, then, boy?"

"Where?"

"Tennessee."

"We're here?"

"Dammit, don't fool me!"

"The girl, sir."

"What girl?"

"The girl with that man."

"The one almost have her throat slit?"

"Yes, sir."

"What about her?"

"She lives here."

"Says who?"

"The man."

"With the knife?"

"Yes, sir."

"So what?"

"I know her."

"That girl?"

"Yes, sir."

"You know *that* girl?"

"Her name's Aurora."

"Aurora."

"I think."

"You think?"

"It's been a while."

"How long?"

"We were kids."

"Oh, Lord—"

"In another country—"

"Get out."

"Really, sir?"

"You ain't no devil."

"No, sir—"

"Just a fool."

"No, sir—"

"The worst kind—"

"No, sir—"

"A fool in love."

"No, sir, I—"

"Get in them woods and pee. The damn dog, too. Then go sit up front. We'll drive into town, find you somethin' to eat."

"Thank you, sir. Thank you so much."

"What you thankin' me for, boy? You just rode two days in the trunk of a car—for a *girl*."

He snickered. "You'd be better off if you's the devil."

29

1952

A BIT OF CATCH-UP NOW (OR AN "ANACRUSIS," THE NOTES that run up to the first downbeat of a song, like the "happy" in "Happy Birthday").

Frankie ran away from the orphanage after reuniting with the hairless dog. In the months that followed, he found work in the Black Bottom section of Detroit, where, despite his age, he played nightly shows with jazz groups in exchange for plates of food for himself and the dog, and a mattress in the club basements. It was there he befriended the trumpeter Marcus Belgrave, sat in with his quartet, and, one night, saved the life of a young blond girl by distracting her attacker with his astonishing guitar speed.

And, although she looked much older now, Frankie believed this blonde was Aurora York, the girl in the tree. The man with the knife had confessed that he'd just met her and said that she was visiting from Tennessee. Which is why Frankie stowed away in a car headed south.

Next thing he knew, he was sleeping on the couch of Hampton Belgrave, Marcus's cousin.

Everyone joins a band in this life.

Some are by accident.

$\wp$

Six months after that ride in the trunk, Frankie had secured his first solo engagement, in hopes of drawing Aurora to him: singing in front of a Nashville automobile dealership.

Cars, cars, cars,
We've got cars, cars, cars . . .

The owner, Mr. Rutland Vines, of Vines Fine Cadillacs, was a baldheaded, double-chinned businessman who liked to hook his fingers around his suspenders. He had hired Frankie (in hopes of luring buyers) at the urging of his mechanic, Hampton Belgrave (who had inadvertently transported the boy to Tennessee).

"My Cadillacs ain't no different from the Cadillacs over at Shimey Motors," Rutland said. "Only difference, I reckon, is the customer experience I give 'em, y'understand?"

Frankie hadn't really understood. But Hampton said the man would pay him and Frankie understood that part.

"Just do the good churchy music, some gospel, like Red Foley, but also that hillbilly boogie like Tennessee Ernie Ford and maybe some honky-tonk, too," Rutland instructed. "Keep 'em happy. Ya got it?"

Frankie nodded.

"And you need to dress right. Get yourself a nice tie. And pomade that hair. You got too much of it popping up. Ya hear me?"

That evening, back at Hampton's house, Frankie planted himself by the radio while Hampton cooked a stew of pork, corn, and onions. The two had been staying together for months, after Hampton phoned his cousin Marcus and Marcus confirmed that Frankie was not, in any way, the devil.

Hampton was a squat man with a short neck and thick elbows, fond of sweet cake, bowler caps, and the blues. He always dreamed of making music, even though, for a living, he fixed automobiles. He played a little harmonica (he took a small amount of me at birth) and at night he put on records as Frankie strummed along.

"You got good ears, boy," he told Frankie. "You hear it, you play it."

That evening, Frankie turned the radio dial from one station to another, teaching himself a fast country repertoire. Much of the music the announcers called "honky-tonk" or "hillbilly" was simple enough, three or four chords, pick the bass note, strum. But the singers weren't easy to imitate, they warbled or drew out the words in a southern accent. Still, Frankie liked this music, because it told stories of heartbreak and love and drunkenness. Also, it was much easier to play than the twelve études of Heitor Villa-Lobos that El Maestro used to put him through.

"Yodel-ley-ee-hee-ho," Frankie sang, trying to mimic a yodeling sound in a song called "Chime Bells" by Elton Britt. "Yodel-ley-ee-hee-h——"

Hampton rushed in carrying a large soup spoon and snapped off the radio.

"Quit that! You about to drive me crazy!" He shook his head. "Get dressed, boy. I'm gonna take you someplace and show you some real music."

The hairless dog rose to its feet.

"Can't take no dogs," Hampton said.

The dog sat back down.

"Yodeling," Hampton grumbled. "Lawd help this world."

That night, Hampton walked Frankie through the streets of Nashville. They passed a redbrick building called the Ryman Auditorium. "That's where they do the *Grand Ole Opry* show," Hampton said. "It's on the radio clear around the country. That place make you about as famous as you can get."

"Can I play there?" Frankie asked.

"I reckon you could, once people see how fast you is."

Hampton rubbed his chin.

"That something you want to do?"

"Sure."

"All right then. Maybe you will."

He walked Frankie to Printer's Alley, an area of night-clubs that featured country music. When the doors opened they heard fiddles mixing with guitars and upright basses.

"You catchin' that sound?" Hampton asked.

"Can we go in?"

"You can. Colored clubs is up the block a'ways."

Frankie didn't fully understand the "colored" rule Hampton often spoke about. But he knew it was unfair. He wasn't even from America, and he could enter places Hampton could not.

"Let's go to those other clubs, then," Frankie said.

Hampton smiled. "Awright, boy. But you can't be playing none of the music you hear up there at the car lot. Rutland will throw you out on your rump."

❧

That night, Hampton took Frankie up and down Jefferson Street, to places called Club Baron, the Del Morocco, Maceo's, Sugar Hill, and Pee Wee's. The boy's eyes bulged at the music he heard, rambling guitars and basses, growling singing, piano players who seemed to be running and walking their fingers at the same time. There was laughing and wailing and people rising from their seats and swinging their hips or yelling, "Go, go, go!" Frankie loved it.

It felt as if the music and the crowd were all on the same stage. Even Hampton, wearing his bowler cap, went out and danced awhile, coming back sweaty and waving his hand like a fan.

"Well, now, Hampton, who's this boy?" asked a man who wandered over holding a drink. "You find yo'self a white son?"

Hampton laughed. "Petey, this boy can play a rope around most pickers in this city. I'm fixin' to manage him. Get him into the Opry."

"Manage him?"

"That's right."

"You a car mechanic."

"For now."

"You know music?"

"I know enough."

"When you gonna start managing him?"

"Once he find what he's looking for."

"What he looking for?"

"What all boys his age looking for?"

They exploded in laughter. Frankie felt himself blushing.

&

Of course, Frankie had not forgotten the reason he'd come to Nashville: to find Aurora York. He was sure she was the girl in that Detroit nightclub. But he had no idea this city would be so big. The world, to Frankie, just kept getting larger, and everyone in it was getting harder to find.

Each weekday morning, he would walk up and down the Nashville business streets, stopping in stores to inquire about a girl named Aurora. Many asked if he had a picture.

"No," he'd say, "but she talks funny. With a British accent."

"Son, you talk funny, too," they would answer. Still, no one could recall her. Pretty soon, having exhausted the businesses, he began to knock on house doors, asking mothers or old ladies if they had seen a blond girl his age. He took the job at the Cadillac dealership and told everyone he was from Spain, hoping someone might get word to Aurora. Surely she would be curious about a guitar player from that country.

As the weather turned hot, Frankie noticed other teens in convertible cars, heading to amusement parks or lakes. He felt pangs of loneliness. Hampton was nice, but he was old, his children scattered, and his wife had passed away. And no one at work really spoke to Frankie. Only the hairless dog gave him hope for happier days. Frankie played constantly with that creature, rolling on the ground and scratching behind its ears.

Of course, when he was truly sad, Frankie came to his

guitar. Hour after hour. Day after day. Practicing, playing, practicing some more, honing the blues progressions that he heard in the clubs on Jefferson Street. For my disciples, the map is simple. All lonely roads lead back to music. I embrace you. I forgive you.

I will never leave you.

Can humans say the same?

⌒

One day, Frankie was standing out in front of the dealership, singing a gospel tune that Rutland was particularly fond of called "By and By."

> *Temptations, hidden snares*
> *Often take us unawares,*
> *And our hearts are made to bleed*
> *For a thoughtless word or deed;*
> *And we wonder why the test*
> *When we try to do our best,*
> *But we'll understand it better by and by.*

A car pulled up and a tall thin man in a cowboy hat stepped out of the passenger's side. He drank from a flask, then wiped his mouth with the back of his arm. Frankie noticed his ears, which pushed out, and the strangely thin line of his lips, which seemed drawn from one end of his cheeks to the other.

The man rested his arms on the hood of the car and nodded along with Frankie's song.

"Ya coming?" the driver asked.

"Y'all go on in, see what they got," the man said. "I'ma listen to the music."

The friend went inside to talk to Rutland. Frankie finished his tune. The tall man clapped.

"Heck of a job, playin' in a car lot."

"Yes, sir."

"Y'all take requests?"

Frankie looked around. There were no other customers.

"Yes, sir, if I know it."

"Play me the saddest song you got."

Frankie hesitated. It was hot, and he felt sweat running down his temples.

"Why do you want to hear a sad song?"

The man took another swig from the flask. "They're more true than the happy ones, don'tcha think?"

"Happy songs can be true, if you're happy."

The man snorted a laugh. "Where you come from, son?"

"Spain," he answered, thinking about Aurora. He checked to see if Rutland was looking. "This is a sad song where I come from."

And he played "Lágrima," the composition by his namesake, Francisco Tárrega, the one his mother hummed, the one he heard Segovia play, the one that Tárrega himself wrote because he was feeling homesick.

The one that means "teardrop."

The tall stranger listened intently, staring at the asphalt as if there were a hole that he was gazing through.

When Frankie finished, the man scratched above his eye.

"Well, son, that was fine, just fine." He looked up. "You do know you're too good to be working here, right?"

"Please don't tell Mr. Rutland I played that," Frankie implored.

The tall man smiled wryly. "Your secret is safe." He approached Frankie. "Can I have a spin on that guitar?"

Frankie glanced inside the store.

"It's all right, son," the man said. "Your boss won't mind."

Frankie handed it over.

"Sturdy instrument," the man said, examining it.

"Yes, sir."

"Good wood. Strong neck. Label's covered up, though. How come?"

"I don't know, that's the way I got it."

The man shrugged. "Okay, then. This is the saddest tune I know."

He sang a song called "I'm So Lonesome I Could Cry." It spoke about a train whistle, and long nights, and birds crying, and the moon going behind a cloud. Each verse ended with the singer saying how lonesome he was, until, by the end, Frankie felt ready to cry himself.

"Whatcha think?" the man asked after the final chord.

"Did you write that?"

"I surely did."

"It's sad."

"Told ya."

"Who did you write it for?"

"My wife. But she ain't my wife no more." He coughed. "You got a girl?"

"I'm waiting for her."

"Here?"

"Yes."

"You might be waitin' awhile."

"You're a really good singer."

The man cackled. "Son, you don't know who I am, do you?"

"No, sir. Who are you?"

The man looked into the store, waved at his companion, then looked back at Frankie and grinned.

"Luke," he said, offering his hand. "Luke the Drifter is my recording name."

"You make records?"

"Sometimes."

Frankie shook his hand. "I'm Frankie Presto."

"Wanna help me pick out a car, Frankie Presto?"

Suddenly, Rutland came rushing out of the store, his smile bigger than Frankie had ever seen it. He looked like a child, Frankie thought, his short, fat legs skipping toward them.

"Ho-leee!" he exclaimed, grabbing for the man's hand. "I can't believe this! Mr. Williams, it is an honor! I mean, I am a follower—a devoted follower of your music. You are the greatest recording artist of our time! Yes, sir! Oh, my! Oh, myyy! Hank Williams!"

The tall man turned to Frankie and winked.

"I am thrilled—honored—I said that already, didn't I?—but it's true," Rutland gushed. "I am honored to sell you a car, sir! A Cadillac, of course! The best we have!"

The man adjusted his hat. "Whatcha got in blue?"

Soon they were walking down the rows of vehicles. Rutland never stopped talking, asking about this song or that song, "Hey, Good Lookin'" and "Move It On Over" and "Cold, Cold Heart" and something called "I Saw the Light," which Rutland said his church choir had tried singing.

"Wonderful tune, Hank, so full of the spirit!"

The man in the hat ran his fingers along the hoods of each car, until he came upon a baby blue model and stopped.

"Whoo, now, she's sweet," he said.

"She could be the one," his companion said.

"Can't do better, Hank," Rutland quickly agreed.

"What do you think, Frankie Presto?" the man asked.

Frankie felt them all looking at him. He spun his guitar over his back and put his hand on the hood. He felt something cold and scary and his face dropped. He pulled back as if shocked.

"What is it, kid?" Luke—or Hank—asked him.

"Don't get this car," Frankie mumbled.

"What's that now?"

"Don't get this car. There's something bad about it."

"Oh, Lord, what does he know, he's just a stupid teenager," Rutland said, shooting Frankie a scowl. "Today's his last day, anyhow. Get on back to your post, boy." He pushed up a smile. "So sorry, Hank. I'm sure we can make an excellent deal for you. She's a fine car. Cadillac. Only the best."

The man in the cowboy hat shrugged at Frankie, and Frankie walked away slowly, the guitar on his back.

❧

An hour later, their paperwork done, the two men emerged from the office and returned to their vehicle. Frankie was alone in the sun, strumming chords and trying not to cry. He didn't want to lose this job. How would Aurora ever find him?

"We'll be on our way now, Frankie Presto," the man said.

"Did you buy that car?"

"Yep."

Frankie looked down.

"It's just a car. Your boss gave us a good deal. And a good deal's hard to come by. I might not need the money, but the people I owe sure do."

The man chuckled at his own joke. Frankie said nothing. The man reached in his pocket for a small vial of pills. He swallowed one and washed it down with whatever was in his flask. Then he slid into the passenger's seat, closed the door, and hung his arm out the window.

"Mister?" Frankie said.

"Yeah?"

"Who are you, really?"

The man scratched his nose. "You wanna keep making music for a livin', son, you're gonna have to be a lot of people. Some you're gonna like being more than others."

He jerked his head back toward the store. "Don't leave before gettin' an envelope your boss got for you."

The car drove away, a small puff of smoke coming from its exhaust. It was suddenly very quiet. The sun baked down without a cloud to soften its heat. Frankie played a little longer. When it turned six o'clock, he entered the office, where Rutland, clearly upset with him, handed him an envelope and told him he didn't need to come back.

"I shouldn't even be givin' you this," he said. "Y'all almost cost me that sale. You'd best learn some respect, you expect to work anyplace again."

On the walk back to Hampton's house, Frankie stopped and sat beside the road. He felt sick. He was afraid of what

Hampton would say about his firing. He should never have talked to Hank or Luke in the first place.

He peeled open the envelope and his mouth dropped. In it, he found $107, the commission on the sale of the Cadillac that Hank Williams had insisted be paid to Frankie and no one else. It was more money than Frankie had ever seen in his life, more than he would have made in half a year at the car lot.

He also found some song lyrics, scribbled on a piece of paper:

Sunflowers waiting for the sunshine.
Violets just waiting for dew.
Bees just waiting for honey
And honey, I'm just waiting for you!

Underneath were the words, "Good luck waiting on your girl," and it was signed "Hank Williams."

Six months later, in the wee hours of New Year's Day, 1953, Hank Williams, his bloodstream laced with morphine, died quietly in the backseat of that baby blue Cadillac. The driver, trying to get Hank to a performance, pulled into a gas station and discovered the singer, cold and unresponsive, beneath a blanket, dead at age twenty-nine.

What Frankie felt on the hood of that car was what I foresaw, what I wanted him to convey, that death awaited, that the singer needed to mend his ways, slow down, stop the drinking and the medication. Do you think me meddlesome? Why? I have told you I love my disciples. I have told you my saddest visits are the ones that come too early. I have told you I can see all futures. Is it beyond me to share this power now and then? Should I always do nothing and let the music die?

30

1969

IT WAS DARK NOW AND FRANKIE STUMBLED THROUGH THE Woodstock crowd until he could no longer see the woman's purple van. It had rained and his feet sloshed. He shifted the guitar on his back. *The stage. He had to reach the stage.* Where was it? How did he get so lost? He heard howling laughter and turned to see a group of young people sliding into pools of mud and squealing as it splashed up on them.

"I'm the Mud King!" a young man screamed.

Frankie lumbered on, past a man handing out bologna sandwiches and a group sharing a jug of water. Gnats engulfed his head. He swatted at them with the egg carton, swerving as if navigating a strange, bumpy planet, passing makeshift tents and rows of sleeping bags and a naked mother washing two children in a pond.

He saw a long line of people and, his mind still cloudy, took a place at the back of it, figuring someone at the front could steer him.

"Who do you have to call, brother?"

"Huh?"

A freckle-faced man was grinning at him. He was shirtless with thick chest hair. The belt around his jeans pushed his flabby waist over the sides.

"It's a phone line, man. Who do you have to call?"

"A phone line?"

"Yeah. They're letting us use the pay phones for free. I gotta call my old lady. I was supposed to be back *yesterday*."

Frankie felt the sweat on his face. He moved his jaw around. Whatever that woman's green pill was, it was having its effect. His bones seemed to be disconnected from one another.

"You trying to get home, too, brother?"

"The stage."

"You're playing?"

"Uh-huh."

"Far out. Far *out*!"

The man squinted. Frankie squinted back.

"Hey, brother?"

"Yeah?"

He pointed over Frankie's shoulder.

"The stage is that way."

31

1953

"The stage is right behind this door," Hampton whispered.

Frankie nodded.

"You get in there, you just make your music. They can't say no to you, fast as you play that guitar."

It was a hot day, in a brisk 2/4 key signature, and the tempo was *vivace*—lively, but *sostenuto*, prolonged. Hampton and Frankie were standing outside the Grand Ole Opry, waiting to audition. Frankie, now seventeen years old, had learned a great deal of country music since arriving in Nashville. He had also grown two inches and looked less a boy than a young man now. Hampton told him, "I reckon you ready for the biggest stage of all."

He'd dressed Frankie for the audition in a gray cowboy hat and a white sports coat with lace trimming. It cost Hampton a week's pay. I should note that the mechanic had asked to be Frankie's manager, and, while Frankie didn't really understand the position, he'd quickly said yes. He liked

Hampton. And seeing that he was feeding Frankie and letting him listen to his radio, Frankie couldn't really refuse.

"Just play the way you played up in Detroit. No way they say no."

"Okay."

"You the fastest thing anyone ever seen."

"Okay."

Hampton seemed nervous. Another hour passed. Frankie wanted to knock on the door, but Hampton refused. "We don't want to seem pushy. They'll come get us."

Eventually, with the sun beginning to set, a man in a suit came out the front door. Frankie ran up and said, "Excuse me," and asked if someone would be greeting them soon.

"Auditions wait at the south door," the man said. "Around the corner. But they're gone now. Y'all need to come back next week."

Frankie glanced at Hampton, whose mouth fell open. Frankie turned back to the man in the suit.

"Sir . . . can I get something that says we were here? For next time? So we can be first in line maybe?"

The man looked him up and down and grinned. He reached into his pocket and pulled out a business card.

"That's all I got, young fella."

The man walked away. Hampton cursed and shook his head. *The wrong door?*

"It's okay, Hampton," Frankie said. "We can try next week."

But the old man kept grumbling, upset by his mistake. He was sweating heavily. On the ride home, he banged the steering wheel many times. Then, after turning at a traffic light, he gripped his arm and fell against the door as the car veered to the curb.

"Hampton!" Frankie screamed, grabbing the wheel and steering wildly. "What's the matter? Hampton! Hey!" He threw his leg over the man's legs to brake the car with a screech.

"Oh no, no, no, no," Frankie implored. He pulled open Hampton's collar. His eyes were rolled back. He was moaning. Frankie screamed out the window, "Help! Where's a hospital?"

Minutes later, he was pulling Hampton through double doors, his arms wrapped around the old man's chest. He kept saying, "You're all right, you're all right," but once inside he again screamed, "Help!" A nurse ran out to assist him, but a doctor with close-cropped hair and a barrel chest raised his hands.

"Hold up," he said. "Y'all need to take him to the colored hospital."

"Please!" Frankie yelled.

The doctor shook his head. "The colored hospital will take care of him."

"But he's in trouble!"

"Then you better get moving."

Frankie's breathing quickened. He squeezed his eyes

closed. And something inside him snapped. Perhaps because of Baffa, or El Maestro, or never finding his mother, or any of the many precious things that had been taken from him in his life, he felt a force surging, a noise between his ears, like an angry glissando from one end of the keyboard to the other.

He would not lose Hampton, too.

"Now you listen," he said, raising to within inches of the doctor. "I just came from the Grand Ole Opry. So did he. This is an important man."

The doctor snickered. "Y'all came from the Opry?"

Frankie pulled the business card from his pocket and slammed it in the doctor's palm.

"That's right. I'm playing there Saturday night. I will leave you four free tickets in the front row if you take care of this man right now."

Even as he said it Frankie felt as if he were listening to someone else. Where did he find these words?

The doctor sniffed as he read the business card. It belonged to a high-ranking events manager.

"You really playin' the Opry?"

"Look at my clothes," Frankie said.

The doctor pursed his lips. He nodded at the nurse.

"In the back," he said.

℘

A few hours later, Frankie sat near a bed, softly strumming his guitar, a blues progression that seemed to make its own rhythm.

"Keep playin' boy. It soothes me."

Hampton Belgrave, at seventy-seven, had suffered a heart attack, but the quick medical attention he'd received had stabilized him. He would live.

"You really promise that doctor tickets?" Hampton whispered.

Frankie nodded.

"To a show you ain't doing?"

"Yeah."

Hampton smiled and shook his head.

"You a lot smarter than when I found you in my trunk."

Frankie fingered a chord. Hampton choked up.

"Ain't no tellin' what mighta happened to me."

"You'll be all right, Hampton."

"Thanks to you."

"Nah."

"I'm going to sleep a bit now. Maybe say a prayer."

The old mechanic closed his eyes, so he did not see what happened next: the D string on Frankie's guitar turned a burning shade of blue. Frankie stared at it. He felt a chill run down his arms and legs. You have wondered about the critical passages in my child's story? Here is one:

In the quiet of a hospital room, to the sound of an old man's breathing, Frankie Presto finally understood that, somehow, through those strings, he held life in his hands.

⌁

Two weeks later and eight pounds lighter, Hampton returned home. He sat Frankie down and told him that managing a musician was obviously too strenuous for him, and "maybe you oughta consider someone with a better head for these things."

Frankie was sad. He liked Hampton, and he wanted to see the inside of the Grand Ole Opry. But the truth was, he didn't care for the cowboy clothes. And he never found Aurora York in Nashville, which was the reason he had come. The closest he came was the makeup counter at Harvey's department store, where a middle-aged woman remembered a blond girl with a British accent who said she was moving to New Orleans.

It wasn't much to go on.

But it was something.

So one morning, a few months after the Opry incident, Frankie took twenty dollars from the money left in Hank Williams's envelope, and hid the rest in Hampton's drawer, as a way of thanking Hampton for looking after him. Then he put on his sunglasses, gave the old man a hug, and walked off—with his guitar, his suitcase, and the hairless dog—to the Greyhound bus station, where he purchased a one-way ticket to New Orleans.

As he went to board, the bus driver said, "No dogs allowed unless you're blind." Thinking fast, Frankie put his hands out in front of him and said, "Why do you think I'm wearing these glasses?" He and the creature were allowed to get on. The bus pulled away. An older woman sitting across from him tapped him on the arm and stuffed a ten-dollar bill into his hands. "May God help you with your affliction," she said.

Frankie thanked the woman. He heard the dog whimper. He wondered why God was always mentioned in the most unusual moments of his life.

32

1954

ABOUT THAT DOG.

Frankie was now eighteen years old, which meant his four-legged companion was even older. In the life of a canine, that is rare. But this was an uncommon animal, and its life span was clearly determined by need, not years. The dog was there to pull Frankie from the river. It was there to distract soldiers at the sardine factory. It was there to keep Frankie company when Baffa was arrested. And somehow it was there, in Detroit, outside the orphanage, when Frankie desperately needed a friend.

Down in New Orleans, the dog waited nights in hotel rooms while Frankie earned money playing with doo-wop groups and jazz quartets. During the day, the creature followed Frankie up and down the streets, waiting outside storefronts while Frankie asked about Aurora. Each time my child emerged dejected, with no new information, the dog rose, its tongue panting, and accompanied him to the next stop.

But as 1954 drew to a close, Frankie noticed his companion slowing down. It took longer to walk those streets or to navigate the high grass below the Huey P. Long Bridge, which straddled the Mississippi River. Frankie practiced beneath that bridge three hours each day, as the trains passed overhead. He'd become quite skilled at rhythm and blues, and he strummed to the beat of the wheels when they hit a gap in the rail joints. The hairless dog would look up at the noise.

"Chuckutty, chuckutty," Frankie would sing.

But in recent weeks, nothing Frankie played could raise the creature's head off its paws, not even when he imitated the high warble of a young Elvis Presley and the scrubbing rhythm of his new record called "That's All Right (Mama)."

"You are a tough audience," Frankie said.

The dog sneezed.

"What do you want to hear?"

The dog blinked and looked directly at him.

"Mmm? Something slow and pretty?"

Frankie leaned against a tree and began picking at a 2/5 progression. The air was warm and the sun ducked behind a single white cloud. Frankie's memory drifted. Before he knew it, he was fingering "Maalaala Mo Kaya," the song he'd once played to honor the buried dead in a Spanish field. Frankie hadn't tried this piece in many years, and he was surprised by how easily it came back to him. Its simple melody was soothing. The hairless dog gave a big, silent yawn.

When Frankie finished, the animal came to him and Frankie scratched its ears. The dog licked his fingers.

"Thanks," Frankie said, smiling. "Now I'm all sticky."

The dog turned and walked to the river's edge. The muddy current was moving quickly.

"Hey, careful," Frankie yelled, leaning forward, but for the first time ever, the animal turned and growled, causing Frankie to lean back, confused.

There are songs that you play that you have to restart, and songs that you play that you never get right. But when a song is complete, there is no more you can do.

The hairless dog leaped into the water and paddled away.

Frankie watched limply, knowing somehow he was not supposed to follow, even as the last member of his original three-piece band disappeared down the Mississippi River.

A moment later he heard a rustling in the tall grass behind him. He turned his head and squinted into the sun. He saw a figure hovering above him, smiling.

"I hear you've been looking for me," Aurora York said.

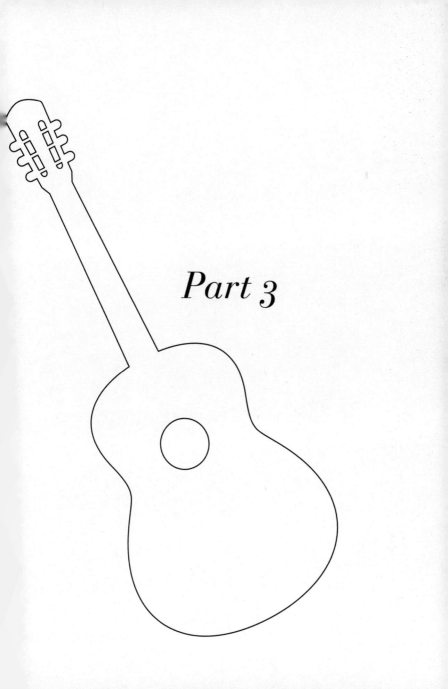

Part 3

Cecile (York) Peterson

Sister to Aurora York; retired mathematician, London School of Economics

OUR FATHER WAS A SPY.

That's how we got to Spain, my dear. He was a spy during World War Two, and he thought we'd be safer here than in England. And I suppose, given the Blitz, he was right. Father worked for British Intelligence on Operation Fortitude. It's quite famous, actually. They distracted the Germans from the Normandy invasion by pretending the Allies were planning bigger attacks elsewhere. . . . Oh, yes, dear. They've written books about it. Look it up.

Father worked with a Spanish double agent whom the Germans trusted. It was all rather productive—but not for our family. Father left us in a small house near Valencia, my mother, Aurora, and me. Then he left us for good. He was murdered in 1945, eight months after Normandy. They found his body in a Barcelona hotel room, strangled by a wire. I suppose he was double-crossed. One never knows.

"Secrecy is part of the life we've chosen," Father used to say.

My sister and I were quite different. Aurora was a free spirit. She dressed in odd, mismatched clothes; she liked to dance about first thing in the morning; liked to climb trees, run out in the rain, smear tomato paste on her face, things like that. I was more studious. Proper decorum. Stay dry. My mother's daughter, I suppose. Numbers intrigued me. Math. Science. I preferred things orderly. Aurora liked things messy.

You could describe Aurora and Frankie that way. Messy.

To be accurate, I'd heard of "Francisco" years before I met him. My sister encountered him when she was quite young, in the woods here in Spain. I don't know what they said or did that afternoon, but whatever it was, he became part of her vocabulary. *"One day, when I marry Francisco . . . ,"* she would say. Or *"When I get a house one day with Francisco . . ."* Honestly, I thought he was imaginary. She was only seven or eight, and you know how young girls are. Anyhow, being the daughters of a spy, truth and lies were often indistinguishable in our home.

It wasn't until she ran away in America that I realized "Francisco" was an actual person. Aurora was a teenager by this point, and that summer she'd gone to Tennessee with our mother and new stepfather for a medical conference. He was a physician. Scottish. Awful temper. He and Aurora were constantly fighting—she hated the idea that my mother would replace my father—and they got into a horrible row during that trip. She had this new yellow suitcase, and when my mother came back to the hotel room, the suitcase was gone and so was Aurora. They stayed a few weeks searching, but eventually gave up and came home.

I remember them walking in the door, two people, not three, and feeling so cheated, as if they'd driven off with all my things and returned empty-handed. What childhood I had left with my sister, my stepfather took away. I never forgave him for that. Perhaps I never forgave Aurora, either, leaving Mother and me alone with that man.

Over the months, we got postcards saying she was all right, but with precious few details, except that she believed "Francisco" was somewhere in America, too, she could feel it. I dismissed that as more ramblings from my nutter sister. I frankly don't know how she survived.

Then one day, in 1955, she rang up our flat in London. I must have been twenty-three, so she would have been, what, eighteen or nineteen? I answered the phone and I heard her say, "Cecile, you must come over. I'm getting married!" Not even a hello. I was stunned to hear her voice. I said, "Aurora? Is that really you?" And she said, "He finally found me, Cecile." And I said, "Who found you?" And she said, "Francisco, of course!"

That's the way it worked between the two of them. Long periods of absence—then crazy, intense romance. I do believe she and Frankie belonged together, even if they rarely stayed together. It was as if they had a secret they were bound to, which made them joyful most of the time and insane the rest.

But in love? Oh, yes, dear. Frankie and Aurora were more deeply in love than any two people I have ever encountered, and that included my own marriage, which lasted forty-two years. I remember Frankie practicing or composing, and my sister would come up behind him and kiss his ear—always his ear—and he'd say, "Aurora means dawn," and they would laugh, whatever that was about. They sang little duets together. There was this one Spanish song about a railroad car. *Laaaa-paaan-de-ro la-la-la, la-la-la-la-la.* Do you know it? . . . I just thought, being here in Spain . . . Well. Anyhow.

They were at their happiest just before Frankie became famous, which is when they had their wedding. They were living in New Orleans. I booked passage to be Aurora's maid of honor. My stepfather forbade my mother going. Can you believe that? He said, "The little scrubber has caused us enough headaches." Honestly, the man was poison.

So I traveled to the United States by myself, but when I got to New Orleans, I discovered that since neither Frankie nor Aurora had the proper paperwork, they could not be legally wed.

That didn't stop them. They threw their own wedding—at a nightclub in the French Quarter. . . . No, I can't recall the name. But I remember it began at two a.m.— after the establishment closed. There were lots of musicians there. Fats Domino played the piano. He was a friend of Frankie's. And quite a few jazz artists, too.

That was the first time I heard Frankie perform. He was brilliant, really. I understood why my sister fell for him. He sang like a nightingale and was severely attractive. At the time, he was working with a group of—is it "doo-wop music"? Yes . . . Exactly . . . Each of them had a different vocal tone, one very low, one very high, one in the middle, and they did a song called "Earth Angel" for my sister. Frankie actually got down on one knee when the song asked, "Will you be mine?" and Aurora started crying when he put a ring on her finger. I was truly glad for her. She was my sister, after all. And when Aurora was happy, no one could be happier. She would grab your hands and swing your arms and say, "Isn't this wonderful!" as if she were a little girl.

Maybe that's why she and Frankie were attracted to each other. They were hardly allowed to be children when they were children, so when they were adults, they often acted like, well, children. Let's just say it. Sleeping late. Missing appointments. Always laughing and apologizing their way through things. But they weren't children, were they? And that's where their troubles started.

When she would leave him for long stretches, I would

scold her, but she always had an excuse, that he needed to work on his music, or she needed to get through something. He would send her money. She would send it back. He would phone. She would hang up. She knew there were other women. It didn't faze her. I would say, "Aurora, if he's your husband, you belong together," and she would say, "Oh, Cecile, we are together. We're just apart."

They kept a lot of secrets. Father would have approved. But it left me in the dark about many issues—including whatever the big split was about. To this day, I couldn't tell you. I imagine the marriage to that actress did not help. I won't even say her name, it upset me so much. I don't know what Frankie was thinking. Have you seen photos of my sister when she was younger? Prettier than any actress, my dear. Aurora could have had any man she set her mind to. She chose Frankie. There it is, really.

Do you know the Latin motto at the London School of Economics? *Rerum cognoscere causas.* That means, "To know the causes of things." But there was so much I didn't know about Frankie and Aurora, so perhaps I'm not being very helpful for your report. I can only confirm that he was the cause of a lot of joy for her—and a lot of heartache. Maybe because of that, he didn't think I liked him. Whenever they visited, he would hug me and say, "Cecile, let me play you a song." And I would say, "No, that's quite all right." I wasn't going to let his music charm me. Artists believe that art makes all behavior acceptable. I do not agree. And I told him so.

Looking back, perhaps that was harsh. But I've always been the practical one. Aurora understood that. She used to laugh and say, "You're better off if he doesn't play you his music, Cecile. It only takes that boy and his guitar a couple of minutes to change your life."

33

FRANKIE AND AURORA. A SYMPHONY IN ITSELF.

I have spoken before about love and music, the tangled duet. Suffice it to say, there was a reason that, for all his amorous adventures, Frankie Presto felt empty with nearly every woman he was with.

Mea culpa.

The truth is, I do not share well. I want you to myself. And you, my precious acolytes, want me, too—even at the expense of others. You follow me to lonely practice rooms, faraway stages, late hours inside smoky recording studios, your weary fingers banging piano keys, your tired lips clamped around a mouthpiece, playing on, forsaking those who love you and who you should love back. They will lure you. I will lure you more. It is the price I exact. And the one you pay.

Frankie saw this early on. One night during his time with Duke Ellington, the famous bandleader had two attractive women waiting in a long black car.

"Do you like those pretty ladies, Francisco?"

Frankie grinned.

"I agree. They are fine. But music is my mistress. Do you know what that means?"

Frankie shook his head.

"It means those ladies will be gone by morning, but my piano will still be here."

As a boy, Frankie did not understand. As a man, he understood completely. Over the decades, no matter whose bed he landed in, I was Frankie's mistress. And I could steal him back from anyone.

Anyone.

Except Aurora York.

e⁓

Frankie fell in love with Aurora as a child and he would never love anyone that way again. It was that simple. He thought about her, he pursued her, and every time he lost her, he pursued her again. From that first day in the Spanish woods to that fateful night at Woodstock, theirs was what you humans label a true love story.

But all love stories are symphonies.

And, like symphonies, they have four movements:

- *Allegro,* a quick and spirited opening
- *Adagio,* a slow turn
- *Minuet/Scherzo* short steps in ¾ time

- *Rondo,* a repeating theme, interrupted by various passages

I always knew where Frankie and Aurora were heading. Given his musicality, how could they not follow form?

34

1955

THEIR FIRST MOVEMENT. *ALLEGRO.* QUICK. LIVELY. IT BEGAN in Spain and picked up speed in Louisiana. They found a place to live, renting a one-room apartment above a New Orleans drugstore. Aurora slept in a single bed and Frankie slept on a couch in the other room, still shy to the ways of love and mindful of Aurora's warning that "Everything up to now does not count. We are starting fresh."

Each night, over red beans and rice, Frankie told Aurora about his adventures, his boat ride from Spain and meeting Django on the docks and the orphanage and Hank Williams and the Grand Ole Opry. She leaned in with her cheek in her hands, marveling at all the places he had been. She did not say much about her own travels, and Frankie did not ask about the bearded man in Detroit, or any other people she might have been with. But sometimes, in the morning, while he was practicing his guitar, she would look at him and cry a little. Once he asked, "What's wrong?" and she said, "Why didn't you find me sooner?" And he said, "I ran after you that night," and she said, "I was ashamed," and he said, "It didn't stop me," and he told her about going door to door with the hairless dog in different cities.

"Thank you," she said.

"For what?"

"For not giving up."

"Why would I give up?"

At night, sometimes, they walked along the Mississippi River and shared fried dough from inside a paper bag. Music could be heard from the clubs in the French Quarter and Frankie would sing along. Or he would do a song the children in Villareal used to sing when chasing the train through town.

La pan-der-o-la-la-la
La pan-der-o-la-la-la

Aurora would laugh and rest her head on his shoulder, and Frankie remembered a conversation he'd once had with his guitar teacher:

"How do you know you are in love, Maestro?"
"If you are asking, you are not."
"Were you ever in love, Maestro?"
"Who wrote 'Recuerdos de la Alhambra'?"
"Francisco Tárrega."

"What technique must be used in that song?"

"The tremolo technique."

"These are the questions you should be asking. Not love questions."

"Where does tremolo come from, Maestro?"

"From the word 'to tremble.'"

"What does tremble mean?"

"To shake. To quiver. To be scared or nervous."

"When does this happen?"

El Maestro paused. "When you are in love."

⁓

Frankie made a great deal of music in New Orleans, a city I infuse more than most. He sat in with blues bands. He played jazz at the Dew Drop Inn. Aurora went with him to small bars and outdoor stages, even a recording studio in the back of an appliance shop in the French Quarter. Frankie's guitar versatility made him a favorite there, and the owner would tell his clients, "Whatever you need—*presto!*—this kid can play it! That's why they call him Presto!"

One summer night, Frankie was in that studio when a wiry black man with high hair and a thin mustache came to record some songs. It was mostly blues numbers, which were easy for Frankie to follow, but he could tell the producer was not happy with the results. After several hours they took a break.

The singer, whose name was Richard Penniman, stepped into the alley behind the studio to have his shoes shined. He seemed frustrated. Frankie followed him out. The shoe-shine boy was a six-year-old named Ellis who adored Frankie because he showed him how to make chords on the guitar.

"Want a nice shine, Mr. Presto?" Ellis asked, but Frankie told him to do the new man's shoes first.

"Thank you," Richard Penniman said.

"Sure."

"That your girl in there? The blonde?"

"Yes."

"Whooo-eee."

Frankie smiled.

"You a good-looking thing yourself," the man said. "You perform?"

"I mostly play guitar."

"Mmm-hmm."

"What?"

"Nobody gettin' famous playing guitar. You wanna be big, you better get singin'. Out front. By yourself."

Aurora came outside and said she was going for ice cream. She asked if they wanted any.

"How about a cone of tutti frutti?" the man said.

Frankie laughed.

"What's so funny?"

"Tutti-frutti. That's Italian."

"For what?"

"All fruits."

"Hmmph. Wish I'd known that before."

"Before what?"

"Before I wrote my song."

"What song?"

" 'Tutti Frutti.' "

"About fruits?"

"It ain't about fruits! It's about, you know . . ."

He did a little headshake and moved his hips.

"Wanna hear it?"

And there, on the shoe-shine stand, he sang a verse—a loud, fast boogie-woogie melody—and Frankie nodded, his eyes wide, and even little Ellis the shoe-shine boy grinned.

"Maybe," Frankie suggested, "you should be recording *that*."

A few minutes later, he was. It was thrown together quickly and the energy in the room was palpable and Richard Penniman screamed "Aaaaah" to let the saxophone player know it was time to solo. The words were deemed too racy, so a woman at the studio quickly made up some new lyrics, and fifteen minutes later, the final song was recorded. (Quick creation, remember? My gift to you?)

"Tutti Frutti" (with Frankie playing an uncredited guitar lick) became a hugely successful record, and forged the career of the mustached man, who became better known as Little Richard.

Nobody noticed when Aurora returned with the ice cream.

"What did I miss?" she asked.

e~

The *allegro* continued. Frankie saved up money from his music jobs and, just before Christmas, bought a small ring, two hearts connected by a diamond chip. The next night, he and Aurora walked along Canal Street, past the Maison Blanche department store, where, in the window, as part of an annual tradition, there was a large papier-mâché snowman named Mr. Bingle, depicted as Santa's helper. Aurora loved this odd creation, with its small hat and round black eyes.

"Santa can't go do anything without Mr. Bingle," she announced, her face against the glass.

"Aurora?"

Frankie opened the ring box.

"I can't do anything without you, either. Marry me. Please?"

Aurora inhaled. Tears fell down her cheeks. I was keenly aware of a lack of music, but Frankie, ever reliable, softly sang the words to "Earth Angel" and the moment was complete.

Earth angel, Earth angel,
Will you be mine?

"Santa and Mr. Bingle are always together," Aurora whispered.

"Always," Frankie said.

"No matter what."

"No matter what."

"All right. I'll marry you."

They kissed sweetly and she put on the ring and Frankie tipped an imaginary hat to the papier-mâché snowman, which made Aurora laugh.

♪

They scheduled their wedding at a nearby church, and it was not until the week of the event that they realized their lack of paperwork. Both Frankie and Aurora had existed on the fringes; neither had a driver's license, the money they earned came mostly in cash, and from what I could gather (such details bore me), the proper filings would have caused a long delay.

Instead, they canceled the church and used a friend's nightclub, and a violinist who had once attended divinity school blessed their union at 3:07 a.m. Aurora's sister, Cecile, was her maid of honor, and young Ellis, the shoeshine boy, served as Frankie's best man. There was food and drink and Fats Domino played the piano and Richard Penniman sang his wild songs and Hampton Belgrave came down from Nashville and sat in on the harmonica.

In the early morning, when everyone had gone home, Frankie and Aurora, still wearing their wedding clothes, took a walk along the river.

"Do you remember the day we met?" Aurora asked.

"In the woods," Frankie said.

"You were so scared."

"No, I wasn't."

"Yes, you were."

She removed her shoes. A flock of birds flew over the water.

"That was the last day you saw your father."

"He wasn't my father."

"I'm sorry he wasn't here."

"Your mother wasn't here, either."

"You're right. She wasn't."

She took his hand. They walked in silence. Off in the distance, a man in an apron threw a bucket of water onto the sidewalk and began sweeping away the night's revelry.

"Francisco?"

"Yes?"

"We both have a family now."

"You and me?"

"Always."

Frankie sang the first line of "Always," a popular tune recorded by the Ink Spots and Frank Sinatra. Aurora pulled his arm across her chiffon-covered shoulder.

"Not everything is a song."

"Yes, it is."

"Okay. Everything is."

As the sun rose over the east end of New Orleans, they retired up the stairs to their apartment above the drugstore, and lay down together on the same single pillow. Later, Frankie fell asleep with his nose in her blond hair and his arm around her waist. He had joined many bands. This one was his favorite.

35

1969

THE MUSIC GREW LOUDER IN THE DARKNESS OF WOODSTOCK, and from the heavens Frankie heard the scratchy voice of a blues singer named Janis Joplin. Even in his cloudy state, he could decipher the 1/4/5 chord pattern of a song called "Piece of My Heart," and a crashing chorus in which the singer screams for her lover to take it, take it, take another little piece.

"Stage?" Frankie yelled at a crowd.

"That way!" someone yelled, pointing.

"Stage?" he screamed a minute later.

"That way!"

He had a direction. He had the eggs. He willed a forward march to his legs, which, thanks to the green pill, he had to mentally maneuver through his knee joints, as if he were a marionette. Lift, stretch, plant. Lift, stretch, plant—

"Can I try your guitar, Mister?"

Frankie looked down. There was a towheaded boy in

a striped shirt and white underpants, shoeless, maybe six years old. Next to him was a girl, even younger, also in her underwear. Both were playing in the mud.

"Can I try after him?" the girl said.

Frankie rolled his neck, trying to process. *Kids. Night-time. Playing in the mud.* He had to keep going. But for some reason he kneeled down and reached around his back.

"This?" he asked

"Yeah," the boy said.

"Do you know how to play it?"

"Sure."

"Me, too," his sister echoed.

"My mommy's boyfriend plays one."

"Where is your mommy?"

"Over there."

The boy pointed to a circle of people draped in blankets, passing pipes. Frankie tried to guess which one was the mother. He scratched his head. *Keep moving*, he told himself.

"Do you want some mud?" the boy asked.

"Huh?"

"You can have some."

"Okay."

The boy put a glob of mud in Frankie's hand.

"Thank you."

"Now can I play your guitar?"

"You're too young."

"No, I'm not."

Frankie remembered being in a Villareal music school, Baffa Rubio arguing with the owner.

"No, you're not," Frankie mumbled. "You're right."

He thought about Aurora on the blanket. What was he doing out here? Why wasn't he with her? Who were these children? What were the lyrics of this song he was hearing? Take it? Take it? The stage. *Keep moving.*

"Go find your mother," he mumbled.

"But we want the guitar."

Frankie rubbed the mud back in the boy's hand and stood up. He stumbled off in the direction of the music, and another little piece of the heart being taken.

36

1956

FRANKIE AND AURORA'S SECOND MOVEMENT. *ADAGIO.*

The slow turn.

Frankie's talent put him in high demand. Live performances. Studio recordings. He played with, by my count, forty-six bands between the years 1955 and 1958. At first, this was not a problem (at first, it is never a problem). Aurora joined him wherever she could, and in between she cozied inside their small apartment, which featured a balcony with an iron railing and old wooden fixtures in a pastel-tiled kitchen.

Aurora was happy there. She cut Frankie's hair and helped pick out his clothes. At the concerts, she began to notice that the girls who came to scream for Jimmy Clanton or Sam Cooke would also make eyes at her husband, the sultry guitar player with the grape black pompadour. It did not bother her. She waited for Frankie after the shows and he always took her hand and they walked through the city and got home in the wee hours and listened to records until they drifted off, curled around each other. Aurora would wake with the sun strong in the sky and make tea and nudge him, saying, "Get up, sleepy. You have to practice."

It was about this time that Frankie told Aurora about the strings. Leaning against their mattress one night, he showed her his guitar and recounted the three incidents: the docks with Django, the hospital room with Hampton, and, of course, the night Aurora was threatened by a knife until Frankie distracted her attacker.

"You saved me."

"I guess."

"I would have died."

"Don't say that."

"And the string turned blue?"

"Yeah."

"For how long?"

"A few seconds."

"Why blue?"

"I don't know."

"Can you predict when it happens?"

Frankie shook his head.

"What does it mean?"

"That I can affect things, I think."

"Whenever you want?"

"No. Just . . ."

"What?"

"If it really matters, I guess."

"So I really mattered?"

Frankie smiled. Aurora moved closer.

"I think it's something else, Francisco."

"What?"

"Where did the strings come from?"

"My teacher."

"Before that?"

"His wife."

"Where did she get them?"

"Who knows?"

"That's where your answer is."

"Three of them have broken."

"The three that turned blue?"

Frankie nodded.

"Maybe they're used up. Maybe you're getting six chances." She looked off. "Six souls."

"What are you talking about?"

"In the woods, remember? You made your strings into flowers? And we put them on the graves?"

"So?"

"You did something for strangers. A kindness for six strangers. Maybe it's coming back to you."

"I doubt it." He shrugged. "I'm just a guitar player."

Aurora held his gaze.

"No, you're not."

37

1957

AS THEIR *ADAGIO* CONTINUED, FRANKIE AND AURORA increasingly saw the same thing differently. One day, he got a call to play at Pontchartrain Beach, an amusement park on a lake near New Orleans. Elvis Presley was scheduled to perform, and the band wanted a backup guitar player, because while Elvis wore a guitar, he barely used it. Aurora attended that show. The screams were deafening. After the final number, she tried to get backstage, but there were so many hysterical young girls, she gave up and went home.

When he returned that night, Frankie was relieved to see her. "Where were you? I looked all over."

"It was too crowded," she said.

"Did you like the music?"

"I couldn't hear it."

"They want me for more jobs."

"At the beach?"

"Shreveport."

"That's a little far."

"It's not too bad."

"What was it like?"

"It was crazy!"

"Is Elvis nice?"

"He didn't talk much. He said he liked my haircut."

Aurora smiled. "Of course."

In the simplest harmonies, notes move up and down together, keeping the same distance, like the edges of a railroad track.

A more complex version is counterpoint, where two musical lines move independently of each other, still a harmonic balance, but no longer attached as if by an axle.

In the three years following their wedding, Frankie and Aurora moved from harmony to counterpoint, as the *adagio* completed its slow turn. Frankie made a trip to New York City. Aurora took a job in a flower shop. Frankie secretly replaced Elvis for a show in Vancouver. Aurora joined a church. Frankie went to Los Angeles, met the agent Tappy Fishman, and signed a contract. Aurora learned to cook crawfish.

When he came home, Frankie said, "I've got big news. We're moving to California."

What followed was a two-week argument, common to

human couples when one wants to go somewhere and one does not. Finally, at the end of the month, they packed up boxes from their apartment over the drugstore and, with grim expressions and little conversation, filled the back of a used Plymouth Belvedere that Frankie had purchased after Tappy Fishman helped get him a driver's license.

As they pulled out of New Orleans, only Aurora looked back.

In earlier days, they would have spent the ride holding hands. But the car was cramped with instruments and clothing and two very different ideas of the future. They drove for three days, from the American South to the American West, and when they reached the coast, just before dusk, Frankie noted that the sun looked like a giant orange.

38

"YOU'RE *NOT* GOING TO PLAY YOUR GUITAR?" AURORA ASKED.

"Leonard doesn't want me to," Frankie said.

This was just before Christmas, in an undecorated apartment on a treeless street in Los Angeles.

"Why doesn't he want you to play?"

"It interferes with my dancing."

"But you're a guitarist."

"I sing, too, Aurora."

"You sing wonderfully. But . . ."

Frankie held out his palms.

"What?"

"I like when you play guitar."

"I play when I'm in a band."

"Won't you be in a band?"

"The band will be behind me."

"Behind you?"

"Like Canada. I sang some songs without the guitar that night."

"So?"

"It felt different. I liked it."

"You weren't being you in Canada. That's why it felt different. You're not him, you know."

"I know."

"You're not Elvis Presley."

"I know."

"But you felt like you were."

"Why do you say things like that?"

"Because they're true, Francisco."

He frowned. "Frankie."

"Frankie. Another idea from Leonard. Or Tappy. Whatever his bloody name is."

Aurora grabbed her bag and fished through it. "Why do people need more than one name?"

"He's helping me."

"What did your teacher call you?"

" 'Boy,' mostly."

"What did your father call you?"

"He wasn't my father."

Aurora found a pack of cigarettes.

"Do what you want," she said.

"It's not what you want?"

"Does it matter what I want?"

"Yes."

"Then it's not what I want."

Frankie's leg tapped quickly.

"I won't forget how to play the guitar."

She plopped to the floor.

"No. I don't imagine you could."

"Leonard has ten shows booked already. With lots of people. The Drifters. The Everly Brothers. Big shows with big crowds. They don't care if I play guitar. They want to hear me sing. I have the recording session coming, and—"

"All right."

"A record could make a big diff—"

"All right, I said."

Aurora's voice had softened.

"All right?" Frankie asked.

"Do what you want."

"Are you sure?"

"Can we stop talking about it?"

Frankie forced a smile.

"You'll see. It's going to be good. *Fantástico*."

"How long is this tour?"

"I might get famous—"

"How long?"

"One or two months."

Aurora lit her cigarette. "You mean three."

"Why do you smoke?"

"I miss New Orleans."

"This is a nice apartment."

"It's too new. I like old things."

Frankie walked across the room and opened his case.

"Look. A guitar," he said, trying to joke.

" 'Parlez-Moi d'Amour,' " Aurora said.

"That *is* old."

"Please. Play it for me."

"All right."

Frankie strapped the guitar over his neck and picked the strings gently. Then he kneeled down and sang the song Aurora requested, written nearly thirty years earlier by a French composer.

"Parlez-Moi d'Amour," the title states. "Speak to me of love." But speaking of love is like sticking words to the wind. Aurora waited for the final stanza. A small tear formed in her eye.

Du Coeur on guérit la blessure
Par un serment qui le rassure

It means, "We heal the wounded heart, with an oath that reassures it."

Frankie promised he would call when they reached the first stop.

But Aurora knew she would be gone.

39

C

1969

AT LAST, FRANKIE SAW THE WOODSTOCK STAGE. IT LIT UP like a square in the darkness, illuminating a massive field of spectators.

"Hey, man, watch it—"

"Wuhh?—"

"Easy, brother—"

"Sorry—"

The green pill now had him swerving from side to side, bumping into people, things getting blurry then clearing again. He felt the guitar slapping against his back. When Frankie had been a student, El Maestro taught him to block out distractions by humming the melody he was trying to play, so that his mind and fingers would be one.

Now, as he lumbered down the long, sloping hillside, past tents and latrines and people sitting cross-legged or lying against each other, he repeated three words, "Aurora . . . baby . . . breakfast."

He picked up speed, determined to make things right.

"Aurora . . . baby . . . breakfast . . ."

"Ow—"

"Aurora—"

"Look out."

"Baby—"

"Easy—"

"Breakfast—"

Suddenly, he was running, or it felt as if he were running, the lights getting larger, the music louder, the comments blowing past as he progressed.

"Excuse me!"

"Aurora—"

"Did you see that guy?"

"Baby—"

"What guy?"

"Breakfast—"

"With the guitar. That's . . . whatisname! Presto! Frankie Presto! That was *him*!"

40

NOT FAR FROM THIS CHURCH IN VILLAREAL IS A SMALL
museum dedicated to Francisco Tárrega. Inside are many
photographs, some of his guitars—and a large plaster bust
of his image. That bust was once the prize possession of
a poor neighborhood in Castellón called San Félix, nick-
named the "Gunpowder Quarter" for its tough, working-
class citizens. Those citizens thought so highly of Tárrega
that in 1924, fifteen years after his death, they made him
their patron saint.

Every October, while other towns hoisted images of traditional Catholic figures, the people of San Felix marched
Tárrega's bust through the streets in a religious procession,
surrounded by young women, horseback riders, and a cart
full of flowers. Magic powers were attributed to that bust. It
was even taken to the homes of sick neighbors to heal them.

Other towns disapproved. How could a guitarist become
a deity? they asked. But is it much different from fame today? Your world is full of artists turned to gods, their very
presence inspiring screams of devotion.

Once Aurora York disappeared from his life, Frankie Presto had his own such period. From August 1959 through October 1964, he sold over three million records, recorded five albums, and had four songs attain a top-ten position on the musical charts, including two that reached the very peak. "I Want To Love You" and "Shake, Shake," both of which Frankie composed. The crowds at his concerts grew from hundreds to thousands to tens of thousands. He performed on *American Bandstand*, *The Ed Sullivan Show*, and *The Kraft Music Hall*. His face was on the cover of magazines and billboard advertisements. He dressed in colorful suits and matching shoes, his dark, thick pompadour combed back and wavy. Sometimes locks of hair would tumble onto his forehead when he sang, and they would shake when he danced, causing young girls to scream, *"Frankie! Frankie!"*

In record stores across America, fans held up his albums just to stare at his handsome face. One of those albums, *Frankie Presto Wants To Love You*, featured Frankie in a convertible car, wearing a tan sports coat and a pink-collared shirt, as he leaned out the window to sign the hand of an ecstatic young brunette. It looked like a scene outside one of Frankie's concerts, but it was actually staged by a professional photographer. The brunette, a shapely woman with almond eyes, was a model from the state of Texas, personally chosen by Tappy Fishman.

Her name was Delores Ray.

She was, to me, no different from the many other women who shared time with Frankie. No threat to his heart. Only Aurora York could rival my grip there. But Aurora, as I mentioned, was gone during these years, her yellow suitcase missing when Frankie returned to their California apartment.

At first, he'd been angry. Hurt. He'd tried drinking to forget her. Then Tappy put him back on tour and didn't let him stop for two years. Aurora's absence paralleled Frankie's rise to fame, and while it may seem coincidental, I assure you it was not. She knew she was sharing Frankie's heart now, not only with me (which she could tolerate) but with ambition (which she couldn't). I admired the foresight with which she departed, knowing how success would soak Frankie like a wave, and its undertow pull him away.

So she left first.

Meanwhile, Delores Ray, thanks in part to that album cover, was cast in a television series called *The Adventures of Dee Dee* and soon became wildly popular on her own, with Tappy Fishman directing her career. She starred in movies and was romantically linked to more than one actor. But her passion remained strongest for Frankie, whom she kissed the night of that photo shoot, calling him "the most exotic thing I've ever seen." She seemed infatuated with my beloved child (why not, given all of my draping?), and while Frankie did not love her, she was quite seductive. Tappy Fishman encouraged their involvement, knowing the public was always interested in the pairing of attractive, well-known celebrities. He even paid for meals they shared at restaurants, calling photographers to alert them to the couple's whereabouts.

Eventually, he suggested they marry.

That was in late 1964. By then, Frankie's popularity had begun to wane. His records sold less and less. Public taste is as fickle as a child's attention span, and a new wave of popular music, this time from Great Britain, was now dominating sales. Frankie was no longer writing all his own material. Instead, he was forced to record songs written by others. When he objected, Tappy reminded him that it was part of a big contract he had signed with the record company, which viewed him as "a teen idol," a title as fleeting as it sounds.

As for his guitar? He barely played it. His magic strings went ignored, the guitar itself shut away in a dark closet of a big new house, which, to my accurate count, had five bedrooms, two pools, and sixteen mirrors.

I would like to tell you that, as his star dimmed, Frankie did not care, that top billing was, to him, the same as second billing, that selling a million records was no different from selling half a million, that only one thing mattered, me, Music, my sonic deliverance. But fame is addictive. And without the guiding forces of his life, without El Maestro, Baffa, Hampton, or Aurora York, Frankie was adrift.

Once, floating down the river, he'd grabbed the leash of a hairless dog. This time, he grabbed for something else.

$\sim$

"A wedding?"

"Hawaii, on the beach!" Tappy said. "I'll spring for it. My present to the happy couple."

"But, Leonard—"

"What?'

"I'm married to Aurora."

"Says who? You have a license? You told me yourself, you couldn't get the paperwork. And when was the last time you saw her? Four years ago? Five? For God's sake, Frankie. She's not coming back."

"Don't say that."

"It's not like you've been a monk, kid."

"Leonard—"

"Hey, I make no judgments. But Delores is nuts about you. We all know you guys have a thing."

"Who says she wants to marry me?"

"Trust me. Ask her."

"I don't even have a ring."

"I got you all set up at a jewelry place. Go anytime this week. Go today if you want."

What Tappy did not say was that the marriage, in his

view, was more for Frankie's benefit than Delores's. He feared his singer was using up his spotlight, that the townspeople who once worshipped him would put down his bust and no longer scream his name. Frankie Presto was on the decline, Delores Ray was on the rise. Her light could replenish his.

"I don't know, Leonard—"

"What's to know? You have a problem coming home to that woman every night?"

"It's not that—"

"What I wouldn't give."

"She's all right, but—"

"Frankie. Listen to me." He put his hands on Frankie's shoulders. "It's good for your career."

I do not know who invented this phrase. I do not know who invented that word. I can only tell you I have been on earth since mankind's inception, and have produced sounds for every stitch of life's tapestry, sounds that invoke awakening, pain, love, the four seasons. But in my countless creations, there has never been a sound for "career."

Why do you let it affect me so?

౷

The marriage took place and created the headlines Tappy wanted. The couple honeymooned in Hawaii, where photographers were dispatched daily. Sure enough, sales of Frankie Presto records rose, albeit briefly. Delores was cast in another major film. She moved into Frankie's large house, and put his guitar in a smaller closet. Frankie watched her do this. He thought about Aurora. He started drinking again. He took bottles with him to the patio or the swimming pool.

One day in the summer of 1965, Tappy called Frankie to his office. There was a man there he had never seen.

"Come here, kid," Tappy said. Frankie approached and Tappy reached over and mussed his hair, until it filled his forehead with bangs.

"What do you think?" Tappy said to the man.

The man nodded. "He should wear it that way."

"This is Allan Edgars. He's a director. We're gonna put you in a movie, Frankie. How about that?"

Frankie shrugged. He didn't like his hair mussed up.

"With Delores. You and her together. Romantic leads. Beats working, huh?"

The director laughed.

"Here's the best part. We're shooting in London. It's Allan's idea. The hell with this British Invasion crap. We'll invade *them*! How about that? You ever been to England, Frankie?"

Frankie looked down. He remembered his journey on the ship from Spain. He remembered being wrapped in a blanket, placed atop cargo, and rolled onto the Southampton docks, where he was instructed to "stay quiet." He remained there for hours, listening to the sound of his own breath, too frightened to move. Finally, he felt something moving on his stomach. He shed the blanket and a seagull flapped past his face. He screamed as it flew up into the cloudy white skies.

"No," Frankie said. "I've never been to England."

"We leave in three weeks.

"I still have songs to record."

"After the movie."

"What about the next album?"

Tappy looked at the director. He looked back at Frankie.

"We're gonna make the movie first, kid. It'll be good for you. Fun."

Frankie said nothing, but he felt a burning in his stomach. He took a comb from his back pocket to fix his hair.

"Leave it," Tappy said. "It looks better that way."

Frankie put the comb back, the burning growing hotter.

Roger McGuinn

Guitarist, singer, founding member of the Byrds; inductee,
Rock and Roll Hall of Fame

MY BEST FRANKIE PRESTO STORY? WELL. I INTRODUCED HIM to the Beatles. That's a pretty good story.

It was the summer of 1965. The Byrds were on our first tour of London, and Frankie was there shooting a movie. He saw one of our shows. Afterward he came backstage to ask about my twelve-string Rickenbacker. I had seen him in concert when I was in high school. I thought his hair was cool. I had no idea he was such a great guitar player. But I was about to find out.

The Byrds were really popular in '65. Our record "Mr. Tambourine Man" was number one on the British charts, which is why we went to London. But it wasn't a great tour. They were billing us as "America's answer to the Beatles," and that's hard to live up to. The press was out to get us.

Anyhow, the night after Frankie came backstage, the real Beatles came to see us play. Our publicist, Derek Taylor, used to be their publicist, so he arranged the whole thing, and afterward, we were supposed to all meet in a room upstairs from the club.

We were really nervous. Our bass player had broken a string during the show—that almost never happens. He must have been hitting it so hard he didn't realize it.

Anyhow, we go into the room and John Lennon and George Harrison are there, and John says, "That was a great show," and I felt like I had to apologize. I said, no, it wasn't very good, and he mocked me a little. Then he said, "What's with your tiny specs?" meaning my round glasses. He tried them on. And as everyone knows, he started wearing glasses like that and made them pretty famous.

At one point, I mentioned that Frankie Presto had come around the night before, and John sang a little of "Our Secret" and said it was one of the coolest ballads he'd ever heard. He also said that Frankie Presto hadn't made a good record since.

The next night, I met with Paul McCartney at this private club, and he took me for a ride around London in his new Aston Martin DB5. I mentioned Frankie to Paul and he got all excited and said somebody told him Frankie had been in Elvis Presley's band. There was a party later that week at one of the Rolling Stones' houses—at that time, all the big British bands hung out together—and Paul said I should bring Frankie so he could ask if it was true. Everyone looked up to the Beatles, but the Beatles still looked up to Elvis.

So the next day I found out where they were shooting Frankie's movie, and I dropped by. It was a warehouse off Carnaby Street, where we got our clothes back then—you know, the stretch jeans and the black zipper boots? I found Frankie just sitting by himself in one of those director chairs, sort of half asleep. He perked up when he saw me. He introduced me to his wife, Delores Ray, who was a big TV star in America.

I told Frankie about what Paul McCartney said, and Delores seemed really surprised. "When did you play with Elvis?" she asked, and Frankie said it was just a stupid rumor. When I invited him to the party, Delores got excited. She said, "The Beatles *and* the Rolling Stones? We're coming!" But later, when she was shooting a scene, Frankie said he didn't think it was such a good idea. I got the feeling his wife embarrassed him.

We talked more about guitars and I asked if he wanted to come by that night and jam at the hotel. He showed up a half hour early. He had this really old case and he pulled out a beat-up acoustic—I don't even know what make it was, the label was covered—and we started playing. I noticed his hands were huge. A lot of great players have big hands, you know, like Jimi Hendrix, the way he could get his thumb over the neck? It gives you great control.

Anyhow, up to that moment, I thought I was a decent guitarist. But after twenty minutes, I didn't even want to play. Frankie took these solos and created these really unique voicings and when I'd ask him, "What was that?" he'd mention some classical composer—Giuliani, Haydn—and then I'd say, "What was that?" and it would be Antonio Carlos Jobim or Wes Montgomery. And he wasn't trying to show off. He was just so good, he couldn't hide it.

We did the basic stuff you jam on, like "Midnight Special" and Jimmy Reed's "You Got Me Dizzy." And we played some Beatles songs. He had their arrangements down cold. At one point, he started smiling and I said, "What's so funny?" and he said, "Nothing, I just haven't really played guitar in a while." And again, I wanted to crawl in a hole, because if this was how he sounded when he *hadn't* played, you know? But I got the impression that he felt he'd sold out. I'm sure a lot of early rock and rollers felt that way, because in those days, everyone wanted you to do the same thing, over and over.

Frankie said he missed being in a band and I joked that he could join the Byrds if he promised not to break a string when the Beatles were in the audience. He looked at his guitar and he said, "Roger, do you know how old these top three strings are?" I said no. "Twenty years," he said. No way, I said. They hadn't broken? That's not possible. And he shook his head and said, "I know. But it's true."

So, okay . . . the Beatles story. The party was in one of the Stones' houses, maybe Keith Richards's, sort of a fancy brownstone, three stories. I remember they showed us how the butlers would roll joints for them and leave them on the steps in the morning. There were a lot of drugs at that party—at *any* party during those years.

About an hour into it, Frankie showed up. I said, "I thought you couldn't make it," and he said, "I can't stay long." So I introduced him around and everyone was pretty cool. I remember me, Frankie, George Harrison, and Eric Clapton got into a discussion about Leadbelly, the old blues player, and Frankie knew all about him because he'd lived in Louisiana. He said that Leadbelly was so good he got pardoned from prison *twice* after the wardens heard him sing— once for killing a man! We laughed and said we should try that if we ever got busted.

I remember Frankie met Paul and Ringo, and they got along fine, even though Paul was disappointed when Frankie denied playing with Elvis. But when Frankie met John, John made some remark about his hair, because he was wearing it kind of mop top. John laughed and said, "The great Frankie Presto. Are you trying to look like us now?" I don't think he meant anything, but it bothered Frankie, you know? He left soon after that.

I saw him a few days later and he still seemed upset and I told him to forget what John said, he was just that way. I said he should really get back into his guitar playing, he was so good, and if he ever wanted to jam on our records, we'd be lucky to have him.

We went back to America that week. I don't know what happened with the movie Frankie was doing. I heard he walked out. I also heard he split up with his manager. The next time I saw him was the last time I saw him, maybe four years later, in a club in Greenwich Village. He was with this rock band, just standing in the back, playing rhythm. He didn't sing. He had on dark sunglasses. I wasn't even sure it was him until after the show. I went up and said, "Frankie?" and at first he seemed happy to see me, but after talking for a few minutes and remembering that party, he sort of clammed up. I asked if he wanted to jam sometime, but he said he couldn't, he had a lot going on, his wife was expecting a baby. Maybe he was embarrassed to be playing in such a dive. I really don't know. He asked if the Byrds were going to play at Woodstock and I told him no, we'd done enough festivals for a while. Then he excused himself to go to the bathroom and he never came back.

I felt awful when I heard he died. I was touring in France and I thought I owed it to him to come to his funeral, because he made me a better guitarist. He really did. That first night we played, I realized how far I had to go. Music can be competitive that way. Iron sharpens iron, like the proverb says.

Someone told me he made it to Woodstock, but I never found out for sure. . . . We would have known about that by now, right?

41

ALLOW ME TO ANSWER MR. MCGUINN'S QUESTION. FRANKIE did indeed make it to Woodstock. He would even play. But it was not the way anyone imagined it. He was not invited. No one asked him to be there. He went in the deluded hopes of recapturing what he once had, large crowds cheering his music. But no bands needed him, and, as you are about to hear, things went terribly wrong. His attendance became a sad chapter for a man who lost his way—and the end of a major movement in his symphony with Aurora York.

It was the *minuet/scherzo*, conducted in 3/4 time. If you tap your fingers to illustrate—1-2-3, 1-2-3, 1-2-3, 1-2-3—you sense an almost giddy rhythm. Indeed, the word *scherzo* translates to "joke."

It was a word Frankie had begun to apply to himself in the mid-1960s, "A sad joke." (Is there sharper counterpoint than that?) He felt his music was no longer taken seriously. He felt his desires were not being heard. That burning feeling he'd experienced in Tappy Fishman's office had intensified and the comments John Lennon made about him being an imitation had heated it to an angry boil. In its bubbly wake, these are the things Frankie Presto did in the remaining months of 1965:

He walked away from the movie in London. That destroyed his film opportunities.

He walked away from Tappy Fishman. That destroyed his business opportunities.

He walked away from Delores Ray. That destroyed his marriage, and left him entangled in legal and financial complexities, most of which, to his detriment, he ignored.

He cut his hair.

Like Samson pulling the pillars down around him, Frankie crumbled all the things he'd become attached to in an effort to be free of them. Then, in the years that followed, he lost himself in the rubble. He fell into substances, believing, as I have lamented, that my truer powers might be discovered inside them.

He took up residence in New York City, in a dimly lit, ground-floor apartment on West Twelfth Street in Greenwich Village. He kept odd hours. He slept badly. He practiced incessantly, and when not practicing, was often in an altered state. He worked for whatever group would pay him, played in whatever studio session would use him, took cash for leaving his name out of royalty reporting, and if they didn't have money, he accepted pills, smoke, alcohol.

He found himself thinking about his childhood.

"*Why do you drink so much, Maestro?*"
"*This is not a music question.*"
"*Are you sad, Maestro?*"
"*Again, not a music question.*"
"*I am sad sometimes, Maestro.*"
"*Practice more. Speak less. You'll be happier.*"
"*Yes, Maestro.*"

Everyone joins a band in this life.
Sometimes, they are the wrong ones.

42

1968

——

BUT BACK TO THE LOVE STORY. THE *MINUET*. A SHORT DANCE.
One December day, Frankie answered his door in Greenwich Village, half dressed, bleary-eyed, and there she was, Aurora York, wearing a scarf and gloves, her blond hair tucked under a hat.

"Are you done with that actress?" she asked.

"Yes."

"Paperwork finished?"

"Yes."

"We can get married now?"

"If you want."

"The real way?"

"The real way."

"I just came to make sure."

"Will you stay?"

"No."

He didn't see her again for several weeks. On a Thursday afternoon, she knocked again.

"Are you practicing?"

"Yes."

"Are you playing?"

"When I can."

"Are you taking drugs and drinking?"

"Sometimes."

"You have to stop."

"I know."

"Then do it."

"Will you stay?"

"No."

The next month, she came again. This time she spent a few hours. The next month, she came and spent the night.

She repeated this pattern, short dances—a *minuet* defined—throughout the winter and into the spring, until, on a Monday morning in the middle of a blowing rainstorm, she appeared again. This time, she was holding an umbrella in one hand and her yellow suitcase in the other.

Frankie smiled.

"Will you stay?" he asked.

"I'm pregnant," she said.

43

1969
———

IT IS TIME WE FINISH THE WOODSTOCK JOURNEY. FRANKIE had finally reached the backstage area. By this point, the festival had dissolved into mass confusion. Helicopters had brought the performers to a landing area, where they traversed a wooden bridge to reach the stage, but they were left waiting for long stretches, and many did not know when they were supposed to play. The rain wreaked havoc with the electricity. Amplifiers frizzled. Supplies ran out. By the dark hours of Sunday morning, the event had the feel of a lingering party, one that had no real end anymore, just hordes of people fighting sleep and trying to keep dry.

One story often told is that the drinks backstage were laced with hallucinogenic drugs. I cannot confirm this. But I do know that when Frankie finally got there, he was beyond thirsty and drank the first thing he saw, from paper cups arranged on a fold-up table. His face was streaked with mud and his white shirt was filthy. He rolled his head from side to side.

"Aurora . . . baby . . . breakfast," he kept mumbling.

He stared at the other musicians, who smirked at him or looked away. A large bucket of water sat near some paper towels. Frankie splashed his face and wiped off the mud.

Finally, amid the blaring music of a band named Sly & The Family Stone, singing a song called "Stand!" Frankie twisted left and right, and began his final *minuet*.

"Aurora!"

He yelled it spinning. He yelled it staggering. He held up the egg carton.

"Aurora! I'm back! Aurora!"

He slipped. He got back up. His screams were swallowed by the music, and when a vocal popped or a guitar screeched, you could not hear him at all.

"Stand! . . ."

"Aurora!"

"Stand! . . ."

"Aurora!"

"Stand!"

She was nowhere to be found.

And so finally, when the band finished to great applause—it was 4:05 in the morning—the stage lights went off. All was black.

And Frankie decided to play his guitar.

To draw Aurora to him.

And change their fate.

❧

What happened next is not pleasant to recount and, in defense of my cherished disciple, he was not himself. His body, mind, and heart were in three separate places. He stumbled up the ramp and approached the giant stage. No one stopped him because he had a guitar around his neck and moved like a musician who knew where he was going. A few workers had begun setting up for the next act (the celebrated British band The Who) but it was late and they were exhausted and paid no heed to the long-haired musician moving purposefully toward the wall of amplifiers.

Mumbling to himself, Frankie picked up the jack end of a gray cable and slammed it into the output of his guitar, which he had equipped with an electric pick-up. He could not hold the eggs and play, so he lay the carton down. The top popped open. In the limited moonlight, he could see that all the eggs were broken.

His eyes welled up with tears.

❧

What you cannot know—what no one knew—was what happened a few weeks earlier, the night Roger McGuinn saw Frankie in New York. Aurora, pregnant, had moved into his apartment, under the strict agreement that Frankie straighten up, come directly home after playing, and prepare to be a good father to their baby. No drugs. No drink. No other women. She was five months along and their new arrangement had worked for a while. But Frankie, upon seeing McGuinn, was reminded of London and 1965 and the Beatles and the party and how far he had fallen from his once-worldwide fame—playing in this dank and smelly nightclub—and his ego was bruised and he grew depressed and he stayed out until dawn, drinking and smoking with musicians in the club's basement.

Just after sunrise, he stumbled back to his apartment, ashamed of his relapse and preparing for a confrontation. But it was dark inside and he was quiet entering the bedroom, and he slipped under the blanket while Aurora slept. His movement nudged her slightly awake, and she rolled over to put an arm around him.

"Francisco," she mumbled.

"Aurora," he whispered.

"It means dawn."

"I know."

"I'm hungry. If you love me, you'll make me breakfast."

He sighed deeply. He was safe. She didn't know. He would never do this again. He swore it to himself.

"I'll get some eggs," he promised.

All he had to do was stay awake.

But his eyes closed.

The night had done him in.

❧

An hour later, having woken to find Frankie snoring into the pillow, Aurora decided to get her own breakfast and make something for him as well. There was nothing in his refrigerator, so she pulled on a jacket, took her handbag, and left the apartment. She purchased a carton of eggs and an onion at a grocery. On her way back, a block from home, she was accosted by three young men who sprang from an alley, pushed her, and grabbed for her bag. The strap was hooked on her arm and as she pulled back on it, she spun directly toward one of the attackers, who raised his leg and kicked her hard in the stomach. She fell to her knees, the bag still on her shoulder. He kicked her again to snap it loose. The other two cursed at him and ran away, and he turned and ran as well.

A taxi screeched to a halt. A man jumped out. Aurora made a small gurgling sound, then dropped to the pavement and began to shake.

❧

Frankie slept through the first phone call from the hospital. He slept through the second. By the time he got to see his wife, a stillborn child had been delivered and wrapped in a blanket, given to the mother to hold for a minute and then taken away. Aurora was staring out the window when Frankie entered. Her face was bruised and she was bandaged in several places. She turned her head and Frankie stood like a statue. He felt guilt in every pore.

"Who did it?" he mumbled.

She shook her head.

"How did they . . ."

She shook her head.

"Why . . ."

He was out of words.

"Where were you?" she whispered.

From that moment to the moment he started playing at Woodstock was a blur of weeks, and while Frankie could barely recall a thing, I can attest to the fact that he had not been sober a single day of them. He couldn't face her. He couldn't face anything. He staggered home from the hospital, grabbed his guitar and didn't come back. He hitchhiked to upstate New York, taking any drug he could to avoid thinking about what happened. But his tortured mind could not forget. Instead, he imagined Aurora every day in every way, until reality and fantasy lost their distinction. Finally, at Woodstock, he imagined her sleeping on that hillside ("*If you love me, you'll make me breakfast.*") and set out on a pointless quest for eggs.

And now, in the darkness of the stage, wanting only to

see her once more, he tried the last thing he could think of to change what had happened.

He stepped away from the broken shells and angrily spun the volume knob on his guitar pickup. He heard a hum from a giant amplifier. An empty beer bottle was sitting on top of it. Somewhere in his blurry memory, Frankie recalled a trick Hampton Belgrave had shown him. He smacked the beer bottle on the amp's edge, breaking it cleanly in two, then took the neck portion and slipped his ring finger through the spout, creating a glass "slide"—a device blues players use to affect the strings' pitch and vibrato. The moisture felt good on Frankie's skin and he tapped his foot twice and ran the slide up the neck and fired a screaming B-seventh chord, as if to jangle the music loose.

Offstage, musicians looked up, because the chord rang out so cleanly. But all they saw was darkness. Frankie began playing like a ghost, a tangle of arpeggios that got faster and faster, then sliding down the neck as if crashing a rocket. He used the pedals at his feet to create distortion, fuzz, wah-wah. He held a high D note, shaking his hand as if strangling every breath from the fret board, then ran a blazing blues scale up and down and up again. There were no other instruments playing, no drums, no bass. Most solos are played over a melody line, or against a rhythm section. But this was a singular guitar performance, and the melodies within Frankie's riffing made it all the more remarkable. He was a man swimming against raging waters, and in all my time inside him, I cannot recall a greater battle. I was flapping in that solo like a sheet in a windstorm. Pieces of Leadbelly, Mozart, Chet Atkins, Segovia. Frankie conjured up every musical influence he knew and delivered the notes with such emotion, tears streamed down his cheeks and fell onto his fingers.

And all the while, he stared at his strings and screamed, "Change! . . . "Change!"

He wanted them to turn blue.

In his waffled mind, he believed he could undo that awful night, save his child, bring Aurora back to him. Didn't he have that power? What was the point of these strings if not *now*?

"Change!"

His fingers flew. His solo blew out of the amplifiers.

"Change!"

The last surge of notes came gushing forth, a theme from Vivaldi, a Chuck Berry lick; his guitar was all but choking, the emotion raw and endless. To the side of the platform, a stagehand mumbled, "I'll go get this guy," but as he walked past members of The Who, their guitarist, Pete Townshend, grabbed him and whispered, "Don't you dare."

All told, Frankie played for two minutes and seventeen seconds. He ended by whipping his right hand like a flapping butterfly as he slid chords down the neck, which sounded like a giant engine dying, then streaked the glass slide up and down and twanged a howling low note and three harmonic overtones, followed by the finale.

Bum-bum-bum.

Dummmmmmmmmmmmmmm.

The strings remained unchanged. He sank to the floor.

As there had been no lights, no one saw him play. And, as it was nearly five in the morning, many in the crowd were asleep. To the sounds of lightly scattered applause, a few stray whoops, and one man yelling in the darkness, "BRING ON THE WHO!" Frankie sensed that nothing in his life was going to get better. It was black and dark and he was alone.

So on his knees, already in a praying position, my beloved child leaned forward, and held out his left hand as he had always been instructed, straight and open as if asking God for help.

And then, remembering El Maestro's words ("Stupid boy! God gives you nothing!"), he stabbed the jagged bottle neck into his palm, again and again and again, slicing open the hand that fed him, until he couldn't see his fingers for the blood.

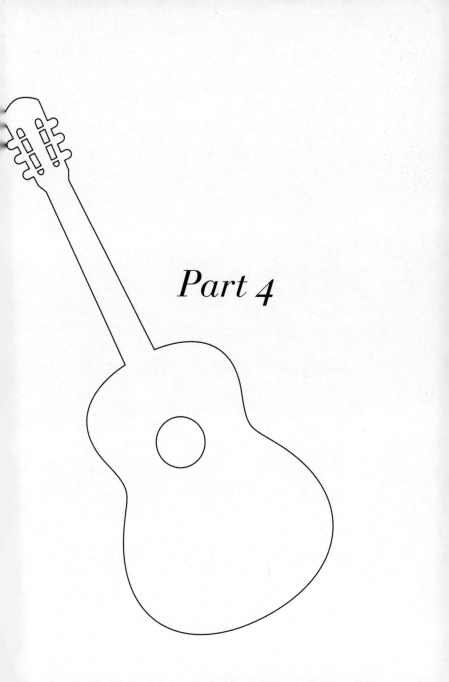

Part 4

Pau Sanz

Inspector Jefe (chief inspector of police), Cuerpo Nacional de Policía

I GIVE YOU TALK NOW.

Just a short, okay? . . . My English is not so well.

I am Pau Sanz. Inspector Jefe. I am chief of investigation for death of Francisco Presto.

Eh? . . . No yet. All we know is he die when he fall from very high at the Teatro Municipal. Is festival for Tárrega. We have every year. Never a problem. Never before.

Eh? . . . *Sí,* this our question also. How he does rise? Why he does fall? Maybe someone push him? Maybe someone want him to die?

We find no wound. Scars on hand, but no wound. No *balas,* how you say . . . bullets? Nobody shoot him.

We must ask questions. We know is a church. We respect. But is job of *policía,* someone killed, yes? Must ask questions.

Eh? . . . No suspect. No yet. But people say they see

him with person in morning, and this person wear many clothes and cover face. Maybe this person do the bad thing to him? Is possible, no?

To me, case is simple. Is a murder. Must be.

Man do not fly.

44

1981

THE FERRY PULLED INTO THE BAY AND THREE YOUNG MEN
gazed up at the green cliffs.

"It's like Never Never Land," one of them said.

"From Peter Pan?"

"Maybe we're the Lost Boys."

"Good band name."

"I'm Captain Hook."

"You're Tinker Bell."

"You're hysterical."

"Shut up."

The calendar year was 1981, the month of January, on
a small landmass called Waiheke Island in the Hauraki
Gulf of New Zealand. The three young men, recent college graduates and members of a country music band, went
by the names Lyle, Eddie, and Cluck. They wore jeans and
loose cotton shirts, their hair thick, their bodies thin. Lyle

was taller than the other two. He and Eddie carried guitar cases as they stepped off the boat and walked up a hill.

"Gidday, boys."

Inside an old Jeep sat a large man with a robust, reddened face, close-cropped silver hair, and a tattoo on his forearm. His hand rested over the steering wheel. He smiled, revealing several gold teeth.

"Lookin' for transportation?"

"Yes, sir," Lyle said.

"Hop in."

They piled in the back.

"I'm Lyle. That's Eddie. He's Cluck."

"Cluck? Whoo-hoo." The man laughed.

"Everyone's a critic," Cluck mumbled.

"What's your name?" Eddie asked.

"Keeyvin."

"Kee-vin?"

"K-e-v-i-n."

"Oh. Kevin. Okay."

"From the States, are ya?"

"Texas."

"Good on ya. Here we go."

Within seconds, they were bouncing along the island's one main road, passing large sections of undulating grass and rocky coves that broke small waves into the shore. They noticed how Kevin waved at every passing car or pedestrian.

"A couple ankle biters there," he announced, waving at two small children.

"Aw, hard yakka there, mates," he said, pointing at bare-chested field workers.

"What is this guy saying?" Eddie whispered.

"Beats me," Lyle said.

"Been in Oz, then?" Kevin asked.

"Excuse me?"

"Australia."

"Oh. Yes, sir. We landed there, then flew here."

"You know what they say. Australia's the lucky country, but New Zealand is God's own."

"Really?"

"It's true, mate. She's beautiful. Look at that water. Lovely, isn't it?"

Hot air blew through the open windows. The road zig-zagged through one luscious cove after another. There were no traffic lights and Kevin barely had to touch his brakes.

"God's own," he repeated to himself.

"Do you know a cheap hotel?"

"Aw, there's heaps, mate. On holidays, are you?"

"Just finished college."

"Good on yas! What brings you to the island?"

"We're looking for someone."

Lyle slapped Eddie's arm.

"Who's that?" Kevin asked.

"A guitar player."

"And a singer."

"Kiwi?"

The boys looked at each other.

"He's American. Well, Spanish first. Do you know a lot of people on this island?"

Kevin smiled, the creases on his face pulling up like a window blind. "I reckon I do."

He pointed out the window. "That fruit stand is owned by Curtis Mormont. He's a hardcase. . . . That blue house up there? That belongs to an Irish fella, comes down for the warm weather. Mulligan. Milligan. We call him Red. . . . That bach over there, the tiny house? That's my mate, Tim. 'Terrible' Tim, we say. But only when he's drunk. . . ."

The Jeep curled around rolling fields that dropped off in lumps toward the sea. Every turn revealed a new, picturesque bay.

"What's this guitar player's name?"

Lyle looked at Cluck who looked at Eddie.

"Presto. Frankie Presto."

The man scratched his forehead just above his eye.

"Nah, mate. Don't know that one."

He glanced in the rearview mirror.

"So you boys are musicians, too, eh?"

"We're in a band."

"Aww, good on yas. What do you play?"

Cluck slapped on the back of the seat. "Drums."

"Guitar," said Lyle.

"Bass," said Eddie.

Kevin slowed the Jeep. "Look, mates. I've got an idea. Why don't we stop by the house? Meet the wife. She's lovely. We'll have some food, then get you on your way. Nothing flash. Just bubble and squeak."

"What's that?" Cluck asked nervously.

"Leftovers," Kevin said.

"You don't have to do that for us," Lyle said.

"No worries, mate. If not for you Yanks in World War Two, we'd all be speaking Japanese."

"How far is it to your house?"

"Nothing's far on Waiheke."

"What's the fare?"

Kevin shook his head and smiled.

"Aw, I'm not a cabbie, mate. I just live here."

⁓

Hours later, the moon hung over the water and countless stars could be seen from Kevin's patio. Lyle, Eddie, and Cluck had bellies full of chicken, olives, cheese, and tomatoes. And wine. Lots of wine. Planning only to stay for a few minutes, they had eased into the Kiwi hospitality and remained past sunset. The humid breeze seemed to slow their pace and their skin glistened slightly with sweat.

They had confessed to Kevin and his wife, Robbie, about

their quest to locate Frankie Presto. They were hoping to meet him and perhaps hear him play.

"He's kind of a legend," Eddie said.

Indeed, by this point, twelve years after Woodstock, a small mythology had developed about my cherished disciple. A critic had written a bestselling book claiming Frankie was "the most gifted guitarist in early rock and roll," and the Byrds' Roger McGuinn, in a film documentary, had recounted playing with Frankie and being astonished at his skill. Although his anguished guitar solo in the darkness at Woodstock had not officially been recorded, a tape recorder had been running offstage, and bootleg copies of the two minutes and seventeen seconds had become a collector's item, with many guesses as to the artist, including Jimi Hendrix, Jerry Garcia, Pete Townshend, and Carlos Santana, all of whom were present at the festival, all of whom denied being the player. More recently, Frankie's name had been postulated, but as he had disappeared from public life, no one could confirm it. And the less you humans can solve a mystery, the more interesting it becomes to you.

Lyle, Eddie, and Cluck were fascinated with the Frankie Presto enigma. They even developed a theory as to his whereabouts: Eddie's cousin, who worked at a music licensing company, traced a royalties check for the song "I Want To Love You" to a forwarding address at a post office box on Waiheke Island, New Zealand. Eddie, Lyle, and Cluck, whose band was called the Clever Yells, had planned this trip as a postgraduation adventure, in hopes of being the first to find the elusive guitarist.

Lyle seemed particularly infatuated. He tried to explain it to his curious Kiwi hosts.

"Frankie Presto was real popular when I was a kid," he said. "My parents had his records and I hung the album covers on the wall. He was just so cool to me. He had everything—voice, looks, skill. And then he quit. Disappeared. Some people say he was better than anybody on the guitar—ever. And he just up and went."

"So why do you want to find him?" Robbie asked.

Lyle looked away. "Well, ma'am, maybe it sounds stupid. But I really want to make it in music, and I've been writing songs, trying to sell them. Every time someone says no, it's like they kicked me in the gut. I go crazy trying to figure out why they didn't like it. I guess I thought if I met Frankie Presto, he could teach me something."

"How to sell a song?" Robbie asked.

"How to not care so much," Lyle answered.

Kevin looked at his wife. "These Yanks are very deep."

She laughed and he laughed and he said, "Good fun, eh?" and Lyle grinned but looked away. It was late when they finished talking and Kevin said the hotels would have closed. He insisted the visitors sleep on his couches. They were too tired to argue.

Early the next morning, with the sun just rising, Lyle felt a push on his shoulder.

"Get up, mate," Kevin said softly.

Fifteen minutes later, the three musicians were in the back of the Jeep, wiping sleep from their eyes, as Kevin steered off the main road and drove down toward a hidden bay. He came to an opening in the trees. The Jeep stopped and Kevin pointed to a small path.

"Through there."

"What's through there?" Lyle asked.

"What you're looking for."

❧

Minutes later, the three of them were pushing away vines, stepping over moist ground, and moving forward in near darkness caused by thick overhead branches. They saw an icebox in a tree. They saw two old speakers wired together between ladders. As they edged forward and rays of light increased, they heard a distant rumbling sound, and realized they were approaching the surf.

"Get down," Eddie whispered.

The three of them dropped low.

"What is it?" Lyle said.

"Look."

"Where?"

Eddie pointed to the left. Through the clearing of brush they saw a man, sitting in a hammock, hunched over a guitar and facing out to the water.

"Is that him?"

"Jesus."

"I can't believe it! We found the guy!"

"Wait." Lyle put a finger to his lips. "Listen."

They leaned forward, trying to distinguish musical sounds above the small waves lapping the rocks.

"Do you hear that?"

"What?"

"What he's playing. It can't be him."

"What's he playing?"

Lyle shook his head.

"Scales. Like a kid."

45

1944

"*Maestro?*"

"*Yes?*"

"*Is my papa coming home?*"

"*I don't know, Francisco. Pour me my drink.*"

"*What if he never comes home?*"

"*Do not think such things. Now pour.*"

"*But what if he doesn't?*"

"*Then you will have to start over.*"

"*At the beginning?*"

"*No. You cannot be a baby twice.*"

"*Then how do you start over?*"

"*The way a composer starts a new piece. Where is my drink?*"

"*I don't want to start without my papa.*"

"*Do not cry, boy.*"

"*But—*"

"*Stop it right now.*"

"But—"

"Listen to me, Francisco. Do you think I wanted a life of darkness? Do you think I wanted not to see my fingers or the frets or the tuning pegs, to have to poke around like a lost animal?"

"No, Maestro."

"No, I did not. This is life. Things get taken away. You will learn to start over many times—or you will be useless."

"Yes, Maestro."

"As you are useless right now, since I do not have my drink."

"I am sorry, Maestro."

"Never mind it. Return to your arpeggios. This is all I will say on the matter. Are you listening?"

"Yes, Maestro."

"Stop crying. Start playing."

46

FEW IN HUMAN HISTORY GRABBED MORE OF ME AT BIRTH than Ludwig van Beethoven. My color drew him instantly and his two-fisted clutch assured a musical existence. But when his drunkard father would wake him late at night and demand that he practice, a frightened Ludwig could hardly bring me forth. Later in life, when he went deaf as a stone, I remained in his soul, steadfast as always, but producing music without hearing it was a burden I could not lighten, not even for a favorite child.

Likewise with Frankie Presto, whose left hand was badly slashed on the Woodstock stage. All I could do was observe. Bloody and dazed, he'd been evacuated from the festival via army helicopter, thanks to a woman who rushed him to the medical area. Military personnel tended to his cuts. An army surgeon operated, saving what he could.

In the hospital the next day, the drugs finally flushed from his bloodstream, Frankie realized what had happened. He looked at his bandaged hand and cried until he couldn't look anymore. That night a nurse entered with his guitar case, saying someone from the festival had transported it. He asked if his guitar was inside. She undid a clasp and peeked.

"Yes, it is," she said. He felt his chest well up before telling her, in a cracking voice, "Take it away, okay? Just take it away."

In the days that followed, he learned about other Woodstock casualties, a young marine who died from heroin use, a teenager who'd been run over in his sleeping bag by a tractor. He saw LSD victims stumbling in, most of them barely out of high school, being whispered to by volunteers who rubbed their arms as they screamed or cried. At some point, a nurse with a clipboard asked Frankie his age, and, staring at the young patients, he answered, "Thirty-three." He felt old and ridiculous.

In time, he was released and he returned to New York City, but the apartment on Twelfth Street was empty, as he knew it would be. Aurora was gone. So was her yellow suitcase. And this time he did not try to find her. Instead, he sold most of his equipment—the electric guitars, the amplifiers, the tape machines—keeping only his childhood acoustic and its mysterious strings. He drifted for months, staying in hotels, sleeping late to avoid the empty hours of staring at his hand. He longed to drink, to lose himself in substance, but he knew that was how he'd fallen into this hole. *You will have to start over many times*, Maestro had warned him. But he'd always had me to run to before, to lose his troubles in the trance of his guitar. Frankie

listened to cassette tapes in his car, songs by young composers named Randy Newman and Warren Zevon and guitarists Grant Green and Freddie Robinson. But listening
was not the same. He missed playing. He missed practicing
just as much.

After a while, he filled the hours watching television.
He saw young people protesting the war overseas. Frankie
hated war, yet he knew it was the army that had airlifted
him to safety and stitched him back together. He felt
indebted—particularly to the surgeon, whom he continued
to visit, a muscular man in his midforties who kept reminding Frankie of great musicians with handicaps.

"Did you ever hear of a jazz guitar player named Django
Reinhardt?" he asked. "He only had two good fingers. But
his playing was amazing."

Frankie looked away. "Django was unique."

"He couldn't sing. You can."

"Mmm."

"Would you consider singing your songs again?"

"No one wants to hear my stuff."

"A certain audience might."

"It's a whole new scene now."

"Maybe here." The doctor smiled. "But I wasn't talking
about here."

Phone calls were made. Introductions arranged.

Nine months later, Frankie Presto went to Vietnam.

〜

The United Service Organization, or USO, had been bringing entertainers to American troops for decades, starting with the Second World War. Singers like Bing Crosby and the Andrews Sisters made the journey. Even my magnificent violinist Jascha Heifitz took part, and once played for a single soldier sitting in a rainstorm. Jascha called it his greatest performance ever.

Music and war have long been intertwined, from ancient trumpets to the fife and drum, and late in the calendar year 1970, Frankie Presto continued the tradition, joining a Christmastime USO tour with the comedian Bob Hope, the singer Lola Falana, a group of dancers called the Golddiggers, a baseball player, a beauty pageant queen, and a big band that Frankie helped arrange. He also sang two of his famous numbers, "No, No, Honey" and "I Want To Love You." The tour played in various military bases. Trucks rolled out, stages were built, the show took place, then everything was packed up, moved out, and done again.

Wherever the tour went, Frankie befriended soldiers, and asked them to drive him as close to the front as they could get. The misery he witnessed helped diminish his own. He saw Vietnamese children on the side of the road, their eyes vacant. He saw large gun tripods that looked like tepees. He saw explosions from a rooftop, and a sniper who was killed and fell from a window.

But the day I must recount, for purposes of our story, came in the final week of his tour, following an afternoon show in Long Binh, a major United States army base. The crowd was large, nearly two thousand people, and soldiers climbed poles for a better view. They cheered and whooped—particularly when the women danced. The Golddiggers performed in the background when Frankie sang and some troops yelled out, "Lucky you, Presto!"

After the show, as the band was breaking down, Frankie heard a voice screaming his name.

"Mr. Frankie! It's me, Ellis!"

A strapping soldier was at the edge of the stage, smiling and waving in his green fatigues. Frankie blinked in disbelief. Ellis Dubois had been the shoe-shine boy in the alley back in New Orleans (the one who had listened to Little Richard sing "Tutti Frutti") who later served as best man in Frankie's impromptu wedding to Aurora York. At the time, Ellis was six years old.

Now he was twenty-one.

"Ellis, I can't believe it," Frankie said. "You're all . . . grown up."

"Yes, sir."

"Well . . . come here!"

They hugged and spoke rapidly, trading details and questions. Frankie asked about the young man's health (good), his path into the army (drafted), and the old New

Orleans recording studio in the back of the appliance store (moved to another location). Ellis asked about Frankie's hit records (Ellis owned all of them), and *The Ed Sullivan Show* (he watched it both times), and, of course, Miss Aurora.

"We're not together anymore," Frankie said.

Ellis said he was sorry, because he remembered all the times Miss Aurora brought him sandwiches and beignets and sweet tea.

Then Ellis revealed that he was about to be wed himself. He had fallen in love with a Vietnamese woman, and he was marrying her before his tour was over in hopes of bringing her to America and providing a better life. The marriage process was long and drawn out, but there was a reception that evening with the woman's family. Ellis begged Frankie to come.

"Please. Is there any way you could play a song for us?"

Frankie showed him his scarred left hand.

"I can't play anymore, Ellis."

"What happened?"

"Long story."

Ellis was used to seeing wounds. But this one he found profoundly sad. His memory of Frankie was of a man inseparable from his guitar.

"I'm awfully sorry, Mr. Frankie."

"Thank you, Ellis."

"I got an idea . . . What if you sing and I play?"

"Ellis, you play now?"

"Don't you remember teaching me chords in the alley? You showed me D, G, and A. The rest I taught myself. I'd sneak in and listen to you all record. You guys were so good, you inspired me to join a band and everything."

Frankie smiled. "Don't blame me."

"Please? Come and sing?"

"All right. I'll sing for you and your girl."

"Cool. Um . . . Do you have a guitar?"

A few hours later, they were in the back lawn of a Buddhist temple, in front of three tables filled with Vietnamese family members. There was food and drink and women in traditional dress and a few U.S. soldiers who had to leave their guns outside. Ellis strummed Frankie's guitar (yes, Frankie still took it everywhere, heeding the words of Django Reinhardt) and played the chords to Frankie's hit, "Our Secret." And for the first time in years, Frankie sang that song, a simple, acoustic performance, much like the day he wrote it, with Aurora in mind:

One day our secret
Will not be a secret
Because everybody will see
That my secret,
Is your secret
I will love you
And you will love me, too.

The guests clapped politely. Frankie sensed the family was not happy about this union; he could see it in their faces. But they were cordial and Ellis and his bride-to-be seemed very much in love.

e⌒

After several hours and many drinks, Ellis insisted on accompanying Frankie back to the hotel where the show personnel were staying. He arranged for a taxi and when it finally arrived, the two men got in the backseat. En route to the hotel, they agreed how nice it was to see a familiar face in a foreign war.

"This was the best wedding gift, Mr. Frankie."

"I hope you two will be happy."

"We will be. I'm gonna get her back to New Orleans and open my own shoe business."

The driver began pointing and saying something. He pulled over toward a gas station.

"No gas. Hotel," Ellis instructed.

The man kept pointing at his gauge.

"No gas!" Ellis yelled. "Hotel! Straight!"

The driver was speaking quickly in Vietnamese, tossing in, "Short time, short time," and he stopped the car and got out, waving his hands to reassure them that they should wait. He went toward the gas station.

"Man, I'm sorry, Mr. Frankie," Ellis said, sighing. "The people here, you know?"

Frankie watched the man through the window.

"Ellis, why is he running?"

Ellis's eyes, softened by alcohol, blinked lazily, then sprung open wide. "Get out! Get out! Get out!" he screamed and Frankie pushed the door open and they both started running, because Ellis remembered the times he'd been warned to never stay in a vehicle in Vietnam if the driver leaves it, as they sometimes wired cars with explosives to kill U.S. troops. As he and Frankie ran, they heard a lone voice screaming in Vietnamese and then a moment of silence and then a huge explosion that propelled them both forward. Frankie threw his guitar case over Ellis as they hit the ground and everything was dust and noise and their ears were ringing and their eyes burning and they couldn't see anything for the smoke.

Then, just as suddenly, all was quiet. Someone yelled. Dogs barked. The car had indeed been wired. Perhaps someone wanted Ellis dead for taking a Vietnamese bride. I lack such details. I only know that Frankie helped Ellis scramble up against a building and when an army jeep came zooming in, looking for soldiers, Frankie flagged it down. Ellis was bleeding slightly from his leg but otherwise was all right, just scraped and bruised, as was Frankie. They got into the jeep, and Ellis screamed that Frankie was a VIP and they had to get him back to his hotel immediately. Both men were breathing hard. But Frankie was now looking at his guitar case, and when the vehicle passed under a streetlight, Ellis saw why:

There were small chunks of shrapnel stuck in it.

Realizing that the shrapnel might have hit him instead, Ellis touched the case. His voice choked.

"Oh, Jesus . . ."

"It's all right," Frankie said.

"That could have killed me."

"Don't think about it."

Ellis started crying.

"I'm sorry, Mr. Frankie. Lord, I'm so sorry . . ."

"Don't be sorry. You're alive."

He heard the words as he said them—*Don't be sorry. You're alive*—as if he were meant to hear them himself. He slid the case between his legs and opened it.

"What's that light?" Ellis said.

Frankie stared. The guitar's fourth string was glowing blue. He felt a lump in his throat and shut the case, then ran his hand over the shrapnel holes.

"It's OK," he said. "It's nothing."

But of course, it was not nothing. A future had been altered. Saved from the explosion, Ellis would go on to marry his Vietnamese bride, and they would settle in New Orleans and open a shoe business and raise three children and nine grandchildren, one of whom would become a famous composer.

None of this would have happened had Frankie not found Ellis again. The fourth string told that story.

Everyone joins a band in this life.

Sometimes they reunite.

47

1981

THE TEXAS BOYS REMOVED THEIR SHOES, LIFTED FROM THE
brush, and walked slowly onto the sand, approaching the
guitarist from behind.

"Mr. Presto?"

Frankie looked up. His beard was full and his skin was
tanned.

"We're from America."

Frankie squinted. His silence made them speak faster.

"Actually, we're from Texas—"

"We've got a band—"

"Sorry to bother you—"

"This guy, Kevin, told us—"

"He dropped us at the woods—"

"We didn't even know—"

"That you were here—"

"We love your music—"

Frankie held up a hand, which silenced them, although

he didn't mean to do that. He was actually beckoning a little girl, maybe four or five years old, who came running across the beach. She had braided hair and wore no shoes or shirt and Frankie beamed as she entered his arm at her belly. He swung her up. She seemed to laugh, but made no sound. When she landed, she saw the three strangers and her expression changed. She went running back, silently, the way she'd come.

Lyle, Eddie, and Cluck looked across to her destination: a small house by the back of the beach, enveloped by trees, where a blond woman was now emerging, wearing a colorful wraparound robe.

"What's going on?" the woman said.

"Uh, we're sorry, ma'am, we'll come back later," Lyle stammered, as he and the others scurried back into the trees.

Tony Bennett

Singer, painter, Grammy winner, Kennedy Center honoree

WELL, FIRST OF ALL, THIS IS TRAGIC NEWS, HIS DEATH. IT'S a tragedy for the entire music world. This was a beautiful man. Did you know him? If you did, you were lucky. I mean that. Frankie Presto was a true artist. Very gentle. Very thoughtful. And the most purely musical guitarist I ever met.

I'll tell you why I say this. I've been singing since the late 1940s. Frank Sinatra, Nat King Cole, Billie Holiday, these people were my influences. I loved jazz singers. That's how I saw myself. But when it came time to make money, I was told I couldn't do it as a jazz singer. Understand? That's how the business worked. They once told Duke Ellington they were dropping him from his record label. He said, "Why?" And they said, "You're not selling enough records." And he said, "You have things confused. It's my job to make the records. It's your job to sell them." Duke Ellington. Can you believe that?

Well, I hit a period in the early 1970s where I wasn't selling enough records, either. And I wouldn't do the music they wanted me to do. Under duress, I had recorded an album of rock songs. A terrible fit for me. Even making it, I got physically ill. It was a tough time. I felt like I was locked out of the thing I loved the most.

I left my label and went to London and wound up staying there for nearly two years. It was the greatest period of my life, because I just did the music I wanted to do.

While I was there, I stayed at this one hotel, and every morning when I got up, the drapes were opened in the outer room that looked out on a park. And there was always a man sitting on a bench with a guitar. He never played it. He just held it on his lap.

So after a few weeks, I got curious. On my way back from a walk, I passed him and I thought I recognized his face. I said, "Excuse me, I see you here every day—" and before I could finish, he looked at me and sang a verse of "Love Letters," which was a song I recorded on my very first album. And his voice was beautiful. Perfect tone.

"Chuck Wayne was your guitarist," he said.

"That's right," I said.

"That was a great record."

"Thank you."

"There's another song called 'Love Letters.'"

"Oh?"

"Django Reinhardt. It's called 'Billets Doux.'"

" 'Billets Doux.' "

"That's the French. It's an instrumental."

"Can you play it?"

"No." He looked at his guitar. "Not anymore."

That's when I saw his left hand, which was all scarred. And I said, "Is that why you sit out here every day, but don't play?" And he looked at me and said, "I'm waiting for someone." And I said "Who?" And he said, "My wife." And I said, "Is she coming soon?" And he shook his head and said he wasn't sure, he didn't even know if she lived in London anymore.

Well, we got to talking, and I realized this was Frankie Presto. He'd been off the scene for years. He told me his real name was Francisco, and I said, "Hey, my real name is Benedetto, maybe we're cousins!" We laughed and had a good chat.

I always thought he was a rock and roll guy, but it turned out he and I knew a lot of the same people. Frank Sinatra. Bob Hope. He'd even met Duke Ellington when he was a boy, did you know that?

The next day he was sitting there again. I had a car picking me up, so I invited him to come with me to the set where we were doing a TV show called *The Talk of the Town*. It was a terrific experience, with Robert Farnon, the greatest arranger in the world (everybody called him "the Governor"), and we performed songs and talked about music every week.

Francisco—he liked that I called him that—came along that day and sat in the studio and listened. He never opened his guitar case. I invited him the next day and a few more times, and every time we got into the car to go, he took one last look around, as if his wife might be coming.

But she never did.

So about two weeks later, we were practicing for the show, and I was singing a Kurt Weill tune called "Lost in the Stars" with just a piano player accompanying me. It's a beautiful but sad song. You know it?

Before Lord God made the Sea and the Land
He held all the stars in the palm of his hand
And they ran through his fingers like grains of sand
And one little star fell alone.

Suddenly, I heard the most beautiful guitar chords, one strum at a time. I looked over and Frankie Presto was playing. Every chord seemed to be a struggle. You could see it on his face. But the tempo was very slow and he had time to make the finger changes. I kept on singing. I didn't want to stop, because I could sense this was important to him. We did a few verses and we got to the end:

But I've been walking through the night and the day
Till my eyes get weary and my head turns grey

And sometimes it seems maybe God's gone away . . .
And we're lost out here in the stars.

He hit the final chord, and I saw tears roll down his face. Even the stagehands clapped. I said, "That was nice." I didn't want to embarrass him. But I was lying. It was more than nice. It was spectacular.

At the end of that summer, I decided to return to the States. The car came to get me, and there was Francisco, as usual, sitting on his bench. I told the driver to wait and I went over and sat down next to him.

"I'm going," I said.

"Where?"

"Home."

"Thanks for taking me to your shows, Mr. Benedetto."

"How long are you going to wait here?"

"I don't know."

"What if your wife doesn't come back?"

"She will."

"Well, if you ever feel like it, I would be honored to record with you someday."

He almost laughed. "I can't play anymore."

"You can. You did."

"Just some chords."

"Not chords. Music."

I told him that as long as he had that kind of music

inside him, nothing could keep it from coming out. I meant it.

And then I asked, "When was the last time you were home?"

And he said, "I don't really have one."

And I said, "Everyone has someplace they call home."

He held up his guitar.

"All I ever had was this," he said, "and her."

48

ONE OF FRANKIE'S FAVORITE SONGS WAS THE DRIFTERS'
"Save The Last Dance For Me." The lyrics—which tell a
woman it's all right for her to dance with others, as long as
she remembers who is taking her home—were written by
Doc Pomus, a polio victim. He wrote it recalling the night
of his wedding, when other men danced with his bride,
while he had to watch from a wheelchair. He scribbled the
words on the back of their wedding invitation.

I have told you all love stories are symphonies, and the
final movement is the *rondo*, repeated themes with episodes
intervening. Frankie and Aurora, with their *rondo* of arrivals and departures, had saved their last dances long enough.
Finally, in the calendar year 1974, they were reunited for
good—thanks to, of all things, a radio program.

Yes. A radio program. Mr. Tony Bennett (or Benedetto)
did one final favor for the wounded Mr. Presto. Departing from London that day, he'd shared his limousine with
another passenger, a presenter from the BBC. The two
men conversed en route to the airport, and Mr. Bennett

recounted some of Frankie's story, omitting his name, but mentioning that every morning, this man waited for his wife with his guitar in his lap.

"Isn't that something?" Bennett said.

"Extraordinary," the presenter agreed.

Moved by the sad tale, the BBC man told it himself on his radio program that week. The program was heard on the drive to work by Cecile (York) Peterson who, upon reaching her office at the London School of Economics, phoned her sister, Aurora, and said, "I think your husband is back in town."

The following morning, in a steady rain, Aurora York stepped off a bus and walked toward the park. She spotted Frankie and ducked behind a post, waiting for an hour, watching him get wet. She counted the raindrops hitting her umbrella, and assigned to each one a reason that she should not go to him. When she ran out of reasons, she closed the umbrella and let herself get soaked.

Then she crossed the street.

Frankie looked up as she approached, the rain dripping down her face. She moved his guitar and lowered into his lap.

"Will you stay?" he asked.

"Yes," she said.

Music can soothe a soul. The body is another story. Aurora York spent months seeking the finest specialists for Frankie's wounded hand. For this, I am most grateful. She used her sister's connections. She paid for another surgery. She made him do rehabilitation exercises every day. She nursed my beloved disciple back to the point of utility, after which, my allure rekindled in him.

Meanwhile, returning to their affections (the *rondo*, remember?), Frankie and Aurora pleasantly discovered the barriers between them had melted away. Fame was no longer an issue, nor was traveling, late nights, or other women. Aurora discarded all remnants of narcotics or alcohol in Frankie's life.

Then she set out to find a home.

"Do you want to stay in London?" Frankie asked.

"Absolutely not," she said.

"Where then?"

"Someplace far away," she said. "And quiet."

They drove to various outposts in England. None of them pleased her.

"Farther," she said. "Quieter."

They flew to New York, where Frankie retrieved two guitars.

"Farther," she said. "Quieter."

They flew to Los Angeles, where Frankie retrieved money from a bank and Aurora refused to even leave the airport.

"Farther," she said. "Quieter."

They flew to Australia.

"Farther. Quieter."

They took a boat to New Zealand. Spending the night by the Auckland harbor, she saw an old ferry sailing off in the moonlight. When she asked where it was going, a clerk told her a place called "Waiheke," whose Maori name, "Te Motu-arai-roa," meant "long and sheltering island."

The next morning, she and Frankie were on that ferry with all their possessions. An hour later, when they reached the docks and saw the high green cliffs and heard the quiet lapping of water, Aurora turned to the love of her life and looked him in the eyes.

"Here," she said.

49

1981

THE TEXAS BOYS HAD DRAWN STRAWS. ONE OF THEM WOULD try again. (The three of them together, they decided, was too intimidating.) Lyle drew the shortest straw, and the following evening, with the sun setting, he walked through the brush and trees, and edged out alone onto the beach. Frankie was sitting with his shirt off, the guitar strap around his bare, tanned skin, playing scales in the key of F: major scale, minor scale, Dorian, Phrygian, Lydian, ascending, descending.

"You can come around," he said, not looking back.

Lyle edged forward, hands shoved in his pockets.

"Hello, sir."

"My wife said you'd be back."

"Sorry about last time. . . ."

Frankie kept playing the scales, slowly, deliberately.

"I just . . . I never thought I'd actually meet you, Mr. Presto. My name is Lyle."

Frankie moved to the F sharp scales.

"I play guitar, too."

Frankie nodded.

"Not like you, of course."

Frankie nodded.

"Was that you playing the famous solo at Woodstock?"

Frankie nodded.

"Really? Because nobody could confirm you were there."

Frankie kept nodding until Lyle realized he was not responding to his questions, but rather moving with the rhythm of the breaking waves, as if following a drummer.

"Are you practicing? I mean. Sorry. Dumb question. Why scales? Why are you practicing scales?"

Frankie stopped playing.

"Huh?"

"Why scales?"

"Retraining."

"Retraining?"

"My fingers. My ears. It's a long process."

Lyle wanted to ask a hundred questions, but as Frankie resumed, he stayed quiet and listened. When Frankie completed the B flat and B natural rotation, he stopped again.

"I messed up my hand. I'm working on finding it."

"Finding what?"

"The beauty. Left hand finds the beauty."

He held out his palm and Lyle noticed the scars.

"Oh, man."

"Not much beauty."

"What happened?"

"Not sure I remember."

"An accident?"

"Can't say that."

"When?"

"In '69."

"That's Woodstock. So you *were* at Woodstock?"

"Sort of."

"Was that you playing?"

"Playing what?"

"The solo. The one I just asked you about."

"Sorry. I wasn't listening."

"It's famous. I mean, with bootlegs, it's famous."

Frankie stared at the young man.

"Bootlegs?"

"Recordings. You can get them if you ask around."

"Of a solo?"

"It's the most amazing solo ever. I couldn't play it if I tried. Nobody can."

Frankie's breathing seemed to accelerate.

"It wasn't me."

He looked down at his feet.

"You should go now. I have a lot of practicing to do."

c~

Several days passed. Lyle and his bandmates tried three more visits, but the beach was empty each time.

"Maybe we scared him off," Eddie said.

"He said it wasn't him," Lyle said.

"You believe that?"

"I don't know. He plays pretty slowly."

"How'd he hurt himself?"

"He wouldn't say."

"What should we do now?"

They looked at each other.

"Drink," Cluck said.

Ten minutes later, they entered a pub called McGinty's and ordered beers. They found a table.

"Is that the Yankee rock and rollers?"

They looked up to see Kevin, the driver, grinning from behind the bar.

"You're a bartender, too?" Eddie asked.

"Aw, no, just helping myself. So. How's the adventure going?"

"It's not," Lyle said glumly.

"He's disappeared," Cluck added.

Kevin pulled up a chair. "You know, mates, people usually move to an island to be left alone. If they wanted to be found, they wouldn't pick Waiheke, that's for bloody sure."

"Then why did you take us to him?"

"Dunno. He's been here a long time. I thought he might

like knowing there were people who hadn't forgotten him."

"You knew who he was? That he was famous in the sixties?"

"Aw, sure. 'I Want To Love You'? We heard that song in the army. Whoo-hoo! Makes you shake your hips, eh?"

"Then why did you say you never heard of him?"

"First rule of friendship, mates. Learn how to keep a secret."

The three boys slumped. They sipped their beers.

"That's why I went by his place that night. To make sure it was all right."

"Wait," Lyle said. "He gave you *permission* to bring us?"

"Not him, mate. Her."

"His wife?"

"Aurora. She's lovely. She thought it was a good idea."

ℰ

Bolstered by this news, the Texas boys decided to stay on the island through the weekend, which featured an annual tradition known as Race Day. Horses, ponies, and tractors all competed on a large beach, while the islanders gathered in the sun, eating steaks from McGinty's and drinking beer from barrels. Music was part of the festivities, and it took very little for the Clever Yells to arrange to play a few songs in the late afternoon. (The other musicians were a small brass band and a man with an accordion.) The stage had a crude arrangement, with an old drum set in the center, and small amplifiers and microphones that were used for council meetings. But Lyle, Eddie, and Cluck were anxious to play—bands that get together after an absence are as giddy as lovers at an airport—and once they'd plugged in their guitars and offered a quick greeting, they opened with a country song, written by Lyle, which was met with robust applause. They did "Jambalaya" by Hank Williams and a version of "Twist and Shout," all of which seemed to mix well with the sun and the beer and the general noise of children squealing and drunken men laughing.

"We'd like to do one more," Lyle said. "An old one, but a good one for sure."

Cluck pounded the drums, and, with the guitar playing an old familiar line, Lyle broke into the opening verse of Frankie Presto's biggest hit:

I want to love you,
I will be true,
No one will love you
The way I do.

The crowd immediately clapped along, as people do on

songs they recognize. Lyle looked at Eddie, who smiled as he sang background. Their affection for this music was apparent. But a quick glance over the crowd took the smile off Lyle's face.

In the back stood Frankie, with the little girl on his shoulders.

In the middle of the song, he turned and walked away.

ᕙᕗ

I should explain about the child.

Frankie and Aurora had found the peace they were searching for on the island. Land was cheap and they purchased a small plot on the beach and built a tidy home from local materials with a deck that overlooked the water. In the mornings they walked the shoreline and in the evenings Aurora barbecued fresh fish while Frankie practiced scales and arpeggios to regain his dexterity. They dressed in shorts and old cotton shirts and found the island residents to be a collection of artists, drifters, and colorful characters, none of whom cared about Frankie's former celebrity.

About a year after their arrival, Frankie and Aurora were returning from a walk when they heard an animal crying. In the brush, they saw a stray dog. It had white fur and was hunched low, staring at them. When they approached, the animal whimpered and backed up a few steps. Behind it, they discovered, wrapped in a gray blanket, a tiny baby girl, no more than three months old.

"Who are *you*, sweetheart?" Aurora whispered, gently lifting her.

Frankie watched. The child made no sound. Aurora held her against her chest, but the baby's eyes remained open, looking at Frankie.

"Someone left her to die," he said. The words just came out. Inside all humans is the entirety of your memories, the ones you can access and the ones you cannot. Somewhere in the deep of Frankie's mind was his own abandonment, his own gray blanket, his own whimpering dog.

"We need to get her someplace safe," Aurora said.

They hurried to their car, and never saw a heavily clothed figure, hiding in the woods.

❧

They took the child to the nearest church, a small, single-level building. The attending nun, a thick-necked woman with a stern expression, seemed surprised by their arrival, and she took the child and told them to wait. Soon a police officer arrived. He grilled them about the details. Where? How? When? Who were they?

"Why are you asking us so many questions?" Frankie said.

"Because that baby was left here two days ago, mate," the officer replied. "Someone abandoned her in the vestibule, with a note asking that the church take care of her. And then, this morning . . ."

He paused. "She vanished."

Frankie looked at Aurora.

"We didn't have anything to do with that."

"We told you what happened."

"We just found her."

"That's the truth. In the woods. A dog was guarding her."

Since the baby was unharmed, the officer eventually accepted their story. He allowed them to go home. But that night Aurora dreamed about the child. And the next day, she insisted Frankie go with her to the church.

"Hello, precious," Aurora cooed, leaning over the crib.

"Don't expect no response from that one," the nun said.

"Why not?"

"Something wrong with her."

"What?"

"Can't make a peep. Just grunts a little. May be deaf. That's usually the reason. Poor thing. We're taking her to the mainland tomorrow."

Aurora looked at Frankie.

"Get your guitar," she said.

෧

Frankie returned with his acoustic. He strummed the open strings. The child did not react.

"Play her a song," Aurora said.

Frankie played the elementary notes of "Hush Little Baby."

"Sing," Aurora whispered. So he did.

Hush little baby, don't say a word,
Papa's gonna buy you a mockingbird.

The child looked over. Aurora sang the next line.

And if that mockingbird don't sing,
Mama's gonna buy you a diamond ring.

The child opened its mouth.
The adults sang together.

And if that diamond turns to brass,
Mama's gonna buy you a looking glass.

They stopped. The child turned her head. She started to cry, her eyes squeezed tight. But hardly a sound came forth. Just small, muted grunts, almost painful to hear from such a tiny creature.

Frankie started playing again.

And she stopped crying.

"You see?" Aurora said to the nun. "She's not deaf. She

can hear." She turned to Frankie. "And she likes it when you play."

"Well, I don't know . . . ," he said, smiling.

But I knew. I knew exactly what was happening. I see the future of all my children, and I saw in this future a discussion, a decision, an adoption, and the clearing of space for a small crib in their tidy house. A new band was forming with Frankie Presto at its center.

This one was a family.

50

BUT TO FINISH WITH THE BOYS FROM TEXAS.

Frankie and Aurora had named the baby girl Kai and they raised her with love, sand, seawater, and music. As near as the doctors could tell, she was mute, a congenital malfunction in her vocal cord development. But her hearing was sharp, and so were her eyes, and those eyes followed Frankie as he walked around a room. When he sat down with his guitar, she clapped the base of her palms together.

Kai provided inspiration for Frankie's recovery. She was there when he finally played a Giuliani piece without error. She was there when he mastered (for the second time in his life) the twelve études of Heitor Villa-Lobos. And she was on Frankie's shoulders when the Clever Yells did their version of "I Want To Love You" at the beach races.

She was also there, two weeks later, holding Frankie's and Aurora's hands, when they entered a cramped recording studio in downtown Auckland called the Last Laugh, Frankie carrying his old guitar. At Aurora's urging, he had agreed to record a song with the young men from Texas, in exchange for their departing the island and leaving him alone.

"It won't hurt you to play with them," Aurora had said.

"I'm not looking to play with anyone."

"But it's time."

"Time for what?"

"To grow your audience beyond your wife and daughter."

Lyle had been so excited, he wasn't able to sleep the night before. He wrote out charts for the song they would record, a rock composition that he felt was his most commercial.

"Sorry, I know this isn't the greatest studio," he said to Frankie, "but the equipment is good. And they're only charging us fifteen dollars an hour."

"No names," Frankie said.

"Sorry?"

"I don't want my name anywhere. Not on the tracks or the credits or anything."

Lyle was disappointed, as he had hoped that telling people Frankie Presto was on his record would make it more marketable.

"Of course. Sure. Whatever you want."

Frankie nodded stiffly. He sat down and opened his old guitar case. Handed to him by El Maestro himself, the case was now almost forty years old, and it showed the wear and tear, with security stickers from countless airports and tape over the holes that once held shrapnel.

The guitar itself remained the sturdiest of partners.

Frankie took great care to polish its fret board and oil the tuners. There were a few nicks in the rosewood body that had been repaired but remained discolored. The ebony neck had stood the test of time. And of course, the strings. The bottom four had been replaced many times. But Frankie's eyes fell on the top two, the remaining originals, the ones yet untouched by the combustible blue magic.

He recalled a conversation with his teacher.

"Why do the strings make different sounds, Maestro?"

"It is simple. They work like life."

"I don't understand."

"The first string is E. It is high pitched and quick like a child.

"The second string is B. It is pitched slightly lower, like the squeaky voice of a teenager.

"The third string, G, is deeper, with the power of a young man.

"The fourth string, D, is robust, a man at full strength.

"The fifth string, A, is solid and loud but unable to reach high tones, like a man who can no longer do what he did."

"And the sixth string, Maestro?"

"The sixth is the low E, the thickest, slowest, and grumpiest. You hear how deep? Dum-dum-dum. Like it is ready to die."

"Is that because it is closest to heaven?"

"No, Francisco. It is because life will always drag you to the
   bottom."

Frankie asked for the chart. Lyle fumbled with the paper
and dropped it. Frankie picked it up. Then, seeing what
was written, he leaned his own guitar against the wall and
picked up a Fender Stratocaster.

"All right if I use this?" he asked, motioning to the curly-
haired engineer who was standing behind the glass. The engineer gave him a thumbs-up sign.

"All right, let's go," Frankie told Lyle.

"Don't you want to rehearse it? We can run through it a
few times to show you where—"

Frankie shook his head.

"Just roll the tape."

❧

The song was a fast number called "What the What?" Cluck
played the drums at a frantic pace and Eddie's bass was like
nervous pounding. Frankie's part was just four chords repeated with heavy distortion, and he only had to strum four
beats to a measure. It was, in my view, more rudimentary
than was worth his talent. But he fulfilled his obligation,
repeating the song five times while Lyle tried different vocal approaches. Through the glass, Frankie saw his wife and

daughter, and Kai was shaking back and forth with the beat. Aurora moved her head in exaggerated motion, as if banging it against a wall, and Frankie half-grinned.

"What do you think, Mr. Presto?" Lyle asked when they were finished.

Frankie nodded, but did not make eye contact.

"I mean, I'd like to know your opinion," Lyle said. "Honestly."

"Honestly?"

"Please."

"Why are you doing this song?"

"What do you mean?"

"I mean, your voice doesn't seem suited to it. And it doesn't sound like you really feel it."

Blood rushed to Lyle's face, turning it red.

"Why do you say that?" he asked.

"Well, you did five takes," Frankie said, "and every vocal was different. That tells me you're still searching for the tune. Why not do stuff like you did at the beach? At least that sounded like you enjoyed it."

There was an uncomfortable silence. Lyle glanced at Eddie and Cluck and they took their cue to leave the room. Frankie exhaled and glanced at Aurora and Kai through the glass. He had already been here longer than he wanted to be.

"I know what you're saying is right," Lyle said, lowering his voice. "But I'm trying to make it in the business. And this is what they're buying. They want a driving beat. They want edge."

"Edge?" Frankie said.

"Yes, sir. Like your solo—or, the solo everyone thinks is you. The one I thought was you. That kind of edge."

Frankie rubbed a palm over his eyes. He sighed.

"That wasn't edge. That was pain."

Lyle looked up.

"It was you?"

"A different version of me. You don't want to be that."

Frankie put down the Stratocaster, and leaned back in the chair.

"I had a teacher who was blind. Sometimes, when he was in the bathroom, I would bang around on the guitar, making noise. And he would yell, 'Stop it, stupid boy! No one wants to listen to ugliness.' I would defend myself by saying, 'In school, they teach us that God listens to everything.' And he'd yell back, 'God may listen, but I will not.'"

Lyle laughed and Frankie broke into a smile.

"The point is, you have to decide who you are playing for. I wanted him to think my playing was beautiful, so I stopped making noise and made music instead." He rubbed his chin. "What do you really like, in your heart?"

"Probably more country, or folk."

"Then play that," Frankie said.

"Even if it doesn't sell?"

"Money and music are not friends." Frankie chuckled. "I know something about that."

Lyle thought for a minute. "It's funny, I actually have a song that's like what your teacher said. It's about forgiving someone who's cheated, and how God will, but I won't, and God does, but I don't."

"Sounds good," Frankie said.

"Can you play it with me? Please? I'll write up a chart right now. It won't take long. Could you just stay and do that?"

"Then you and your friends will go back to the States?"

"I swear."

"And leave me alone?"

"Absolutely. We'll sleep at the airport if you want."

Frankie jerked his head. "Go on."

Lyle sprung to his feet and pushed open the door. Aurora and Kai were on the other side.

"Oh, sorry. Excuse me," Lyle said.

Frankie motioned his family inside.

❧

What happened next would prove both important and—as sometimes occurs with milestone events—totally unexpected.

Aurora was pleased that Frankie was advising the young band. "You're helping them. They're nice boys."

"I'm only doing it because you said to."

Aurora smiled. "That's a good enough reason."

"Come here, Kai," Frankie said, lifting their daughter into his lap. Aurora popped open a small bottle of juice. The little girl took one sip, then jumped away.

"And she's off!" Aurora said.

They watched Kai circle the room, giddy but silent. She came back and lifted the electric guitar toward Frankie. She had a curious expression on her face.

"Show her what you can do, Francisco," Aurora said.

"Yeah?"

"How's the hand?"

He raised his eyebrows. "Let's see."

He plugged a cord into a nearby amplifier and tested the effects pedals. Then he lifted his chin toward his daughter.

"Kai?" he said. "Are you listening?"

♈

What would you give to remember everything? I have this power. I absorb your memories; when you hear me, you relive them. A first dance. A wedding. The song that played when you got the big news. No other talent gives your life a soundtrack. I am Music. I mark time.

That day in Auckland, Frankie played his own memories. He opened with a verse of a children's song, "Billy Boy," before speeding into a jazz version (as the pianist Red Garland had once done with Miles Davis). He played it easily and, to his surprise, without pain. He improvised for two minutes, pushing himself, then ended with a speedy flick of his wrist.

Little Kai clapped, her face a portrait of silent delight.

"Want more?"

When she nodded, he played "Tea for Two" and "A-Tisket A-Tasket," songs he listened to on the phonograph with El Maestro, each time beginning simply, then taking it to far corners and beautiful colors. Aurora tried to suppress her grin. If I had a mouth, I'd have done the same. For the first time in years, Frankie was playing freely again, nearly as fast as before, but better, richer, because his music now was passionate, more thoughtful, the notes more carefully chosen, the way a great painter chooses not just a color but the perfect shade.

He did parts of many rock songs, including "All Along the Watchtower" by Bob Dylan and "You Really Got Me" by the Kinks, slowing them down then revving them up, playing as if he were the drums, bass, and guitar all in one. When he finished on the electric, Kai lifted the old acoustic guitar that now connected her childhood with his.

"That one?" Frankie said.

She nodded.

"'Parlez-Moi d'Amour,'" Aurora said.

Frankie obliged, playing it soulfully and humming along. He also played "Nuages" by Django Reinhardt (which the gypsy guitarist had shown him in a Cleveland hotel room) and two blues numbers he had learned in Louisiana; and "Träumerei" by Schumann, which he once played on a beach; and the tremolo-infused "Recuerdos de la Alhambra" by Tárrega. He even played a challenging composition by the Brazilian guitarist known as Garoto, who was once labeled "the man of golden fingers."

One song rolled into the other, and Frankie's playing opened up like spreading sunlight. The look on his daughter's face inspired him the way no audience ever had, and in between joking and laughing with Aurora, he played for them a musical score of his life, with new shadings and interpretations, using flat ninths, suspended fourths, and chord inversions that he'd never attempted. I could feel myself coursing through his veins and releasing through his fingers in passion and dexterity and creation.

It was glorious.

He finished with a song he loved, the achingly beautiful "Nature Boy," a mysterious piece written by a drifting composer who never again had a song as popular. It tells the story of an enchanted boy who, like young Frankie, travels the world and holds a secret. The last two lines were the only lyrics Frankie sang that afternoon, looking gratefully into the eyes of the two people who had brought him back from despair:

"The greatest thing, you'll ever learn
Is just to love, and be loved in return."

He concluded with a slowly picked final chord, a D minor, adding a sixth, a ninth, and a sharp eleventh up in the highest reaches of the guitar neck, then playfully popping his eyes at his daughter. Little Kai was so pleased she scrambled over and patted on the frets.

"Careful," Frankie whispered, smiling, "those are magic strings."

Unseen, through the glass in the control room, the curly-haired engineer jotted those words on a piece of paper. *Magic strings.* A budding guitarist himself, he had been listening the whole time, alone behind the console, nearly frozen by the music coming through his speakers. He glanced over at the reels of two-inch tape on the main recorder and exhaled in relief.

They were still spinning.

The whole thing had been recorded.

"We're ready to go," said Lyle, bursting into the control room, Eddie and Cluck behind him.

"New tape?" the engineer said.

"Yeah, everything new," Eddie said. "We're starting over."

"What about the old tape?"

"Forget it. Don't want it."

The engineer nodded. "All right, mate. Whatever you say."

He rewound the reels, put the spool in a box, and grabbed a marker.

"Hey," he said to Cluck, who was tying his sneakers. "What's the bloke's name on the guitar?"

Cluck smiled mischievously. He looked left and right.

"That's Frankie Presto, man. Don't tell anyone."

"Why should I?" the engineer said. "I never heard of 'im."

Cluck frowned and went into the studio. The engineer wrote on the side of the box "The Magic Strings of Frankie Presto" and put it on a shelf.

51

THE FIRST SOUND RECORDING CAME IN THE MIDNINETEENTH century, when an inventor made noises into a cylinder and diaphragm, moving a stylus that etched lines onto soot-covered paper.

Twenty years later, Thomas Edison created the phonograph. And ever since, you have been capturing me in all types of mediums, from shellac plates to vinyl records to magnetized tape to data-encoded discs. I make no judgments. I am a talent. I care no more about the recording format than Painting cares about a blank canvas.

But how those recordings affect my disciples—that is of interest. The song the Clever Yells recorded that day in Auckland was more satisfying than its rock-styled predecessor. It suited Lyle's unusual vocal style, a sparse, plaintive voice that infused a yearning into his music. That song—called "God Will"—was rerecorded a few years later and included on the young man's first album, called *Lyle Lovett*.

And, never forgetting the message of the Kiwi who took

him to Frankie ("*First rule of friendship, mates: learn how to keep a secret*"), Mr. Lovett, now a successful artist in your world, never revealed Frankie's whereabouts or spoke of the solo at Woodstock.

As for the box of two-inch recording tape, it remained in the hands of the curly-haired engineer, until someone he met offered a tidy sum of money, which he quickly accepted and spent on a new mixing board.

Soon, pressed copies of a vinyl album in a plain white jacket began to appear around the South Pacific, purchased privately and marveled at by musicians and nonmusicians alike. Its title, in simple words across the back cover: *The Magic Strings of Frankie Presto.*

But by the time that happened, Frankie and Aurora had left the island of Waiheke. They departed shortly after Kai's eighth birthday, when she suddenly, inexplicably, woke up and asked Aurora, in a rasp of a voice, "Where's Daddy?"

The doctors were baffled by her sudden speech, making reference to "selective mutism," hidden lung problems, neurological issues, or the child's inability to reveal symptoms prior to what seemed to be a miraculous recovery.

All Frankie and Aurora knew was that they now had a daughter asking questions. Like a musical piece that adds strings and horns, their lives grew richer and more complex, as the child's little universe expanded.

"Pack some clothes," Aurora said one night.

"Where are we going?" Frankie said.

"We need to take her off this island for a while."

"Why?"

"Because today she asked where you and I came from. And I think it's time she knew."

And just like that, the next morning, they were boarding the ferry, suitcases in tow, on a journey of rediscovery, the three members of Frankie Presto's family band—and a fourth, unseen party, a heavily clothed figure, walking fifty feet behind them and watching everything.

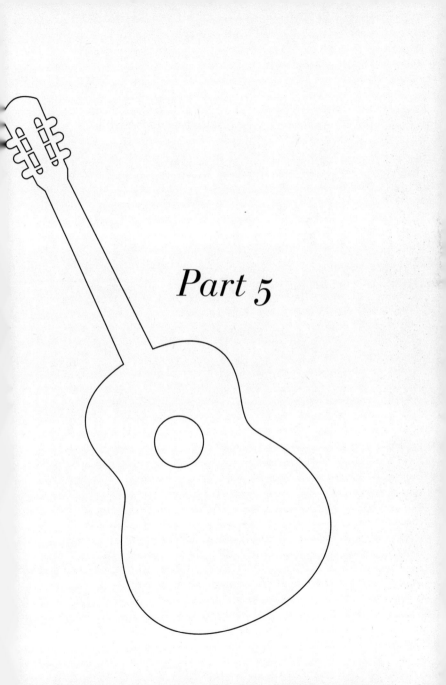

Part 5

Paul Stanley

Guitarist, singer, founding member of KISS

SURE. I'LL TALK TO YOU ABOUT FRANKIE. . . . HE AUDITIONED
for KISS once, you know.

I'm serious. It was . . . what . . . 1984? In Los Angeles.
We were looking for a lead guitarist to replace Vinnie Vin-
cent.

KISS had always auditioned guys. We'd bring them into
the studio, let them play with a couple of our tracks. We
knew right away if a guy could hack it musically. But he
also had to have the right look. We're such a visual act. And
then, if he had the looks *and* the chops, we'd try and get to
know him, because you're going from dating to marrying
when you put a new guy in a band.

Especially a band like ours.

Anyhow, we needed to do this fast, so we had three guitarists come on the same day. We'd already seen the first
two—both pretty good—and then the last guy walks in.
He looks old. I can't remember who or what agency sent

him over, but he's wearing a ski cap and carrying a case. He doesn't even open it. He sits down, sees a couple loose guitars in the studio, picks up a Japanese electric model, a Riverhead, little diamond-shaped body, and says, "All right if I use this?"

And we said, "What's the matter with yours?"

And he said, "Ah, that's just an old acoustic."

Already I'm thinking, "You're kidding me. That's what you bring to a KISS audition? Let's just go home now." But he pulls off the ski cap and pushes his hair back and I lean forward and say, "Holy crap," and Gene Simmons says, "What?" and I say, "That's Frankie Presto!"

Now, I should tell you that, as a kid in New York, Frankie Presto was *it* for me. I liked voices like Dion and the Belmonts, Bobby Rydell, Jimmy Clanton. They could all sing. But Frankie sang *and* played *and* wore cool clothes *and* could really dance. I watched him on *American Bandstand*. He did that move with the mike stand where he'd push it forward, then pivot it back with his foot—Joe Tex was famous for that, too. So cool.

I was like eight years old when "I Want To Love You" came out, and it was the first record I ever owned. I must have played it until it shredded. A year or two later, when "Shake Shake" was big, I convinced my parents to take me to see Frankie at a rock and roll show. The Fox Theatre in Brooklyn. He only did a few songs, but he played guitar and just *killed* it. He took a solo that I can still remember. Not only were his fingers flying, but at the end he hit these four big chords that just rang out, one after the other, bang, bang, bang, bang! And it filled the place up. It was like the Sermon on the Mount for me. To this day, when I play, there's nothing like exploding one big chord and just *owning* the building.

Anyhow, the other KISS guys didn't even want to audition Frankie. "He's too old," they said. But I said, "Let's give him a shot. He was there when it all started." He still had a good face, strong cheekbones, all his hair. I thought it could work.

We played him one of our older tracks called "Creatures of the Night," and told him to try something like the solo on that. And I swear, he played that solo back *note for note*. I don't know how. He only heard it once. But he made every note scream right where it had screamed before, hit the whammy bar perfectly, almost like he was tracing the music.

So I said, "Okay, this time do what you want." And he laid out a solo that was even better. What impressed me most was that he didn't show off his speed. One or two licks proved how fast he was. But he made it musical. You could almost *sing* the solo once he'd played it.

We didn't need to hear any more—not as far as his playing went. But age was still an issue. And what was he like? Gene was busy that night, so I offered to have dinner with Frankie. Deep down, I wanted to ask him about the old days.

We went to a little hamburger place in Santa Monica, and I confessed to seeing him in the sixties. He was pretty

shy about that, like it was from another life. He said he'd
been away from the stage for a while, and he hadn't had a
recording deal in a long time. I said, "Is that why you want
to be in KISS?" And he looked down, almost sheepish, and
he said, "No. To be honest, my daughter loves you guys."

I said, "How old is your daughter?"

He said, "She's eight. She loves the outfits and the makeup
you guys wear. And she's never really seen me onstage. So
I thought, if I were in a band that she liked, that would be a
good memory for her."

And I said, "Are you kidding me?"

And he smiled and said the older you get, the more you
want your kids to know about you.

Well, I'd heard a lot of people say why they wanted to be
in KISS, but that was a first. I wasn't sure how to respond.
But I did tell him, "You know, Frankie, we're not wearing
the makeup anymore." And he was stunned, like his daughter would be heartbroken.

"Why not?" he asked.

"Some people think makeup means we're not serious."

"Little Richard wore makeup," he said. "Jimi Hendrix
wore makeup. David Bowie, too."

I said, "You played with those guys?" And he said oh yeah,
he'd played with all of them.

I couldn't believe it. It was like talking to rock and roll
history. Finally, I said, "Where have you been, man?" And
he said, "On an island." I thought he was joking, but he was

serious. I said, "You flew in all the way for this?" And he said his family was taking a long trip, working their way to Europe, and someone he knew in L.A. told him about the auditions. Then he looked at me and said, "You're *really* not wearing the makeup anymore?"

To be honest, I wanted him in the band—I thought it would be cool to have some history in KISS—but in the end, obviously, it didn't work out. He went wherever he was going and we went with a guy who was, like, twenty years younger than Frankie, and that was that. But a couple weeks later, I got a letter from him thanking me for the opportunity to audition and wishing us well. You know how often that happens in rock and roll? Never.

And at the bottom, in some crayon scribble, was a line from his daughter, saying "I love KISS!"

It's funny. In 1999, I got a chance to play the lead in *Phantom of the Opera* in Toronto. I'd never tried anything like that. But I went for it, partly because my son at the time was about five years old. And I remember thinking, "I want him to see me in this."

And then I remembered Frankie talking about his little girl. And he was right. At a certain point, your life is more about your legacy to your kids than anything else.

52

FOLLOW ME.

Up these steps.

The seats below are filling, and the priest is greeting the mourners. The funeral mass will begin shortly. Our story must soon finish. But there is a history in this basilica that we need to complete it.

Look inside this empty chamber. See the concrete floor and naked walls? This is where Frankie was born. It is also where, nearly four hundred years ago, a man named Pascual Baylón died. A poor Spanish monk with little education, Baylón was later canonized for his humble devotion to God—and the small miracles that happened around him. It is said that during his own funeral service, his eyes popped open to observe the Eucharist ceremony.

For centuries, his body lay interred in this church—until the night it was burned to ashes, the same night Frankie's mother, Carmencita, lost her life giving birth in this very chamber, bestowing Pascual's name on her son—Francisco de Asís Pascual Presto—in the hope that it might protect him.

But it already had.

There is a reason more people were not killed that night, a reason the church was nearly empty when the raiders arrived. Hours before, San Pascual performed one last miracle, this time from the world of the dead.

He signaled the church members to flee.

By clapping inside his tomb.

They heard the sound clearly.

Clap. Clap. Clap.

And they ran.

Warning music.

When Frankie returned to Spain, it should have been sounding again.

e⌒

"Maestro, could we visit the river today?"

"Why would we do that?"

"My papa took me once, to see the Pastoret statue. The little shepherd boy."

"So you have seen it. No need to go again."

"Do you know the story of the statue, Maestro?"

"Everyone in Villareal knows that story."

"Is it true?"

"Get the guitar."

"Is it true a little shepherd heard music from a cave?"

"The guitar—"

"And inside he found a statue of the Blessed Mary?"

"Francisco—"

"Is it true he brought the statue to the city—"

"Such foolishness—"

"And the next day it disappeared?"

"Enough—"

"And when the people went back to the caves, they heard music and found the Mary statue again?"

"Enough! Does music come from caves?"

"No, Maestro."

"No, it does not. It comes from practicing. Which you are not doing."

"So the story is not true?"

"I will tell you what is true. If Mary wanted to stay in a cave with her music, why does the shepherd need to disturb her?"

"Yes, Maestro."

"Why do people need to disturb other people?"

"Yes, Maestro."

"Don't go back looking for things. Leave well enough alone in this life. Understand?"

"Yes, Maestro."

"Now start playing. I am not getting any younger."

The family stepped out of the airport and into the blinding sunshine. Frankie's eyes began to hurt. He found his sunglasses, and as they drove down the coast, he gazed out the window, realizing he had forgotten much of his country's color; the pastel houses, the orange groves, the whitecaps breaking up the blue Mediterranean Sea. What he had not forgotten, he had buried in his mind, including all his memoires of Baffa Rubio, having never forgiven the man's deceptions.

It was Aurora's idea to return. They had already visited California, New Orleans, and London, where Aurora saw her mother for the first time in years. Around an oblong wooden table, they shared a dinner of roasted beef and cabbage, and Aurora endured her mother's glares at the foreign child they were calling their own.

"If I can handle that," Aurora told Frankie that night, "you can handle Spain."

"It's not the same."

"Do you think your father is alive?"

"He's not my father."

"So you won't see him?"

"He's not alive."

"What if he were? Wouldn't you speak to him?"

"And say what?"

"And say you lived. Say you have a wife and a child. Say thank you."

"You don't thank people for lying."

"Francisco—"

"I don't want to go."

"We're going."

"Why is this so important for Kai?"

"Not just Kai."

"I don't want to go."

She hooked her fingers in his.

"You said that already."

On his own, he would never have made the trip. But with his wife holding one hand and his daughter holding the other, he was led back to this hot country.

And all the secrets it held.

$\sim$

Spanish life had changed dramatically since the 1940s. The dictator Franco was dead, and the country he'd held down for so long was slowly rising. Frankie barely recognized Villareal. The streets were paved, and cars commanded the roads where horses and bicycles once traveled. There was a sports stadium now and a large hospital and many new shops along the Calle Mayor.

Frankie walked his family through a busy plaza, past a weeping willow garden, and along an irrigation canal into which Francisco Tárrega had once been thrown by his caretaker, just as Frankie had once been thrown into a river. He avoided sharing any stories about Baffa Rubio, although he could feel Aurora's silent urging as she walked beside him.

In the end, it was young Kai who changed Frankie's mind. They had gone to a park to see La Panderola, the old steam train that had stopped running decades earlier. Only the engine and a passenger car remained, lodged under an awning.

"We used to chase this train," Frankie told Kai.

"Who?"

"The children."

"Why?"

"It was fun."

"What if you fell on the tracks and the train was coming?"

"That would not happen."

"What if you ran like this"—she darted in front of the old car—"and you fell, ooh."

She dropped, laughing, and Frankie swooped in and lifted her high.

"Then my papa would save me at the last second!" he bellowed.

When he put her down, he noticed Aurora looking at him, her eyebrows raised. Frankie sighed.

"Come with me, Kai," he said. "I'm going to show you where I grew up."

ᄋᄉ

The house on Calvario Street had been painted a lemony shade, and the windows were new. The lower door frame still contained two slots for cart wheels. Otherwise, the place seemed as modern as the homes surrounding it.

"There it is," Frankie said.

"You lived there, Papa?"

"As a boy."

"Who else lived there?"

"The man who took care of me—and our dog."

"Where were your mama and papa?"

"In heaven."

He opened his palms to Aurora as if to say, "Enough? Can we go?" but the child darted free and banged on the door.

"Kai, why did you do that?" Frankie yelled, grabbing her arm.

"Stop," Aurora said. "She's just curious."

The door eased open. A smallish woman with a shawl on her shoulders peeked out.

"*Sí?*"

Frankie straightened up, then spoke in Spanish.

"I am very sorry, señora. We did not mean to disturb you. My daughter was—"

"Do you speak English?" Aurora interrupted.

"A little," the woman said.

"*No es necesario*—" Frankie said.

"My husband used to live here as a boy. In this house. Your house."

"*Sí?*" The woman looked at Frankie. "Ah," she added, her expression widening, "I see you before."

"Where?" Aurora asked.

The woman held up a finger. She disappeared for a minute, leaving the door open, then returned dragging a large box along the floor.

"Come, come," she said.

The three of them stepped inside, Frankie last. His heart was beating quickly. He glanced around, expecting to be hit with a wave of emotion. But everything was different. The paint. The photos. The furniture. Rooms are rooms, after all, as a music staff is a music staff. How you fill them is what makes them your own.

"*Mira*," the woman said. She lifted a thin blanket from atop the box, and pulled out an old record album. "Is you, yes?"

It was the cover to Frankie's first release, a Spanish import.

"Papa, look!" Kai exclaimed, grabbing the record. But Frankie's eyes had already shifted to some other contents of the box. An old radio. A dog leash. And his *braguinha*.

"Was that your guitar?" Aurora whispered.

"Where did you get this?" Frankie asked the woman.

"A man bring. Long time ago. He say leave in house if family come to get. No family come."

"Which man?"

She wiggled her fingers, searching for the word in English, then gave up.

"*El hombre del cementerio.*"

"What did she say?" Aurora asked.

"The man from the cemetery," Frankie said.

୧ン

Music has long been a part of your death rituals. Requiem masses. Hymns. A bugler blowing "Taps." As a talent, I cannot grieve. But you certainly grieve through me. Your most passionate compositions are often inspired by loss.

The requiem for Baffa Rubio arrived late, in the form of his adopted son, Francisco, who wandered through the Cementerio Municipal, searching crypts for a name. It was not a place young Frankie had ever visited. During his childhood, the Franco forces would pull citizens from their homes and line them up against the cemetery's exterior walls, then shoot them dead. Many of them carried pieces of my talent, and were buried with their songs unsung. Their bones fill an anonymous tomb, and bullet holes in the walls are their only markers.

Baffa had kept his son away from such a place. But now, inside it, Frankie searched for Baffa's name, walking past burial vaults stacked four high, some marked by images of Jesus or the Virgin Mary, others boasting fresh flowers. He found nothing. No record of a Rubio. And no one could recall who might have delivered a box of his possessions to the house on Calvario Street. Too many years had passed. All clues had vanished. The son was left wondering, once again, where his papa could be.

Aurora and Kai had waited outside, to allow Frankie his private discovery. When he emerged, as vacant as he had entered, he saw them sitting on a bench in the sunshine, little Kai clinging to his old record album. He tried to imagine what Baffa must have thought when he first saw that disc. Did he discover it in a store? Did someone give it to him? Did he wonder why Frankie's name had been changed? Why he never got in touch? Did Baffa listen to the music? Could he hear inside the slick production the voice of a boy who once sang in his garden?

Frankie grew dizzy from the breadth of it all and leaned back against the cemetery's wall. When he touched it, he felt a sudden rush of horrible memories, as if those bullet holes were screaming a thousand silent stories into his soul. One of them, he sensed, belonged to Baffa.

He jerked away.

"Francisco?" Aurora said, seeing him. "Are you all right?"

He staggered forward, embraced her, and held her for a full minute. He saw Kai staring up at him lovingly, the record album leaned against her mouth. He realized, at that moment, that this little girl was not his flesh and blood, yet the way she looked at him was the way he once looked at Baffa Rubio, wide-eyed, trusting, loving, secure. He also realized that, had it not been for the fat sardine maker, Frankie might have never heard music, never learned guitar, never known the hairless dog, or been in the woods to meet Aurora—and if that had never happened, there would be no little girl right now, holding his album and squinting in the sun.

He wiped his eyes and walked his family to a nearby fountain. They sat down.

And he told them everything about his papa.

53

HAD THEY ALL LEFT THAT DAY, OUR STORY WOULD BE different. But then, had many of you left places even one day earlier, the landscape of your lives would be rearranged. You cannot unplay your notes. Time, like music, is indelible that way.

They were heading back to England, Frankie, Aurora, and Kai, to visit Aurora's sister and then return to New Zealand. On their last night at the hotel, Frankie had a vivid dream. He dreamed about walking behind Baffa, up the stairs above a laundry. He saw Baffa wiping his brow, and urging young Frankie to sing. He saw a door opening, and got his first look at a tall, bearded figure with dark glasses.

And then everyone was gone.

The next morning, Aurora awoke to see Frankie sitting by the window.

"What's wrong?" she said.

"There's something I need to do here."

"So we'll stay."

"I should do it myself."

She narrowed her gaze.

"Everything's all right," Frankie assured her. "Go to your sister's. You already have the tickets. I'll be there in a few days."

"Promise?"

"Promise."

He drove them to the airport, kissed them good-bye, then drove back to Villareal.

To search for El Maestro.

                      ᶜ⁓

Perhaps you are wondering why this did not happen sooner? A fair question, for Frankie had never stopped thinking about his teacher. He remembered every instruction, every scolding. Each time he lifted the guitar, he pictured El Maestro's face, the tousled dark hair, the unkempt beard, the dark glasses. Was he still alive? What might he look like? How would he get around? A blind man in his seventies? Would he even remember the child he took in?

And what would he think of Frankie's career?

It was this last question, in truth, that had kept the former student away this long. For all his successes, his gold records, his concerts, Frankie was sometimes ashamed of how he'd achieved them. El Maestro had lectured him on the purity of music, the dedication to playing the guitar and the dangers of silly distractions. Yet Frankie had become hugely popular (and wealthy) on relatively simple songs. The guitar hardly mattered. His voice and good looks were what sold him to the public. His dancing only added to his popularity. Some of what he'd done, Frankie feared, might actually disgust his mentor.

"Why did you behave like a fool?" he could hear him say. No amount of fame or wealth diminished that. His time in El Maestro's small flat above the laundry had been the closest Frankie ever came to my stark beauty, my melodic seduction. In drifting from that, he feared he'd drifted from El Maestro's grace.

This, I should note, is often the relationship between mentor and mentee. Witness my French composer Henri Duparc, who grabbed a considerable piece of me at his birth in the nineteenth century. He created some inspired works, beautiful blends of orchestra and voice. Yet he so revered his mentor, the German composer Richard Wagner, that in 1885, when Duparc was just thirty-seven years old, he stopped composing altogether and eventually destroyed all his work, burning his transcriptions, certain they were not worthy of the man he looked up to.

A teacher's shadow can hover for life. Of course, Frankie could not know that this teacher was also his father. Nor could he know that, in searching for him now, he would not like what he found.

Instead, he rose early, had an espresso in the hotel, and retraced a familiar course through the streets, a journey he had often made with a green wagon and an oversized guitar. How many times had he walked this route, wearing a cap and short pants, mumbling the information he was certain El Maestro would demand? "*Which composer wrote that piece? . . . What is the* rasgueado *technique in flamenco?*" Those memories flooded back now with each step Frankie took. He could feel his pulse quickening like the nervous student he once was.

But when he turned the corner onto Crista Senegal Street, his body sagged. The laundry was gone, replaced by a square office building with a P sign for parking. No blue shutters. No steps to climb. Just a glass-enclosed entrance and a yellow-gated garage.

It was as if someone had bulldozed his memory.

Frankie sat on the curb. He felt the morning sun on his neck. He could not give up so quickly. Where else? he thought. Only that last day had they ventured far from this corner. He reconstructed, in his mind, their final stops, but he could not recall the location of the stores, the restaurant, or even the guitar maker who had handed El Maestro the instrument that Frankie still played today.

But he remembered the *taberna*.

He wondered if it was still there.

ℰↄ

"A blind man, you say?"

   "Yes. Tall. Dark hair."

   "No, señor. I do not recall."

   "It was a long time ago."

   "My father was the owner then."

   "Is he still alive?"

   "No, señor—"

   "It's important I find this man—"

   "—but *you* look familiar."

   "That does not matter."

   "Wait . . . You are the American. The actor!"

   "No—"

   "The singer?"

Frankie pursed his lips.

   "Ah! I am right? Yes?"

   "Yes."

   "Your name is Presto."

   "Yes."

   "You are from here, señor?"

   "As a boy."

   "Villareal?"

   "Yes."

   "This I did not know."

   "I had a different name."

   "This is why you speak Spanish! *Increíble!*"

The owner yelled to his bartender, who was setting out chairs. A dishwasher looked up as well. They nodded at the news.

" '*I want to love you,*' " the bartender bellowed. " '*I will be true . . .*' "

His accent sounded like a bad imitation. Frankie forced a smile.

"Señor, please, would you honor us by playing on our stage?"

"Playing?" Frankie said.

"Tomorrow night. We have the large band on Fridays. They would be most happy to include you."

"I'm not here to play—"

"You will be our guest—"

"I only wanted to—"

"You were here as a boy—"

"Yes, but—"

"You return as a man! Is perfect, no?"

Frankie exhaled. He looked around the *taberna*, just opening for business, the chairs being taken off the tables. The place was dimly lit and smelled of alcohol and bleach. Frankie did not mention that he had already played here once. Or that he remembered it vividly. He felt it every time he stepped on a stage. The cheers turning to boos. The banging glasses. The way El Maestro forced him to take a bow.

Maybe he should play, he thought. There were demons in this place he had long sought to silence. He had made a certain peace with his papa's memory. Was it time to do the same with that final night?

"I'll think about it," he said.

"Please do," the owner replied. "We will make a special meal for you. Lovely food. Drink. Music."

"Is there anyone else who might know the man I'm looking for?"

The owner scratched his chin. "Perhaps the musicians. Some of them are quite old. They work cheaper that way, eh?"

He grinned and raised a glass of orange juice. "To your return, señor!"

Frankie nodded and walked out the door.

⁓

Later that day, Frankie went to the Villareal city hall, to see if there were any records of his teacher. He had to fill out a form and was told it would take several days for a response. When Frankie mentioned El Maestro was a guitarist, he was directed to a round-faced man named Jacinto, who served as a cultural delegate. Jacinto said he could not recall a blind guitar teacher, but offered to show Frankie a room honoring the beloved guitarist Francisco Tárrega. There were photos and letters and sheet music and the large plaster bust that was once carried through the streets of San Felix. There were also several of Tárrega's beloved guitars in glass cases, including the first one he had made by the venerable Antonio de Torres Jurado, the famous nineteenth-century luthier from whom most acoustic guitars today can trace their roots.

Frankie noticed it was damaged, with breaks and stains that had not been repaired.

"Do you know the story of this guitar?" Frankie asked Jacinto.

"I do, señor," the man said, straightening up as if making a presentation. "It was one of Tárrega's favorites. He played it for twenty years. When he was forced to replace it from too much use, he sought out a man to restore it. After many attempts, the man succeeded."

"And?"

"Tárrega and his guitar were reunited."

"So he left it behind when he died?"

"Yes and no, señor. Tárrega left the guitar to his family, but in time, his brother Vincente sold it. He thought he was selling it to the famous musician Domingo Prat, a disciple of Tárrega's who lived in Buenos Aires. So he put it on a ship and sent it to South America.

"But when it got there, it did not go to the great Domingo Prat. Instead, it went to a ten-year-old girl. Over the years, it fell into disrepair."

"In South America?" Frankie said.

"Yes."

"How did it get back here?"

"A former student of Tárrega's discovered it years later in Buenos Aires, in a house, lying on a couch. He helped arrange for its return to Spain."

Frankie gazed at the guitar, which had a break in the body near the neck, and was missing pieces of the rosette that framed the sound hole.

"Why did he bother? It's broken."

"Just the same, señor," the man said. "It belongs back where it made its best music, does it not?"

Frankie stared at the instrument. He wished El Maestro could have seen it or, even better, played it in its healthier days. Connected to the great Francisco Tárrega? How he would have loved that! Frankie thanked Jacinto and left the building. But for the rest of the day he thought about that guitar's journey: made here, shipped on a boat, misdirected, knocked about, now returned to native soil.

It belongs back where it made its best music.

He decided he would play at the *taberna*. To honor his teacher.

And, if possible, to summon him.

℮

Homecomings in music are never predictable. Some are raucously successful (the rock musician Bruce Springsteen playing in New Jersey), some are bittersweet (the Russian pianist Vladimir Horowitz returning to Moscow after sixty years of exile), and some are, frankly, less than they were hoped to be.

Frankie's homecoming was hastily arranged, so the crowd would be mostly regulars. Still, Frankie hoped the word might spread; if El Maestro was alive, perhaps he would hear that his student had returned. Villareal was still not that big, right?

He arrived early with his guitar. There were men outside smoking by a row of motorcycles. Inside, he noticed the stage was wider than it had once been, and the house band, slowly arriving, was a nine-piece ensemble, whose musicians ranged from middle-aged to quite old. Frankie went over material with the bandleader, a thin-armed piano player. Unlike forty years earlier, foreign songs were now commonly performed in Spain, and the man nodded with each of Frankie's selections.

Frankie chose a variety of material. Determined to erase the bad memories of this place, he selected a few of his own compositions, "I Want To Love You" and "Our Secret," but also instrumentals like "St. Louis Blues," "Tiger Rag," and Django Reinhardt's "Parfum," along with any other song he could remember from El Maestro's last performance on this stage.

The crowd shuffled in. Seats were taken. Drinks ordered. The lights went down.

Few people noticed a heavily clothed figure taking a chair in the back.

The owner gave Frankie an ebullient introduction, to polite applause, but with each number, the ovations intensified, as Frankie grew more focused on the memory of that last night. He played Ellington, Schumann, and Tárrega as El Maestro had taught him, as if the next best thing to finding his old teacher would be to conjure up his spirit. He blazed through several flamenco numbers, pleasing the Spanish audience. When he sang his famous songs, the patrons cheered, delighted that the man who'd made these records was actually here in Villareal.

Frankie took no breaks. He never left the stage. Drinks were replenished, more cigarettes smoked. For nearly two hours, the guitarist's music grew ever more piercing. An old *jota* melody. A Muddy Waters blues.

For his last number, he chose a very specific song: "Avalon." It was the first thing he'd ever played for an audience, on this very stage in 1945, and the only piece he'd ever performed with his beloved teacher.

As he started the first chords, beads of sweat trickled down his forehead. He pictured El Maestro sitting alongside him, whispering the old words, urging him on.

"Sing the song."
"But I don't want to."
"Why not?"
"I'm scared."

"*Yes. And you will be scared again. All your life. You must
   conquer this. Face them and pretend they aren't there.*"
"*Maestro——*"
"*You can do it. Always remember I said you can do it.*"

As the band fell in behind him, Frankie noticed the
crowd's bobbing heads and tapping fingers. The beat grew
louder, and some patrons clapped along. Frankie sang:

*I found my love in Avalon
Beside the bay,
I left my love in Avalon
And sailed away.*

He looked at the owner, who was clapping with the rest
of them.

*I dream of her in Avalon
from dusk till dawn
So I guess I'll travel on
To Avalon.*

While part of him braced for history to repeat, there was
no protest this time, only enthusiasm, and Frankie found
himself looking left and right, in some deluded hope that he
would see El Maestro at a table, smiling from behind his dark

glasses, a cigarette dangling from his mouth. Deep down, this had been his wish for years, seeking what every student desperately seeks from a beloved teacher: final approval.

It did not happen. Frankie completed his spirited solo and reached the last lyrics like a runner crossing the finish line. He hit three chords to end it, the last one ringing out to the crowd, and he bowed his head. The owner jumped to his feet and the others followed, standing in a noisy shower of appreciation.

Frankie slowly rose and held up his guitar. He thought of Tárrega's long-lost instrument and was overwhelmed suddenly by the deepest longing he'd ever felt in his life: to see his old teacher one more time.

Instead he got an ovation. He forced a smile. Homecomings are never predictable. And there are few things emptier than applause when you feel you don't deserve it.

$e\sim$

A music arranger has a difficult task, coordinating instruments into a mellifluous blend. What happened next in Frankie's story can best be told as a series of arranged sounds, coming together to reach a climactic finish.

There was high applause, like soaring violins, when Frankie finished his show. Then bass lines of adult conversation as patrons discussed it on their way out. There were

the percussive sounds of the band breaking down, pack-
ing up their horns and cymbals, and the soft scribbling of
Frankie signing autographs for older fans who remembered
his records.

There was the enthused baritone of the owner, asking
Frankie to return anytime. There were soft vocals like tick-
led piano keys between Frankie and several musicians, and
questions about a blind man that rose in hope and sank in
disappointment, like a glissando on a flute.

Later, with the place nearly empty, there was the sound
of the back door creaking open as Frankie stepped into the
alley where he'd once escaped in a car.

And, finally, the sound of a match being lit.

℮

"I know you," a voice said in Spanish.

Frankie saw the orange glow of a cigarette tip.

"How do you know me?"

"That song. I have not heard it in many years. But I could
never forget it. You are Francisco."

"And you are?"

"Drunk."

"Your name, sir?"

"You don't know me? I was playing onstage with you all
night. In the back."

An old man wobbled out from the shadows, clearly inebriated. His hair was sparse and curled white. His shoulders were stooped beneath a draping jacket.

"The congas," he said.

Frankie tilted his head curiously. The old man placed two fingers around his lips.

"Years ago, I wore a mustache. You see?"

He lowered his hand.

"I am Alberto."

Frankie's eyes widened. "Alberto," he whispered.

"Yes."

"You drove with us that last night . . ."

"I did."

Frankie felt his heart racing.

"Alberto, please, I have been looking for El Maestro. My teacher—your friend. He—"

"I know who he is."

"Do you know *where* he is?"

Alberto scanned Frankie's face.

"Yes."

"He's *alive*?"

"No."

Frankie felt his stomach drop.

"When did he die?"

"Stop this game. You know the truth."

"What truth?"

Alberto dropped his cigarette. He inhaled with a sniff and tried to stand up straight.

"You want me to say it? Fine. I killed him."

Frankie swallowed.

"What do you mean?"

"What do I mean?" Alberto said, looking away. "What do I mean? You want me to play it on the skins of a drum? I killed him. It is why you are here. Stop playing with me. Get it over with."

Frankie felt his insides shaking, the start of his soul breaking loose from his body. When he spoke, there was no air getting to his lungs, and his voice no longer sounded like his voice.

"Explain yourself, Señor Alberto."

Alberto lifted his eyebrows.

"No one sent you?"

"Sent me?"

"To avenge his death."

"I don't understand."

"I pushed him into the sea. Just after your ship left."

"But why—"

"Money. A bag of money. It was stolen from me a week later." His head dropped. "So now you know."

"But you *liked* him."

"I did."

"He trusted you. . . ."

"A mistake."

"For money?" Frankie whispered.

"Yes. Yes! I am a thief! All right?" When he said it, he seemed beaten, his voice a shaky bassoon. But then it rose to an angry pitch, fueled by alcohol and years of guilt. He began to sway. "For money! For money!"

He reached beneath his coat and whipped out a gun. He pointed it straight at Frankie's chest.

"Give me yours!"

"No, please—"

"Give it to me! If you won't take revenge, then I will take what you have. Give me your money. Or maybe I'll kill you, too."

Frankie held up his hands. He opened his fingers. In the lamplight, Alberto saw the scars covering Frankie's left palm. He leaned in, blinking.

"What did you do to yourself, Francisco?" he whispered. "How can you play that way? . . ."

Frankie grabbed his arm and jerked it up quickly. The old man was wobbly and no match for Frankie's strength. He dropped the gun. It fell to the pavement. He squeezed his fists around Frankie's shirt collar.

"Kill me, Francisco." His voice was a guttural plea, and tears rolled down his cheeks. "Forty years, I live with this sin. Forty years, I wonder if Maestro comes for me. Take his revenge! Now!"

Frankie stared at Alberto's face, the crying eyes, the rotted teeth. He felt blood rushing to his brain. This was his answer? El Maestro was gone? A weeping conga player had killed the most powerful man he'd known?

A silent rage descended on my disciple. He pushed away from the old man.

"Nothing?" Alberto said. He stumbled off, drunkenly. "Then good-bye to you, stupid boy."

Frankie stared.

"Señor Alberto."

"Stupid . . . stupid . . ." the man mumbled.

"Señor Alberto . . ."

Frankie picked up the gun. Alberto turned. Frankie held the barrel high.

Alberto charged toward him.

"No, Francis——!"

Frankie pulled the trigger three times.

Alberto crumpled.

Frankie dropped the gun, stunned. A wisp of smoke came from its mouth, the shape of a music rest.

Inside the *taberna*, an old guitar leaned against a wall, its fifth string now a burning shade of blue.

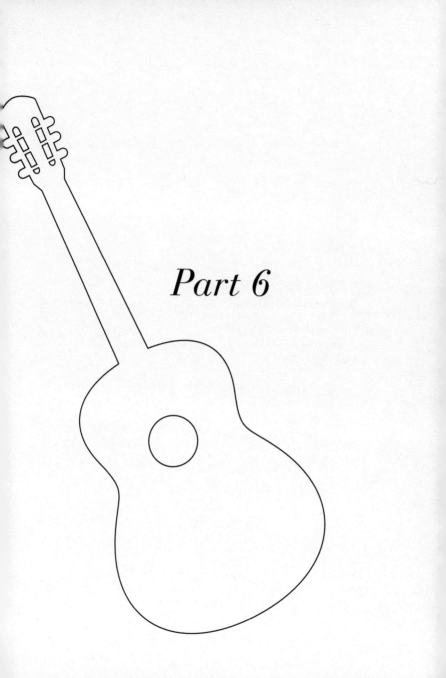

Part 6

54

1943

"Maestro?"

"What is it?"

"I have done something wrong."

"What?"

"I have broken a string."

"Were you throwing your guitar?"

"No, Maestro."

"Were you using it as a toy?"

"No, Maestro."

"How did you break it?"

"I was practicing."

"Your scales and exercises? Or the silly songs I have warned
   you to stay away from?"

"Not the silly songs."

"So you were doing the proper thing?"

"Yes, Maestro."

"And a bad thing happened."

"Yes, Maestro."

"Give me the guitar."

"Here, Maestro."

"We will repair your damage."

"Yes, Maestro."

"Help me run a new string through the tuning peg . . ."

"It is through now, Maestro."

"And you tied it off?"

"Yes, Maestro."

"Now listen to how you tune. The string starts low. But you
  turn the peg and the tension makes it rise."

"I see, Maestro."

"You turn until it sounds like this . . . You hear? . . . That
  is how a new string finds its place."

"What if you kept turning and turning?"

"The string would snap. You cannot ask things to do what
  they are not meant to do, Francisco. Eventually, they
  will break."

"Maestro?"

"Yes?"

"I did a bad thing."

"You have told me this."

"I was not doing my exercises. I was turning the peg until
  the string broke."

"So you lied to me?"

"Yes, Maestro . . ."

"And you also broke the string."

"Yes, Maestro."

"And now you feel guilty."

"I'm sorry, Maestro . . . I'm sorry . . ."

"Cry. You should cry. Cry like the lying boy you are."

Wynton Marsalis

Trumpeter, composer, Grammy winner; artistic director, Jazz at Lincoln Center

FRANKIE PRESTO DIDN'T SPEAK FOR THREE YEARS. HOW many musicians can say that? Three years, man. Not a word. Just played his guitar in a monastery. That's where I met him. He blew me away. The key to learning music is humility, see? If you want me to talk about Frankie Presto, I have to start with that. I mean, it takes a very rare humility not to talk for *three years*. . . .

Spain? Yeah. I come here a lot. I spent twelve years writing a piece for a festival in Vitoria—Spanish music with American blues—and when I finished, they built me a statue. I'm serious, man. A statue. They love their jazz here.

But my first visit was in 1987, and I'll never forget it. That's when I found Frankie. We'd done some shows and we were driving back to Barcelona when I spotted this castle up in the hills. The translator said it was a monastery. She asked if I wanted to see it. I said absolutely. I'm from

New Orleans. It's not every day you see monks walking around.

Well, this place was exquisite. Nine hundred years old. The architecture, the stones, light pink, faded gold, like nothing you see today. And man, it was *quiet*. Dead quiet. I wandered off, got a little lost. When it's silent like that, I like to walk and get ideas.

All of a sudden, I heard music. I said to myself, "I must be crazy, because that sounds like the blues." Like Leadbelly or Albert King. I thought maybe some jazz angel was gonna pop out and start a conversation, you know?

I came down past this fountain, under a little bridge, and that's when I saw this guy, by himself, with a guitar. He had his back to me, so I just froze and listened. Man, it was some of the most beautiful playing I've ever heard. Not only the speed and the dexterity. But the *story* it was telling. Music is about communication, see? It's about baring your soul in the notes, telling your tale. That's how you play. I didn't even know this guy, but from his music, the way he was bending those strings, I could tell he was hurt and was searching for something.

When he stopped, I said, "Excuse me," and he spun around. I didn't want him to jump and run away, so I put my hands in front of me like I'm praying, and he's watching me get closer, and I whisper, "I'm very sorry to disturb you." He doesn't respond. "Your playing is beautiful." Now

I'm a few feet from him. His head is shaved, he's got blue eyes, nice-looking older Spanish guy, you know? He's wearing a robe, but not the white robes like the other monks.

I say, "My name is Wynton Marsalis. I'm a musician from America. I play the trumpet." And he looks at me real hard—for like ten seconds he just stares at me—and then I see he's starting to cry. And I say, "I'm sorry. Did I say something wrong?" And he's shaking his head, still crying, and I keep saying I'm sorry and he's got a little pad and paper, and finally, he writes down four words.

"I knew your father."

Well, come on, now! I'm in Spain, in the mountains, in a monastery, and this monk is playing the blues and saying he knew my father? That's some crazy stuff. So I say, "What is your name, sir?" And he writes down, *"Frankie"* and then *"Presto."*

And it all comes back to me.

My father's a musician, too, you know, and he *did* know Frankie Presto, back in New Orleans, in the fifties, when they were both kids and gigging around town. They used to play jam sessions at this joint called the Dew Drop Inn. When I was growing up, I heard the name "Frankie Presto" more than I wanted to—like whenever I didn't want to practice my horn. My father would tell me about this young white guitar player and how, when he was my age, he was already gigging—and he didn't have a mother or father to push him. And how he created a different sound, a sort of classical/blues blend, and other cats came out just to hear him. In New Orleans, if you can play, musicians know it. Doesn't matter how old you are. Music tells the truth. And they said Frankie Presto could make a guitar spit out the truth, even though he left eventually to become a rock and roll act.

So here we both were, years later, in this monastery, about as far from the French Quarter as you can get, you know? And I said, "Are you allowed to talk?" And he nodded. And I said, "It's not against the rules?" He shook his head. "But you're not talking?" And he shook his head again. "How long?" I said. He held up three fingers. And I said, "Three months?" And he shook his head no. "Three years?" And he nodded yes.

Man, listen. Three years of silence? Part of me just wanted to leave him alone. But part of me felt like I had come there for a reason, because it was all too much coincidence, you know? So I asked him, "Why are you in here, Mr. Presto?"

And he wrote, *"Penance."*

Now, I've known a lot of guys who have been in trouble, a lot of cats I grew up with were incarcerated, so I'm not shy about it. I just asked him straight out, "Did you kill somebody?" Because that's how it was shaping up to me. And he shook his head no, then he wrote, *"But I was ready to."*

I said, "That's not the same thing."

And he tapped his heart, as if to say, "*It is in here.*"

Later, I understood that. He was talking about intentions. That's important in music, too. Critically important. What you're thinking about can be what you become. Good *and* evil. But sitting with him, it seemed like he had done his time. Three years, man? For *thinking* about doing something bad? I asked if he had a family, and he nodded, and I asked, "Do they know you're here? Do you write to them?" and he nodded again and I said, "Don't they need you with them?" And he didn't say anything, but I could tell I'd hit a nerve. He was crying now without making a sound, tears falling like from eyedroppers, you know? I felt terrible for this guy. I said, "Mr. Presto, the music world could use you. I would love to record with you." And he wrote down, "*I don't want to perform anymore.*"

So I said, "Maybe you could teach."

For some reason, that ended the conversation. He took his guitar and walked away. I had to sit and absorb what had happened. I'm telling you, man, that was one of the craziest encounters I'd ever had—and no one else was there. I was wondering if anyone would believe me.

When I got back to the translator, I asked if we could talk to somebody in charge. She got me to an older monk and we sat down on a little bench in the refectory where they ate, and I said I knew Frankie Presto from a long time ago. The man said he couldn't discuss any of the brothers there. I asked if he knew what happened, who Frankie almost killed? Again he said he couldn't discuss anything. So I said, "What would it take to get him out of here?" And he seemed surprised. He said, "A novice can leave any time he chooses. He just has to walk out the door."

So after that, I went looking for him. I went back to the fountain and the bridge, but I couldn't find him. It was getting late, so we walked back to the little parking area, and there he was, sitting against the car, in regular clothes, holding his guitar case. He stood up and looked at us, and he spoke, for the first time, in a real weak voice, like every word was scratching against his throat.

This is all he said. One sentence.

"Can you help me get home?"

55

LOOK. THE PALLBEARERS ARE GATHERING. THEY WILL CARRY Frankie's coffin to its final resting place. Do you see them there?

I will tell you who they are.

What they meant to Frankie.

And how he died.

But then I must be gone. There are new souls to tend to. New talent to dispense. So let us play this final movement in an *allargando* tempo—slowing, yet growing more majestic. It is worthy of the story, for the years, in the end, did elevate Frankie Presto.

I see one of the choir's selections is "Come to the Water." How fitting for a child once thrown in a river. Water was also the gateway to Frankie's journey home. Although Mr. Marsalis offered a plane ticket for his newly discovered friend, Frankie, coming out of monastic seclusion, was not yet ready for a rapid return to the world.

Instead, he went to the Barcelona harbor. There, seeking work for his passage, he joined a cargo ship, doing kitchen labor, and sailed with it to Italy. He joined another ship and sailed to Sri Lanka. Another took him to Singapore. And another to Australia and finally to New Zealand. He took solace in the vastness of the sea and how small his problems seemed in its wake. Each morning, he would gaze at the water, imagining the soul of El Maestro at rest; each night he sang devotionals on the deck, his prayers joining the splash of waves against the hull. Fellow sailors marveled at his voice. Some climbed up to sing along, another in Frankie's long list of bands, this one vocals only.

All told, he sailed for five months and 19,000 miles. Over those weeks, he made a certain peace with his less than peaceful past. For the first time in a long time, Frankie slept through the night. He found himself dreaming of Baffa Rubio, and the oranges they would share from a paper bag, and old Hampton, making Frankie pork stew in his tiny kitchen, and even the nuns in the orphanage and the meals they would serve after mass. He realized how many people it takes to keep one child alive in this world.

His final water journey was the shortest, a one-hour ferry, at sunset, from Auckland back to the island of Waiheke.

Where Frankie ended his exile.

ℯ

He stepped off the boat, carrying only his guitar case and a folded shirt. His skin was browned from the sun, his hair had grown back long, and his thick beard was flecked with gray. He moved slowly behind a group of passengers toting shopping bags or briefcases. In his mind, he envisioned the walk up the hill and around the road to the small beach that he last called home. He had not written that he was coming. He had not been sure, until that morning, that he felt ready for—or worthy of—a return to his old life.

But when the people cleared in front of him, he stopped, and his heart jumped.

There, sitting against the ticket booth, arms around her knees, was Aurora.

$$e\sim$$

She wore a long green dress, leather sandals, and dark sunglasses, which, upon seeing him, she removed. But she did not rise.

Frankie approached slowly.

"Aurora means dawn," he said.

"Not anymore."

"Do you come here every night?"

"I wait for the final ferry."

"How long do you wait?"

"Until the last person gets off."

"And then?"

"I go home."

"For three years?"

She looked away.

"Did you find what you were looking for, Francisco?"

"No."

"Will you keep looking?"

"No."

"You are done with that?"

"Yes."

"And you will stay with us?"

"Yes."

"We are not kids anymore."

"No."

"We are not in a tree."

"I know."

"You have a family now."

"You're right."

"You wrote that you were innocent."

"Of killing, I was."

"Yet you punished yourself."

"It was not punishment."

"It was to us."

"I know."

"Who killed that man?"

"They wouldn't tell me."

"Do you care?"

"I should always care."

She watched a gull land on the dock. It pecked at something then flew away.

"What does Aurora mean now?" Frankie asked.

"Glowing light."

"Why?"

"A teacher told Kai about glowing lights in the southern sky. They're called 'the Aurora.' "

"And?"

"Kai said that was me. I was a glowing light. And as long as I stayed in one place, you would find us and come home for good." She raised her eyes. "Is that what you've done?"

Frankie felt a choking in his throat. He had not known, when he stepped off the boat, what life would be there for him. Or any life at all. But Aurora's love had waited for him, as he had once waited for it. *Save the last dance.* He thought about that song. He looked at the cliffs. He looked at the small boats. He looked at Aurora, as beautiful as she ever was.

"I'm so sorry," he whispered.

"Do you want to see your daughter?"

"Desperately," he said.

She bit her lip. Then she grabbed and kissed him, as he grabbed and kissed her. Had you returned an hour later, you would have found them still there, locked in that embrace, refusing to let go.

╰

The mystery of Alberto the conga player I can only partly explain. Frankie had not killed him. That is true. He had lifted the gun, and as Alberto charged him, Frankie contemplated the worst thing he might ever do. But in the end, he'd fired into the air, three times, wanting only for Alberto to halt. When the old man went down, Frankie thought he'd fallen.

As it turned out, Alberto *had* been shot—but someone else had pulled a trigger, the bullet's noise melding with the sound of Frankie's shooting.

After forty years of inner torture, Alberto got his mortal peace.

By someone else's hand.

The police held Frankie for two days. Then they let him go. They said the real killer had come forth, that the bullets matched, and that Frankie's story about warning shots proved true. He demanded to know who the assassin was, but they would not tell him. Only that the person had surrendered voluntarily and was locked away. And it might be wise if Frankie left Villareal for a while.

He departed on foot that afternoon, lost in a swirl of disbelief: a man died in front of him, a gun was in his grip, the last witness to his childhood was gone, El Maestro had been dead all this time. Who killed Alberto? Had Frankie really been ready to take a man's life? He stumbled along the main road out of town and past the Mijares River, where a sardine maker and a hairless dog had once saved him. After days of walking and exhausting himself in thought, he came upon the monastery. He climbed the steps and asked if he could stay. The monks saw his guitar and inquired as to his church.

"Santuario de San Pascual Baylón," he answered.

They nodded with approval. Pascual Baylón had practiced the guitar himself, they noted, as a shepherd, more than four hundred years ago. They didn't know he had died in the same room where Frankie was born.

56

THERE IS ONE MORE MOMENT I MUST DETAIL FROM THE island years.

Shortly after Frankie returned, he was able to attend his daughter's twelfth birthday celebration. A table with a cake was set up on the beach, and a group of children joined Kai for the party. Reunited with her father, she was all but skipping on air.

As the sun went down, Frankie called Kai to the table and told her he had a gift for her. He fetched his battered guitar case.

"Papa, I don't want your guitar," she said.

"I know," he answered. "But maybe you want your own."

He opened the case to reveal a most unusual-looking instrument, a red guitar with white tuning pegs, its body colorfully painted with the image of a Spanish horseman and a beautiful young woman.

"Oh, Papa, is it for me?"

"All yours."

"Where did you get it?"

"Another country."

"Look at the horse!"

"And the señorita."

"So pretty."

"Like you."

"Will you teach me to play it?"

"If you want."

"Yes!"

She grabbed it and ran off with her friends. Aurora watched until they were out of earshot, then leaned over and touched Frankie's shoulder. "Where is *your* guitar?"

"I don't have it anymore."

"What did you do with it?"

"I left it behind."

"But the strings. Their power—"

"That's *why* I left it behind."

"It did good, Francisco."

"And bad. A string turned blue when Alberto died."

"You didn't kill him."

"He'd be alive if I hadn't gone there."

"That just means you affect people."

"I don't want to affect people."

"You can't help it."

"I can try."

"It was a gift—"

"I know—"

"From your teacher—"

"So is my playing——"

"And what your playing does to others."

"I am done with it, all right?"

They sat in silence. The tide splashed against the rocks.

"Francisco?"

"Yes?"

"What if something . . . happens?"

"Happens?"

"What if you need to affect someone else? What if you need to save a life?"

"Yours?"

"Hers."

She nodded toward their daughter, up the beach, shaking the guitar for her laughing friends.

"I'll have to do it myself," Frankie said.

And that was the last they spoke of it. In life, as in music, there are measures to play and measures to rest. For the first time since he was nine years old, Frankie Presto was without his precious guitar, which remained halfway around the world, under a bed inside a Spanish monastery.

With one blue string to go.

⁓

"Papa?"

"Yes, Kai?"

"My fingers hurt."

"Music is pain."

"Really?"

"It's something my teacher told me."

"What are these things?"

"Those are calluses."

"Why am I getting them?"

"Because you're learning. The more you play, the harder they will get."

"Yesterday they were bleeding."

"Yesterday you tried a lot of songs."

"I was terrible."

"No, you weren't."

"I'll be better today."

"You will."

"Can I get as good as you?"

"Maybe better. Are your nails cut short?"

"Yes . . . What's this chord?"

"That's a G."

"I like it. It's easy."

"Play your scales."

"The do-re-mis?"

"That's right."

"Papa?"

"Yes, Kai?"

"Did you always want to play guitar?"

"Maybe not. Maybe, at first, I just wanted to make my father happy."

Kai smiled. Her teeth had come in straight.

"Me, too."

"Back to your scales."

"These calluses are ugly."

"They will go away."

"And they'll stop hurting?"

"Soon."

"So music isn't pain?"

Frankie looked at his daughter, holding her first guitar. He felt a welling in his heart.

"Not always, no," he said.

Ingrid Michaelson

Recording artist, singer, songwriter

ALL RIGHT, BUT IT HAS TO BE QUICK . . . I'M SO LATE. THEY
haven't started, right? I just landed this morning and it took
a long time to get a car. . . .

Yes . . . uh-huh . . . my name is Ingrid Michaelson, I'm
from the States. I knew Frankie . . . well, when I knew
him, I didn't call him Frankie. He was Mr. Rubio. That's
what everyone called him. We didn't even know he was the
same guy.

A teacher . . . He taught guitar. There was this music
store where I grew up in Staten Island . . . It's a borough
in New York City . . . Yes, technically, it's an island, but
so is Manhattan . . . Anyhow, this music store was like every music store, I guess. Big, cramped, amplifiers lining
the walls, a room for drum sets, a room for keyboards, and
always a few teenage guys in the corner banging electric
guitar riffs.

It was like its own little theater, and I was into theater

when I was a kid—and music, since my parents made me take piano lessons—so I'd wander around the store, kind of watching the characters and listening to what everyone was playing. And they had these lesson rooms in the back, four or five rooms down a hallway, and you'd see kids lugging in instruments that were too big for them, oboes, violas—if they were lucky, they played the flute, because that didn't weigh much.

So one day I'm in the store, and this tall kid with a Mohawk is trying out a big Marshall amp, and he hits a guitar chord so loud my head almost explodes. I move to the rear to get away from the noise, and down the hall, in one of those lesson rooms, a door is open and I hear someone playing guitar. Classical. And then the Mohawk hits another E seventh or something—*whaammm!*—and I go deaf for a second, and then I pick up the classical playing, and a few seconds later, another explosion from rocker boy, and then the classical again. It was so weird, juxtaposing those two sounds. But also kind of cool.

I was curious about who was playing classical music—especially in that store. So I walk down the hall, pretending like I'm going for a lesson, and I peek in the door. There's this older guy with long hair just playing away, not minding all the noise. I come back the other way, another peek, he's still going, I turn, come back again. This time, he's playing these Spanish-sounding passages that were so fast but so melodic, like two hands playing at once, that I just stop dead in the middle of the doorway, hypnotized. And he looks up—I'm busted—and he says, "Barrios."

And I say, "Huh?"

"The composer is Barrios," he says. "It's called 'La Catedral.' You should always know whose work you are playing."

I just nod my head. I mean, I'm fourteen years old. He smiles, puts down the classical guitar and picks up an electric that's plugged into a little Fender amp—he's got, like, ten guitars in this room—and he starts playing some crazy wild rock. And he says, "Hendrix."

And I kind of shrug, because I didn't know Jimi Hendrix music back then. So he switches to something else. "Stevie Ray Vaughan?" he says. Again, I don't know it. Then he plays a lick from "Walk This Way" and says "Aerosmith?" and I'm like, yeah, I heard of that one!

And then I just blurt out, "Do you know any show tunes?"

Looking back, that was really lame, even if I *was* into theater. I mean, "Do you know any show tunes?" It's like something your grandmother would say. But he didn't mind. He picked up another guitar and played "Somewhere Over the Rainbow" so beautifully, it gave me chills. I loved Judy Garland anyhow, and I always loved that song, but I'd never heard it so melodic. When he finished, I said, "Can you teach me how to do that?" The way he played, you just wanted to *experience* it, to know what it felt like to have that kind of music come off your fingers.

He said I'd have to sign up for lessons, that was the store's policy. When I went home and asked my parents, they said I was already studying voice and piano and doing theater. That was plenty. Plus, a guy working in the back of a music shop wasn't what they had in mind. My father is a classical composer.

"But, Dad," I said, "he played Barrios." And my father was surprised. He said, "Agustín Barrios?" and of course, I couldn't remember the guy's first name, so that ended that little boast.

Anyhow, I went back to the store, like, a week later, and he was there again, in his room, and when he saw me he said, "Hey-hey, Miss Show Tunes," and he played a song from *Finnian's Rainbow* and sang a little. I asked him how he knew all this stuff and he said when he was a kid in Spain, he listened to the same records over and over again until he memorized them. I asked why he was living in New York if he was from Spain, and he said his daughter was also a guitar player, and she had gotten into Juilliard, so he and his wife moved up here to be with her.

I thought that was cool, that a whole family would move so their daughter could study music. I kept coming by, and eventually he said I could bring my guitar on Thursdays because some kid had paid for a whole year of lessons then disappeared, so he was free for that hour—as long as the kid didn't change his mind. He taught me some amazing things.

He could play anything with strings. Bass. Banjo. He was the first person to show me the ukulele and later I ended up using it a lot in my recordings.

But like I said, I had no idea that he was Frankie Presto. He said his name was Mr. Rubio, and that's how everyone referred to him. I only knew his first name because one day in the winter his wife brought him a sweater. She had an English accent and she said, "Layers, Francisco, layers. That's how you stay warm." *Lay-uhs, Francisco, lay-uhs.* I loved that.

Anyhow, they were the coolest old couple to me. She was really beautiful and British, he'd grown up in Spain, they'd lived on an island—a New Zealand island, not Staten Island—and they were supporting their daughter and he knew all these songs and he was still kind of cute, even at whatever he was, fifty-five or sixty years old.

I went there on Thursdays on and off for a couple of years. Sometimes we just talked about school or boys or having a career in music or theater. He mostly listened. He never told me that he'd been a rock star. Not once. The only advice he gave me, over and over, was, "*Don't let your music get out of your hands.*"

It didn't mean much then, but years later, when I started making records, it did. It was one of the reasons I kept the rights to my material, even when industry people were advising me differently.

I'll say this about Mr. Rubio. He kept a good secret. Looking back on it, I did notice some unusual "students" start to come into the store after he'd been there for a while. Older guys. Jazz musicians. One night I dropped by and I swear I saw Jon Bon Jovi going down that same hallway and ducking into Mr. Rubio's room. And Lyle Lovett—I mean it had to be him, he's pretty unique-looking. But I was still a teenager and was kind of clueless about the whole thing.

I went off to college at SUNY Binghamton, and one summer I came back and he was gone. The room was cleared out. When I asked what happened to Mr. Rubio, they said he and his wife had moved away, somewhere down South.

I never had a chance to say thank you or good-bye. I only found out who he really was when *Rolling Stone* did a story a couple of years ago about that bootleg album, *The Magic Strings* one? Crazy, huh? There's actually a few lines in my songs that were inspired by Mr. Rubio, like the line about sharing a sweater in "The Way I Am" or the line about moving to an island in a song called "Far Away." Over time, I guess all your teachers find their way into your music, right?

When I heard about how he died, I thought I should be at his funeral. For years, I'd been meaning to find him, to tell him how impressed I was that he never used his past to brag or to feel above teaching some awkward teenage girl how to play "Somewhere Over the Rainbow." I mean, how many people are really like that? Not many.

Oh . . . you hear that singing? I've got to get inside. . . .

57

FASTER NOW. THE SERVICE IS BEGINNING. LET US USE PASSING tones—notes in the melody that are not of the chords but connectors between them, like people you twirl during a square dance before returning to your partner. I will sum up the passing tones of Frankie Presto's remaining years—and detail only the major pillars—then bring us to his final days. Double time. A 2/2 signature.

Passing tones. In the calendar year of 1994, Frankie's family left the island of Waiheke (as you just learned). His daughter, Kai, was accepted into the prestigious Juilliard School in New York City (thanks to daily guitar lessons with her father.) Aurora and Frankie rented a row house on Staten Island. He was using the name Francisco Rubio now. The bootleg recording of *The Magic Strings of Frankie Presto* had grown legendary in guitar-playing circles and there were many people searching for the mysterious, missing guitarist—young musicians, opportunistic journalists, even a documentary filmmaker. Frankie had no interest. The past was the past. How strange, he thought, that the more he ran from the limelight, the more it pursued him.

But for a blissful stretch, it did not find him, and in his seven years on Staten Island, he lived a happily ordinary existence: he gained twelve pounds, purchased prescription sunglasses, saw his hair turn silver-gray, hurt his foot running, visited the coast of Maine, learned to make penne pasta with eggplant (Aurora's favorite), taught himself every solo by guitarist Charlie Christian, practiced yoga, fixed up vintage amplifiers, and purchased stacks of used CDs at a store in lower Manhattan, playing them for Aurora as she cooked late breakfasts.

He brought home a different guitar each week from a local music shop, where he'd taken a part-time teaching job, always returning the instrument after a few days' use.

"You will never be happy with any other guitar," Aurora would say.

"I'm happy right now," he would answer, disarming her by taking her hand.

Waters calm in even the stormiest seas, and Frankie and Aurora enjoyed these restful years with quiet gratitude, like climbers exhaling upon reaching a summit. They shopped each day at a local food market. They made friends with their neighbors and a woman who owned a Greek bakery. They discovered a park with a carousel for children, which Aurora would sometimes gaze at as if entranced. Frankie worried that she was thinking about the baby she'd lost, being back in the city where it happened, so he would take her hand and say, "Let's get a root beer," which had become her favorite beverage.

For her part, Aurora worked four days a week at a charity thrift shop, took up oil painting, rode her bicycle along the river, and spoke to Kai on the phone every evening, if only to say good night. On weekends, Frankie would sometimes play her new songs he had written and mix them in with old ones composed by someone else. She never failed to guess which were his.

"How do you always know?" he would ask.

"I can hear you in anything," she said.

She had encouraged her husband to teach, believing, with the Rubio name, he could keep his anonymity while still pursuing his passion. But over time, Frankie's copious talent became common knowledge at the music store (you cannot hold me down) and after the owner introduced him to a visiting young rock star—and the two men played several blues songs together—word spread that a master guitarist was laboring in a Staten Island retail outlet, and accomplished players, some very well known, began dropping by when they came to New York, some for tips, some for collaboration, some just to see if the rumors were true. The owner did not mind, as it brought prestige to his establishment, and he sold more guitars.

"Rubio" was how he was known (*"You going to see Rubio?"* *"I heard Rubio was cutting it up!"*), and at one point, Frankie wondered if it wasn't getting to be too much. He enjoyed the chance to play with talented artists away from a stage. But he was taken aback at how they pursued him. He had become, to his surprise, a rather good teacher, sharing small tips that went back to his days with El Maestro. Over a two-year span, by my count, Frankie was visited by—and consulted with—eighty-three professional musicians, including members of Bon Jovi, Pearl Jam, and the E Street Band, as well as the bassist Christian McBride, the guitarist Earl Klugh, the rhythm and blues singer KEM, and the singer/songwriter Warren Zevon.

Only a handful of visitors, including Lyle Lovett and Darlene Love, knew who he really was. They vowed to keep the secret and they kept their word.

But one day, at their rented house, the phone rang, Aurora answered, and a man who said he worked for *Rolling Stone* magazine asked, "Is Frankie Presto living there?"

Aurora quickly hung up.

ℓ◡

Passing tones. Kai graduated with highest honors. She joined a conservatory in Boston. With their daughter gone, Frankie and Aurora moved back to New Orleans. That phone call had concerned them. And Aurora had always been happiest in the Crescent City, where Frankie proposed marriage in front of the Mr. Bingle window display.

They bought a small apartment in the Garden District. Aurora made coffee for Frankie in the morning, and he made tea for her at night. One afternoon, she took him to a community center where she'd been volunteering, teaching art, and she told the children that Mr. Rubio was a musician. Before you knew it, he was guiding a young ensemble that included a piano, an electric bass, two drummers, a trumpet, and a chunky teenage boy with a trombone. They played funk and jazz and the drummer liked to rap. They called themselves the "Big Mess Band." Frankie found himself looking forward to their young enthusiasm, even if their technique was less than accomplished.

By my count, which is always accurate, this was the 372nd band that Frankie Presto had played with.

There would only be two more.

$\mathcal{e}$

The guitarist Les Paul was one of my disciples, blessed with gobs of me inside him and a curious mind that led him to innovations in the electric guitar, tape recording, and over-dubbing. As a teenager, he stretched a single string across a railroad tie and tried to amplify it with the insides of a telephone receiver. A few years later, he took a chunk of pine, attached a pickup, and invented a guitar they affectionately called "the log," the precursor of solid-bodied electrics played around the world today.

Yet his greatest gift was his perseverance. A car crash in 1948 left Paul and his wife, Mary Ford, in the bottom of a ravine, undiscovered for three hours. His ribs, nose, spleen, pelvis, and collarbone were damaged. But worst of all, his right arm was broken in multiple places, and the doctors considered amputation before finally setting it at a permanent right angle. He never stopped playing. Not then, not decades later, when arthritis chewed his body until his hands were more like claws. He continued to make music into his nineties, playing in a small club, refusing to let go of me.

In New Orleans, Frankie Presto saw his own body start to deteriorate, making his playing a challenge as well. Stiffness in his left hand was now a constant, and humid weather made it painful to complete a song. He needed reading glasses to follow musical transcriptions, and his lower back, from years of hunching over, left him permanently in distress, reaching behind with both hands when he rose and bending backward with a groan.

"I'm creaking," he would sigh to Aurora.

"Someone's getting old," she'd say.

"But not you."

"Nope. I could still climb a tree."

"Mmm," Frankie would grumble.

58

IN THE CALENDAR YEAR OF 2005, ONE YEAR BEFORE FRANKIE turned seventy, a great storm descended on the state of Louisiana. Homeowners were warned to evacuate, but many remained. Aurora had joined a nearby church, a small congregation in an old brick building. When forecasts of the storm became dire, most of the members departed, but the elderly priest vowed not to leave, no matter how high the water.

"You have to go," Aurora implored him.

"I started this church fifty-two years ago," he said. "If God wants me to perish here, so be it."

When Aurora told this to Frankie, he shook his head. All his life, he'd seen devotion and suffering go hand in hand.

"We're not staying," he said. Aurora agreed. But when Frankie pulled up with their loaded car, she was gone. Rain had already started. He drove quickly to the church, and found her there with several younger members, boarding up windows.

"What are you doing?" Frankie said.

"If he's going to stay, we have to help him."

"They're calling it a hurricane now. We need to leave."

"Just a few minutes."

As the winds outside blew stronger, Frankie helped where he could, holding up boards as others frantically drilled and hammered. Two teenage boys hurried a large wooden beam up adjoining ladders, rushing to get it positioned by the big window. They swung it too fast and it smashed through the glass. Rain blew in, and the first teen lost his balance and threw the beam in the air to grab the ladder, causing the other boy to do the same. The first boy fell off the ladder anyway, thudding to the ground, and others yelled, "Are you okay?"

"Yeah, yeah," he said. "Just landed hard."

Only then did Frankie hear a moan and look over to see Aurora on the floor, holding her head. The thrown beam had struck her from behind.

"Good Lord," the priest yelled, rushing to her.

Frankie pushed everyone out of the way and leaned over his wife. She was bleeding slightly from her scalp, and blinking her eyes.

"Help me get her to the car," Frankie yelled.

"It's fine, I'm fine," she said.

"Come on!"

A half hour later, dripping wet, they were in the emergency room of a hospital, where a doctor stitched the gash as Frankie watched the halls filling with patients, many of them older, arriving in fear of the storm that was upon them. Aurora was assured that the cut was not deep, but she had suffered a mild concussion, and was assigned a bed and instructed to stay awake for observation.

"I feel all right," she said. "Just a headache."

"Will we be safe here?" Frankie asked the doctor. "With the storm that's coming?"

"Yes, yes, of course," the doctor said, rushing off to other patients.

Within hours, the hurricane was blowing hard through New Orleans. That night, certain levees protecting the city broke. Rushing waters from Lake Pontchartrain (where Frankie first played with Elvis Presley) and the Mississippi River (where Frankie and Aurora walked as newlyweds) flooded the streets and raised water levels higher and higher, climbing the walls as if bringing their past back to them. The hospital became a repository for not only the sick and wounded, but for those seeking shelter, food, or protection. Power was lost. Doctors operated by flashlight. Food dwindled. Supplies were not replenished. Everyone from the lower floors was moved to upper ones, and the crowding made things even more uncomfortable. It was late summer and the heat became stifling. Some fixed windows were smashed for ventilation.

Throughout this pandemonium, Frankie never left Aurora's side. In the corner bed of a crowded room, he kept her awake with stories, conversation, even singing.

"I'm fine, you know," she whispered.

"I know."

"I'm not leaving you yet."

"No way."

"But I am going first."

"Is that right?"

"A long time from now."

"A long time."

"But still first."

"Not fair," Frankie said.

"Yes, fair," she replied.

"How do you figure?"

"If you die first, what do I have?" Aurora asked.

"You have Kai."

"True." She looked off. "But daughters have their own lives. You can't smother them. She'll get married. Have children."

"Well, I can ask the same thing," Frankie said. "If you go first, what would I have? Besides Kai?"

She looked at him as if he was joking.

"You'll have your music."

Frankie snorted lightly, but said nothing. (I, on the other hand, knew exactly what she meant.)

" 'Parlez-Moi d'Amour,' " Aurora said. "Sing it to me. Keep me awake."

"My French is rusty," Frankie said.

"You have to sing it." She grinned. "I'm the patient. It's a prescription."

He sighed and sang her the song as he remembered it, softly, until an elderly woman in the next bed turned their way and said, "Louder, *cher*. You got a sweet voice."

Frankie sang louder and the entire room—with six beds, close together—quieted in the darkness. The patients and their family members pulled open the thin curtains that separated them, grateful for the distraction of his performance.

Parlez-moi d'amour,
Redites-moi des choses tendres.
(Speak to me of love,
Tell me again, the tender things.)

When he finished, they clapped politely and someone said, "Do another!" Frankie rolled his eyes at Aurora as if to say, "Look at what you started," but Aurora smiled and yelled out—in a mock American accent—"Hey, fella, do you know 'I Want To Love You' by Frankie Presto?" An older man said, "That's an oldie but a goodie," and soon Frankie was singing the biggest hit of his career, with no accompaniment but the rain pounding on the windows.

I want to love you
I will be true

No one will love you
The way I do . . .

As he went on, the others slowly joined in, like a camp-fire sing-along, until everyone in the darkened room was contributing to the familiar tune, a high voice, a low one, an off-key screech, singing together in brave defiance of the storm outside.

Oh, if you let me
Show my love to you
Then by tomorrow
You'll love me tooooo!

They held on to the last word, someone rattled a spoon like a drumroll, and the others laughed and yelled, "Whoo-hoo!" It was, to Frankie, the best version he'd ever heard.

Everyone joins a band in this life.

Sometimes just to be brave.

Frankie grinned and looked down at his wife.

"Aurora?"

Her eyes were closed.

59

THE FATAL STROKE, DOCTORS EXPLAINED, WAS MOST LIKELY brought on by the trauma of her earlier blow. They could not be certain; Aurora was sixty-eight years old. Nurses had rushed in with flashlights, but attempts to revive her were futile. She was gone that fast. A young physician offered condolences then rushed to help other storm victims. Frankie slumped in mute disbelief as orderlies entered with a gurney. When they took her body, he fell to the floor and crouched against the wall, rocking back and forth, holding his arms as if freezing. The streets outside were flooded. The hospital was like a war zone. There was nowhere to go. No place to scream. Once again, his life was altered by rushing waters.

It was four weeks before they could bury her.

At the graveside funeral, Kai held her father's hand and wept. Aurora's fellow churchgoers held hands and wept. Cecile (York) Peterson flew in from London and held Kai's hand and wept. She also delivered a warm, economic eulogy

that spoke about her sister Aurora as brave and smart and—
sometimes—the happiest woman she had ever known, a
person who clearly thought of others before herself. The
Big Mess Band from the community center played a funeral
dirge, a New Orleans tradition, performing "Just a Closer
Walk with Thee."

Frankie did not join in any of it. He did not sing a word.
He stood to the side of the service, looking a thousand
miles away.

I have said Aurora York was my only rival for Frankie's
heart. On that day, she vanquished me. Not a note of music was left inside him. His desperate love for her, with no
release, went crashing into his inner walls like the waters
of that flood, drowning me out, rendering him silent. He
kept seeing her face, asking him to sing in the hospital. He
kept seeing her as a little girl, asking him to play in a tree.
He kept thinking about the old guitar he had left behind,
and its one blue string, still unused.

"*What if you need to save a life?*" she had asked.

It was too painful to consider. His mind shut down. His
eyes went glassy. He was empty as a hole.

At the end of the ceremony, he remained by the grave,
waiting until everyone left him alone. Then he squatted,
took something from his pocket and pushed it into the
earth: a small, round flower made from a guitar string. His
eyes welled up and he lost his balance and fell forward, the

wet grass soaking his hands and knees. He whispered her name again and again.

"A long time from now," he gasped. "You said '*a long time from now.*'"

Everyone joins a band in this life.

Some of them break your heart.

60

THE REMAINING YEARS OF FRANKIE'S LIFE WERE SPENT AS far as he could get from his memories, in the city of Manila in the nation of the Philippines, teaching classical guitar at the University of Santo Tomas. His daughter, Kai, at her father's request, had used her symphony connections to secure an interview.

"It's so far away," she protested.

"I know," he said.

Frankie's Catholic upbringing was helpful in his hiring. He never told his new employers that he had given up on prayer, church, and God. Instead he took the teaching position, which paid modestly, and lived in a small apartment on España Boulevard, which allowed him to walk back and forth to campus, crossing to the Plaza Intramuros under the massive, baroque-style Arch of the Centuries.

He found Filipino students polite and respectful, and he taught them one on one, patiently, firmly. They admired his knowledge. But he rarely played for them. Nor did he join an ensemble or a faculty orchestra. He was there for one reason, to be someplace nobody would find him.

Only at night, alone by a window that overlooked a bus terminal, did he touch a guitar. He played slow baroque melodies by Gaspar Sanz and old blues by Robert Johnson. But his fingers now hurt all the time, the arthritis ravaging his nerve-damaged left hand, and a permanent stiffness had settled into his shoulders and neck. He no longer ran. He no longer cooked penne pasta. He no longer restored amplifiers or made tea or took part in any routine he had shared with his wife. Loneliness was like an ogre hovering over those activities.

Aurora had once said that, besides Kai, he would have his music when she was gone, and she was right. But I brought him little comfort. He wrote one song in the months after her death and he never wrote anything again.

In the calendar year of 2009, Kai came to visit at the close of a symphony tour, and informed Frankie that she had been selected for the prestigious International Francisco Tárrega Guitar Competition in Spain. It was a celebrated festival, more than forty years old, and this year was a special honor since it marked the hundredth anniversary of Tárrega's death. Because of that, the festival and competition would be held, for the first time, in the town of Tárrega's birth, Villareal.

"Papa, I want you to come."

"No, Kai."

"It's important to me."

"I can't."

"You taught me Tárrega. It was the first thing you taught me. Everything I know about his music is from you."

"There are too many . . ."

"What? Memories?"

"Yes."

"Memories are not in places, Papa. Memories are in your mind. They're here, too. In this"—she looked around—"stupidly tiny apartment."

Frankie rubbed his face and pushed back his hair, which, although thinned and gray, still mussed over his forehead.

"Do you ever use a brush?" Kai asked, trying to make him smile.

"Who for?" he said.

She looked away.

"I miss her, too, Papa."

"I know."

He stared at his daughter and how beautiful she had grown, in her early thirties now, peaking as he was shrinking.

"Will you stay a few days?" he asked.

"I'm here until Friday."

"A few days after that?"

"I'll have to make a call."

"You can use my phone." He motioned to a desk.

"I have a phone, Papa. Everyone has a phone now."

"Oh. Right."

She leaned in and rubbed his knee.

"Are you okay?"

A rush of love and anguish hit him at the same time, like converging waters.

"When is the festival?" he asked.

John Pizzarelli

*Jazz guitarist, singer, composer, son of famed guitarist
Bucky Pizzarelli*

YES, CERTAINLY. . . . MY NAME IS JOHN PIZZARELLI, I'M A
musician, I live in New York City. I'm here because Frankie
Presto was an old friend, and because he asked me to do
something before he died. . . . He asked me to find the original tapes of *The Magic Strings of Frankie Presto* and give them
to his daughter. . . . They're in this suitcase. . . .

Frankie and me? A long time. He first knew my father,
Bucky Pizzarelli. They met in the mid-1960s, after Frankie
appeared on *The Tonight Show*, where my dad was in the
band. Being guitar players, they got to talking, and Frankie
tried my dad's seven-string and knocked his socks off. Dad
loved him. He'd say, "And he ain't even Italian!" We thought
he was one of us. "Presto," you know? It *sounds* Italian.

Anyhow, the next few years, if Frankie came through
New York, he'd drop by our house and jam with Bucky and
the jazz guys who came around after their gigs, mostly to

eat my mom's rigatoni. I was probably six or seven the first time I met him. He looked different from the older guys. He was handsome and had black hair and wore sunglasses. He was kind of like Elvis to me. Or as close as I was gonna get. I was learning the tenor banjo and after Frankie played a song on his guitar, I held up my banjo and said, "Yeah, but can you play this?" Obviously, I was a smart-aleck kid. But he took it and winked at me and played "La Malagueña," that famous Spanish tune, and he went faster and faster until I was like—gah!—my eyes were bugging out. And this was the banjo, which wasn't really his thing. He finished and said, "How was that?" And I said, "Pretty good," and he said, "Pretty good is pretty good."

He used to call me "LPJ," for Little Pizzarelli John, because the president at the time was Lyndon Baines Johnson, LBJ. So I was LPJ. He loved to watch me play with my dad. I guess he didn't really know his father, so the idea of father and son playing together was special for him.

Then, for a long stretch, we didn't see Frankie. He came by once in the seventies, when he was married to Aurora and they were passing through New York. My mom made her pasta. I was in high school and had a big mop of wavy hair—I was really into Peter Frampton—and he said, "Is that LPJ under all that flop?" and I said, "Yeah," and he said, "How you doing?" and I said, "Pretty good," and he said, "Pretty good is pretty good." And then he said, "Have you learned 'La Malagueña' yet?"

It was a long time before I saw him again—not until I was in my thirties, already recording and traveling around the world. I heard that he was teaching in a music store in, of all places, Staten Island, under a different name. I drove out there, and sure enough, it was him. He made me close the door, and then he gave me a big hug and asked how my father was. He told me about his daughter and the Juilliard thing and why he was lying low, because all these people were curious about him. I was playing in the city at that time, and I begged him to come sit in with us—I promised I wouldn't introduce him—but he declined. He said maybe he and Aurora would come by the house one night, but they never made it.

Then they moved to New Orleans, and we lost touch.

The last time I saw him was a year ago. Our band was doing some gigs in Asia, and we had a show in Manila. Afterward, a student from the university was hanging outside the stage door, and he said he had something important to tell me. A message from a man who used to eat meatballs at my house. And he said the words "La Malagueña" and gave me an address. Like something from a James Bond movie, right? But it wasn't far from where we had played, so I asked a cabdriver to take me there. I went up to the apartment. No doorman or anything. I just knocked.

And Frankie answered the door and said, "Hey, LPJ."

I did a double take. He didn't look healthy. He was bent over and really thin and he was wearing reading glasses and his hair was all mussed up, like a discombobulated professor. I didn't know Aurora had died. Once I heard that, I understood. They were so crazy about each other.

We talked for a while and he asked about my father, like he always did, and he wanted to know if we still played together and when I said yes, he seemed happy. I asked if he was recording or writing or anything, and he said he'd only written one song since his wife died. I asked if I could hear it. He sang it for me, and it was short enough that I can remember the whole thing.

Yesterday
I saw a bird
Whose tree had disappeared,
The clouds lay claim
To a moonless sky
You are gone
I'm here.

It broke your heart, it was so sad and beautiful. I asked if he was going to record it and he looked at me as if that was never going to happen and he said, "You can have it if you want."

That's when he asked me the favor. He said this bootleg of him playing guitar called *The Magic Strings of Frankie Presto* had been out there for years (I didn't tell him every guitarist I knew either had it or had heard it) and he really needed to get the original tapes. I figured he wanted the money that was due him.

But I was wrong. He didn't care about that. He wanted the tapes because he remembered that his wife and daughter were in the studio with him that day, and they talked and laughed in between him playing, and the original recordings would have all that stuff on it. He said when he died, he wanted Kai to have that happy memory of her parents.

Well, it took me a year to track the tapes down. But I did. Somebody in New Zealand had sold them to somebody in Australia, then England, then Japan. I was in Tokyo last month, and I found the engineer who had them, and he got kind of scared when I told him I was representing the real Frankie Presto—he said, "I thought he was dead"—and he just handed me the tapes after I signed something in Japanese that promised he wouldn't get sued.

Once I had them, I called Frankie's number in the Philippines. But I guess he'd already left to come here. I missed him by a couple of days.

That's typical Frankie Presto timing, isn't it?

61

FRANKIE AND KAI FLEW TOGETHER TO SPAIN. THEY WAITED at baggage claim for her guitar to be unloaded. Frankie did not bring an instrument, just a small suitcase. He was there as a father, he reminded himself. The less he had to do with music, the better.

The first day, he mostly slept in the hotel, while Kai registered and attended festival events. Frankie's arthritis was bad and he took pills for the pain. That evening, Kai asked him to listen to her practice, so he sat in a chair, his shoulders slumped, his shirt unbuttoned, and gazed at her rapidly moving fingers, astounded at how proficient she had become, particularly at the music of his youth. As she played the most complicated passages by Spanish composers—the tremolos, the *rasgueo* fingerings—he nodded slowly.

"So?" she asked upon finishing. "Any tips?"

"Did I tell you how much I love you?"

"That's not a tip, Papa."

He shrugged.

"Ah, well," he said.

❦

Kai performed wonderfully in the first two days of competition and easily advanced to the final round. That morning, Frankie woke before the sunrise. His neck cricked. His knees ached. Feeling restless, he dressed by a lamp and left the hotel, hoping some fresh air would boost his spirits.

Villareal was shrouded in mist, like the morning Carmencita met the gypsies who gave her the strings. Frankie walked along a wide street then turned down a narrow one, barely able to see two steps ahead. The city was as quiet as a cave.

Frankie's mind drifted. He was scheduled to depart the next day, and was certain this would mark his final visit to Spain. As the first wisps of sunlight broke through the haze, he found himself in a small park centered by a statue.

He stepped up and squinted. Looking down at him, from atop a stone pedestal, was a large bronze sculpture of the great Francisco Tárrega.

It was like watching one of my children meet the other.

Tárrega had been cast in midperformance, his left foot on a small stool, his hands perfectly positioned on the guitar, which was pitched upward at the classical angle. Frankie studied the face of the master, now dead for one hundred years, the long beard and flowing hair slightly unkempt, reminding Frankie of El Maestro.

His eyes dropped to read the inscription. Then he glanced to the side and blinked.

There, resting against the stone base, was his guitar.

At least it looked like his guitar. But that was impossible, wasn't it? He looked around as if someone might be coming. Then he lifted himself awkwardly over the low railing that surrounded the statue, catching his pants on a spoke and tearing a small cut in his skin.

"Ahh," he groaned.

He put his hand on the guitar's neck, and experienced a blinding flash of imagery, the faces of Django, young Aurora, Hampton, Ellis, and Alberto. He pulled back as if stung.

And he realized he was not alone.

Hiding behind the rear of the statue, holding a cane, was a hooded, heavily clothed figure.

"It is your guitar, Francisco," a voice whispered. "Take it."

62

FRANKIE ASSUMED HE WAS LOOKING AT A MAN, BUT AS THE hood lowered, he realized it was a very old woman. Her hair was wispy, cut short and mostly white, with rusty patches as if once red. Her eyes, lined with creases, were a hazel shade. When she opened her mouth, Frankie saw a gap between her front teeth.

"You left this at the monastery," she said.

"I don't want it."

"Just the same."

"Why have you brought it?"

"You are not finished playing."

"Who are you?"

"Once, I was known as your mother."

"My . . . *mother*?"

"It was undeserved."

She bowed her head.

"I left you to die. The rest of my life, I have been forsaken."

❧

The old woman stared at the ground beneath the statue. Her face was weathered in deep lines and her skin hung loosely beneath her chin. When she spoke, it was in slow, deliberate tones, as if she had practiced this story many times and was now, finally, getting to deliver it.

"My given name is Josefa. In 1935, when I was sixteen years old, my parents came to Villareal to hide me in a convent. They were poor but pious, and the revolutionaries were hunting them, especially my father, who they called 'El Pelé.'

" 'You will be safe here, daughter,' he told me when he left. 'God will reunite us soon.'

"I never saw him again.

"I found comfort with the sisters of the San Pascual basilica. I took part in mass, folded laundry, and helped tend to the tomb of our patron saint.

"On the night our church was destroyed by militia I had been outside taking food to a needy family, something only a novice was permitted to do. When I returned, nearly everyone had fled. I was preparing to run myself when I saw someone enter the front doors and kneel by the candles. A woman. Young and pregnant. As I approached to warn her of the danger, she collapsed and began her labor.

"That woman was your real mother. Her name was Carmencita. She came to pray for your safe arrival. But once your birth began, there was little she could do. The raiders had arrived. I rushed her upstairs to the chamber of San Pascual and I prayed his spirit would protect us.

"Minutes later, you were born, with evil below and the good Lord above. Your mother gave you your name, honoring our patron saint, and she held you only briefly. To keep you from crying, she hummed a song. It saved your life.

"And mine."

Frankie was shaking.

"What happened to her?" he whispered.

"She could not move. She was weak and bleeding. I heard the men screaming. I extinguished the candles. In the darkness, I sensed her reaching out, and when her hand found my head, it pulled me in close. She whispered in my ear, just three words.

" *'Save my child.'*

"I did all I could. I removed my tunic, because my life would surely end if they knew what I was. In those days, a nun could be murdered in the street. I took your mother's clothes and wrapped her in mine. I whispered a prayer. And I ran out the back steps, carrying you in my arms."

"You left my mother?" Frankie said.

The old woman looked at her feet.

"I have done worse."

∼

She coughed harshly, gripping the cane. The more the day-light spread over them, the older she appeared, and Frankie realized the great effort it must have taken for this woman to bring herself here. But she seemed determined to finish her tale.

"For many months, I raised you as my own. I lied about my past. I gave you all I could. But there was no work and no money and very little food. I was still a child myself. I did not understand an infant's crying. I felt damned for leaving your mother and dirty for living a lie. I never slept. I heard devilish voices. The church had been my salvation, but I could no longer go there. With no family and a screaming baby, I was outcast. Alone. And so, one morning . . ."

"What?" Frankie said.

She took a breath.

"I threw you away, Francisco. Forgive the way I say it, but I do not deserve to say it more kindly. I put you in the Mijares River. And I ran. I ran until my chest could no longer take air. I collapsed in a thicket of muddy bushes. The world went black and for a moment I thought I would die. That is what I wanted.

"But then I heard the sound of something breathing and I opened my eyes to see a dog standing over me, dark, with no hair. It never made a sound. It just stared at me. A voice called out and the dog ran away. I saw, in the distance, a bald man carrying you off, the animal beside him."

"Papa . . . ," Frankie whispered.

"Baffa Rubio. I knew then that God had forsaken me, but he had not forsaken you. I was a wretch. Undeserving of a child. My punishment would be living with what I'd done. But my penance was clear."

"What penance?" Frankie said.

"To guard you from afar. To honor your mother's final request. *Save my child.* It was my only path to salvation. It gave me a reason to rise from that muddy brush. I followed behind Baffa Rubio until I witnessed him entering his home with you in his arms. From that moment forward, I became your sentinel. I vowed to keep watch no matter where your life took me. And that is what I have done."

Frankie stared in disbelief. "For how long?"

She put both hands on the cane.

"Until this moment."

~

Robert Schumann's haunting composition "Träumerei" ("Daydream") is a piece he wrote to recall his childhood. Frankie learned it from El Maestro. It features a repeated four-note passage, followed each time by a different chord that changes the music's mood. It is simple yet captivating, evoking the dreams of a child. But the entire piece hangs on one crescendo, a remarkable sound that follows the final four-note build, a chord so piercingly beautiful that everything before only makes sense once you've heard it.

For Frankie Presto, the nun's tale was that chord. It pulled him out of the cloudy dream that for so long had shrouded his story, tumbling details into place like the pins of a turned lock.

This woman, he learned, had been less than a mile from him for much of his life, a silent partner in nearly every band he'd joined. It was Josefa who distracted the police when Frankie stole the phonograph as a boy. It was Josefa who paid a gypsy to stop his cart as Frankie ran from soldiers. It was Josefa who trailed Frankie to England, who found him on the docks in Southampton and who sometimes dropped coins in his guitar case to keep him from starving.

It was Josefa who followed Frankie to America, bringing the hairless dog she had rescued from Spain. It was Josefa who shadowed the boy after Baffa's sister rejected him, and who told police that he was sleeping in an alley, so they would bring him to an orphanage. It was Josefa who took work in the orphanage kitchen, to watch him as he grew, and who left the kitchen window open so the sad child and the hairless dog could be reunited.

It was Josefa who witnessed Frankie's blue string incident at the Detroit nightclub, and Josefa who followed him to Nashville and New Orleans and informed a young Aurora York that a Spanish guitarist had been playing under a bridge and had been asking about her. It was Josefa who urged medics to the stage at Woodstock, to get a bleeding Frankie Presto to the helicopters, and it was Josefa who, working as a housekeeper in a London hotel, left the shades open every day in the room of a singer named Tony Bennett so that he might see Frankie sitting on a park bench and perhaps help him return to music.

Decades later, on a New Zealand island, it was Josefa who took an abandoned baby from the church and left it in the woods, knowing Frankie and Aurora would make a family.

And on that family's fateful return to Villareal, it was Josefa, dressed in the heavy clothing that she used to disguise herself, who came to Frankie's show at the *taberna*, and who hid in an alley after it was over, knowing that an old conga player was lurking there as well.

"Then . . . you killed Alberto?" Frankie said.

"May the Lord forgive me."

"You turned yourself in."

"I could do no less."

"You went to prison."

"For nineteen years."

"Why did you shoot him?"

"Because I thought he would harm you. I knew he could be violent. I witnessed it before. So I took a weapon. My life, my entire existence, was to protect you, Francisco. He was running your way. I shot."

She covered her mouth, as if the memory still stunned her. Tears fell quickly down her spotted skin.

"In the end, it was justice. That is what I tell myself.

What he took from you, no man should take."

"He killed my teacher," Frankie said.

"Not just your teacher," she whispered. "Your father."

❧

Suddenly, Frankie couldn't breathe.

"What are you saying?"

"The man you called Maestro? His real name was Carlos Andrés Presto, the husband of Carmencita. He was once the most promising guitarist in all of Valencia. But he lost his sight fighting in the war. And when he lost your mother— and, as he thought, the baby she carried—he lost himself."

"That can't be true," Frankie whispered.

"It is. But church bells chimed when you were born, Francisco. God gave you a new father in Baffa Rubio, and in time, unaware, he returned you to your real father. It was Maestro who visited Baffa in prison. It was Baffa's money that Maestro used to send you to America. It was that money Alberto stole when he pushed Maestro into the sea. And it was that money I stole a week later from Alberto, a great deal of money, enabling me to watch you all these years. Everything is connected, Francisco. My father used to tell me a gypsy expression '*Le duy vas xalaven pe.*' The hands wash each other."

"You stole the money back?" Frankie said.

"There are few sins I did not commit in my sworn protection of you. But to what matter? The greatest sin, I committed first. I let you go.

"During my years in prison, I could only pray for your safety. I thought I would never again see your face. But now, by His grace, the Lord has brought you back to this place, so that I may make my final request."

"What do you want?" Frankie said.

She lowered her eyes.

"To ask your forgiveness."

Frankie's head rolled back, heavy. He rubbed his temples. This was too much to comprehend. He kept imagining scenes he was not a part of, his mother dying in a burning church; his teacher being pushed into the sea; Alberto being robbed; and this woman, this old, broken, gap-toothed woman, somehow being there for all of it, playing his life's strings like invisible fingers. He felt manipulated. He rose slowly and glared at the shriveled person who claimed to be his guardian. He had not asked for her. She had toyed with his existence, making all that he thought he knew some kind of lie.

"No," he said. "I don't forgive you. Go. Now."

"Francisco—"

"Leave me alone. Forever. Do you hear me? I don't need you. I never needed you."

"That is not true," she whispered.

But he was already limping away, putting the woman, the guitar, and Francisco Tárrega behind him.

63

FRANKIE NEVER RETURNED TO THE HOTEL. HE DID NOT EAT.
He did not drink. He wandered in a trance toward the edge
of the city, and sat down near the hermitage on the banks of
the Mijares River. His frustration was burning in his chest.
He imagined himself being thrown in this water. Imagined
Baffa Rubio finding him. Imagined the disgraced nun lying
in muddy brush, seeing him taken away. Whose life was
this? It felt like an opera with his name on it, but one he had
not written.

He stayed near the river most of the day, by the old water
mill and the shepherd boy sculpture. Finally, with the afternoon sun losing its heat, Frankie entered a small church
once frequented by refugees hiding in the caves.

No one was inside. His footsteps echoed. He moved to
the altar and lowered himself to his knees. For the first time
since he was a child, he opened his hands for something
other than the guitar. And despite El Maestro's warning
that "God gives you nothing," he asked the Lord for some
sort of answer. Some clarity. Some peace.

He waited. Listening. A child of mine expects a sound.
He heard only silence.
As his teacher had predicted.
He rose slowly and made his way back toward the city.

℮

The festival's last night was held in the sold-out Audi-
torio Municipal. By the time he got there, Frankie was
exhausted. He hadn't eaten. He didn't have his ticket. He
went to the back of the building, familiar, as musicians are,
with stage exits and entrances, and found a door to slip
through. Down a hallway, he saw performers getting ready,
and he caught a glimpse of Kai, wearing a red dress that had
once belonged to Aurora.

"Papa?" She hurried to him. "Where were you?"

"You look beautiful."

"I was really worried."

"I went walking."

"Are you all right? You're all sweaty."

"I'm all right. You just think about your playing."

"Do you have your seat?"

"Maybe I will stay back here. Is that all right?"

She found him a chair.

"Rest, Papa."

"Go prepare," he said. "I'm fine. Good luck."

Kai disappeared down the hall.

Minutes later, the competition began. Frankie heard the orchestra on the other side of the wall, the rise and fall of the strings and the winds, and the quiet passages where the guitarists were featured. He remembered the first time he ever heard such sounds, as a boy in the wings of a Cleveland theater, listening to Duke Ellington. But he could no longer rouse that youthful wonder. His eyes stayed locked on his muddy shoes. He had never felt so tired.

When it was Kai's time to play, he moved slowly to the wing of the stage. The last of the competitors, she selected a pair of Tárrega compositions, difficult for most guitarists, but part of her life growing up. And, I am proud to say, she performed them flawlessly. The orchestra fell in behind her as if they'd played together for years. When she finished, spectators nodded vigorously and rose to their feet, whooping and clapping. Had the judges chosen anyone else, the crowd might have revolted.

When she was announced as the winner, Kai stepped forward and bowed, and Frankie felt a surge of pride exceeding anything he'd ever felt for himself. She was led to the front of the stage and given two bouquets of flowers to go with her award.

"Thank you so much," she said into a microphone, in perfect Spanish. "I am most honored to play the works of Villareal's native son, the great Francisco Tárrega."

More applause.

"But I would not know a single note on the guitar if not for another of your native sons. He is my father."

The crowd murmured. She turned and waved at Frankie. He had not expected this. He felt dizzy.

"Papa. Please come out."

He shook his head no.

"Papa . . . Please . . ."

He squeezed his fists, then locked them behind his back. He walked onto the stage with his head lowered. The crowd applauded.

"Here is my father, who you might know better as . . . Frankie Presto. He grew up in this city and he learned his music here."

The applause deepened. This was a surprise. Frankie nodded meekly at the crowd. He realized he had not been on a stage in many years.

"Papa, today someone brought us this," Kai said, pointing to an approaching stagehand. "Your guitar from when you were a child here. It is a miracle."

Frankie swallowed. He did not want to correct his daughter. Or tell her the truth.

"Would you play a song with me?"

Before he could react, the audience roared, urging him on. Kai handed him the guitar. Someone slid a chair into place. Someone else brought a footstool. They quickly exited, leaving father and daughter alone. Kai sat down, putting her guitar on her knee. She smiled and motioned for Frankie to do the same. He shook his head no.

"Papa," she whispered, "it's time to make music again."

Frankie held still, dumbfounded. Finally, he sat down alongside her. The auditorium quieted. Even the stray coughs were silenced. Frankie positioned the old guitar as he had done a million times before. But suddenly, he could not stop shivering. His throat was dry. His vision blurred. His fingers locked up. Kai looked at him, concerned. He closed his eyes and exhaled. As his chest sank he heard the voice of his teacher—his father—in one final memory.

"When will I be finished learning music, Maestro?"

"Never."

"Never?"

"You will never know all there is to know. You will learn until your final days. Then you will inspire someone else. This is what an artist does."

"What does inspire mean?"

"It means you will make someone love music the way you love it."

"And they will want to play like me?"

"Perhaps."

"Can I really do that?"

"Not with all this talking."

"Lo siento, Maestro."

"*English.*"
"*I am sorry.*"
"*All right, then. Begin . . .*"

Frankie put his fingers on the strings. He looked at his daughter.

They began.

It was a sweet and lively Tárrega duet, one they'd done many times over the years. It was called "Adelita," and Frankie's strings intermingled with Kai's, supporting, accenting, taking the lead. She moved slightly, as did he, remembering the many times they'd played this in the back of their house on the island.

When their piece was complete, they let the last notes ring, then lowered their hands at the same time, as if choreographed. The crowd cheered, and Frankie felt his heart swell. Even the orchestra rose in appreciation. It was the last band Frankie Presto would join.

But it was not his last song.

Kai swept a hand toward him and the audience responded loudly, wanting more. She kissed him on the cheek before stepping away and whispered, "Now you. Something for Mama."

Frankie watched her step offstage. He sat back down. His breathing calmed. He knew there was only one song left to play.

"Lágrima."

Death has no ears. Someone wrote that when Tárrega died. If it did, it could never rob the world of his music.

As Frankie Presto played that night, the world again heard something only death could ignore. Frankie was connected to me in the rarest of ways, from the inside out, so that he was no longer playing the notes of that song, he was playing its tears, the tears that fell from Tárrega's eyes as he composed it, the tears that dripped down Carmencita's cheeks as she hummed it, the tears that welled behind El Maestro's dark glasses when he realized he had passed on my beauty to the son of a sardine maker.

The world had never witnessed so strong a connection between music and memory. As Frankie came to the final stanza of "Lágrima," he glanced to the wings and saw his daughter, covering a smile. Then he noticed, behind her, the old woman Josefa, her head lowered.

He stared until she looked up, with the sadness of a life rebuked. All that Frankie had known, this woman had, in some way, given to him: his father, his wife, his daughter, his dog, his safety, his health, his music. Yes, she had once turned her back on him. But he had done the same to her, denying her even the decency of forgiveness.

He suddenly stopped playing. As the crowd watched in curious silence, he stood up slowly and lifted the guitar toward the old woman, as if offering a sacrifice. Deep inside, Frankie heard the voice he had been waiting to hear at the church that afternoon.

And he knew what to do.

"I do forgive you, kind woman," he said. "And I thank you."

"You thank *me*?" she whispered.

"For my life."

He looked at his daughter and smiled.

"My whole, amazing life."

Josefa's lips parted slightly. At that moment, she looked strangely like her father, the gypsy who had once given a gift of magic strings. With her eyes closing peacefully, she pulled the hood over her head. Suddenly the lights in the auditorium went out like a blown candle. Frankie heard a gasp from the crowd. He looked down and saw a thin glowing line.

His top string had turned blue.

The audience, thinking this was part of the finale, began applauding vigorously. In the darkness, Frankie felt a blissful surrender, a draining of both his power and his worries, as if someone had unplugged him from the heaviness of this world. Those strings, he now understood, did indeed have lives inside them, but it was not his playing that turned them blue; it was his heart.

With the ovation growing louder, Frankie lifted his head. He saw now, high in the rafters, the spirits of El Maestro,

Baffa, and Aurora, beckoning to him. He reached for them and a pain gripped his chest. His guitar clanged to the floor.

And then, as some have told the authorities, he appeared to rise to the ceiling.

I shall clear that up now. Frankie's body never rose. That was his soul. But so great was the desire of the world to hear his splendid music—to keep it even a few more seconds—that his spirit was tugged, momentarily, between heaven and earth.

There can be but one victor in such a struggle.

Seconds later, he was gone, and only his body was left behind, thudding to the stage as if a puppet's string had been cut.

Look at the time. Look at the church. Look at the pallbearers, each of them one of Frankie's students over the years, younger men and women, sad faces in dark clothing. I said at the start that I would sprinkle Frankie's talent on other souls. But he has done it already. It is inside those young ones who carry his casket, and in the older musicians who traveled all this way to say good-bye, and in the millions of people who have heard his songs or tried to imitate his playing, and in the hearts of his adoring daughter and the children she will bear, and their children, and their children's children, who will hear Frankie's greatest playing—and laughter with his family—from tapes made long ago.

I leave you now, and return to my eternal task, awaiting newborns and their tiny open hands.

Did you know that once, years after his death, Francisco Tárrega's body was exhumed from its grave, so that it could be moved closer to home? The famed guitarist Andrés Segovia came to bear witness, standing at the foot of the opened casket. Segovia wept at the sight of Tárrega's remains, in homage to the talent that had so influenced him.

I am flattered. But as I depart, I should confess. It is not in the bones. Nor in the lips or the lungs or even in the hands. I am Music. And Music is in the connection of human souls, speaking a language that needs no words.

Everyone joins a band in this life. And what you play always affects someone.

Sometimes, it affects the world.

Frankie's symphony ends.

And so, at last, we rest.

Acknowledgments

MANY AUTHORS, IN THEIR CLOSING PAGES, WRITE "THIS BOOK would not have been possible without. . . ." It's a good practice and I will repeat it here.

But with this novel, the words "This book would not have been possible without" truly do apply—to the numerous artists who agreed to let me stitch Frankie Presto into their real lives. They trusted me to write in their voices and give an alternate universe to their personal histories. And for that not only am I grateful, but I feel compelled to add a few special notes:

Marcus Belgrave. He was a treasure. My last conversation with him was to tell him of this book and his inclusion. He was in a doctor's office—yet typically upbeat and encouraging. He passed away a few months later, and his horn will be missed. He was a huge part of Detroit's jazz legacy.

Darlene Love. "Today I Met The Boy I'm Gonna Marry" was the song my wife sang at our own wedding. I've been a sucker for Darlene's music for years. Her life story is incredible, and Frankie probably should have kissed her while he had the chance.

Burt Bacharach. I've known him for a little while, and he's as elegant as his music. One of the twentieth century's greatest songwriters, he could make the phone book melodic. How one man could compose "Baby It's You" and "I Just Don't Know What To Do With Myself" is beyond me. A deep thanks for his participation.

Roger McGuinn. His humility about his guitar skill was an inspiration for Frankie. Roger is a walking history of rock and roll. The story of meeting the Beatles—and of the party—is all true. And I didn't even write about the night he, Eric Clapton, and Jimi Hendrix jammed in an apartment. Roger also slums with our band, the Rock Bottom Remainders, proving the old adage about pearls to swine.

Lyle Lovett. We met a few years back and became friends. I've always loved his music and lyrics. "Clever" is a word that jumps to mind when I hear songs like "Her First Mistake" or "God Will," so I made his fictional band the Clever Yells. Lyle is as humble as he is talented, and he said yes right away to this story. His trust means a great deal to me.

Paul Stanley. I hadn't met Paul before this book. He was gracious enough to have me at his house, and told me countless rock and roll anecdotes, including how one would audition for KISS. ("Going from dating to marrying" is his actual quote.) Paul is poetic, reflective and kind, and he took this novel very seriously, reviewing his encounter with Frankie with great care. Behind those booming guitar chords is a generous, sensitive artist to whom I owe a debt of thanks.

Tony Bennett. A national treasure. I sat with him backstage one afternoon as he imagined what he would tell a musician who had given up. I wove that into his "encounter" with a damaged Frankie in London. If anyone could inspire a return to music, it would be Tony Bennett. Just listen to him sing "Lost in The Stars" and you'll know what I mean. I love him and am proud to call him my friend.

Wynton Marsalis. Wynton and I have been buddies since the day his band challenged my radio crew to a basketball game. They killed us. (Who knew jazz musicians could shoot?) Wynton said OK quickly to inclusion in *Magic Strings*, and he texted me his enthusiasm after reading his Frankie episode. Jazz music has no stronger musical force than this man, and I'm sure he grabbed with both fists when he came into this world.

Ingrid Michaelson. We met and I floated this idea to her all in a single early morning in New York City, where she had to perform before her coffee kicked in. With her talent, wit, and smarts I thought she'd be a perfect student for an older Frankie. Listen to "Far Away" then "How We Love" to see the amazing span of her gifts. She could have taught Mr. Rubio a few things about songwriting.

John Pizzarelli. John was the first person I spoke to for this book, so it's fitting he was the last guest. John is one of those musicians who has melded into his instrument, and his playing is as effortless as it is infectious. We've been friends a long time, and he is so generous and humble, that it's no surprise he'd go around the world to secure the *Magic Strings* tapes for Frankie. He's a hero to me, so it was fun to make him a hero on the page.

As for the creation of this book, I must begin with my time

in Spain. Marta Armengol Royo was the dream researcher and translator, as precise as she was enthusiastic; and Jacinto Heredia, our Villareal-based historian, was an invaluable source of knowledge and anecdotes. (And, yes, that is him in the book showing Frankie the Tárrega material. It's the least I could do for all his help.) The wonderful people of Villareal, the Tárrega exhibit at the city museum, and the basilica de San Pascual were instrumental in creating the mood and spirit of Frankie's roots. It's an amazing city and I highly recommend a visit. (A big thanks to my Spanish publisher, Maeva, for giving the whole trip a jump start.)

Closer to home, much credit goes to Karen Rinaldi, my angel publisher-editor at HarperCollins, for believing in a book that is tough to explain at the start, and to Brian Murray, Michael Morrison, and Jonathan Burnham for giving their blessings. The Harper family has made me feel quite at home at this stage of my career, and I thank all of them, notably Milan Bozic (another beautiful cover), John Jusino, Leah Carlson-Stanisic, Josh Marwell, Doug Jones, Brian Perrin, Leah Wasielewski, Stephanie Cooper, Kathy Schneider, Hannah Robinson (no more edits, yay!), and Leslie Cohen (for her past and future efforts in bringing Frankie's story to the world).

David Black is now approaching thirty years as my literary agent and friend, so I guess it's working out. Antonella Iannarino is a precious resource on a million levels. Susan Raihoffer is taking Frankie global. Additional thanks to Sarah Smith and Jenny Herrera.

Jo-Ann Barnas did incredible research for this book, from sitting with guitar players to digging into Django's set list in

1946, and through her efforts, I must also thank John Alvarado, of the Indiana Society of the Classical Guitar; the folks at the Hank Williams Museum in Montgomery, Alabama; Amy Hauser, with the Maersk Line (for all the ships Frankie sailed on); Kay MacConnachie, Michigan Hand and Sports Rehabilitation Center; Ian F. Hancock, University of Texas at Austin, and William A. Duna, of Minnesota (for their knowledge of gypsy culture and history); the Vietnam Veterans of America; Gordy Lupo, of Gordy's Music in Ferndale, Michigan; Joshua Bronnenberg, the Ryman Auditorium museum manager, and Brenda Colladay, the Ryman Auditorium curator; Fr. Lawrence J. Delonnay, pastor, Our Lady of the Lakes Catholic Church, in Waterford, Michigan; Sr. Dianne Short, Order of Saint Clare, in Cincinnati; Russell Barber, of Westland, Michigan; Mary Kay Slusher, Louisiana Department of Health and Hospitals, Bureau of Media and Communications.

A special thanks to Vito Lafata, a brilliant guitar player, who read this book at least three times and offered his expertise. A shout of gratitude to the folks at Republic Records, Avery Lipman and Tom Mackay in particular, who saw a real-life record deal for Frankie Presto's *Magic Strings*. Kevin and Robbie Martin are real people who make all visitors feel at home on Waiheke Island. And a deep appreciation for all the public figures who made appearances in Frankie's story, expected or not. All representations, from Django to Elvis to Little Richard to Hank Williams, come from a deep admiration of their gifts.

And then the home team: Kerri Alexander holds everything together, all the time. Marc "Rosey" Rosenthal juggles the world so I have time to write. Mendel keeps the numbers, but he is still, with all due respect, a bum. Chad Audi continues to exemplify that no matter how creative you get, doing for others is the most amazing legacy. Trisha, Rick, Ali, and Jesse gave Frankie his first reviews. And the highest thanks, always, goes to my family, who endured my music long before they endured my writing: Dad; Cara; Peter; all the uncles, aunts, and cousins; and my mother, who went to heaven during the creation of this book, leaving me to empathize with Frankie and Carmencita.

I must also thank every band I've ever been in, for teaching me that bandmates behave like family, good and bad. (Those bands include the Crystal Reflection, the Lucky Tiger Grease Stick Band, the ones in college, Streetwise, the Rock Bottom Remainders, and about a dozen I can't even remember.)

And finally, as always, deepest thanks to Janine, my girl in the tree, who listened to every note of this novel through the less-than-Frankie voice of its author, reading to her while she sat in a chair, both of us rocking in the unique rhythm of storytelling.

About the Author

MITCH ALBOM is a bestselling author, screenwriter, playwright, and nationally syndicated columnist. He has written six consecutive number one *New York Times* bestsellers—including *Tuesdays with Morrie*, the bestselling memoir of all time—and his books have collectively sold more than thirty-five million copies in forty-two languages. He has founded eight charities in Detroit and operates an orphanage in Port-au-Prince, Haiti. He lives with his wife, Janine, in Michigan.